KU-638-052

ACKNOWLEDGMENTS

Crafting a story may be a solo venture, but preparing a book for publication is a well-choreographed group effort. I've been blessed to have some great people guiding me through this process, first with *Collecting the Dead,* and now with *Whispers of the Dead.* Three key movers and shakers in this endeavor are my editor, Keith Kahla, my assistant editor, Alice Pfeifer, and my brilliant agent, Kimberley Cameron. I couldn't ask for better.

There is also an army of unsung heroes behind the scenes, like the proofreaders, copy editors, publicists, and sales reps, not to mention those creative geniuses in the art department at Minotaur who keep coming up with gorgeous covers.

This book is as much theirs as it is mine, and they have my profound thanks.

I'd be remiss if I didn't thank my wife, Lea, and my

daughters, Mary, Katie, and Abby. They've been my biggest fans and longest supporters. And a special thanks to three friends who continue to provide me with an unending stream of insights: Detective Kevin Bowhay, Special Agent Thom LeCompte, and retired homicide detective Marc Ganow.

Finally, thanks to my unofficial team of first editors, those family and friends who are constantly forced to read my writing and yet still consider me a friend. Thank you Cheryl, Kristin, Stephanie, Altavia, Wendy, JoAnn, and anyone else I may have forgotten.

EAST DUNBARTONSHIRE LIBRARIES

3 8060 07004 606 5

WHISPERS OF THE DEAD

"This ... good, old-fashioned gruesome murder mystery with a touch of the supernatural ... fantastic."
—*Criminal Element*

Praise for Spencer Kope and *Collecting the Dead*

"Kope hypnotizes the reader in this brilliant debut, not only for its addictive storyline but also by creating, in Steps, a good man blessed and plagued by his particular talent. Endlessly frightening, occasionally funny, *Collecting the Dead* portends a great future for author and hero in a promised sequel—and beyond."
—*Richmond Times-Dispatch*

"This fascinating debut will place Steps Craig alongside Walt Longmire, Jack Reacher, and Charlie Parker as an enduring literary hero."
—*Kirkus Reviews* (starred review)

"Thrillingly original." —*Toronto Star*

"With a hint of the supernatural à la Stephen King, this is a gripping crime drama. . . . Readers who enjoy serial killer novels will be talking about this book for months." —*Library Journal* (starred review)

"An auspicious debut . . . Kope's dry, unexcitable style, with its streaks of offbeat humor, further raises expectations for a *Collecting the Dead* sequel."

—*Chicago Tribune*

"Kope's debut thriller is tightly plotted and moves quickly. . . . Readers who like strong characters like Charlie Parker and Jack Reacher will find much to enjoy in Magnus Craig, and will eagerly await his next appearance."

—*Booklist*

"Like the best books of the thriller genre, this one is driven in equal parts by characters and plot. It's difficult to put down, given that Kope has constructed one loudly ticking clock."

—*Bookreporter*

"Steps is a welcome new series protagonist, not only because of his unusual talent but also his sense of humor and personality. . . . a humane and captivating character."

—*Shelf Awareness*

"*Collecting the Dead* is a white-knuckled, breathtaking thriller with one hell of a cast of characters."

—*Open Letters Monthly*

"Spencer Kope has introduced a tortured soul who's a welcome addition to the library of crime fiction heroes."

—*Publishers Weekly*

"Fascinating and compelling! Spencer Kope's *Collecting the Dead* reenergizes the crime genre with the introduction of 'human bloodhound' FBI Agent Magnus Craig, whose special skills puts him on every serial killer's trail, but also in at least one psychopath's sights. The twists and turns will leave you breathless!"

—Lisa Gardner, *New York Times* bestselling author of *Find Her*

"I love stories that walk that very thin line between the natural and the supernatural. Intriguing and smart, *Collecting the Dead* veers off the well-worn path and lures us into the deep, dark woods of the unexplained. I hope we get to spend more time with FBI tracker Magnus 'Steps' Craig, the compelling and gifted man at the center of Spencer Kope's sinister, twisty debut."

—Lisa Unger, *New York Times* bestselling author of *Ink and Bone*

"*Collecting the Dead* introduces Magnus 'Steps' Craig, a member of the FBI's Special Tracking Unit who has a special gift known only to a few—but will it be enough to stop a killer who seems to be one step ahead of everyone? Kope's debut is a well-written thrill ride that introduces a very appealing hero. Hopefully Steps will be back in action soon."

—Phillip Margolin, *New York Times* bestselling author of *Violent Crimes*

ALSO BY SPENCER KOPE

Collecting the Dead

WHISPERS OF THE DEAD

Spencer Kope

St. Martin's Paperbacks

NOTE: If you purchased this book without a cover you should be aware that this book is stolen property. It was reported as "unsold and destroyed" to the publisher, and neither the author nor the publisher has received any payment for this "stripped book."

This is a work of fiction. All of the characters, organizations, and events portrayed in this novel are either products of the author's imagination or are used fictitiously.

WHISPERS OF THE DEAD

Copyright © 2018 by Spencer Kope.

All rights reserved.

For information address St. Martin's Press, 175 Fifth Avenue, New York, NY 10010.

ISBN: 978-1-250-30840-5

Our books may be purchased in bulk for promotional, educational, or business use. Please contact your local bookseller or the Macmillan Corporate and Premium Sales Department at 1-800-221-7945, ext. 5442, or by e-mail at MacmillanSpecialMarkets@macmillan.com.

Printed in the United States of America

Minotaur hardcover edition / April 2018
St. Martin's Paperbacks edition / February 2019

St. Martin's Paperbacks are published by St. Martin's Press, 175 Fifth Avenue, New York, NY 10010.

10 9 8 7 6 5 4 3 2 1

To my mother, Mary Joan Kope (Hogan).
Thank you for the dance.

EAST DUNBARTONSHIRE
LEISURE & CULTURE TRUST

3 8060 07004 606 5	
Askews & Holts	27-Mar-2019
AF	£7.99
BIS	

PROLOGUE

Darkness—nearly complete.

Overwhelmed and surrounded, a single incandescent bulb pushes back defiantly against the stygian black. Its feeble light barely reaches through the emptiness, but what illumination it brings reveals the length of a man secured horizontally to a low bench with leather straps and restraints.

The man's panicked eyes dart left and right and his fingers curl and uncurl in jerking fits; nothing else moves, such is the completeness of his bondage.

The chamber feels cavernous and open, its ceiling and walls lost in the murk. Aside from the light and its immediate surroundings, there's little discernible in the empty dark, just the man, the bench, an ominous black structure that looms over him . . . and a whisper-quiet shadow that moves about without word or worry.

The shadow glides this way and that, checking

bindings, tinkering with machinery, tending its business. The smell of blood and fear flavors the air.

When all is ready, all but one small thing, the shadow pauses to study his victim with unseen eyes. Moving closer, he walks a slow, ritual circle around the binding bench, pausing one last time to check a strap. The victim's gaze follows every move, his eyes wide with horror. Indistinguishable sounds issue from someplace deep in his throat, no doubt begging, pleading, for mercy.

The shadow stands still for a long moment, and then, slowly, it moves even closer and a face presses forward from the gloom. For the first time the shadow is recognized as human—all but the eyes; they surrendered their humanity long ago. With deliberation, the shadow opens its mouth and breathes out four whispered words: "Thou shalt not kill."

Utter silence follows, and then the shadow smiles. A single metallic click breaks the darkness, instantly followed by the scraping *whoosh* of steel coming to life. The sound lasts but a moment, the screaming . . . much longer.

What *was* a human bound to a bench becomes a writhing creature, wailing in agony, shrieking in pain, straining against bonds that simply will not give.

The shadow watches.

Intolerable seconds pass into a nightmare of minutes and the creature weakens, falling into delirium; his cries soften until all that's left is a final push of whispered air from spent lungs . . . and then all is still.

Thou shalt not kill.

In the cavernous darkness there remain but two sounds: the steady *drip drip drip* from the tainted bench, and the quiet, measured breath of the shadow.

CHAPTER ONE

Interstate 5, Southbound from Bellingham—
September 2, 11:47 A.M.

The siren wails its lonely dirge.

It's a mournful song, rising and falling, and I know every musical pitch of it by heart. The red and blue emergency lights flash in accompaniment, reflecting off signs and windows, but there is no synchronization to this oft-repeated play. The lights and the siren coexist because they must, though they don't always dance together.

They are the harbingers—the raven and the lightning; bearers of bad news or bad deeds. Today it's both.

Jimmy—that's my partner, FBI Special Agent James Donovan—weaves the black Ford Expedition expertly through the parting sea of traffic as we make our way south on Interstate 5, past Lake Samish and eventually into the flat farmland of Skagit County. The speedometer reads ninety-seven; I try to ignore it.

Jimmy is riding the left shoulder now.

It's clear as far as the eye can see and traffic is pressing to the right to get out of the way. Motorists stare from their vehicles as we pass, and the draft from the SUV shakes the smaller cars. As we continue south and the drone of the siren begins to fade, the sea of people in our wake share a common emotion: relief.

The raven has passed them by.

The lightning didn't find them.

Someone else wasn't so lucky.

Three hours ago, Burlington PD responded to a residence on Ash Way and found the body of Krystal Ballard on her living room floor, her life drained out on the beige carpet in a series of red stains. The cause of death: stabbing. And not the typical two or three jabs, either. She had been stabbed in the chest eleven times.

Eleven times!

Two or three is a kill—eleven is overkill.

Overkill speaks of anger or jealousy or revenge; it speaks volumes about the killer. I've seen it before, the sudden outflow of emotion at the point of a knife, relentless and punishing, until the wielder gets tired of hearing the soft wet thud of the blade and steps back to stare at the mess he's wrought.

It's almost always a *he*.

Knife work takes strength. It's personal and up close.

It comes as no surprise that the ex-husband is already in custody—that's what happens when you drop your cell phone during the commission of a crime. CSI found it on the living room floor halfway under the couch. It's surprising how often that happens: someone drops a cell phone, a wallet, even court papers.

"Why, exactly, are we going to a crime that's already

been solved?" I ask Jimmy as we race down the freeway. The baying of the siren and the roar of air rushing past the SUV are giving me a headache; Jimmy just takes it in stride.

"It's complicated," he says after a moment.

"Really? That's your best response?"

He glances at me quickly, annoyed, and then turns his attention back to the road. "I got a call from a friend," he says. "He's a detective with the Skagit County Sheriff's Office."

I wait for more.

I wait for the friend's name, or the special circumstances of the case, or the reason the unnamed friend needs a tracker when the body has already been recovered and a suspect is in custody, but there's nothing but silence from the driver's seat.

"*And?*" I finally blurt when I can take it no longer.

Jimmy stiffens in his seat, but doesn't say anything. He can drive ninety-seven miles an hour on a crowded freeway and look like he's relaxing in a hot tub, but I press him for info and suddenly his spine goes rigid and his knuckles turn white around the steering wheel.

That's his tell.

Now I *know* something's up. Jimmy's not the secretive type, especially when it comes to tracking. Whatever it is, it's going to be bad, maybe even really bad. I open my mouth to press him further, but before the words come out, Jimmy cuts me off.

"Leave it be, Steps," he insists. "I don't know enough to give you the full brief, all right? I know just enough to piss you off, and I don't need that right now. We'll be there in a couple minutes and then we'll both know a little more." With that off his chest, he relaxes a little and gives me a forced smile, saying, "Cross my heart."

Cross my heart!

I was wrong; it's a catastrophe.

The two-story houses are lined up like dominoes on each side of the quiet street, each identical to the one next door and across the road except for paint scheme and the personalized décor spilled out upon the flower beds and yards.

It's a neighborhood of twenty-four cookie-cutter houses on twenty-four miniature lots, with twenty-four double-car garages opening onto two alleys, one behind each row of homes.

The regimented sameness of the neighborhood has its little charms—emphasis on *little*. It's the type of neighborhood where barbecue grills are standard, where kids play ball in the street until annoying hours of the night, and where having a car up on blocks in your driveway for more than a day is a stoning offense.

As soon as we turn onto the street I spot our destination. It's the tenth cookie-cutter on the right, a charming clone dressed in forest green with tan trim that looks like it has a hint of olive blended in.

The yellow police tape is not part of the décor.

Neither is the mobile command vehicle parked in front, nor the dozen marked and unmarked patrol vehicles scattered along the street and down the back alley, enveloping the crime scene in a dizzying kaleidoscope of flashing lights.

Jimmy pulls his black FBI-issued Ford Expedition to

the curb and puts it in park. A few of the neighbors glance our way briefly, but then the crime scene draws their eyes back. Even though there's nothing to see, they stand on their lawns and watch the sad green house at the end of the street.

I start to get out and Jimmy grabs my arm, pulling me back into the SUV. "What's up?" I say, glancing down at the four fingers and thumb gripping my forearm like a vise.

"Just . . . tread softly," Jimmy says.

"Tread softly?" I scrutinize Jimmy through half-closed eyes, my head tilted back as I stare down my nose at him. "Now, why do I suddenly have this little itch at the base of my skull? Maybe it's time to fill in some of those details?"

Jimmy's mouth is tight and pushed to the left. His words come in slow, cautious chunks. "Fine. There are two things you need to know. First, this search . . . it's not exactly . . . official."

"What's that mean, *not exactly*?"

"We weren't invited," Jimmy blurts, "not officially."

A smile creeps up my cheek. "We weren't invited." I give a little nod and Jimmy's already shaking his head. He knows what's coming. "Yes, that's interesting," I continue. "So, then, Mr. Protocol, Mr. FBI-to-the-Core, what are we doing here if it's not official, if we weren't invited?"

"It's a long story."

"I tread more softly when I know the facts," I say.

Jimmy turns to face me. "You really can be a pain—" He suddenly stops and points through the windshield. "Here he comes; he can tell you himself."

"Wait, what about the second thing? You said there are two things I need to know."

Jimmy's already out the door, but hesitates. For a moment it looks like he's going to slam the door and pretend he didn't hear me, but then he sticks his head in the gap and speaks so fast he sounds like an announcer reading the legal disclaimer at the end of a drug commercial: "Hector Pastori is incident commander. He's inside the command vehicle and doesn't know we're here, so be quiet and move quickly."

The door slams.

Hector Pastori!

I sit and stare out the windshield as a twitch starts in my left eye and works its way to the right. It was smart of Jimmy not to tell me; if he had, I'd be back at Hangar 7 right now watching a movie in the break room.

There's nothing wrong with Hector that a weeklong colonoscopy wouldn't cure. He suffers from chronic envy, the constipated kind that you just can't get rid of. We first met years ago on a search-and-rescue mission in Mount Rainier National Park that was getting national media attention. He's a good man-tracker, I'll give him that, and up until the point when I arrived he was enjoying all the attention.

Our relationship since has been, well, strained.

It's not my fault if I made him look stupid.

The higher Hector rises through the ranks and the more authority he has, the more he seems to focus in on me whenever our paths cross, which, thankfully, isn't often.

I watch Jimmy cross around to the front passenger

side, where he leans against the fender. A man wearing a crisp white shirt, burgundy tie, dark gray slacks, and black shoes sloppy from the rain is crossing the lawn in our direction. On his belt is a gold detective's badge, but the brown paper shopping bag he carries by the handle is not department-issued.

As he draws near he glances nervously over his right shoulder at the command vehicle, and I realize he's part of the unofficial noninvitation. Intrigued, I step quickly from the SUV and join Jimmy at the fender just as the detective comes up and extends a welcoming hand.

"Nice to see you, Kevin," Jimmy says, taking the hand and shaking firmly.

"Thanks for coming," the detective replies. "It means a lot."

Jimmy throws a thumb in my direction. "Kevin, this is Operations Specialist Magnus Craig. He's our lead tracker."

"Magnus," Kevin says, repeating the name so he won't forget it. It's a good memory trick, especially for a detective. "Thanks for coming," he says, thrusting his hand out.

"Call me Steps," I say, taking his hand.

"Steps?" He gives me a quizzical look.

I shrug. "It's a long story."

"This is an old friend of mine, Detective Kevin Mueller," Jimmy explains. "He's been with the Skagit County Sheriff's Office probably longer than he cares to remember. We used to be on the same softball team."

"Softball? When were you on a softball team?"

"During a different life," Jimmy replies dryly. He scowls up at the ugly, weeping sky a moment before turning his eyes back to the crime scene. "Why don't you tell us why we're here, Kevin?"

He does.

It's the same old script: love betrayed, money pilfered, and murder most heinous, just retold a different way—and Kevin doesn't spare the details. As it turns out, the suspect, Archie Everard, is a high school friend of his and, according to him, incapable of harming a soul, despite his six-foot-six linebacker build.

"He's a gentle giant," Kevin says, wearing out an already overused cliché.

I've heard it all before, the same sentiment, the same conviction, and if there's one thing I've learned it's to never underestimate the dark shadow that lies upon every human heart. Sometimes it's small and buried deep, other times it's all-consuming.

Every so-called gentle giant is just one beanstalk away from becoming a raging titan.

Archie Everard has every reason to be a raging titan. Four years ago he married Krystal Moon Beam—yeah, her parents were hippies—and for the first year he thought life couldn't get any better.

Then Krystal convinced him to sell a forty-acre blueberry field for a hefty sum. Archie had other fields, 235 acres' worth, so the loss of the smaller parcel wasn't a big blow to his farming operation, but it was land that had been in the family for eight decades. The sale came with a lot of personal guilt on Archie's part.

It wasn't long before the money started to disappear from the happy couple's investment fund in five-thousand- and ten-thousand-dollar chunks. By the time

Archie discovered the loss, $655,000 had been siphoned off. When he confronted Krystal about the withdrawals, she didn't even blink.

"She broke his heart," Kevin says. "Told Archie she wanted a divorce, which he gave her, with a verbal agreement that she return half the money. She didn't, of course. She moved here"—he lifts his chin at the house—"and then six months later she marries this guy from Seattle named John Ballard."

"Ballard?" Jimmy chews the name. "Where's he?"

"According to the neighbor, he spent last night at his condo in Seattle, something about an early audition to-day."

"Audition?"

"He's an actor," Kevin replies.

"So he's unemployed," I say.

Kevin laughs; it's short, but from the belly. It's a good laugh, the kind that puts a smile on your face. "Yeah," the detective says, "I think that qualifies as unemployed. He used to deal blackjack at the casino, but that didn't last long. We asked Seattle PD to do the death notifica-tion a couple hours ago. Last I heard, one of their sup-port officers was driving him up here." He glances at his watch. "They should be here anytime now."

"How can we help, Kevin?" Jimmy asks. "Archie's already under arrest. I've got to think they have more than just the cell phone."

"They do." The words crawl up his throat like bile. Kevin shakes his head and you can see that he's hurt-ing, that he can't believe what he's about to say. "They found his fingerprints on the back doorknob." The detective seems to deflate as he exhales the words, and then silence fills the void between us.

"Has Archie visited Krystal since she moved here?" Jimmy asks in a soft tone.

"No," Kevin replies. "He's adamant about it."

Jimmy and I exchange a troubled glance. If Archie has already locked himself into a statement by saying that he's never been to the house, it's going to be nearly impossible to explain away his fingerprints.

"He's innocent," Kevin insists. "I'll take my badge off right now and retire if I'm wrong. You told me last year how amazing your partner is at murder scenes." He looks at me—studies me up and down. "All I'm asking is if you'll take a look around and see if we missed something."

Kevin looks down, flicking his finger against the handle of the paper bag. "Archie can't go to prison. It's just not right." He hands me the bag. "Jimmy said you needed this."

There's always a shoe.

It's become part of our search ritual, not because we need to check the pattern on the sole or the size of the foot. Those are some of the excuses we use, but the real reason is more complicated.

Since the age of eight, the year I died and was revived, I've had the ability to see what I call *shine*. Others might call it the human aura, or even life energy, but I prefer shine; it sounds less bizarre, and it's an actual tracking term, though the shine that trackers see is far different from what I see.

To me it looks like neon color and comes in every imaginable hue. Often, multiple colors will populate the shine, though there is always one that dominates. I call this color or combination of colors the shine's essence. Every shine also has a texture. It could be sandy, rough, glassy, rusty, bubbly, muddy, woven, fuzz, or a million other textures.

Each shine stands unique.

It's like fingerprints or DNA: I've never come across a shine that duplicates another. It allows me to walk onto a crime scene and see where everyone walked, what they touched, and where they left behind blood or semen or saliva. Sometimes I know who the shine belongs to because I have a shoe, or because they're present; other times the owner of the shine isn't revealed until the case develops further.

Weird, I know.

What makes it stranger is no one can know about it, and for good reason. Imagine sitting in the jury box during a murder trial and hearing a so-called expert tracker talking about some magical glow that only he can see. Not only would the case be tossed out, but the judge would probably order an involuntary mental health evaluation.

So I pretend.

I've learned the art of "real" man-tracking to gloss over my secret. When we're in the field I study the ground intently, looking for the real clues along the path of the shine. If the suspect brushed up against a plant at some point and broke a stem or branch, the shine points the way and I can highlight the damage as a sign of passage.

There are only three people who know my secret: Jimmy, my dad, and my boss, FBI Director Robert Carlson. Dad and Carlson were best friends and coworkers in the U.S. Army in West Germany in the late seventies. I grew up calling him Uncle Robert . . . and still do to this day. Jimmy has a coronary every time; it's hysterical.

I suppose it's no surprise that Dad told Uncle Robert about my special ability. My mother doesn't even know, but the director of the FBI knows; go figure. So here I am, standing on wet pavement under an overcast sky, staring at a blue-and-white size 11½ Nike taken from Archie Everard's closet.

"Jimmy said you needed to examine it before you could start a track," Detective Mueller says, gesturing toward the shoe.

"Jimmy . . . is . . . correct," I say, releasing the words one at a time as I turn the shoe slowly in my hands. "It looks like Archie has high arches," I say, running my finger along the outside edge of the sole. "See the wear pattern? That's supination; he's not rolling his feet inward enough when he walks. You should warn him about that. He could end up with knee problems or plantar fasciitis. That's actually kind of ironic; a guy named Archie who has high arches." I pause for effect. "Archie . . . arches, get it?"

"I think Archie has bigger problems at the moment. Steps," Jimmy says.

No one gets my jokes.

"Let's get to it, then," I say.

Getting the Nike was just a ruse to identify Archie's shine. People are generally a little squeamish about wearing someone else's sweaty shoes, so it's a great way to identify shine when the subject isn't standing in front of you. I saw it as soon as I took off my glasses. In addition to high arches, Archie has shine that radiates deep turquoise. The texture looks like waves of heat. It's an interesting combination.

"Take this," I say, handing the shoe to Jimmy.

When I was young I learned to dim the pulsing mass of superfluous shine that constantly clutters my vision, filtering it down so that just one shine remains. It's pretty effective, but gives me wicked headaches. With my glasses still in my hand, I block out all but Archie's unique turquoise shine and I let my eyes walk slowly over the front of the house.

"Who found the body?" Jimmy asks.

I don't know if he's trying to buy me time or is just curious. Either way, I'm grateful for the distraction.

"The neighbor," Detective Mueller says, thumbing toward the town house next door. "She was hyperventilating and pretty freaked out when we got here. Said the back door had been standing ajar for about an hour so she came over to close it, thinking the wind pushed it open. When she looked down the hall she saw a foot sticking out from the living room."

"How'd she know Krystal was dead? Did she go in?"

"Didn't have to, there was blood everywhere."

Finding no evidence of Archie's unique turquoise shine on the street, in the yard, or up the steps to the front door, I turn to Kevin. "Can we go around back?"

"Lead the way," he replies.

Following the sidewalk to the end of the block, and then to the right, we soon find ourselves at the alley that runs behind the row of houses. It's cordoned off with yellow police tape and guarded by a Skagit County deputy.

We stop at the perimeter and Kevin vouches for us. We show our FBI credentials and our names are dutifully added to the log sheet of personnel entering the crime scene, then Kevin lifts the tape and we duck under.

The house is on our right, just ahead.

Passing the gate into the backyard, I make my way to the open rear door—and there it is: a splash of turquoise. The doorknob glows with it. It's Archie's shine, there's no doubt about it, but what I'm seeing just doesn't make sense. I pull Jimmy aside, out of earshot.

"I've got a match."

Jimmy's shoulders slump. "That's it, then. Archie's our guy."

"Maybe not."

Jimmy's head jerks around. "How do you mean?"

"The shine is on the doorknob," I say.

"That makes sense. That's where they got the print."

"*Only* the doorknob," I stress.

It takes a moment for this to register. "How's that possible?"

"It isn't," I say. "Not unless he's got a magic carpet hidden away somewhere. I've got no tracks leading to the door, no elbow brushes against vegetation, no handprints on the gate, no footsteps leading inside the house. It doesn't make any sen—"

Jimmy's phone suddenly bursts into song.

It's Diane—I can tell by the ringtone. She's the third and final member of the FBI's Special Tracking Unit, or STU, and a call from her means one of two things: either she has information for us, or a new mission.

The conversation lasts less than a minute before Jimmy ends the call and slides the phone back into his pocket. "Les and Marty are fueling up Betsy," he says, referring to the Gulfstream G100 corporate jet parked at our office—Hangar 7—at Bellingham International Airport. "We're heading to El Paso."

"El Paso? They find a body?"

"Not exactly."

"What's that mean?"

"It means not exactly. I'll explain on the way. We need to wrap this up in a hurry." He lowers his voice to a whisper. "Is there anything you can do?"

"I don't know," I say resignedly. "I need to see the victim."

We make our way into the house. Though built just three years ago, it's now tainted by murder, and that's a stain that lingers. Kevin runs interference for us as officers from three different jurisdictions cast curious, sometimes annoyed eyes our way. A crime scene investigator is busy taking photos when we step into the living room.

I shudder, wrapping my arms across my chest.

When it comes to corpses, I'll take fresh bodies any day over those that have been percolating for days or weeks. This one is only hours gone, so it's not the smell—that hint of iron in the air—that makes me shudder.

The body is a bloody mess.

No, *bloody mess* doesn't go far enough describing what we find. Krystal Ballard is prone on the carpet and red from head to toe, like someone painted over her with a heavy brush as some sort of twisted art project. Her clothing is red, her hair is red, her shadow is red.

I can still see the suspect's shine, though.

And it's not turquoise.

A moment later I feel Jimmy's hand on my shoulder. "We save the ones we can," he says quietly. It's our mantra, our clarion call; words meant to remind us that we have a job to do and spur us into action, despite the horror that lies before us.

"We may be too late for her," I say to Jimmy, "but we can still save Archie." Turning my gaze to Detective Mueller, I say, "You're right; he didn't do this."

It's all clear to me now—like neon in the night, but without hard evidence it's going to be difficult to prove what I know. Meanwhile, Pastori is going to be hard-charging against Archie. Who could blame him? The physical evidence is compelling.

"I need a piece of paper and a pen," I say, snapping my fingers anxiously. Jimmy hands me a pen and Kevin hands me his notebook. Walking into the kitchen, I pull up a barstool and scratch out some notes and instructions. Two minutes later I tear the sheet from the notebook, fold it in half, and hand it to Kevin.

"Everything you need is in there: the suspect, how he did it, and how you can prove it. I'd get out of here right now and get started before Pastori has you standing perimeter or booking evidence for the next two days."

Kevin unfolds the note and I watch as his eyes walk across the words. At first he frowns, but then his whole demeanor changes and he actually smiles. Taking my hand, he shakes it briskly. "I don't know what to say." He shakes Jimmy's hand next, clapping him on the shoulder, and then he's out the door, off to solve a mystery.

Jimmy's dumbfounded. "What did you write?"

I shrug and hand his pen back.

"No, seriously, what did you write?"

"You'll see when he's done."

Jimmy just stares at me. "Really? You're not going to tell me?"

I shake my head and give him a grin. "That's what you get for not telling me about Pastori." Jimmy's still standing in the kitchen, hands on his hips, as I make my way out the front door and back to the Expedition.

I'm halfway across the lawn when I sense an ill wind stirring nearby. My eyes drift to the command vehicle just as Hector Pastori comes stumbling out, cursing the metal steps for making his feet oversized and clumsy. I quickly look away and tuck my head down between my shoulders as far as it will go.

A second later, I'm at the Expedition. I'm home free, my hand is on the door handle, just another second or two . . . and then Jimmy comes bumbling out the front door. He doesn't even look up as he starts down the walkway, which is unfortunate because Pastori isn't looking up either. They nearly collide fifteen feet from the door.

"Youuu," Pastori says. It's his fire-breathing dragon imitation; he says a word all long and drawn out and puts every ounce of his breath into it.

"Youuu," Jimmy mimics, not missing a beat.

"What are you doing here, Donovan?" Pastori demands. "Did I call you? I don't remember calling you. Yet here you are in the middle of my crime scene."

"Relax, I'm leaving. Sounds like you already have a suspect in custody anyway." As he starts to pass Hector, Jimmy pauses and leans in. "Are you sure he's the guy?"

"He's under arrest, isn't he? I don't need the FBI teaching me how to do my job like I'm some kind of incompetent. Speaking of which, where's that wannabe tracker you call partner?"

His eyes are already searching; he knows if Jimmy's here, I'm somewhere close by. Rather than give him the pleasure of spotting me slouching next to the Expedition, I start across the lawn toward him.

"Hey, look, it's Pastrami," I say loudly as I draw near and put my arm around Hector.

"It's Pastori, you degenerate." He throws my arm off.

"That's a very unusual name, Pastori Yudegenerate. Are you still looking for missing people on the wrong side of the mountain?"

"SERGEANT!" Pastori bellows, jabbing a finger at an officer near the front door. "Get these sons of bitches off my crime scene, and do it now. If they come back, arrest them for obstruction."

As he storms off, I say, "Geez, Hector, lighten up, buddy."

His steps falter and his shoulders rise up and he whips around on us with startling speed. "You're not the only ones with powerful connections, you know."

"Yeah," I shoot back. "Ours is the director of the FBI; yours is Wi-Fi. Congratulations."

He fumes at me with wordless anger, his face red and quivering, ripping my hair out strand by strand with his eyes. After a moment he turns and marches off without looking back.

I just shrug.

It's a good day after all.

Closing the door on the Expedition, I buckle up and then fish my glasses out of their case and slide them on. "You never answered me earlier," I say to Jimmy.

"About what?"

"The call you got from Diane, about going to El Paso. I asked if they found a body and you said, *Not exactly.* Remember?"

"Yeah, I remember."

"Well? Did they find a body?"

"Not exactly."

CHAPTER TWO

El Paso, Texas—September 2, 5:52 P.M.

Evening is settling over El Paso when Les and Marty—our pilot and copilot—land the Special Tracking Unit's Gulfstream at the El Paso International Airport. Nicknamed Betsy, the Gulfstream may look like a waste of taxpayer dollars, but it only appears so. Time is critical when responding to incidents; sometimes it's the difference between life and death. And so we try to get from one place to the next as quickly as possible and with as little grief.

Betsy makes that possible.

Six hours ago we were in Bellingham, now we're in El Paso—a two-thousand-mile journey in the course of an afternoon. Besides, flying around in the sleek Gulfstream is my favorite part of the job.

* * *

It's an hour until sunset, but already the El Paso sky is splendid with color. A hundred shades of yellow embrace a thousand shades of orange against the intermittent backdrop of robin's egg blue. It's a stunning wash of color that reflects off every window and casts a glow upon the city.

The air is blistering when Jimmy pulls to the curb in front of the El Paso Medical Examiner's Office on Alberta Avenue. Heat rises in waves from the road, which is lined with medical facilities on both sides: Texas Tech Health Science Center, University Medical Center of El Paso, El Paso Children's Hospital, Thomason Regional Laboratory, and more. Ironically, a large cemetery wrapped in cyclone fencing sits at the end of the street.

I'm sure it's just coincidence.

As we exit the rented gray Ford Focus, a stubborn wall of heat slams into us, feeling a lot like a swift gut punch that knocks the wind from your lungs. Unless you're a heat vampire, El Paso is one of those places where you walk from your air-conditioned house to your air-conditioned car to your air-conditioned office without too much lingering in between.

It's after hours, so Jimmy presses the buzzer next to the door and we sweat under the burnt sky for several minutes before a face appears in the door. Jimmy doesn't say anything, just presses his badge and ID against the window, and then we hear a loud click. Mr. Face pushes the door open and holds it long enough for us to slip through.

"They said you were on your way," Mr. Face says, "they just didn't say when." Wiping the wet tips of his fingers on his used scrubs, he extends a hand. "I'm Dr. Jimenez . . . Paul. Just call me Paul." When neither Jimmy nor I hurry to take his hand, he suddenly grins and holds them up, palms out. "It's just mustard and some pickle juice," he says. "You caught me in the middle of a sandwich."

We share a laugh and take turns shaking hands. Paul has a contagious grin, a robust laugh, and a sense of humor that seems out of place in a morgue, but then I realize it's not much different from cop humor. As we follow him down a pristine white hall he shares a coroner joke with us and laughs like someone else told it.

You can't help but like the guy.

Leading us into a large autopsy suite, Paul slips on a white gown over his scrubs and pulls on some gloves. "I'll fetch the remains from the cooler," he says as he heads out of the room. Pausing in the doorway, he points a finger at Jimmy, then me, saying, "Since I'm heading to the cooler, anybody want a beer?"

We stare at him.

He suddenly bursts into laughter and waves us away. "You guys are so easy." Then he's gone and we hear him whistling as he makes his way down the hall.

The autopsy suite is similar to a hundred others I've seen. There's the examination table, the sinks, screening tables, hanging scales, movable lighting, rinsing hoses, and more. The two dominant colors—almost the only colors—are white and stainless steel.

It's not long before we hear whistling in the hall, accompanied by the metallic rattle of a wheeled body cart. When Paul pushes the conveyance into the room, I'm immediately puzzled by its contents—or lack thereof.

"Well, this can't be good," I mutter.

The cart is nearly empty.

There's a white sheet draped over it, but instead of outlining the rough topography of a corpse, it covers a two-foot-by-two-foot rubber pan resting in the center of the stainless steel top.

"Let me guess," I say. "A head?"

"No," Paul replies with a grin, "that would make our job too easy, wouldn't it?" He whips off the white cloth like a magician pulling a tablecloth from under porcelain plates and half-full wineglasses.

Nestled in the center of the rubber pan are two feet still in their size 9½ gray Converse sneakers and white socks.

"Okay, you got my attention," I say.

Reaching under the cart, Dr. Jimenez retrieves a white Styrofoam ice box, one of those cheap ice chest substitutes you can buy at most stores, especially during the summer. He sets it next to the feet.

"What's that?" Jimmy asks.

"That," Paul replies, "is what they were found in, sitting in the middle of County Judge Jonathan Ehrlich's living room." He chuckles. "Couldn't have happened to a nicer guy." He shoots us a grin. "You didn't hear that from me."

Jimmy's curious. "Tell us about him."

Paul pauses, looks over his shoulder toward the door, and then leans in close. "He's the part of the foreskin you throw away after the circumcision, know what I mean? The guy's as useless as a warning label on a junkie's syringe. Still, he's got political connections and somehow got nominated to be a federal judge, if you can believe it. That was last month. He's still got to make it through the confirmation hearing, but he'll probably get rubber-stamped—God help us."

"You think this might be a message, something related to his nomination?" Jimmy asks. He's leaning over and checking out the inside of the ice box. I'm not interested in the ice box; I'm keeping my distance. Styrofoam freaks me out. I don't know why, it just does. I have issues, okay?

The only thing that freaks me out as much as Styrofoam is your standard everyday forest. Anytime large numbers of deciduous and evergreen trees start milling about together, you know it can't end well.

"I suppose it could be some sort of message," Dr. Jimenez replies. "Still, this *is* El Paso. All options are on the table."

"What about the cartels?" I ask.

"That's one option," Paul replies emphatically, "though they tend to use heads when they want to send a message. Still, who knows? It wasn't long ago that Mexican authorities found a van abandoned in the desert a few miles south of the border, east of Juárez. The Federales recovered fourteen bodies. The only reason they knew there were fourteen bodies was because that's how many torsos were inside. Even at that, they somehow ended up with fifteen left arms." He scratches his chin and shakes his head. "How's that happen? Fifteen left arms, fourteen torsos?"

"How much trouble would it be to take off the shoes and socks?" I ask. "Actually, I don't need to see both feet, one will do."

"No trouble at all," Paul replies. "I've already given

them a cursory examination for trace, but came up empty." He retrieves both shoes from the rubber bin and sets them on the examination table, where they immediately begin to puddle. "Did I mention they were frozen?"

"Frozen?" Jimmy says.

"Yep. Based on the rate of thaw, they'd been out of the freezer for about two days when we found them— starting to get a little ripe, too." He wrinkles his nose, and then gets to work unlacing the left shoe. He pulls it off with a bit of a tug, gripping the stump of the ankle in the process. "Freezing complicates things a bit," he says as he works. "For starters, it makes it impossible to estimate time of death or time of crime. This guy could have died six months or six days ago. I have no way of knowing for certain."

The left sock comes off next and I get my first good look at the foot, but it's not really the foot that I need to see, it's the shine: mocha brown, speckled with wisps of lime green. The texture is that of pumice; it's porous, vesicular, ugly.

I don't know where the rest of him is, but I know he's dead. That's one of the peculiar aspects of shine: it vibrates and pulses with energy when the subject is alive, but lies flat and dormant once they're dead.

Other shine is present, of course.

These likely belong to the factory workers who made the shoes, socks, and ice box, the clerks who displayed them and sold them, the killer who cut them off the victim, and the crime scene investigators who recovered them. Most of it is older, and I can filter it out easily enough. That still leaves three distinct examples of shine on the shoes, and four on the ice box, one of which is Dr. Jimenez—a very pleasant shade of purple, simple and clean.

Of the remaining shine, only one is on both the shoes and the Styrofoam box. It's bright and piercing: ice blue with flecks of black and the texture of smooth plastic, a shine so cold my bones shudder at the sight.

"Any idea what was used to sever the feet?" Jimmy asks, pointing to the flesh and bone at the unfinished ankle.

Paul nods with appreciation. "It's a clean cut, isn't it? I'm thinking some kind of industrial equipment, maybe for food processing or something along that line. Whatever it was, it sliced through the bone without a problem."

"Does a butcher have equipment that would do that?"

"Honestly, I don't know," Paul says with a shrug. "There's no indication of saw marks, though, so it looks like a clean chop."

"How about DNA?"

"I sent a sample to the lab, but it's going to be a while before we get results—that's provided he's in CODIS," Paul says, referring to the Combined DNA Index System. It houses the DNA of sex offenders and subjects arrested for or convicted of various other crimes. CODIS also houses DNA from unsolved rapes and murders, running those profiles against new additions to the database on a daily basis.

"Would you mind sending a sample to the FBI lab as well?" Jimmy asks.

"Aren't you guys backlogged worse than us?"

"Probably, but we get priority processing."

Scratching out an address and instructions, Jimmy hands the piece of paper to the doctor. "Make sure you include the line *Attention: Janet Burlingame*. She's the lab tech who does all our processing. She'll make things happen."

"Roger dodger," Paul says, stuffing the note in his pocket.

We have everything we came for, which was really only two things: the shine of the unidentified victim, and the shine of his killer. We thank Dr. Jimenez and say our goodbyes, leaving him in the autopsy suite. As we're exiting the front door, he hurries up behind us.

"You guys will let me know if you find the rest of him, right?" he says, holding the door open for us. "DNA match or not, I need to ID this guy as soon as possible or these feet are going to sit in the cooler taking up valuable space."

"We'll call you if we find him, or if we figure out who he is," Jimmy says, shaking Paul's hand a second time.

"Beers on me next time," the doctor says. Then he chuckles as Jimmy and I exchange glances. "No, for real. I know this great little pub."

He's still smiling as we exit the parking lot.

Vista Hermosa Drive lives up to its translation: Beautiful View.

It's a fairly straight road of well-tended asphalt that juts right into the western slope of the Franklin Mountains, near the southern tip. It's a street of high-end houses, high-end cars, and high-end career professionals; home to the well-to-do of El Paso. Judge Jonathan

Ehrlich's house is in the cul-de-sac at the end of the street, snug up against the base of a mountain.

The crime scene still hasn't been released and the spectacle of yellow police tape is an unpleasantness to which the residents of Vista Hermosa Drive are unaccustomed, as is the police car in the driveway. Even now we see faces peering out windows at our approach, more fodder for the text- and Twitter-driven rumor mill.

As Jimmy eases the Ford carefully up to the curb, we both spot a young city officer, probably fresh from the academy, maintaining perimeter at the open front door. We notice him because he's getting an unpleasant earful from a short, rotund man in his mid-to-late fifties.

"Judge Ehrlich, I presume," Jimmy says under his breath as he slips the Ford into park and gives the ignition key a twist and pull.

"He seems nice," I say in a singsong voice before unbuckling my belt and pushing it aside. Taking my special glasses off, I stow them safely in their leather case and leave them on the center console. I have an identical pair in my travel bag, which is still in the trunk, and two more at home. The lead-crystal lenses in the glasses are the only substance I've found that completely blocks shine. As such, the glasses are the only thing keeping me sane.

Still, I can only wear them six or seven hours before a throbbing headache ensues—the same thing happens if I stare at shine too long. So I alternate: two or three hours with the glasses, a half hour to an hour without.

As Ehrlich continues to rant and even bellow, the city cop keeps his mouth shut and doesn't react. That's the one thing about being in law enforcement: someone's always mad at you. Someone always wants to fight or argue or scream. The second thing about being in law enforcement is that someone is always blaming you for something you didn't do or aren't responsible for.

The city cop is getting a truckload of both.

It takes patience to be a cop.

As we make our way up the sidewalk, Red-Faced-Angry-Man spots us and immediately rampages in our direction. Imagine you're on safari in Africa; you're on foot for some ridiculous reason and you stumble upon a herd of wild elephants. Spooked by your presence, the elephants suddenly stampede in your direction, trumpeting and bellowing as they come.

Red-Faced-Angry-Man is scarier.

Closing the distance with frightful speed for someone with his drag coefficient, he's on us in seconds. "Are you the two incompetents I've been waiting for all day?" he demands, spit flying from his mouth in seven different directions.

"Special Agent James Donovan, FBI," Jimmy says calmly. "Are you Jonathan Ehrlich?"

"*JUDGE* Ehrlich," he replies tersely. "I am. And what are you going to do about this crime scene? My house is wide open; you've got police tape cluttering the place up and making an eyesore of it; and my wife says she won't step foot in this house until someone's caught and behind bars." He crosses his arms and glares at us, looking me up and down like I'm some kind of troll that just crawled up through the business end of an outhouse. "When is that going to be, I wonder? Hmm?"

"*Judge* Ehrlich," Jimmy says, "we just got here. Let us do our job. Trust me; we want this over as quickly and as painlessly as you. We just need to examine the crime scene and we'll be on our way."

He just stands there with his arms folded.

"Hurry up," he finally snaps. Whirling around, he moves back to the front porch so he can harass the El Paso officer again. As we pass, I give the poor guy a quick wink, a gesture of solidarity for a fellow member of the Jerk of the Month Club.

The house is expansive, about four thousand square feet in all. As we make our way through the foyer and into the living room, we see a spot outlined in tape on the carpet, courtesy of CSI. We crouch down next to the tape, side by side, and I walk Jimmy through it.

"Looks like he came in there," I say, pointing to the far wall where a French-door-style slider opens onto a large deck. "He walked straight here, set the ice box down, and left the way he came; no detours; in and out in seconds. He didn't even bother to look around or stare at the family photos on the wall."

"He's organized," Jimmy says. "Mission oriented; task oriented."

"Looks like it. And there's no shine suggesting he's ever been here before. This was his first visit." Pushing myself upright, I say, "Let's check outside, see how he approached the house."

Through the slider, I follow the ice-blue shine east across the deck and then up and over a decorative rock wall at the back edge of the property. From there the trail goes up the western slope of the mountain range, into Franklin Mountains State Park. The park itself covers over twenty-four thousand acres and is completely contained within the city limits of El Paso.

It's not an overly steep climb, but the trail is littered with loose rock, baked earth, and a sampling of lowland vegetation, including desert grasses, creosote bushes, and a variety of cacti. Two hundred feet into our climb, we discover the unexpected: a road.

The ice-blue shine with its black speckles turns abruptly and follows the road south. From where I stand, my eyes follow the glow until the road veers left and disappears around the corner. "He came and went from that direction," I say, pointing south, "which means he either walked up from the other side of the mountain, or he drove in and parked somewhere up ahead."

Jimmy's on his smartphone pulling up maps—should have thought of that before we walked up the cacti-strewn mountain. "There's a scenic overlook with a small parking lot," he says, his eyes quickly scanning additional images. "It's just around the corner, probably less than a quarter mile." Stuffing his phone in his pocket and without another word, he starts marching to the south.

"Whoa! Hold up," I shout after him. He pauses long enough for me to catch up. "How about we finish at the house first?" I point down the hill where the whole community is laid out before us. "The road starts just north of the judge's place. We can grab the car and follow IBK in a climate-controlled environment."

"Air-conditioning," Jimmy scoffs, always up for a good hike, regardless of the weather. "It's already cooling down—wait, did you say IBK?"

"Uh-huh."

"What's IBK?"

"Ice Box Killer."

"Ice Box Killer? Really? Do we always have to give them names?"

"Just the weird ones," I say with a shrug. "We always name the weird ones; in fact, you named the last two, if I remember correctly. Besides, if we don't, the press will . . . you know they will."

He gives me a harrowed look.

"What?" I say, raising my hands up like I'm pleading for clemency. "You want me to call them *unsubs* or *perps* like they do on TV? Seriously, in the last five years how many times have you heard a cop use the word *unsub* or *perp*? Hmm? Zero," I say with authority, holding up a circle with my thumb and index finger.

"*Suspect* works just fine," Jimmy replies.

"I-B-K works even better," I say, drawing out the letters. Jimmy doesn't argue it further, which means I win by default.

"Whatever," he grunts. "Let's get a move on."

"No, wait!"

Jimmy's already a half dozen steps away and slows only long enough to whirl around mid-stride and say, "Come on, Steps, we're losing the light."

"Seriously, Jimmy, hold up," I say. "Besides, we've already lost the sun." I point to the western horizon as he stops, shakes his head, and then walks slowly back. "You know as well as I do that there's a ninety-five percent chance we're going to walk around that corner and the trail's going to come to an abrupt end where he got into a car. It may be a quarter mile; it may be five miles. The point is that it's not going to add to what we know."

"We still have to follow it to the end," Jimmy says.

"Maybe the guy dropped his wallet when he got into the car. Maybe there's a camera monitoring the area where he parked—who knows?"

"Yeah, I know all that. I'm just saying we should go back to the house and finish with Judge U-lick—"

"Ehrlich."

"That's what I said; and then we can finish the track in the car. Besides, the poor cop at the door looked like he could use a break. If he has to put up with U-lick much longer we may have another homicide on our hands."

"We're already here," Jimmy argues. "Why not just trudge on?"

A dusky tint settles upon the mountain as we speak, and shadows deepen and come to life, creeping across the landscape from every cactus, rock, or bush. From the edge of the road thirty feet ahead of us something moves; just a small movement at first, but enough to catch my eye in the failing light. As Jimmy and I talk, I tilt to the right, looking past him as a thin strip of blackness moves slowly out onto the road.

"Do they have rattlesnakes in these parts?" I ask.

Jimmy chuckles. "If you want to go back that badly, just say so."

"No." I grab Jimmy by both shoulders and spin him around, pointing up the road. "Do they have rattlesnakes in these parts?" I repeat.

Jimmy stares up the road for a good thirty seconds and then fumbles for his smartphone; it only takes a few seconds to find the answer. "Not only rattlesnakes, but tarantulas, scorpions, and poisonous centipedes."

We're fifty feet down the mountain when something

occurs to Jimmy. Rather than keeping the thought to himself, he decides to share: "What if we're walking right through them?" he hisses.

Now all I can think about is a poisonous centipede crawling up my pant leg and nesting in my underwear. Frankly, I'd rather get bitten by the rattler. We pick up the pace until we're practically running down the mountain, barely able to see the obstacles in front of us. When we reach the rock wall at the back of the judge's property, we vault over it like Olympians and don't slow down until we reach the deck.

I'm bent over, catching my breath; Jimmy's holding up the wall with both hands. A minute later he brushes his clothes off and stands erect. "Let's clear the crime scene," he says in a calm, almost ho-hum voice, as if nothing had happened.

Entering the house through the rear slider, I'm instantly aware of what sounds like a muted riot issuing through the open front door and reverberating off the walls and ceiling. The caterwaul only grows louder as we cross the living room and enter the foyer. There's no doubt as to the source of the discordance, though how a would-be federal judge learned to whine so prodigiously is beyond me.

The target of Judge Ehrlich's abuse, of course, is the young rookie.

As we step out behind Ehrlich, relief washes over the officer—you can see it on his face and in the way his shoulders rise up from a slump. He's been taking a steady verbal beating since we arrived.

"Go ahead and collect all the police tape," Jimmy

tells the officer. "Close down the crime scene; we're done here."

"Well, it's about time," Ehrlich fumes, stepping in front of Jimmy and getting in his face. "It's beyond me what could take so long and why this process has been dragged out all day." Jabbing a finger hard into Jimmy's chest three or four times, he says, "I want your names and badge numbers. Couple of worthless FBI flunkies—" The finger jabs again, but this time Jimmy steps to the side and grabs the judge's extended wrist. In one swift, smooth motion he spins the judge around and plants him face-first against the side of the house with his arm bent up his back.

"Assaulting an FBI agent," Jimmy hisses in the judge's ear, "is a federal offense; I could lock you up for that. I suggest you get inside before I place your ass in handcuffs and file charges." He lets go of the judge and pushes him toward the front door. "How would *that* look during your confirmation hearing?"

Ehrlich is spitting mad . . . and I swear there's a bit of foam building up at the corner of his mouth.

He's no dummy, though. You can see him processing his options as he stares Jimmy down with venomous eyes. Without a word, he turns abruptly and walks briskly into the house, slamming the door behind him. We listen as his heavy steps thud down the hall, and then the porch grows quiet.

The El Paso officer is the first to break the silence.

Hurrying over, he cups Jimmy's hand with both of his and blurts, "I've never seen anything like that." He has a huge grin on his face as he adds, "That was a friggin' *judge!*" He's still shaking his head in disbelief and grinning with glee when he hurries off to clean up the crime scene, eager to be out of there before Ehrlich makes another appearance.

"*Place your ass in handcuffs?*" I say to Jimmy after we get back into the car and buckle up. "A little vulgar for you, isn't it?"

"The guy's arrogant and abusive. I lost my cool."

"Obviously," I say, letting the word linger a moment. I could leave it at that, but this is too rare an opportunity to let pass. Jimmy doesn't believe in polluting his "higher mind" with profanity and vulgarity, so for someone to elicit an *ass* out of him is a significant accomplishment.

"I get it," I continue, "the guy's a real piece of work. But this is the third time you've said *ass* in recent memory. I'm just not sure I can continue working under these conditions."

"*Shut up!*" He starts the car and turns the headlights on. "And stop grinning at me; you look like Gary Busey when you do that."

"Who?"

"Gary—ah, never mind."

The GPS in the rental tells us that the road looping around the southern tip of the Franklin Mountains is Scenic Drive. It's an appropriate name for the road, since the sweeping view is . . . well, scenic.

We pick up the Ice Box Killer's trail where we left off, and although there's no sign of the meandering rattlesnake I keep my window up and the door locked.

I'm from the Pacific Northwest; what do I know about rattlesnakes? Maybe they can jump through windows, maybe they can't. I'm just not going to risk it.

We follow the ice-blue neon path to the south for a quarter mile and then east around the southern tip of the mountain range. The scenic overlook is just ahead and, as expected, the trail of shine terminates in the parking lot.

I get out.

"He parked over there," I say, pointing to a spot half-way down the limited parking strip, which has room for maybe ten cars. "It looks like he didn't go straight to his car after he finished," I add, studying the ground.

And then I start walking.

Jutting out from the parking lot is Murchison Park, a recreational area complete with picnic tables, coin-operated binoculars, and ample observation points for looking down upon the city of El Paso, and to Juárez on the other side of the border. There's a wall around the entire park, probably to keep the overly curious from taking an unexpected tumble.

It's a pleasant area—in a rocky, arid sort of way—and my eyes follow IBK's trail as it makes its way along the paved footpath that parallels the western wall. He stopped halfway to the point; halfway to the tip of the observation area where the whole city is laid out to the east and to the west.

There's nothing unique or particular about the spot where he chose to stop, but he stood there a long time; I can tell from the shifting pattern of his feet on the ground and the array of handprints on the wall. They're the signs of long ruminations, of someone with a lot on his mind and the need for a solitary place to sort it all out.

"Is it guilt?" I ask Jimmy after pointing this out.

Jimmy has a master's in psychology, and though he's not a profiler, he could be. He's pretty good at reaching into a person's head and pulling out the stuff that matters.

"It could be guilt," he replies. "Or fear, or frustration. For all we know, he just liked the view."

We stand in silence for a while, looking out over the city. "I have to say, it's a beautiful view," Jimmy declares at length. "Probably better at night than it was for him during the day."

He's right.

The city is awash in the warm glow of artificial yellow light. Any imperfections are masked and made trivial by the golden hue until all you see is a shimmering city on a high desert plain. Just beyond El Paso is Juárez; if it wasn't for the border running between them, they'd be the same city.

All of Mexico lies to the south.

It's a beautiful sight.

The night makes all things mysterious.

CHAPTER THREE

River Belmont Hotel, Room 227—September 2, 10:12 P.M.

There's an unspoken truth in business travel: if you've seen one standard hotel room, you've seen them all. There are always décor differences, of course, but the basic rule applies. Some travelers have had the misfortune of staying in hundreds of hotel rooms, as Jimmy and I have, in which case they all seem to homogenize into a generic box with one or two beds, a TV, a hair dryer attached to the wall, a big mirror over the sink, and the ever-present DO NOT DISTURB placard hanging off the inside of the doorknob.

When your hotel rooms start to homogenize, it means you're probably not spending enough time with your family. I don't know how my partner does it. Pete, Jimmy's son, was a year old when the Special Tracking Unit was established. Now he's six. Half of that time,

Jimmy and I have lived out of hotel rooms while chasing down some of the sickest minds in the country.

Jane, his wife, is one of the most patient, self-reliant women I've ever met, but it has to get to her, Jimmy being gone all the time. These constant absences—it's too much to ask of a person, no matter how important the job.

He's out on the balcony right now talking to Jane and Pete. It's a nightly ritual when we're on the road. I could go to my room, give him some privacy, but my room is boring.

Twenty minutes later I'm propped up on his bed, eating some of his dry-roasted peanuts, using his clipboard as a lap desk, and writing a letter on tan stationery, when he comes in from the balcony and closes the slider behind him.

"How's Jane?" I ask, not looking up.

"Good . . . well, a little upset that we had to bug out. We had dinner plans tonight." He shrugs. "I'll have to make it up to her when we get back."

"You said that last week," I reply, shaking my head. "I thought tonight was supposed to make up for that one. And you still owe her for the wedding you missed last month. I know because she keeps complaining about how she had to dance with your weirdo second cousin, Elmo."

"Elmore," he corrects.

"Same difference."

Jimmy's my brother in every way except biologically. Our shared experiences include so much more than just working together: we travel together, commiserate together, weep together, scheme together, brainstorm together, and, ultimately, solve horrific crimes together. The bond between us is almost as strong as the one I share with my brother, Jens. That's what happens when your history includes near-death experiences, gunfire, serial killers, and a freight train of emotional baggage.

I remember not really liking Jimmy when we first met.

He was too stuffy, too straitlaced-FBI—a walking, talking stereotype in polished shoes. We're polar opposites in so many ways, which makes our friendship that much more unusual. For starters, he's athletic, into sports, and likes being out in the woods—camping, hiking, you name it.

I rarely watch sports, and though I'm in great shape, I believe that sweating is something one should never do intentionally. As for hiking and all that happy-camper stuff, you can keep it. I can't stand the woods; clusters of trees freak me out. It's a condition called *hylophobia* and stems from that incident when I was eight—more emotional baggage.

While the differences between us seemed immeasurable, those first days and weeks together also turned up a surprising number of similarities. Fragmented conversations on the road and in the air painted a picture of a man I could like, even respect. By the end of the first month, respect had turned to admiration, and the seed that would grow into an unseverable bond was planted.

Jimmy is my brother; Jane is my sister; Pete is my nephew.

Sometimes family has nothing to do with blood.

I set my pen down for a moment and wait for Jimmy to look at me. "We can ratchet this back, you know. We don't have to take *every* case they throw our way. What are they going to do, fire us? Good! I'd welcome it."

"Easy for you to say," Jimmy replies with a smirk. "You're the human bloodhound, remember. Without you there *is* no Special Tracking Unit. Me, I'm just the handler. Handlers are replaceable."

"You're joking, right?"

Jimmy doesn't answer; he just steals the jar of peanuts back and plops down into one of the two generic chairs in the corner and proceeds to stare at the ceiling.

I knock on the clipboard until Jimmy glances at me—irritating, I know, but it's effective. "We're a team," I say. "You go, I go. No exceptions." I stare at him until he again pulls his eyes from the ceiling and looks at me. "We've talked about this," I say firmly. "Give the word and I'll quit right now, this minute. We can go be private investigators or something like that."

Jimmy snorts. "We can't quit."

"Sure we can," I reply forcefully. "We can do whatever we want."

This sets him back, but only for a moment. "Thanks," he says quietly, and then his eyes return to the ceiling. I just watch him in silence. "I can't give it up yet," he eventually says. "It's not because I enjoy it," he adds, "it's because I know that people will die when we finally stop. People we could have saved."

He pulls his eyes from the ceiling and looks right at me. "That's why you can't stop either, despite your claims to the contrary. You probably need the STU more than I do, you just won't admit it."

There he goes again, pulling that stuff out of my head. I smile and give him a single nod, the type of gesture that acknowledges his words without confirming or rejecting them.

He's about to continue when his phone rings.

Looking down at the calling number, he says, "This should be good," and answers the call with a friendly, "Hey, Kevin, how's the investigation going?" The voice of Skagit County Detective Kevin Mueller murmurs from the phone, but I can't make out the words. "Yeah, he's right here," Jimmy says a moment later. "Let me put you on speaker." He pushes a button and sets the phone on the bed between us.

"Your information played out perfectly, Steps; exactly as you described it," Kevin begins. "We checked Archie's house and found that his doorknob is the exact same brand and model as the victim's back door. As you suggested, we checked John Ballard's debit and credit card activity and found he made a purchase at Home Depot a week ago for $27.32 using his debit card. It didn't say what he purchased, but using the date and time stamp from the debit card we were able to pull surveillance video."

"Which showed him browsing the doorknob aisle," I say.

"Exactly! He spent some time sorting through the shelves and kept checking a piece of paper in his hand. Eventually he picked out the exact model of Kwikset polished brass entry knob that's on Archie's back door."

The doorknob? Jimmy mouths in my direction. His face is conflicted, stuck somewhere between impressed and puzzled. It's only then that I remember I never clued him in on any of this.

"Nice," I say, trying not to grin too much. "Do you have enough for PC?"

Probable cause, better known as PC, is the ever-present standard that must be met to make an arrest. It's a simple standard that requires enough reasonable suspicion, supported by circumstances and evidence, so that a prudent and cautious person would believe that the facts are probably true—hence the word *probable*.

"We didn't at first," Kevin replies, "so we went back to Archie's hoping to pull Ballard's prints off the doorknob or the door itself, but no luck."

"Still, you have the debit card transaction and the surveillance video," I say. "That's got to count for something."

"Oh, I can do better than that," Kevin says. "Archie's garbage can was on the side of the house and for some reason I looked inside. There, right near the top, was an empty Kwikset box, and when we dusted it for prints Ballard was all over it. The fool didn't want to throw it in his own garbage can so he tossed it into Archie's."

"Nice work," Jimmy says with a pleased look on his face. He keeps looking at me, and then back at the phone. "Did they cut Archie loose yet?"

"Yeah, they released him an hour ago." He chuckles. "I hope you guys like blueberries, because I think you're going to get buckets and buckets of them for the rest of your lives. Oh, and speaking of the rest of your lives, you two might want to stay clear of Pastori for at least that long."

"He's not happy with us?" I ask with exaggerated inflection.

"Let's just say I've heard the term 'spitting mad' plenty of times," Kevin replies, "but I don't think I've actually seen it until today. For a while there, he refused to release Archie, despite the evidence. It wasn't until Archie's lawyer threatened to sue him for violating his civil rights that he finally relented. After that, your names were kicked around so often and so hard you would have thought a one-man soccer match was under way."

I chuckle . . . twice.

"Well, we're glad it worked out for Archie," Jimmy says. "It wasn't really looking good for him; I can only imagine what he's been through."

"Well, we owe you big; you have no idea."

"No sweat. Take care, Kevin. And let us know if you need anything else."

"Thanks. You guys are geniuses."

There's a click and the line goes dead. Jimmy picks his phone up and slips it back into his pocket. His face has regained its normal lines and curves, with just a hint of puzzlement at the corner of his left eye.

"Geniuses," I say, letting the word roll from my mouth slowly. "Or . . . genius?" I add, tapping myself twice in the chest. I give a little nod and then pick up my pen and turn my attention back to the stationery on the clipboard.

"Switched doorknob, huh?"

"Yep."

"How'd you come up with that?"

I roll my eyes toward him, pulling my head along for the ride. "I'm a genius." Then it's back to the stationery, the clipboard, and the pen.

He watches me in silence for a long minute. I can tell he's smiling. I don't have to see him to know; we've been partners so long I can almost sense it.

After a minute he says, "What are you doing?"

"What does it look like?" I reply. "I'm writing Heather."

"Didn't you just spend an hour on the phone with her after we checked in? What more could you have to talk about?"

"This is different."

"I'll say," Jimmy replies. "No one writes letters anymore, Steps. We have these new inventions called texting and email."

"Proof that we've all become too impersonal," I say. "Where's the romance in a text message? We send two- and three-word texts back and forth using abbreviated symbols that don't even look like words and we call it communication: *OMG LOL YMMD*. Frankly, it's a vulgar display of illiteracy. Besides, what happens when you clear the text or email from your phone? I'll tell you: it's gone forever. Even if you try to save a special email, chances are your phone or computer is going to crash at some point and you'll lose it anyway."

"So writing letters is the solution?"

"It is."

"And what brought about this sudden revelation?"

"Geniuses have revelations like that all the time," I quip.

He's shaking his head. "Seriously; why?"

There's no getting around it, so I set my pen down and meet his pressing stare; this must be what it's like when I pester *him* for information. It's a bit annoying.

"Remember about three weeks ago," I say, "when I helped my mom clean out the garage?"

"Yeah, I remember. You said you might have hantavirus because you thought you saw some mouse droppings."

"I *did* see mouse droppings."

"Jens told me it was a couple dead ants."

"Well, Jens is a hantavirus denier."

Jimmy's head is shaking back and forth like a broken washing machine. "Let's get back to the part about helping your mom clean out the garage. Please."

"Right; well, as you know, she's a pack rat."

"She's a hoarder," Jimmy corrects.

"Right, but she limits it to the garage. Still, you can barely walk through the place, so we pulled everything out onto the parking pad so we could go through it. We spent all day sorting through the clutter, and in the late afternoon we came across this old hope chest. It belonged to Grandma Samuelsen and ended up in the garage after she died. I don't think it's been touched since.

"We really had no idea what to expect, since Mom never bothered to look inside when it was put into the garage. When we opened it up, we found stacks and stacks of old letters that Grandpa wrote to Grandma over the years, starting when they were first dating and all the way up to a year before Grandma died. Whenever he was away, Grandpa wrote to her. Mom said it wasn't because he wanted to pass on news, but so she'd know that he was thinking of her while he was away. I'm sure Grandpa got some letters too, but we never found any. Grandma probably saved every letter she ever got."

"On account of her being a hoarder," Jimmy says.

"Exactly," I say, grinning at him. "But in this case, I'm glad she did. We spent the next hour reading the letters to each other. Mom was bawling her eyes out, and I think even Jens got a little misty."

"What about you?"

"Nah, I was stoic."

"I'm sure," Jimmy replies. "I've seen how stoic you are."

I chuckle—only because he's right.

"It got me to thinking, though," I say, trying to remain serious. "With Heather constantly on the road with her job, and me bouncing all over the country tracking bad guys, I thought it would be nice to have that kind of connection. Something she can actually hold in her hand; something she can look at and read if she starts to miss me."

"You're assuming she misses you," Jimmy chimes in.

I just ignore the jab. "Poke at me all you want, but I'm right about this. You should try it with Jane. Trust me, she'll melt. Women love this kind of thing. Heather's been on the road for the last week and I've sent her two letters so far."

"The day I have to take relationship advice from you, Steps, is the day I'm in real trouble. Now, out of my room so I can get some sleep."

"Really? *Hunger Games* is coming on in a few. I thought—"

"No! You've seen it thirty-seven times, Steps."

"Six or seven times," I correct.

He just shakes his head. "Do what you want, but do it in your own room. It's been a long day and I need sleep." He looks at me with a corner of his mouth twisted up. "When we woke up this morning we were still in Whatcom County. Since then we've investigated a murder in Skagit County, flown two thousand miles, examined some severed feet, and tracked a killer up a mountain."

"And beat up a judge," I add.

"And beat up a judge," he says with a little too much satisfaction. "Get out."

I'm halfway out the door when I remember something.

"Diane called while you were talking to Jane. Our liaison with El Paso PD is Detective Tony Alvarado. She said he's a real go-getter."

"Detective . . . Tony . . . Alvarado," Jimmy scratches on his notepad. "Got it."

"Sure you don't want to watch *Hunger*—"

The pillow hits the door next to my head and I mutter, "Fine," and make my way back to my boring, homogenized room.

CHAPTER FOUR

River Belmont Hotel—September 3, 8:32 A.M.

Normally I don't sleep this late when we're on the road, but it was a late night after a long day, so I spoiled myself a little. I'm sure Jimmy was up at six as usual. Probably got his workout in, plus a five-mile run, then had breakfast. Right about now he's watching the news and double-checking his notes.

I have two new emails on my phone when I step out of the shower: one from Diane, the other from eBay. I open the eBay alert first. I've been bidding on a first edition, first printing of *The Caine Mutiny* to add to my collection. The alert is just letting me know that the auction ends soon and I'm still the highest bidder; in fact, the bid isn't even close to my maximum. With luck, I'll get this one cheap.

The email from Diane is a little more problematic.

Three weeks ago, on August 13 to be precise, we

responded to a crime scene outside Fairmont, West Virginia. A nineteen-year-old hairstylist named Ally McCully was found dead in a wooded clearing after being reported missing a week earlier. The shine matched that from an unsolved murder in Bellingham eleven years ago.

Long ago I dubbed the killer Leonardo.

It wasn't a name randomly selected. It was derived from that first crime scene itself, from the pattern intentionally placed upon the ground. I didn't see it at first, but as I puzzled over why he would walk a perfect circle around the victim I started to recognize the image—and then I was certain. It was a crude rendition of a drawing by Leonardo da Vinci, a symbol that had, in some way, come to represent humanity.

I was sixteen when I first saw it.

The image is with me still.

My attempts to identify Leonardo predate the Special Tracking Unit by six years, and I've been frustrated at every turn. This new victim three thousand miles away in West Virginia represented the first substantial change in the investigation since it began. What it yields, if anything, is yet to be seen.

That's the sad thing about hunting serial killers: evidence is doled out in batches, each batch paid for with the life of the next victim. The cost is high.

The decade-long span between Leonardo's two known victims begs a question: Is this really his second killing, or are there more victims scattered across the country? More evidence paid for in blood?

Nineteen-year-old Ally McCully was faceup with her

feet together pointing south, and her arms outstretched and pointing to the east and to the west. That's what the cops saw.

My view was slightly different.

I saw where he first extended her arms above her shoulders before bringing them back perpendicular to her body as if she were pointing east and west. I saw where he splayed her legs apart before pulling them together pointing south. I saw where he walked a circle around her still corpse, his oozing black shine encompassing her in a perfect circle.

I saw Leonardo da Vinci's *Vitruvian Man* cast upon the ground.

The only thing missing was the cube that complements the circle. For some reason he doesn't include that. Perhaps it's an irrelevant omission, but I suspect it's by design. He's a creature of ritual and purpose; you don't create the *Vitruvian Man* on the ground with a corpse and neglect to include one of the main elements.

I was startled—*repulsed*—when I saw the image again after so many years.

Turning from the body, I blurted Leonardo's name to Jimmy and a local detective overheard. That led to questions I wasn't prepared for. Jimmy and I tried some quick damage control, and I thought the issue had been put to rest, but a particular detective from Fairmont PD keeps calling. He's persistent, the type of persistent that doesn't quit, which I admire, though it creates a real problem. At some point I'm going to have to give him some straight answers. Fortunately, Leonardo's name hasn't reached the media yet, but that too is inevitable.

Diane's email is addressed to both me and Jimmy. It's short and to the point: *Detective Graham called. Again. Tired of making excuses. Take care of it.*

She's bossy that way.

El Paso Police Department—9:27 A.M.

The El Paso Police Department's Criminal Investigations Division, or CID, is located in the headquarters building on Raynor Street and is home to several specialized units, including the Crimes Against Persons section. As the name implies, the unit handles incidents such as homicide, robbery, sexual assault, and kidnapping.

If you're a detective, you're going to get some ugly cases tossed your way. The good news is . . . you're a detective; you've already proven you can handle it.

Tony Alvarado can more than handle it.

Diane's brief bio says he's thirty-two years old, started with the department eight years ago, and picked up detective just last year. He's single and enjoys building and flying remote-control airplanes. . . . I don't know why that's relevant, but Diane thought it important enough to include.

Detective Alvarado is waiting for us in the lobby when we arrive. He's easy to spot: in a sea of blue uniforms, he's the only dark gray suit. Diane must have done a good job describing us, because as soon as we enter the building he starts across the tile floor.

"Special Agent Donovan?" he says as we come together.

"Call me Jimmy." They shake briskly and strongly, like men do when they're testing one another. "And you must be Magnus Craig?"

"Guilty," I say, taking his hand.

"Magnus? Is that Scandinavian?"

"It is; Norwegian, to be precise. My mom insisted."

"She's Norwegian, I take it?"

"To the bone. She's been in the country thirty years and we still haven't been able to talk the accent out of her."

Alvarado chuckles at this. "Well, it's certainly a unique name."

"I can do better," I say. "Most people just call me Steps."

"Steps?" He stares at me for a moment, utterly baffled, and then I see a change in his eyes, a realization. "Because you're a tracker?"

"Not just a tracker," Jimmy interjects, "the best tracker you'll ever see."

Tony nods. "I believe it. I hear you did some tracking last night." He looks from me, to Jimmy, and then back. "My lieutenant got a call from Judge Ehrlich this morning. I don't know what he said, but it was pretty much a one-sided conversation for the better part of ten minutes." He rubs his hands together. "Lieutenant Kelly said he wants to see you when you get in. He wouldn't say why."

Jimmy sighs.

"Beat up one judge . . ." I say, shaking my head and making a *tsk-tsk* sound with my tongue.

"I didn't beat him up," Jimmy replies. "I restrained him from assaulting a federal officer; there's a big difference." He shakes his head in disgust, and then motions with his hand, saying, "Let's get this over with."

Detective Alvarado leads us down pristine halls and up a flight of stairs. We weave our way through a cluster of desks and cubicles before arriving in the open doorway of Lieutenant Kevin Kelly's cluttered office.

Tony raps twice on the door, but the lieutenant doesn't look up. After a moment, the detective says, "You wanted to see Special Agent Donovan and Operations Specialist Craig when they arrived."

Kelly looks up.

Standing, he tosses his pen down and works his way around the desk. The man looks like a taller version of Mike Tyson, without the face tattoo. As he draws near, I'm waiting for him to either punch me or break into a song. Instead, he plants his towering frame in front of us with his arms folded across his chest. He eyes each of us up and down. Not to be intimidated, Jimmy returns the appraisal, pushing himself higher in his shoes while doing so.

"Which one of you is Donovan?" the lieutenant asks.

"That would be me."

"You the one who roughed up Judge Ehrlich?"

Jimmy doesn't hesitate. "I used the force I deemed necessary to keep the guy from turning my chest black and blue."

"You were wearing a vest, weren't you?" The words are pointed.

"That's irrelevant," Jimmy shoots back. "If someone punched you in the chest, you'd book him for assault on an officer, whether you were wearing a vest or not, right?"

"Yeah, but Ehrlich didn't punch you, he poked you."

"Same difference," Jimmy shoots back. He's shaking his head slowly, and I can tell he's done with this. We don't answer to El Paso PD. Looking the lieutenant straight in the face, he says, "If that bloviating, abusive excuse for a judge wants a rematch, tell him I'm at the River Belmont, room two-twenty-seven. Short of that, I'm done with him."

Deathly silence settles over the room and lingers an eternal moment. Jimmy and Lieutenant Kelly stare each other down, faces blank. Then, in an instant, an explosion of noise shakes the room; a deep-lunged eruption of laughter so strong the windows vibrate. It's almost instantly followed by a multitone cascade of laughter that bounces off every wall—it hits us from every direction. It's disorienting and sets my head to swiveling as I cast about, looking for the source.

I find it in the most unexpected place.

The initial explosion came from Lieutenant Kelly, who has a huge grin on his face. The rippling echo that followed like a shock wave came from the half dozen detectives who had quietly gathered behind us. Suddenly Kelly's shaking Jimmy's hand and clapping him on the back as the others gather to have a go. I hear one of them say, "It's about time someone face-planted that SOB."

Our investigation appears to be off to a good start. Judge or no judge, Ehrlich is learning that karma can be a wicked mistress when you get on her dark side.

Tony's cubicle isn't big enough for the three of us, so he commandeered the conference room. He pre-positioned pens and notepads on the expansive table, as well as copies of the case report and a stack of crime scene photos. He even set up a desktop terminal with access to the National Crime Information Center—better known as NCIC—so we can run criminal history checks through the Interstate Identification Index, commonly referred to as running a Triple-I.

If you've been arrested in Florida for shoplifting, in Maine for driving under the influence, and in Colorado for possession of heroin, the Triple-I is the report that pulls it all together and provides a complete history of one's criminal activity all across the country. It's also the repository for missing person reports, domestic orders, stolen property data, arrest warrants, and a host of other information that is used daily by every cop in the country.

In the center of the conference room table rests an open box of fresh donuts, compliments of Lieutenant Kelly and the rest of the detectives.

Jimmy's been watching what he eats, even more so than usual. Last month he gained a pound. I don't know how you even measure that, but apparently he has special abilities. I've been trying to be supportive of my partner, so I slide the donuts away from him as he takes his seat and I tuck them safely away to my left.

My intent is to ignore the donuts altogether so the sight of me licking sugar glaze from my fingers doesn't tempt Jimmy into partaking. He's preoccupied checking his phone messages, however, and my eyes have a moment to wander . . . coming to rest on a massive maple bar in the corner of the box. I really don't know how these things happen, but the pastry somehow finds its way to a napkin in front of me.

My solidarity has its limits.

Tony walks around the table and hands each of us a file. "I pulled every case the judge heard over the last five years. After eliminating the suspects who are in jail, prison, or dead, this is the list I came up with. I also eliminated those who moved out of state."

"It's still a big list," Jimmy says, thumbing through the report. "What about those with cartel connections?"

"We found a couple, so far. Best we can tell, one of them belongs to Los Zetas, and the other two are somehow tied in with La Línea, which is the enforcement wing of the Juárez Cartel. If you're thinking this was carried out by a cartel, La Línea would be a good place to start looking. Those guys are plain butchers."

"How do they feel about hacking off feet?" Jimmy asks.

"Feet, heads, arms, you name it. One of the leaders of the unit is believed to be personally responsible for ordering more than fifteen hundred killings between 2008 and 2011. They seem to have a preference for cutting off heads and leaving them as warnings."

Pulling the mouse and keyboard near, Tony navigates to a series of folders on the hard drive and starts clicking file names. Images start stacking up on the twenty-four-inch monitor and Tony turns it toward us.

It's not pretty.

"DEA estimates that seventy percent of the cocaine that enters the U.S. comes through right here," he says, "at the Juárez–El Paso border and surrounding area. We're talking at least two hundred million dollars in profits each week; that's a lot of incentive for violence. The biggest fight over the last few years has been between the Juárez Cartel, which has lost a lot of its influence, and the Sinaloa Cartel, which is now the dominant force in Ciudad Juárez."

"You seem to know a lot about them," I say.

"I should." Tony grins. "If you work law enforcement in El Paso, you have to know your cartels . . . and the gangs that support them, like the Barrio Azteca."

"Do you think this is cartel work?" I ask, nodding toward the stack of crime scene photos.

Tony doesn't answer right away, which I find intriguing.

"You don't, do you?"

"Something like this," he says with a slow, exaggerated shrug, "you'd expect it to be cartel . . . just by the ugliness of it. So I'm not saying *definitively* that it's not. . . . It just doesn't seem to fit—for a couple reasons."

"Enlighten us," Jimmy says.

The fingers on Tony's left hand strum the tabletop. "Okay," he says after a moment, "but this is just theory." Reaching for the stack of crime scene photos, he shuffles through and extracts an eight-by-ten close-up depicting the severed feet still in their Converse sneakers and resting in the ice box on the judge's living room floor. Placing the photo in front of us, he says, "Notice anything odd?"

Jimmy and I look at each other.

"Besides the obvious," Tony quickly adds.

Jimmy recites his observations: "He was clothed when his feet were cut off, as evidenced by the shoes and partial socks; Converse shoes aren't expensive, but they're not cheap, either, so that rules out your homeless or illegals; also, there's not as much blood as I would have expected."

"I thought the same thing," Tony interrupts, "like maybe he was already dead."

"Heart stops and there's nothing but gravity to move the blood around," Jimmy says with a confirming nod.

"The dead don't bleed," Tony says matter-of-factly. "But that's not what I'm looking for."

Jimmy picks up the photo and stares at it, letting the image pull him back to the stainless steel table at the medical examiner's office. "The cut is clean," he says after a moment. "Dr. Jimenez suspects some type of industrial equipment."

"Bingo," Tony says.

I look at him. "How do you mean?"

"That's not cartel style—not unless they changed their MO just for this guy. Their enforcers have a morbid fascination with the machete; if this was their work you'd see multiple strikes, cuts in the shoes where they missed, and just a bloody, ragged mess."

Jimmy ponders this. "That's a pretty good argument."

"That's not all," Tony continues. "The biggest miss in this equation is the judge himself; he's not exactly the type the cartel would target. Judge Ehrlich came over from the dark side."

Jimmy raises an eyebrow. "He was a defense attorney?"

"For more than twenty years."

There's an interesting dynamic between law enforcement and defense attorneys; you might call it a 3-D relationship: distrust, disgust, and disapproval. In fairness, some of it is earned—on both sides. There are plenty of respectable defense attorneys, but there are some who border on the atrocious; the type who'll do just about anything—ethical or not—to find that little loophole that will get their client off.

It's easy to hate defense attorneys.

One need only breathe.

Whenever I feel the 3-Ds start to creep up on me, I remind myself that Founding Father and former U.S. President John Adams defended the British soldiers who opened fire on a mob in the streets of Boston in 1770, a little episode that the British referred to as the Incident on King Street and the colonists called the Boston Massacre. Five in the crowd were killed, six were wounded.

Of the eight soldiers charged with murder, six were ultimately acquitted and two were convicted of the lesser charge of manslaughter, thanks to Adams's deft handling of the case. Despite the trouble it caused him, Adams considered it one of the best public services he ever performed. He defended the soldiers not because it was the popular thing to do—it wasn't—but because he knew that for a fair judicial system to function, the accused must have proper representation.

Short of that, we're back to kangaroo courts and lynch mobs.

"Ehrlich started out in the public defender's office and moved into private practice after six years," Tony says. "He spent another fourteen or fifteen years doing that before picking up his judge's robes; made a lot of enemies along the way too."

"Thieves and druggies?" I ask.

Tony shakes his head. "Cops."

The detective leans on the table with both hands and glances at the donut box. "Ehrlich never really made the transition from defense attorney to judge," he continues. "The guilty always fare better in his court, and defense attorneys *love* appearing before him. The odds of getting a dismissal or acquittal go way up. I'm sure it's not intentional, he's just been doing it for so long that it's hardwired into him. He also has a way of getting under your skin, particularly if you're a cop—that part's hardwired as well."

"Yeah, we've seen him in action," Jimmy says.

Tony chuckles at the reminder, but then grows serious again. "Of the three cartel cases I pulled," he says, "one was dismissed, one got an acquittal because of Ehrlich's maneuvering, and the third ended up with a ridiculously light sentence. Not exactly the stuff that sends cartel hit men looking for you."

Tony pulls the donut box over and glances inside briefly before pulling out a French cruller and taking a big bite. Jimmy eyes the box and I swear his left hand twitches, but he controls himself.

"So we need to find the rare case where he actually brought the hammer down hard on someone," I suggest.

Jimmy doesn't seem convinced. "There's something we're missing." Turning to Tony, he asks, "Is there anything else that would make him a target, any skeletons in the closet?"

"Nothing," Tony says with a shrug. "The fact that he's *arrogant* has been out of the closet for a long time."

Jimmy persists. "How about money problems, or a gambling addiction—something that would put him in bed with the wrong kind of people?"

"His wife is loaded," Tony says through a mouthful of donut. "She's old Texas oil money, the type with lots of political connections. She probably imagines her husband as governor someday."

Jimmy ponders this; he ponders the donuts; he ponders how a guy like Ehrlich could get a presidential nomination to a circuit court. "Do you have this in a Word file?" he asks, nodding toward the list of names.

"Yeah, you want me to send it to you?"

"No." Jimmy scratches out an email address on the corner of a page from his notebook and then tears it free. He hands the ragged piece of paper to Tony. "Send it to Diane Parker, our analyst. We'll see if she can come up with something."

Tony's already typing before Jimmy finishes speaking, and a second later the file is attached to the email and on its way. "Done," he says brightly. "What's next?"

I chuckle at his enthusiasm.

"What?" he says, with a wormy grin. "I love this stuff. *This* is why I became a detective in the first place, to figure things out, come up with different angles and ideas. I tell you, I was meant to do this."

Jimmy's got a big grin on his face as he watches the raw emotion flow from Tony. You have to admire the guy's energy and dedication. Some cops burn out after being on the job for too long. Some stop pursuing the leads as aggressively as they did in earlier days, and even stop caring about closing cases. A small few start to coast through each day doing as little as possible— it's referred to as being retired on duty.

But that's not Tony.

"Okay, then," Jimmy says. "What's our next move?"

"How about an RFI?" I suggest, referring to the always useful request for information, a tool that agencies use when trying to identify similar crimes or suspects in surrounding jurisdictions. "Maybe someone will remember recovering a body without feet," I add.

"Yeah, that'd be a little hard to forget," Tony snorts. "How far and wide do you want it to go?"

"Jimmy?" I say, tossing the decision his way.

His head swivels in my direction and he's looking at me . . . but he's not. Jimmy has a way of looking *at* you and looking *through* you at the same time. It's kind of unnerving. "Let's say . . . five hundred—no, make it a thousand miles," he finally says. "That's probably overkill, but better we get too many hits than not enough."

"Do you want to include a photo of the feet?" I ask.

He shrugs. "It's a little gruesome, but we might as well. Curiosity will suck more people in, maybe get them to read the whole thing rather than just skimming through." He looks up at Tony, who's just finishing off his donut. "Any objection from El Paso?"

The detective shakes his head, chews a few more times, swallows, and says, "None. Like you said, it'll get their attention."

"You want to write it?"

"Sure, I got this."

Jimmy's looking at me as he irons out the RFI details with Tony, but my attention is on the floor. It's not that I'm oblivious to his penetrating gaze, I just choose to ignore it. Taking off my glasses, I let my eyes absorb the layers of neon shine that spring to life, painting not just the floor but the whole room in a rainbow of color. That's when it comes to me: our next move.

It's brilliant—if I do say so myself.

"Steps?" Jimmy says in a soft but perplexed tone. Slipping my glasses back on, I give him a big smile. He's going to love this—only problem is I can't exactly spell out the details with Tony hovering over us.

"Where's your bathroom?" I ask loudly.

"Down the hall, take a left, and it'll be right in front of you," the detective says, thumbing absently toward the door. He's already starting the rough draft for the RFI.

"Jimmy, you need to go?" I nod my head and tip it in the general direction of the bathroom, but Jimmy doesn't get it. "No, go ahead," he says.

I sit in my chair a moment, but he doesn't look at me. He's reading through the crime report and studying the photos. "You sure you don't need to go?" I persist, again tipping my head, but with more energy this time.

"What are you, five years old? *No*, I don't need to go." I kick him under the table.

Did I mean to kick him that hard? No.

Did I mean to nail him right in the shin? No.

These things happen.

To Jimmy's credit he doesn't cry out—or scream—he just bites down hard on his lower lip and his face goes three different shades of pale. Thinking it wise to put a little distance between us, I hover near the door to the conference room and wait. When he finally looks at me I don't make eye contact, I just tip my head toward the bathroom down the hall and start making my way in that direction.

I finish checking for feet under the stall doors just as Jimmy limps in. "Dude, sorry," I say with a half laugh.

"I didn't mean to kick you that hard, honest." I have a genuine look of contrition on my face and a sheepish smile.

There's no smile on Jimmy's face.

"It feels like you friggin' broke my tibia," he snaps.

Friggin'? He's even madder than I thought.

"Sorry," I repeat. "I couldn't tell you in front of Tony and you weren't picking up on my nonverbal cues."

"Your nonverbal cues?"

"Yeah, the head-tilt thing; the Jimmy-come-hither thing. You weren't paying attention, so I gave you a little tap under the table."

"A little tap; is that what you call it?"

"Sorry . . . I already said that, didn't I? You should really get that looked at, though. Your bones seem a little oversensitive; there might be a problem. Same thing happens to teeth when they lose enamel; they get really sensitive. Better safe than sorry, I always say. . . ." I realize I'm rambling and decide to just shut up and wait.

Jimmy stares at me a long moment—glares at me, in fact—and then beats out the words like a slow drum: "What . . . is . . . so . . . important?"

Despite his difficult and unpleasant attitude—which, I admit, I may have contributed to—I lay out my genius plan with brief clarity. He understands instantly and I see some of the smolder go out of his eyes.

"That's not bad," he admits grudgingly. He doesn't quite smile, so I give him a big grin . . . which apparently is a mistake, because his face melts back into a scowl and he turns around and limps out the door.

I stay behind; seems I have to use the bathroom after all.

CHAPTER FIVE

El Paso County Jail—September 3, 1:14 P.M.

The El Paso County Downtown Detention Facility is located on East Overland Avenue less than a mile from the U.S.–Mexico border. It's a tall, bland building with nine of its eleven floors dedicated to housing as many as a thousand inmates at any given time; three floors are for women, six for men.

Along with the more impressive thirteen-story El Paso County Courthouse across the street, it's one of a dozen or so high-rises that dominate the downtown cityscape. Like rare teeth in an otherwise toothless mouth, they jut from the earth and stand sentinel over the city.

I'm always nervous when we have to visit a jail or prison.

It's not the inmates or even the possibility of a riot that concerns me, it's that they're so confining. But I guess that's the point. It might be different if I were a county or city detective and had to visit often; I suppose

I'd get used to it. But as things stand, I've been to just nine jails and three prisons in my five years with the Special Tracking Unit.

I remember each one vividly.

This visit will be different.

I'm here to hunt shine. Ice-blue shine polluted with tiny specks of black, the calling card of the Ice Box Killer. If he was tried by Judge Ehrlich, he would have had to pass through this facility. It's unavoidable. If we can determine what cell he was in, we can probably figure out who he is and make a quick slam-dunk of this case.

Heather got home from her latest assignment this morning, and here I am in Texas. It's been a week since I last saw her; seven days too long. I should be intensely focused on the case, but all I can think about is getting on Betsy and flying home. The sooner we find IBK, the better.

As we enter the lobby, Tony turns and says, "I'll check in at the window. It may take a few minutes to get an escort, so grab a chair." Without waiting for an answer, he saunters over to the large reinforced window and explains the situation to the corrections deputy on the other side.

I *did* try talking him into staying at the station to finish the request for information. The last thing I need is an overeager, over-observant detective latched on to me while I'm following shine. Tony's the type that might actually put two and two together.

Lucky for Tony—unlucky for me—Jimmy didn't have the heart to leave him behind. They seem to have a lot in common, and from the way they get on you'd think they were long-parted friends reunited at last.

Meanwhile, I spent the ride to the detention center trying to figure out the second part of my plan, provided the first part works out the way it's supposed to.

"Do you have a pen?" I say to Jimmy as we claim seats across from each other in the stark lobby. Fishing a blue rollerball pen from his shirt pocket, he hands it to me point-first. He seems taken aback when I place it neatly in my shirt pocket, pick up a month-old edition of *Newsweek*, and start thumbing through the pages.

"Steps, can I have my pen back?"

"Yes," I reply, briefly scanning an article that discusses how the government owns the DNA it collects.

"Now," Jimmy presses.

"I'll give it back," I say, looking up and giving him an assuring nod. "I'm going to need it for the next hour or so, if that's all right?"

Clearly it isn't.

"Don't lose it," he says shortly. "I've had that pen for a month; it's probably the best I've ever owned."

"Safe as the gold in Fort Knox," I say, patting my breast pocket.

I'm only halfway through the DNA article when Tony comes strolling over. He's got a six-foot-three, 250 pound trailer named Corey following behind him. "This is Corrections Deputy Corey Fischlin," he says, stepping to the side so we can do the obligatory round of handshakes.

"Just call me Corey," the big guy says. "Tony gave me the names you're interested in and I printed out a record of their housing assignments." He holds up several printed documents as evidence.

So far, so good.

Corey leads us to a dingy gray row of cube-shaped lockers, where Jimmy and Tony secure their firearms. After double-checking each box to make sure the lock is secure, the corrections deputy leads us to an elevator and activates it with a brass key.

Our first stop is the third floor.

Stepping from the elevator, we enter a secure control area where the corrections deputies can monitor the inmates from a wall of windows and from an array of monitors providing live feed from the many cameras mounted throughout the jail. Corey waves us forward and leads us through two secure doors that act as a kind of inmate air lock: only after the first door is completely closed and secure can you open the second door, which leads into the common room.

This particular area serves about thirty inmates and is separate from other common rooms on the floor. The stark, utilitarian design stands out prominently, defining the space. Each of the five tables in the center of the room is made from powder-coated steel with eight seat bottoms welded into the table structure so that the entire ensemble is essentially a one-piece unit.

There's nothing to unbolt or take apart, there's no seat to rip off and throw, there's not even a cushion to beat your fellow inmates with. The entire thing is bolted to the floor with impossible finality.

As soon as we step into the common room, my eyes begin scanning the floor for ice-blue shine, but there's no hint of it. We follow Corey to the first cell on our list and I go through the motions of examining the confined space, paying particular attention to the plentiful graffiti on the wall.

There's nothing, of course, but illusions must be maintained.

We told Tony that we wanted to check the cells for any references to Judge Ehrlich; *a real long shot*, we told him. It's a believable deception. Inmates tend to write and scratch things into their cell walls all the time, whether it's their gang affiliation, vulgar pictures, derogatory comments about a cellmate, or acrimony for some prosecutor, officer, or judge—though this last category is not as common.

After checking three more cells, we move to the fourth floor and repeat. Then we're on the fifth floor, and the sixth. It's not until we reach the seventh floor that I spot something: it's not really what I was looking for, but it'll do.

While our killer's ice-blue shine has been conspicuously absent from the jail, the first cellblock on this floor offers up something almost as important. I notice it as soon as the door opens. It's on the bare concrete at my feet, on every seat at all five tables, and on the cell doors: mocha-brown shine speckled with wisps of lime green.

The pair of feet now thawing in Dr. Jimenez's cooler once walked this cellblock, and based on the shine it was sometime in the last six months.

He was here for a good stretch.

It doesn't take much to figure out which cell he was in, either. Once I filter out the other shine, there's a wide, well-laid path right to block 7C2, cell 011, bunk 4. I grab Jimmy by the elbow and slow his pace so that Corey and Tony are a few paces in front of us. "Cell zero-one-one," I whisper, tipping my head to the open steel doorway. "Give me some cover."

"IBK?" he whispers near my ear.

"The victim." I barely breathe the words.

Jimmy just nods.

Mocha's cell isn't on our list, so I bluff my way through it. "Oh-eleven, oh-thirteen, and oh-seventeen," I say, calling out the numbers as I point to each cell individually.

Corey doesn't even grunt, he just walks to each cell in turn, raps on the doorframe, and says, "Cell check. Clear the room." Most of the inmates are already in the common area and the few that remain in the cells make a hasty exit, planting themselves at one of the tables.

They're all watching us, one way or another.

It was the same on the other floors. Most have the good sense to do it on the sly, but one slack-jawed mouth-breather is seated at the end of the nearest table just staring blankly at us like a fat kid with his face pressed to the candy store window. There might even be a little drool at the corner of his mouth.

It's a creepy look, a Hannibal Lecter look.

After clearing the cells and double-checking for stragglers, Corey gives the all-clear and waves us forward. He's chuckling to himself as we approach, but tries to hide it behind his hand, pretending he's stroking his mustache.

"What's so funny?" I ask.

We're in a crowded jail where anything can and does happen, so I'm not sure I even want to know, but in a straight-up race, my mouth frequently outruns my common sense.

Corey hesitates, and it looks for a moment as if he's not going to share. He tries to swallow the laugh, which goes about as well as giving a gremlin a bath. The laugh just multiplies in his mouth and spills out from behind his mustache-massaging hand. Corey gives up; his demeanor relaxes and he grins. "You have the whole jail buzzing from top to bottom," he says. "They're wondering what the FBI is doing checking cells on every floor. The best theory so far is that you're checking for Al-Qaeda terrorists."

"What's the worst theory?"

He chuckles a bit louder. "Well, let's just say some of these guys watched too many episodes of *The X-Files*." He pauses, and then leans in close to Tony. "And I'm not telling which one is Mulder and which one is Scully."

Jimmy's trying not to smile. "How do they know we're checking cells on every floor?" he asks, sounding a lot like Scully.

"Remember the inmate in the second cellblock," he asks, "the bald banger who asked who you were, and you told him FBI?"

"Yeah."

"Well, you only have to tell one. Information moves quickly around here."

"How's that even possible?" Jimmy Scully says. "They're locked up on different floors and in different cellblocks. There's no internal phones, no cell phones, no texting, no email, right?"

The big guard just nods and walks into cell 013, where he taps the stainless steel bowl of the sink, and then the rim of the toilet. "It's all low-tech, old-school jailhouse communications," he says. "It's kind of like sound-powered phones. They can talk from cellblock to cellblock and from floor to floor using the plumbing.

They've been tracking your movements since you got here."

"Tracking?" I say. "Okay, that's a little unsettling."

"Why would they even care?" Jimmy asks.

"It's nothing sinister," Corey says with a shake of his head. "When you're locked up, you have nothing but time. Any kind of diversion is embraced, and if they kill an hour or two talking to each other about the FBI agents wandering about, and pass updates as you move from cellblock to cellblock, well, that's an hour or two less that they have to deal with the reality of incarceration."

Jimmy shakes his head. "Still creepy."

"Yeah, I suppose it is," Corey says with a grin. "You're good to go," he adds, thumbing toward the open doors.

"Three cells, three of us," I say. "How about we split up; I'll take oh-eleven, Jimmy can have oh-thirteen, and Tony can take oh-seventeen?" The suggestion is accepted without comment and everyone moves slowly toward their assigned cell. We've been here an hour already and our initial vigor is gone, sucked from us by the concrete floors, the concrete walls, and the ever-present mass of inmates sizing us up.

Jimmy plays it perfectly, and just as he's about to step into 013, he pauses and asks Corey if he's a Cowboys fan. It's almost a no-brainer, big guy like Corey who's a native of Texas. Odds are he at least played high school ball, if not college. Of course he's a Cowboys fan. That's more of Jimmy's psychology degree being put to good use.

The ploy works.

Corey follows Jimmy into the cell and a healthy comparison between the Dallas Cowboys and the Seattle Seahawks ensues. I've never been much of a sports fan, but Jimmy eats it up. Though he rarely gets to go to a game anymore, he's got more paraphernalia than most season ticket holders.

With Corey safely out of the way, I pop into cell 011 and find a nice spot on the inside wall where the army of surveillance cameras can't see me. Retrieving Jimmy's prize pen from my shirt pocket, I scratch *187* and *Erlich* into the wall, intentionally misspelling the judge's name the way an inmate might.

The *187* is just icing on the cake.

It's the penal code in California for homicide, and it's widely used by gang members all over the country as a death threat against an individual or a rival gang. In this case it's a clear death threat against Judge Ehrlich.

Yes, I just defaced government property.

Yes, it's a bit juvenile.

No, I don't feel bad.

These two lines scratched into the wall of an already graffiti-rich cell will get me a list of every inmate who occupied this cell in the last year and I won't have to explain a thing; the *187* will do the talking for me.

"Hey, Jimmy?" The words come out high-pitched, with a questioning tone. The combination instills the call with a sense of urgency. It's a bit dramatic, but it gets the job done.

Jimmy pops his head into the cell a moment later, with Corey trailing behind. I don't say a word; I just draw an air-circle around the fresh graffiti. Moving close, Jimmy rubs his fingers over the graffiti and his eyes dart to the pen in my breast pocket. "Well, someone has it out for him," he says, playing along perfectly.

Corey crowds in to get a better look.

He studies the markings intently before giving a knowing nod. "Guess this is what you're looking for, isn't it?"

"It's *exactly* what we're looking for," Jimmy says, snapping a photo of the graffiti with his smartphone. "How long do you think it's been here?" he asks me. What he really means is, *How long has the shine been here?*

I shrug for effect and scrunch up my mouth like I'm taking a wild guess. "Less than a year, I'd say; maybe less than six months."

Jimmy turns to Corey. "How hard would it be to get a printout of everyone who's been housed in this cell in the last year, including DOB and LKA?"

"Not hard at all; it's all computerized. I can give you name, date of birth, last known address. I can also get you photos."

"Perfect."

"Can you also include what bunk they were in?" I ask.

"Whatever you want," the corrections deputy replies.

Fifteen minutes later we're walking out the front door of the downtown detention facility with four pages of possible matches. While we struck out on the suspect, the mocha shine in cell 011 may help us at least identify the victim.

It's a step in the right direction.

Plus, I got a cool new pen; Jimmy didn't want it back after I, as he put it, "carved up the wall." He's funny that way.

CHAPTER SIX

Over Utah—September 3, 6:47 P.M.

Betsy's at thirty-eight thousand feet—flight level three-eight-zero—northbound to Bellingham. It's been just twenty-four hours since we landed in El Paso. In some ways the time has flown by, but as we make our way home, yesterday seems so far away.

We haven't seen the last of El Paso; we're just regrouping and letting the RFI do its work. With luck we'll find the rest of Mocha's body sitting in a morgue in a neighboring county. And with it, another chance to collect evidence, identify the remains, or even identify the scene of the crime. Right now all we have is two feet in a box.

Jimmy is stretched out on one of the Gulfstream's leather chairs in the fully reclined position. He looks like he's sleeping, but I'm pretty sure he's faking it, so I poke him in the arm.

"Go away." His voice is groggy; maybe he was sleeping after all.

"I'm bored."

"I'm tired," he replies.

"I'm persistent."

"I'm annoyed." He opens an eye—just one—and glares at me from his reclined position. After a moment the eye closes again and he begins to drift away.

"Did you know there's a tree in Florida that can kill a grown man?" I say.

He groans and tries to roll onto his side with his back to me. "I don't want to do Plane Talk right now, Steps. I just want to sleep. It's been a long two days."

"We'll be home in a couple hours; how much sleep can you really get?"

"Enough. Why don't you watch a movie or something?"

"I've already seen them all; besides, I invoked Plane Talk."

The rules of Plane Talk are threefold: it can only be invoked while on the plane; once invoked, the other party is obligated to participate; and, most importantly, the subjects of Plane Talk should be as bizarre or unusual as possible.

This final rule isn't hard and fast, since we often find ourselves talking about relatively ordinary topics such as life after death, the origin of the waffle cone, and the Lost Colony of Roanoke Island.

Jimmy's silent, and for a moment I would swear that he's slowly curling into a fetal position. With a loud, extended sigh, he rolls roughly onto his back and brings the chair to its full upright position. His eyes are on me, flaccid and tired.

I give him a big smile; what he returns looks less like a smile and more like the snarl of some wild beast sizing me up for supper. "Tell me about the tree," he growls.

"It's the manchineel tree," I begin. "It's native to parts of Florida, the Caribbean, and the Bahamas, and everything about it is poisonous."

"Fascinating." The word comes out monotone, a flat rail that carries Jimmy's voice from the end of his mouth to the tip of my ear.

"It is," I agree enthusiastically. "According to legend, after Juan Ponce de León returned to Florida in search of gold, he was shot in the leg with an arrow dipped in manchineel sap during a battle with the Calusa tribe. Obviously his death was long and painful."

"Obviously," Jimmy says.

Flipping to the back of my folder, I find my notes on the tree and continue. "It was also used as an early form of torture and even execution. If you stripped the shirt off someone and tied them to a manchineel tree, the physical contact was enough to cause severe burns and blisters—and eventually it would kill. That's not even factoring in what would happen if sap fell on the poor guy's head, especially if it rained. The whole thing's a recipe for slow and excruciating death."

Jimmy's eyes look less groggy—still irritated, but less groggy.

"Do you want to know the worst part?"

Jimmy just stares at me.

"The worst part is the fruit. Supposedly, it was

Christopher Columbus who named it *manzanita de la muerte*, or *little apple of death*. It actually looks like a small green apple and has a deceptively sweet smell, but if you bite into it the burning in your mouth, throat, eyes, and nose is excruciating and can last for up to eight hours. Cool, huh?"

"Cool." Again with the monotone.

"Your turn."

He shakes his head and gives a halfhearted shrug. "I got nothing."

"Nothing?"

"I haven't had time," he shoots back defensively. "Whenever we're home, Jane has me running around getting ready for the kitchen remodel. When I *do* have a free moment, the last thing I want to think about is researching something for Plane Talk. Sorry."

"That's fine," I say, pushing back in my seat. The cabin of the Gulfstream is silent again, so I pick absently at the sewn leather seam on the arm of my chair. Jimmy reclines again, but only halfway. He pulls a worn paperback copy of *Lone Survivor* from his portfolio briefcase and opens to the bookmark.

"Can I run something by you?" I ask.

"What?" His eyes are still tracing across the page word by word.

"It's about Leonardo." That gets his attention and he looks up from his book.

"What about him?"

"Well, El Paso got me thinking that maybe we should put out a nationwide request for information. With the victim in West Virginia, we now have two cases linked to Leonardo that are a decade apart; maybe there are others. We don't have DNA from either case, so there's nothing that would have linked them together except MO and shine. It was just dumb luck that we responded to the Fairmont case; dumb luck twice, actually. First, we were wrapping up another case in Maryland when the body was found. Second, Fairmont is just ten or fifteen miles from the FBI's Criminal Justice Information Services facility outside of Clarksburg. It's just unfortunate that the victim was the niece of one of the records specialists at the facility."

Jimmy moves his seat back to the full upright position and drops *Lone Survivor* back into his briefcase. "Do you think we can describe the MO well enough without delving into shine?"

"We can try. How many bodies are posed with the feet pointing south and the arms extended to the east and west? That's going to sear itself into the mind of every investigator who worked the case."

"Without a doubt," Jimmy agrees. "We've seen our share of body dumps, most of which are fast and crude. A posed body is pretty rare."

"Then there's the circle he walked around both victims," I continue. "It wasn't a casual stroll, either; he was heel-to-toe the whole way and somehow ended up making a near-perfect circle. I think we can articulate that much, at least, without breaking from the tracking narrative."

"That would explain why we named him Leonardo," Jimmy summarizes, "even without the rest of the details. That detective from Fairmont PD—"

"Bobby Graham."

"He's not going to leave us alone until we give him

something. Maybe a good RFI that explains the *Vitruvian Man* element will do the trick." Jimmy churns it over a moment and then nods. "I like it." He reaches into his briefcase and pulls out his notepad and a new pen. Setting them on the table, he says, "Let's get started."

"What, now?"

"You said you were bored." He gives me a penetrating, Vulcan-mind-meld stare as he taps the pen lightly on the table. "The more we do now, the sooner it's out there."

"Okay," I say with a sigh. "Let's do it."

Two and a half hours later Betsy rolls to a stop in the open bay of Hangar 7. As Les shuts the plane down, Marty opens the front hatch and lowers the steps. He gives a slight bow and a sweep of his arm as we exit. "Thanks for flying FB-1 airways," he says with his typical grin. Someone once referred to the FBI as FB-1 and he thought it was hysterical; he's never let it go.

"Marty, set the chocks," Les calls from the cockpit.

The copilot sends a silent salute toward the cockpit and follows us down the stairs. Retrieving the yellow wheel chocks, he goes about the task of placing them on either side of each wheel.

It's a quarter after nine, but the light is on in Diane's office and two figures stand on the balcony outside her door. As Jimmy and I make our way across the hangar floor, one of the figures hurries down the steps and rushes toward us.

When she's fifteen feet away, Heather breaks into a run and throws herself into my arms. Her legs wrap around my waist and she presses her lips to mine as her fingers run through my hair from bottom to top. When she finally comes up for air, she says just four words: "I love my letters."

As her lips find mine again, I see Jimmy out of the corner of my eye. His mouth is open and he's staring in apparent shock or disgust—maybe a little of both—and shaking his head back and forth. After a minute he turns his back on us and makes for the stairs.

I was going to throw my go-bag into the office, but Heather's left hand has found its way inside my shirt and she's working her way up to my chest.

"Get a room," Jimmy calls from the balcony. He's leaning on the rail next to Diane and they're both grinning like two possums hanging from the same branch.

We make it to the parking lot.

We make it to my car.

We make it—well, we make it a good night.

Tomorrow I'm buying more stationery.

CHAPTER SEVEN

The Office—September 4, 11:47 A.M.

Hangar 7 is located at the south end of Bellingham International Airport, near the general aviation hangars, but separate. It's one of the larger hangars and has a parking lot accessible from the street. The hangar itself is built to the standards of an intelligence community SCIF—Sensitive Compartmented Information Facility—which means it has cipher locks on its heavy-gauge steel doors, an alarm system, a white-noise generator, and other features used to deny access to unauthorized individuals and prevent electronic surveillance.

The main hangar area is occupied by Betsy, but at the back is a two-story office complex, built shortly after we took possession of the facility. The upper floor houses three offices, the largest of which is in the middle; that's Diane's. Jimmy and I don't really need offices, but we have them just the same. I'm on the left of Diane, Jimmy's on the right.

On the lower level to the left is a large man cave, technically designated as an employee break room. In the middle is a kitchen, and on the right is a glass-walled conference room.

As the Special Tracking Unit's dedicated intelligence research specialist, Diane Parker runs the office—plus, she has voodoo that Jimmy and I can only dream about. The fifty-four-year-old grandmother of two spits out criminal intelligence analysis better and faster than any three analysts half her age. Her run-of-the-mill tools include the massive public records databases CLEAR and Accurint, as well as law enforcement databases like the National Crime Information Center, the Law Enforcement Information Exchange, better known as LInX, and the Western States Information Network, along with its related Regional Information Sharing Systems.

She also has access to the Automated Fingerprint Identification System, or AFIS, and the Next Generation Identification, or NGI, which is the FBI's massive biometric database that includes a facial recognition component. And we're pretty sure she has an *in* at the National Reconnaissance Office, because on more than one occasion classified satellite surveillance images have found their way to her desk.

We don't ask her how she does what she does.

We've worked with her enough to trust her implicitly and without reservation. When it comes to Diane, our only real duty is to protect the mojo. This generally entails making sure her supply of chocolate-covered macadamia nuts remains constant.

In turn, Diane plays mother hen to the STU.

She bakes us cookies on occasion, and often waits up

for us when we're coming home late, particularly after a bad case. We've never asked her to, but she cleans up the mess we always seem to leave behind in the kitchen and break room, as if we were her teenage sons rather than her coworkers. She's underpaid, overworked, and she's the rock that anchors the unit and protects it through rough times, even when Jimmy teases her about her impending eligibility for a senior discount at the pancake house.

As Jimmy and I enter the conference room, Diane hands each of us a two-page color bulletin from the manila folder in her hand: it's the request for information, or RFI, on Leonardo.

"I sent it out an hour ago," she says. "You'll notice I embellished it a bit. The draft you two put together was pathetic."

Jimmy ignores the barb.

"This looks good," he says as he scans the document. Diane even added a crime scene illustration showing the configuration of the body, which includes a representation of the two positions the arms and legs were placed in, and the circle Leonardo walked around each body. To the right of this artist rendering is a second image: Leonardo da Vinci's *Vitruvian Man*. The side-by-side comparison is stunning.

I tap the Renaissance image with my index finger. "Nice."

"You like it?" Diane says. "I got it off Wikipedia. Did you know they have different versions of the *Vitruvian Man*? I found a Storm Trooper version, and one with Homer Simpson wearing a fig leaf. There's even one with that monster from the movie *Alien*, if you can believe that. Nothing's sacred anymore."

Pulling two more pages from the manila folder, she says, "You'll like this a lot less," as she hands a single page to Jimmy and another to me. We read in silence; the words are fresh, but the story is old . . . and twice repeated.

It was inevitable, I suppose.

The eight-hundred-word article details the disappearance and homicide of Ally McCully in Fairmont, West Virginia. It attaches the name Leonardo to the unknown killer and even draws a connection to an unspecified but similar cold case in Washington; the cold case that has haunted me for eleven years: the murder of Jess Parker.

"Damn," I mutter.

"Detective Graham emailed the link last night," Diane says. "He said he was sorry, but his chief was under a lot of pressure from the media and issued a press release yesterday." She pauses. "The Associated Press picked up the story this morning," she adds, "so it's only going to get more play, not less."

Jimmy sighs. "Guess I should have called him back."

"No, it's my fault," I say. "If I hadn't blurted out Leonardo's name at the crime scene they wouldn't know about the link to Jess's murder. I was just . . . shocked. It's been over a decade and all of a sudden, bam! He's right there on the ground in front of me."

"How can you be so sure it's Leonardo?" Diane asks.

She doesn't know about shine.

It was my decision when the team was first formed:

Jimmy would have to know, but Diane was back in the office, she wouldn't see me operating in the field. The longer Jimmy and I do this, however, the harder it is to explain our results—not just to Diane, but to Heather, who's incredibly astute, and to Dex, the crime analyst at the Whatcom County Sheriff's Office. I've worked with Dex off and on since the STU was founded. Most of that work is focused on identifying Leonardo, but there have been other cases.

Diane, Heather, and Dex are all incredibly shrewd, and each, in their own way, suspects that there's more to my tracking ability than meets the eye.

I should tell them.

The thought is recurring and persistent. It's a daily reminder of the ruse Jimmy and I must play on those closest to us, a deception driven by fear, and the unanswered question: Will they see me as a freak . . . a chimeric aberration . . . a monster?

This thought has kept me silent, but its hold is weakening. Some things must be told, even when the telling is painful. I'm coming to that realization—but the time is not right, not yet.

"It's Leonardo," I tell Diane. "There's no doubt in my mind."

"There's nothing we can do about it now," Jimmy says, handing the printout back to Diane. He takes a seat at the conference table and I follow his lead. "Leonardo's going to have to wait. We need to get this so-called Ice Box Killer sorted out." He looks up at the manila envelope in Diane's hand, then into her eyes. "How's your analysis going?"

"Done," she says with a bit of swagger. Opening the

folder, she extracts two stapled reports, complete with color photos, handing one to Jimmy and one to me. "Of the fifty-seven names you gave me, I've whittled the list down to two."

"Two!" Jimmy sounds impressed.

"It wasn't that hard," Diane says with a casual shrug. "A third of them were in custody when the feet showed up on the judge's living room carpet. Another died of an overdose last month; a dozen or so have no serious criminal history, just DUIs and lesser offenses. Would you like me to go through the whole list or just skip to the two that count?"

"Please," Jimmy says, "skip away."

"That's what I thought." She holds the folder to her chest as she begins walking slowly around the conference room table, reciting the information from memory. "The better candidate of the two is Hector René Ortiz, DOB 2/14/82—he's an Aquarius. He's also an OG, or Original Gangster, with the Barrio Azteca gang. And there's your cartel connection. The Barrio Azteca had their beginning in the El Paso jail back in the 1980s. They're tied in pretty tightly with the Juárez Cartel and Ortiz is . . . well, he could be their poster child. He's bad with a capital *B*."

"Yeah, he looks the part," Jimmy says, staring at a series of booking photos that show full-sleeve tattoos on both arms, plus ink on his chest, back, neck, and face, leaving little room for future additions. "The guy's a regular pincushion," he adds. "What are the small tattoos next to his eyes?"

"Three teardrops on his left eye," Diane says, "which probably represent three people close to him who were killed or died . . . though it could also mean he's killed three people, hard to tell for certain."

"And the right eye?"

"It's the number twenty-one."

"Why twenty-one?"

"Same number-letter transposition we've seen before. Gangs will use the number one for *A*, two for *B*, three for *C*, that sort of thing. In this case, the number twenty-one represents *BA*, short for Barrio Azteca."

Jimmy's holding the stapled report up at eye level and tipping it first to the right, then to the left. "I can't make this out," he says.

Diane walks around and peers over his shoulder. "The tattoo on the side of his head?" she asks.

"Yeah."

"It says Pelón." Her fingers point out the five stylized letters.

"Pelón?"

"It means 'bald' or 'baldy' . . . probably because he's bald," she says in a bland tone. "It's his gang moniker, his street name." Circling the tattoo with her finger, she says, "It stands out like a neon sign, doesn't it? That should make it easier to spot him, even for you two."

"So we have a felon who goes by Pelón," Jimmy muses.

"With a tattoo on his melon," I add quickly.

Jimmy grins. "His girlfriend might be Ellen."

"Idiots," Diane mumbles. Jimmy just chuckles. Taking the report out of his hands, she leafs through to the picture of the severed feet in the judge's living room, taps the image several times with her half-bent right index finger, and then hands the report back to Jimmy.

"Buzzkill," he mutters.

A spontaneous laugh escapes my lips and Diane instantly casts her gaze my way. I sober my face, and say, "Carry on; please. This is fascinating."

She just shakes her head and tries not to smile, but she's not fooling anyone. She's our mother hen, queen bee, camp counselor, and personal Torquemada all rolled into one and she loves every minute of it.

"Any idea why Ortiz would have a beef with Ehrlich?" I ask.

Diane places the folder on the table and leans forward on both hands. Her blue eyes find me, then wander to Jimmy on the other side of the table, then back to me. "That," she says, "was a little more difficult to dig up."

"Do tell," Jimmy says.

"I tracked down the court clerk who was present when Ortiz was tried and sentenced. Her name is Susie, and according to her, Hector Ortiz was less than impressed with Judge Ehrlich, and disrespected him in his own courtroom—during sentencing, no less. What should have been a simple slap on the wrist for a minor drug offense turned into a six-month sentence."

"I'm guessing Hector wasn't happy about that?"

"He said some choice words."

"Sounds like a good candidate," Jimmy says. "What about our second guy?"

"Lawrence Michael Wilson," Diane begins. "DOB 6/27/67. Truck driver, though I don't think he's been doing too much driving the last year and a half."

"That sounds slightly ominous," I say.

"Correct you are. That's because until last month Larry Wilson was locked up in the El Paso County jail for supposedly killing a local woman named Chelsey Lane, who lived three houses down on the same street. They found her at the bottom of some stairs with a fractured skull and multiple contusions."

"How'd it get laid at Larry's feet?"

"Neighbor remembered seeing him coming out of the house. Said he probably wouldn't have noticed, except Larry was acting strange; looking around to see if anyone was watching, that type of thing. He later failed a polygraph and cracked during the interview, admitting to the murder."

"But he was acquitted?" Jimmy asks.

"Yeah, it created quite a stir," Diane says. "One piece of evidence after another was deemed inadmissible and Wilson claimed the confession was coerced. Ultimately the case fell apart. Frankly, I thought about taking him off the list, since it seems like he owes Ehrlich his freedom."

"What stopped you?" I ask.

"Just some comments he made after the acquittal," Diane says. "He went on a tirade about his name being dragged through the mud, called Ehrlich some names, right along with the prosecution. I don't think the guy fully grasps that it was Ehrlich who was responsible for the acquittal."

"Talk about an ingrate," I say.

Jimmy's strumming the table with his index fingers: left-right-left-right-left-right. I know the look: something's bothering him and he's working it out in his head. "Do you have the crime scene photos from the homicide, the Chelsey—what was her name?"

"Lane. Chelsey Lane."

"Right; can we get whatever you have on that case?"

"I suppose," Diane replies, a bit puzzled. "It'll take me a few minutes."

"That's fine. Thanks."

As she exits the conference room and starts up the stairs to her office, I say, "What do you need the crime scene photos for?"

"I don't."

With an understanding nod, I say, "But you needed to get rid of Diane."

"Yeah, for two reasons: first, I think we're forgetting that the guy with the mocha shine is the victim in all this."

"A victim who might be linked to Ehrlich," I add. "I might even go out on a limb here and say with certainty that the victim *is* linked to Ehrlich, because—*hmm*—his feet were found in the guy's living room. That just doesn't happen without reason. Whether it's the gangbanger Ortiz or this Wilson guy, I don't know, but what else do we have to go on? One of them has to be Mocha."

"I'm not saying that Mocha's not involved, I just have a theory that might make sense of it. We didn't find IBK's shine anywhere in the jail, did we; not even in the booking area?"

"No. We didn't."

"Implying . . . what?"

It takes me a second. "He's never been booked."

"*Ding ding ding*," Jimmy says, touching the end of his nose. "So, to recap, the list you got is for a cell occupied by the victim, not the suspect—a suspect who's never been booked, at least at that facility, yet we're still looking for some kind of hostile link between Ehrlich and the two feet in the box. Why?"

I don't have an answer.

"I'll tell you," he continues, using a come-hither finger motion to draw me in close so we can conspire in whispered hypotheticals. The way Jimmy's mind works is sometimes scary-brilliant. I honestly think he could give Diane a run for her money. In hushed tones, he lays out his thoughts as if they were tangible. The words fall from his lips like pieces of a giant puzzle, landing on the table in a pattern that starts to resemble a picture. Then it suddenly makes sense—each piece of it simple and brilliant.

We spend the next five minutes in huddled sequestration until the distinct *clump-clump-clump* of Diane's heels echoes down the stairs. Jimmy and I are now on the same page. It's a page ripped from the middle of a book, so we don't know the beginning, nor can we guess the end, but it's a good start.

It's something.

Just before one P.M., Diane makes a lunch run and returns with some eight-inch subs. My usual—turkey, cheese, tomato, and black olive on wheat—sits unwrapped and half eaten on the conference room table in front of me. Next to it is an eight-by-ten glossy of some severed feet. Above that, and to the right, is another eight-by-ten photo showing a close-up of Chelsey Lane's bloody and battered head.

It's funny what becomes normal with repetition.

Jimmy's phone rings while he's in mid-chew. It rings twice more before he can swallow. "Donovan," he finally says, pressing the phone to his ear. A big smile cracks his face and he looks at me and points at the phone. "Hey, Tony, good to hear from you."

As he listens, the smile slips away and he seems to slump a little deeper into his seat. His left hand rises up and massages his forehead with just the index finger and thumb. It's the type of rubdown you do when you're either disturbed or when a fierce headache is creeping up on you.

"Please tell me you're joking," Jimmy says.

I can hear Tony's voice issuing from the speaker, but I can't make out any of his words. Jimmy pulls his notepad close and says, "Okay, give it to me," and starts scratching away on the paper. "Repeat the last . . . yeah, okay. I got it." I hear the soft buzz of Tony's voice again. "Definitely, we'll keep you in the loop. Okay, buddy. Take care."

Buddy? Since when has Jimmy ever referred to *anyone* as buddy? He doesn't call me buddy. And I *am* his buddy.

He sets his phone on the table and taps absently at the blank screen. After a few seconds he looks at Diane and says, "Can you call Les and Marty and have them get the plane ready?" She just nods and starts for her office. "One more thing, Diane: Can you send Tony the info you have on Ortiz and Wilson? I want him up to speed when we get there."

"We're going to El Paso?" I say.

"No, Tucson."

"Seriously? Jimmy, we just got home last night. I

haven't seen Heather in a week, and your family's going to forget what you look like if you don't spend some time with them."

"I know. I'm sorry."

"Why Tucson?"

He looks at me and shakes his head. "Nothing good."

CHAPTER EIGHT

Pima County Medical Examiner's Office—
September 4, 5:43 P.M.

The autopsy room stinks of bleach and the lingering echo of that too-familiar acrid stench that seems to attach itself to dead bodies. It's a smell I've never gotten used to, and one that's followed me home on more than one occasion.

The afterlife may be beautiful, but death stinks.

"John Doe number one-two-three-J," Dr. Perry Stone says as he wheels the body cart into the autopsy suite and parks it under a perch of lights. The cart is empty but for a small clear plastic bin resting alone on the stainless steel surface.

"Déjà vu," Jimmy says under his breath.

"Recovered on April twenty-seventh," Dr. Stone recites, "from the living room of a residence on Southwind Lane." He checks the time on his iPhone and sets it on the autopsy cart. "No hit from CODIS, and we have nothing else to identify the victim."

"What is it with feet?" I mutter.

"Are you sure it's a John Doe and not a Jane Doe?" Jimmy asks.

"Men's sneakers," Stone replies tersely, reaching down and removing the lid from the box. "Size twelve. A little large for your average woman, I should think."

"Fine," Jimmy replies, a little terse himself. "Have you had the shoes off?"

"Of course."

"But you put them back on?"

"Obviously."

"And what about the Styrofoam ice box?"

"Destroyed."

"Why?"

"Space and convenience," Stone replies. When Jimmy just stares at him he begins to fidget and then uncrosses his arms. Words burst from his mouth like so much bad soup. "We're not exactly swimming in extra storage in the cooler. I've got a hundred and thirty-six bodies stacked six high back there. They come in as fast as we can get rid of them. We need all the room we can get."

"That's a bit much for a city like Tucson, isn't it?" Jimmy's genuinely curious. "Why so many?" he asks.

Dr. Stone misinterprets the question as criticism, and the entire left side of his face scrunches up into a squinting smorgasbord of disgust and annoyance.

"The border, of course," he snorts. "We've got people dying in the desert right and left, and they all end up here." He pauses, shaking his head like some old codger chastising a petulant child. "It's always the same with you Feds, isn't it? You have no clue what's going on down here . . . or in the rest of the country, for that matter."

Jimmy's eyes narrow. "We don't write policy, Dr. Stone. We're with the Special Tracking Unit and we have a job to do just like you." He pauses, and then adds, "Your cooperation is appreciated," pronouncing each word sharply and individually.

To me, it sounds less like appreciation and more like insistence . . . but then, I've known Jimmy longer than Dr. Stone.

"Now, would you mind taking the feet out of the shoes?"

Stone looks at the time on his cell phone again, and then says with a resigned sigh, "We're out of gloves. I'll get some from the supply locker." He pauses in the doorway: "Don't touch anything."

We listen to his shoes as they clump down the hall. For someone who keeps checking the time, he doesn't appear to be in that big of a hurry.

"Well, he certainly brings the gloom back to the room," I say.

A moment later we hear the *clump clump clump* of cheap shoes in the hall, heralding the doctor's return. Stone holds up a new box of gloves as he enters the autopsy suite, perhaps as proof that they really were out.

After tugging up one set of gloves, followed by a second set required by standard operating procedure, Dr. Stone retrieves a plastic disposable apron from a drawer and fastens it around his neck and waist. Next,

EDINBURGH LEISURE+CULTURE

he picks up a face mask that looks like the visor from a riot helmet and settles it into place on his head.

"I'll forgo the rest of the PPE, if you don't mind," he says. "After all, it's only a pair of feet."

"PPE?" I say.

What he replies is, "Personal protection equipment, Mr. Craig"; what I hear is, *Personal protection equipment, you ignorant simpleton.*

It's all in the delivery.

Motioning us away with the back of his right hand, Dr. Stone waits until we're practically at the door before letting out a tiresome sigh and giving us the stop signal. Reaching into the plastic container with both hands, he extracts the feet and places them on the stainless steel table. The laces are untied and hanging loose—apparently he didn't bother to tie them after he had the shoes off the first time around. The feet slip from their covers with ease. Stone places the empty shoes off to the side.

Next he peels off the white athletic socks. The left one has a large hole where the big toe pokes out; the right one has a similar-sized hole in the heel. Either the guy didn't like wasting money on socks, or he didn't *have* money to waste on socks. I'm guessing the latter.

Setting the socks with the shoes, Dr. Stone stands the feet upright and faces them in our direction, a bit like a jeweler would present a watch or a ring for a prospective buyer. He waves us forward to admire his work.

Feet can be ugly; these are no exception.

Taking my glasses off, I slip them into my shirt pocket and lean in, as if to get a closer look. I don't need to, of course. As soon as the glasses slip from my face I see the stunning ice-blue shine—IBK's shine.

It contrasts sharply with that of the victim, which is gray mottled with carmine, overlaying a texture similar to that of a peach skin. It's almost homely by comparison. It's also flat and still, with none of the usual pulsations. Wherever he is, Gray Foot is already dead.

"Anything odd about them?" Jimmy asks Dr. Stone.

"You mean aside from being severed at the ankle and left in an ice box?"

"Yeah, aside from that," Jimmy replies patiently.

Dr. Stone retrieves a clipboard from a shelf under the cart and glances over it quickly. "Mid-twenties Caucasian male. Height and weight impossible to tell for obvious reasons." He glances over the clipboard in case we don't grasp the *obvious reasons* part of his description. "Hmm . . . yes, this was odd," he continues. "Cell structure suggests the feet were frozen—shoes and all. They were completely thawed out when we recovered them, though they were still a bit damp."

Jimmy looks at me with a raised eyebrow. "Just like El Paso," he says. He turns to Dr. Stone. "Anything to indicate whether the victim was alive or dead when the feet were cut off?"

Stone thumbs through the report. "The injuries appear to be perimortem." Glancing over the clipboard, he says, "That means at or near the time of death."

"I know what it means."

"So he was alive when it started," Stone confirms. "How long he lasted is impossible to tell without the rest of the body." He shrugs. "If the bleeding was stopped and the wounds were tended properly, he could still be alive."

No, I tell myself. *He's dead*.

The shine never lies.

Dr. Stone sets the clipboard on the autopsy cart and Jimmy picks it up before the good doctor can object. The information is scant. "Who is this Thomas Mc-Allister, and what is Windhaven?"

"Mr. McAllister is a defense attorney, and Windhaven is a so-called upscale gated community in the suburbs."

"The type of neighborhood that's not easy to get in and out of without being noticed?"

"I suppose so; bit snobbish, if you ask me," Stone replies, scrunching his nose up. The words are almost laughable coming out of this guy's mouth.

"How about the wounds?" Jimmy asks. "Any idea what could have taken the feet off so cleanly?"

"Something sharp."

Jimmy drops his shoulders and just stares. His head is cocked to the right, but his eyes are trained squarely on the doctor—you might say he's burning imaginary holes through his skull.

"What?" Stone blurts after a long, uncomfortable silence. "You can see for yourself. It was something sharp with a lot of force; took the feet off with one stroke. Beyond that, your guess is as good as mine." He waves a hand at us like some womb-weary mother shushing away her children. "You're the investigators, go figure it out. Investigate."

Jimmy's absolutely simmering.

I see it in his face, his posture, his grinding teeth.

Stone stands cloaked in his own self-importance. From the other side of the autopsy table he looks upon us with arrogance and contempt. Spreading his hands wide with his palms up, he asks, "Are we done?"

Opening his wallet, Jimmy extracts a business card and tosses it onto the stainless steel table next to the feet. "I want a copy of your report and any photos. Email them to the address on the card—I'm sure you can do that in the next ten or fifteen minutes, right?"

It's a rhetorical question, and he doesn't wait for an answer.

As Jimmy makes his exit, I look at Stone with a hard eye and make little effort to hide the disgusted curl of my mouth. Without a word I turn and follow in my partner's wake. At the door I pause and lean back into the room. "We're done now."

Residence of Thomas McAllister—September 4, 6:14 P.M.

The guard manning the security booth at the opulent entrance to Windhaven has a contrary visage, like the two-faced Roman god Janus. One of his faces is that of a pubescent lad riddled with acne; the other face is dominated by tired eyes perched above baggy festoons. This second face suggests a severe lack of sleep and an age closer to forty. It's hard to tell which face is true.

His name is Kevin; either that or his shirt is stolen.

When he exits the booth and greets us, his voice is as tired as his face, and it's not with welcoming words that he receives us, but with the raw challenge of a military sentry. "Name and destination?" He has a clipboard in hand, which no doubt holds today's list of expected guests and approved visitors.

Jimmy doesn't waste words. "We're not on your list," he says. Reaching into his pocket, he retrieves his wallet and flips out his badge. "Federal Bureau of Investigation," he says, holding up the credentials so Kevin can get a good look. "I'm Special Agent Donovan, and this is Operations Specialist Magnus Craig. We're here to see Thomas McAllister on Southwind Lane."

"Mr. McAllister arrived home about an hour ago," Kevin says, "but I can't just let you in without approval—"

"Sure you can," Jimmy interrupts, pointing at the badge with his free hand. "See, FBI. We just need to talk to him about his little incident back in April."

"The dismembered body," Kevin says solemnly and with a knowing nod. "I wasn't working here yet, but I heard about it after I got hired. Blood everywhere, they said."

"What exactly did you hear?" I ask, suddenly curious how two severed feet in a Styrofoam ice box suddenly morphed into a dismembered body.

Kevin glances up the street and then over his shoulder, as if talking to the FBI might be construed as gossip, or somehow giving away community secrets. His words come low and fast: "This is just hearsay," Kevin says, sounding very lawyerly, "but Jones and Peña told me the living room was covered in blood when Mr. McAllister arrived home that night. A dozen cops showed up and closed down the street, and some of the residents were evacuated from their homes. From what

I heard, they found a head wrapped in plastic inside Mr. McAllister's fridge—resting right there on the shelf next to a half-eaten apple pie, if you can believe it. The feet, arms, and legs were scattered around the living room, and the torso was lying in the middle of the garage wearing a button-up shirt and tie. They even found a pair of hands in Mr. McAllister's mailbox next to a mail-order catalog and his electric bill."

"That's pretty detailed info."

"Worst thing that's ever happened in Windhaven," Kevin says, giving me a serious look of contemplation. "You don't forget stuff like that."

"I guess not," I say. "And no one heard a thing, huh?"

"Not a peep."

I can tell Jimmy's patience is about gone from the way he's squirming in the driver's seat. "So can you buzz us through, Kevin? We just need to ask Mr. McAllister a few follow-up questions."

Kevin steps over to the booth and reaches for the button, but then thinks better of it and holds up an index finger instead. "Just give me a second. I'll give him a call. I'm sure he won't have a problem with it, he's pretty cool that way." Without waiting for a response he steps into the booth, picks up the phone, and punches in the number. His back is to us, so all we hear is a mumbled one-sided exchange.

When Kevin hangs up the phone he gives us a thumbs-up. "You're good," he says. "Take the second road on the right and he's halfway down the block on the left-hand side; can't miss it." He presses the control button in the booth and the yellow-striped barrier arm suddenly arches up and to the left, clearing the way ahead.

"Thanks, Kevin," I call out, throwing him a wave as Jimmy hits the gas and accelerates through the access point.

Thomas McAllister is waiting on his front porch when we pull into the driveway at Southwind Lane. The home is a large and stunning adobe-style with a cluster of palm trees rising from the front yard. While I'm not partial to the Southwest, I've always loved the earthy Pueblo-inspired homes that are endemic to the region. McAllister's home is certainly a finer example of these.

"Mr. McAllister?" Jimmy says as he greets the middle-aged man with an extended hand.

"Call me Tom, please," the attorney says with a warm smile.

"Special Agent Donovan—Jimmy," my partner says. He extends a hand my way and adds, "This is Operations Specialist Magnus Craig."

I take Tom's hand, saying, "Call me Steps."

He just nods. "Please, come inside." We follow him through the foyer and into the living room, where he motions for us to have a seat on the massive beige couch that dominates the room.

Tom turns away to take a seat and I use the moment to catch Jimmy's attention and give him a discreet nod. The ice-blue shine was evident as soon as we walked into the living room. Like Judge Ehrlich's house, IBK entered through a sliding glass door and stayed just long enough to drop off the Styrofoam ice box before leaving the way he came.

"Jenny ran to the kitchen to whip up some lemonade," Tom says with a grin. "We're both curious what the FBI wants to know about the lost feet that someone decided to leave in our house." He grins as Jimmy and I exchange a look. "Kevin told me the purpose of your visit: the so-called Windhaven Massacre. I guess a couple feet in a box aren't exciting enough; people need to embellish the story so they have something interesting to tell their friends. We were the talk of the community for months. Your visit should get some tongues flapping again."

"Sorry about that," Jimmy says earnestly.

"Don't be." Tom laughs. "I think it's hysterical. Let them squawk all they want. People are funny creatures, don't you think?" Gesturing toward the kitchen, he adds, "Jenny's not too happy about the feet, of course." He just grins and shrugs.

A voice drifts down the hall: "Severed feet, Tom! Severed feet in my living room!" The voice is followed by an elegant woman in her early forties who bursts from the kitchen and down the hall with a wooden tray of glasses filled with ice, a pitcher of fresh lemonade, a plate of brownies, and a gracious smile that belongs in a toothpaste commercial. "It was disgusting," she adds, scrunching her nose. "I had the carpet steam-cleaned—twice."

Her cleaning efforts may have eliminated any dirt carried in by the killer, but it had no effect on the foot-steps I see crossing her living room. That's the odd thing about shine: it imparts a bit of itself in everything it comes in contact with, as if the shine now belongs to the fibers in the carpet or the particles of wood in the subfloor. The only thing that gets rid of it is erosion and corruption: leaves decompose, sand blows, wood rots, and even stone wears down over time, taking the shine with it.

The type of contact is also important. A bare foot leaves a much bolder, deeper imprint than a shoed foot.

Mrs. McAllister sets the tray down and extends a slender hand, saying, "I'm Jenny."

Jimmy and I rise from our seats and take turns introducing ourselves and shaking hands. Jenny insists on pouring us each a tall glass of lemonade. "I use a concentrate," she says, "but then I squeeze in a couple fresh lemons. It gives it a little more bite."

"Wow! That's good," I say after taking a sip. I've never been much of a lemonade guy, but I could get used to this.

Jenny just beams and holds out the plate of brownies.

We spend the next ten minutes making small talk, mostly about Tucson. Jenny insists that we visit Saguaro National Park during our stay. Apparently it has the largest cacti in the county, the big ones you see in all the Westerns. She's also a big fan of the Reid Park Zoo.

Tom has his own passion, which is Kitt Peak National Observatory. "It's an hour west, but worth the drive," he insists. "People travel here from all over the country because we have the perfect conditions for stargazing. Get out of the city a little ways and there's zero light pollution. It's amazing. You'd be surprised how many people retire here—or just move here—so they can watch the night sky."

"Are you one of them?" Jimmy asks with a grin.

"Nah," he says with a small chuckle. "I moved here when I was eighteen and just never left. I didn't catch the astronomy bug until much later."

Eventually we get back to the purpose of our visit,

but reluctantly so. Tom and Jenny are easy to talk to, generous hosts, and decent to their core. With some people you can just tell.

"Yeah, the feet," Tom says when Jimmy broaches the subject. "I was running late that night; thought I'd get home after Jenny, but she had some problems with one of her clients in court that day. Good thing, I suppose."

"You're an attorney too?" I ask, turning to Jenny.

"Divorce and family law," she replies. "I gave criminal law a go earlier in my career, but it was too much. Divorce court is a breeze in comparison, at least psychologically."

"I can imagine."

"So, you got home first . . ." Jimmy prompts Tom.

"Yeah. Nothing was out of order; no sign of a break-in or anything like that. I saw the ice chest sitting in the middle of the living room and didn't think much of it. It looked brand-new and I just figured Jenny left it there, though that's a little out of the ordinary for her."

"I'm OCD when it comes to putting things away," Jenny clarifies.

"I was in the house about ten minutes," Tom continues, "before I got around to picking it up. Soon as I did, I realized it wasn't empty. I'm sure you can imagine my surprise when I pulled the lid off. Geez, and the smell! There was some putrid water sloshing around inside, which was a bit odd, until I learned that the feet had been frozen. Whoever placed it here wanted to make sure they were thawed out when we found them, though. I'm sure of that."

"Can you think of any reason why someone would

do that?" Jimmy asks. "Did anyone make any threats beforehand, or did you have a client that was upset with you? Anything you can remember would help."

"Nothing comes to mind. It's one of the abnormalities of being a defense attorney," Tom says, "the bad guys tend to like me. These days about half my work is pro bono. The legal system in this country can be a bitch if you don't have good counsel. Sure, there's the public defender's office, but they're so overworked and under-staffed they don't have the time to properly defend their clients."

Tom looks at Jimmy, then over at me. "Don't get me wrong, I'm not looking for exoneration for my clients, just a fair shake, a fair punishment, and maybe some treatment. Most of the cases I take on pro bono are drug addicts, and some have done some pretty horrific things by the time I see them. There's still hope for some, though. Or maybe that's just what I tell myself." He pauses, worrying his hands together in his lap, and then he says the most incredible thing: "I used to be one of them."

Jimmy and I exchange a startled look.

Tom nods. "It's not something I'm proud of, but I don't hide it either. Nor do I try to pass myself off as a victim, or claim that I have a defective gene that makes me susceptible to addiction. It was my fault, plain and simple. When I tried drugs for the first time, no one forced me. I chose to partake, and everything that fol-lowed was a consequence of that primary decision. It wasn't long before I was chasing the dragon in a really bad way." He pauses. "Have you ever heard that phrase? *Chasing the dragon?*"

"Doesn't it refer to constantly looking for the perfect high?" Jimmy says.

"Your first high," Tom corrects, "because, for most people, the first high *is* the perfect high. There's nothing like it, and no matter how you try you can never repeat it. Everything that follows seems to fall short, and soon you find that you've spent all your money, alienated friends and family, stolen, even sold your body, all in pursuit of the dragon." Jenny places a gentle hand on Tom's leg, which he quickly cups in his own.

"It's a hell you don't want to know, because even after it rips you apart and breaks you into small pieces, you still love it; you still crave it." He pauses, studying his wife's hand with the vacant stare of one preoccupied with distant thoughts.

"Chasing the dragon," he finally says, the words sounding airy, as if breathed into existence, rather than spoken. "The phrase actually originated in Hong Kong in the 1950s, you know—and had a slightly different meaning. Dragons are almost deified in China, so when addicts figured out they could heat heroin on a piece of tinfoil and inhale the fumes, the practice practically named itself. They quickly learned to keep the foil moving over the flame so the heroin would vaporize properly without burning. This back-and-forth movement caused the fumes to rise in a wispy, zigzag pattern. They'd suck in the vapors with a tube or straw, chasing the fumes along their zigzag course—chasing the dragon."

"But you beat the dragon," I remind him.

Tom smiles and shakes his head. "You don't beat the dragon," he says, "you just build a castle out of your family, faith, and friends and keep the beast out. There are no stronger walls. It's worked for me for more than three decades."

"If you don't mind me asking," Jimmy says, "what helped you get clean?"

"My addiction started with one friend, and ended with a better friend," he says with a smile. "As a teenager I had almost no supervision; typical latchkey kid. My dad was always on the road with his job, and Mom worked to help make ends meet. We were living in L.A. at the time, and it was a friend on the block who introduced me to pot. By fifteen I was using heroin on a regular basis and dabbling in other drugs. I never stole from my mom, but I broke into cars and houses on a regular basis and traded whatever I stole for my next hit. Of course, I got caught.

"It was after my third arrest that I met Parker Jones. He was with the juvenile division of the public defender's office and was new on the job, so new that I was his first case. I don't know who was more nervous, him or me. Anyway, he was the first person to really look out for me, while at the same time giving me the straighten-up-and-fly-right treatment."

He looks directly at Jimmy, then at me. "It was because of him that I moved to Tucson when I was eighteen. I did a couple years for my crime spree in L.A. first, but Parker always kept in touch. He visited once or twice a month and even put some money on my books now and then so I could buy some commissary." He grins. "You've never had a better-tasting candy bar or soda than when you're behind bars.

"Anyway, a year before I was released Parker got a better job in Tucson. I'd been working on finishing high school at his insistence, and before he left he promised to help me get my juvenile record expunged when I turned eighteen, provided I got my diploma. I think he was afraid I'd give up without him around to push me, and I was determined to show him I could do it. I didn't want to disappoint him."

Tom pushes back in the sofa, his hands relaxed in his lap with Jenny's hand still entwined. "He was true to his word, in every way. I had some probation time to serve after my release, but the day it was over I hopped on a bus for Tucson. I can only imagine what he was thinking when I showed up on his doorstep, but if there was any apprehension he didn't show it. He just gave me the proudest smile I'd ever gotten—from anyone. When he went to shake my hand I hugged the guy.

"I started at the community college three months after arriving in Tucson. Two years later my juvenile record was sealed. Four years after that I graduated from the James E. Rogers College of Law, eager to take the bar exam. It was Parker Jones I looked for in the audience when they handed me my diploma."

The smile on Tom's face is warm and penetrating, the type that makes others eager for what he has before they even know what it is. "He's retired now, of course," Tom continues. "Spends a lot of his time in the desert stargazing, which is how I got sucked into that infernal hobby. We still meet every Saturday morning for coffee. That's just a couple days away. If you boys are still in town, you should join us."

"That's very kind of you," Jimmy says, "but we usually don't stay in one place very long; hazard of the job, I'm afraid."

"I understand."

"So all the pro bono work is your way of paying it forward?" I say.

"Yes," Tom says, but he's hesitant. "No, that's only partly true, I suppose. It's more about showing Parker that everything he poured into me was not wasted. He tried helping others, of course, but for every one that gives you hope, there are fifty that break your heart. In the end, there's no such thing as rehabilitation; there's just those who want to change and commit to it, and those who don't. Sometimes you have to bounce off the bedrock pretty hard before you're ready to fix yourself."

When we leave the warmth of the adobe home an hour later, full up on brownies, lemonade, and hope, we linger a moment at the car and exchange a parting wave with Tom and Jenny. Neither of us wants to leave; we could have spent the entire evening and on into the early morning talking with the couple. It's fitting that the desert sky is dusky and the first stars of night are brilliantly ensconced above us.

I look on them with new eyes.

Jimmy and I grab a bite to eat and then make our way to the Best Western near the airport. Marty and Les discovered the motel shortly after we landed and Marty texted Jimmy immediately afterward just raving about the place. It's nice as far as motels go, I suppose; I've just seen too many to judge fairly, too many to care, and right now I just want someplace air-conditioned where I can kick off my shoes.

With our card keys in hand, we're barely thirty feet

from the front desk when Marty pops out of the elevator wearing nothing but flip-flops, blue swim trunks that reveal too much, and a white motel towel draped around his neck.

"Holy cow, Marty," Jimmy blurts, "do the civilized world a favor and put on some clothes!"

Marty is Pacific Northwest to the bone, with legs so white I swear they're reflecting light onto the walls and ceiling as he moves. The rest of him isn't much better. "Hey, guys," he says with a grin, flexing a nonexistent bicep. "Care to join me in the hot tub?"

"It's seven thousand degrees outside, Marty," I say. "Ever hear of heatstroke?"

"Nah, that's what the swimming pool is for; it feels ice cold after the hot tub. Kind of like doing that polar bear thing, you know, where they go out and jump in a lake in the middle of winter."

"Yeah, I'm sure it's just like that," I scoff. "Where's Les?"

"Ah, he's being antisocial; said he's going to write a letter to his wife."

I elbow Jimmy and give an approving nod. He just shakes his head and tries to squeeze past Marty without touching any exposed skin.

"How about you, Jimmy?" Marty presses, moving in a little too close for comfort. "Care for a little hot tub therapy? We can relax and get caught up, just you and me, copilot and super-agent, mano a mano."

"You know that means *hand-to-hand*?" I say.

Marty gives me an odd look. "No, I'm pretty sure it means man-to-man. You know, *mano* . . . it's *man* with an *o* on the end."

"Dude, *mano* means hand; *hombre* means man. If you want to say man-to-man, it's *hombre-a-hombre*." I can't believe I just said *dude*. If I didn't know any better, I'd swear Marty's an IQ vampire: the longer you're around him, the more he sucks the smarts right out of you.

"Hand," Marty says with a chuckle and a shake of his head. "That's pretty funny. So I just asked Jimmy to go hand-to-hand with me in the hot tub."

"Eww," Jimmy says, overexaggerating his facial expressions as he slips into the elevator.

"Whoa." Marty chuckles. "I didn't mean—"

"Ah-ah-ah! Keep those manos where we can see them," I say as I step past him and start punching the number three button on the panel.

"Marty, I'm married," Jimmy says with a perfectly serious look on his face.

"I'm spoken for," I pipe in quickly when Marty turns his failing grin my way.

"Guys, that's not what I meant," he says as the doors close. "Guys?"

We're still chuckling when we get off on the third floor.

After dumping my go-bag in my room, I join up with Jimmy across the hall. He's already got his laptop set up and connected to the hotel's Wi-Fi, but he's having trouble logging into his email. After a minute it finally takes and he finds a half dozen new messages. The two most recent are from Dr. Stone: one has the report; the other has a series of photos.

I read over Jimmy's shoulder as he scrolls through the material. "It seems to fit your theory," I say, referring to his earlier episode of deductive reasoning at Hangar 7. "But like El Paso, we can't be sure until we know who the victim is. So far all we have is feet and more feet." I take a drink from the sweating plastic bottle on the table in front of me and then screw the cap back on tight. "You know what this reminds me of?"

"I'm afraid to ask," Jimmy says without looking up.

"You know all the feet that keep washing up around Puget Sound and up into Canada? There was another one earlier this year in Seattle."

"How could I forget?"

"Well, for a couple years people were speculating that they were victims of organized crime or some serial killer with a foot fetish, especially since a dozen or so were found within about a hundred miles of each other. You don't see that happening in other parts of the country."

Jimmy's smiling, but shaking his head. "They eliminated foul play in a couple of those, you know? Turns out they were probable suicides. My guess is the rest were either suicides or accidental drownings."

"I know, and I'm not saying it's related, or even sinister, it's just that seeing those feet at the ME's office still inside their shoes reminded me of the flyers we got on the floaters. Kind of weird, that's all."

"It's not weird, it's science," Jimmy replies. "The feet wash up because they're encased in rubber-soled shoes that protect them from predation, and also make them buoyant. The fact that they separated from the body is just part of the natural decaying process. After stewing too long in the water, the ankle disarticulates and off floats a foot in search of a beach."

"Yeah, but how come so many wash ashore in the same area?"

"Tides," Jimmy says with a shrug. "Plus, things tend to get trapped in Puget Sound. The only sizable waterway in and out is the Strait of Juan de Fuca. Add to that all the canals, bays, inlets, and islands throughout Puget Sound, and the place is one big sticky swath of flypaper for flotsam and jetsam. Honestly, once a body—or in this case a body part—ends up in Puget Sound, the chances of it finding its way out to the ocean aren't very good." He lifts his paper coffee cup as if to offer up a toast, and then chugs it down in one long pull.

"That's not science; you're just guessing."

"I am," Jimmy admits, "but it sounds good, right? You know what else sounds good?" He swivels the laptop around on the table so I can see the screen, and gives me a double flash of his eyebrows. It only takes me a second to realize what he's up to.

"Really?"

He grins. "Why not? It worked before."

"We got lucky," I say. "When do you want to do this?"

"Relax, princess; you can get your beauty rest. We'll hit it first thing in the morning." Swinging the laptop back around, he adds, "Maybe we can wrap this thing up in another day or two."

"I don't believe in *maybe*," I say, standing and retrieving my soda from the table. "It disappoints me every time."

CHAPTER NINE

*In the Umbra of Bygone Terrors—September 5,
3:03 A.M.*

Something wicked this way comes.

Something wicked this way comes.

Something wicked this way . . .

The cold is upon me, bone-deep with teeth of stone.
The wind gnaws upon my scalp, my cheeks, my hands;
it worries, worries, worries the skin with a thousand
little bites that leave me numb, red, and raw at every
exposed opening. But it's not from wind or ancient cold
that I shiver, nor from teeth of stone upon my bones. . . .
Something wicked this way comes.

At first it's just a shadow, an empty spot in the darkness among the trees, but given time, shadows twist and
convulse. From behind their stygian veil can issue things
both beautiful and hideous. Only the shadow knows
what lies within.

There's something familiar about this, an aftertaste of déjà vu.

I've been here before.

As the shadow begins to take form, my first impression is that of a giant. It's outlined by a lesser tint of darkness, a seven-foot void in the blackness. Its breath mists the air white from invisible nostrils, each exhale akin to the rumblings of a minotaur.

His eyes are upon me.

Though I can't see them, I can feel them slowly dissecting me piece by piece, layer by layer. He's closer now and I recognize the shadow's build—the broad shoulders, the head, but . . . no. It's not him.

That was done and settled years ago.

It's not him.

The moon breaks over my left shoulder. Wrestling free of the clouds, it casts its silver glow upon the snow and marches up to the primal forest. Still he waits, breathing, watching, listening. There's more of him now, this Neanderthal apparition with hams for fists and timber-thick limbs. As moonlight struggles with shadow, I see his camouflage pants, his orange vest, the shotgun under his arm.

It *is* him, and this is *not* done or settled.

Pat McCourt—I killed him three years ago.

"It's a dream," I hear myself say. "Just a dream." And it's one I've had before, one that resurfaces every few months. "Wake up," I say to the darkness, but I don't, and then something changes in the dream.

No, several things change.

First, the moon brightens. It's now a floodlight reflecting off the snow and off every trunk and branch in the forest. Second, Pat McCourt exits the shadows and starts walking toward me, slow at first, then more briskly. Third, it's not Pat McCourt.

"It's a dream," I remind myself, "only a dream; just wake up."

The shotgun barrel sweeps up and fixes on my chest as the creature closes. He's human from the neck down, but what perches on top is a grotesque mask of dead gray skin with a snowman's nose and eyes—coal-black clumps that see and smell nothing.

The worst part is the mouth.

A slithering inch-thick band covering the whole lower half of the so-called head, it droops on both sides to form a sad frown. The frown is fixed yet moves constantly in small parts. It moves because it must, because worms can't remain still, not while they're living.

"Sad Face," I hear myself gasp.

He's on me in an instant. The barrel looms before me and he bears down on the trigger. A shot rings out, echoing in my head.

I can smell the gunpowder.

When I open my eyes I find only darkness, that and the red glow of the motel clock. It's 3:03 A.M. I didn't wake screaming or trembling, nor am I covered in sweat. The dream was similar to others, but now my nightmares seem to be merging together, blending into new and terrifying mixes.

I'm fine, though.

Well, not fine, just better.

I've been talking to Heather about my nightmares; it

seems to help. They don't seem to come as often, and when they do I soon recognize them for what they are. They can still be terrifying, but less so when I feel in control.

Rolling onto my side, I stare at the clock until it rolls over to 3:07 A.M. and then I close my eyes and picture Heather in the passenger seat of my car, her hair tossed lightly by the rush of air from the open sunroof as we drive along Chuckanut Drive.

When sleep finds me, I'm in better company.

Pima County Adult Detention Center—September 5, 8:37 A.M.

"Well, this is . . . pretty amazing," Jimmy says, turning the rented Cadillac Escalade off West Silverlake Road and into the parking lot of the Pima County Adult Detention Center. The corrections facility is located in South Tucson, just blocks from Sentinel Peak, or "A" Mountain, as it's more commonly known, which rises some 2,900 feet in the background. Back home we have hills that are taller, but if they want to call it a mountain, so be it.

The mountain's original name dates to the period after the Presidio of Tucson was built in 1775. For the security of all, a sentinel was posted on the peak to keep a lookout for any approaching Apache raiding parties. Early settlers apparently had little time to waste on coming up with clever names, so the mountain ended up with the utilitarian moniker Sentinel Peak.

That lasted over 150 years, until a 160-foot-tall letter *A* made of painted basalt rock appeared on the eastern side of the peak. Originally built by students from the University of Arizona in 1916, the *A* is normally white, but sometimes gets painted green for Saint Patrick's Day. These days the schizophrenic mountain goes by both names, weighing each equally.

When Jimmy says the place is amazing, however, he's not referring to the mountain; he's talking about the jail. The Pima County Adult Detention Center *is* impressive, with a double exclamation mark. But then, I'm not a subject-matter expert on crowbar hotels.

I may have acted dubious last night when Jimmy clued me in on his plans for this morning, but, honestly, I should have thought of this myself. The jail visit worked well in El Paso, why not here?

This time I'm not going in with expectations of finding IBK's shine; it's probably not there. I'd bet money, though, that we'll find the gray shine of victim number two. If Jimmy's theory is correct, he's a local who would have spent time—probably a good deal of time—at this facility.

His crime would have been significant: we're not looking for someone who was hooked up for shoplifting, purse snatching, or driving with a suspended license.

To find him, we need to go through the motions, like before, and check each cellblock, and each common area. That gray shine with mottled carmine is here somewhere, we just need to ferret it out. To fortify our little ruse, Diane contacted Tom McAllister's office and his paralegal provided a list of all his clients for the last three years.

After showing our badges twice and explaining what

we needed to three levels of supervision, a congenial lieutenant named Doug with a seventies-style cop mustache takes our catalog of names to his office and starts pulling together a list of cells. He warns us that it'll take about a half hour, so we kill time strolling around the lobby and out onto the entrance courtyard.

The more I see, the more impressed I am.

Thirty-three minutes later, Lieutenant Doug returns to the lobby with an Excel printout of names and cells corresponding to our list. Rather than passing off the escort duty to a sergeant or even a corrections deputy, he decides to take us around to the different cellblocks himself. He seems intrigued by our little quest.

"This is an impressive facility," Jimmy says as we start up a flight of stairs. "If it wasn't for the barbed-wire-topped fences and the limited number of windows, you might mistake the place for an office complex. That wall of glass at the main entrance is particularly inspiring."

"It's home," Doug says with a grin.

"How many inmates do you house?"

"Today's count is 1,823," Doug replies, "but we can hold almost 2,400 if we have to. Average is in the mid-1,750s. Seems like a lot of capacity, but we had to build a separate minimum-security facility up the road to keep ahead of the curve. Tucson has a population of more than a half million, and once you get outside the city limits, the rest of Pima County adds another 450,000. So even if our criminal element only accounts for one percent of the county population, that's ten thousand idiots running around doing stupid stuff."

Jimmy chuckles. "I'm guessing it's more than one percent."

"You got that right," Doug replies. "There's a sharp edge between legal and illegal, and a surprising number of people who want to play right on that edge."

Arriving on the second story, Doug points out several cellblocks. "This facility was built in 1984 and was one of the first in the nation to switch to a direct-supervision model."

"Direct supervision?" I ask.

"The whole place has what they call a 'podular' design that allows staff to interact directly with inmates within the housing units. It's supposed to reduce violence against both staff and other inmates, and the empirical evidence suggests that it works as advertised. We certainly don't have any complaints."

"Isn't that a bit dangerous, putting your corrections deputies right out in the open with the inmates?"

"It only seems that way. The design allows a clear view into every area of the pod, and the interaction between inmates and staff helps humanize the facility. You'd be surprised how effective it is."

Without any fanfare, Lieutenant Doug leads us through a pair of security doors, letting the first door close and lock before opening the second, and we find ourselves in the common room of the first pod.

Doug explains that the pod is only partially populated at the moment because most of the inmates have assigned jobs. For some, it's working in the kitchen or laundry; some are assigned a manufacturing job; and others attend classes or mandatory treatment programs.

The inmates in the common room give us barely a glance before returning to their card games, textbooks, letters, or other pastimes.

My glasses have been safely stowed in my pocket since we arrived, and, as expected, I haven't seen a sign of IBK's ice-blue shine. Honestly, I'm not even looking for it anymore, I'm that convinced we won't find it. I'm focused instead on victim number two, the one who's cooling his heels—literally—at the Pima County Medical Examiner's Office.

We visit pod after pod, putting on a good show of examining each targeted cell before checking off another name on our makeshift list. An hour into our search, and with two-thirds of the jail already eliminated, it's suddenly in front of me, and to my left and right: gray essence mottled with carmine. The colors are cast upon the floor and fixed furnishings of Main 4C, layer upon layer of it. When I focus, the neon effect is powerful and omnipresent . . . but flat.

Our gray fellow is dead . . . wherever he is.

But we already knew that.

Judging by the clarity of the shine, he was here sometime in the last six to twelve months. He visited almost all of the individual cells during that time, but he lived in just one, and his bunk isn't hard to find. You can see the history of his handprints on the upright bar where he helped boost himself up.

I forgo the *187* trick I used in El Paso and just ask Doug for the list straight-up; he doesn't even question it. After all, we're the Feds. Fifteen minutes later, Jimmy and I are walking out the front door with a list of ten people who occupied that bunk in the last year; just ten.

That should make Diane happy . . . or sad; I don't know. Sometimes she seems a bit disappointed when the information we provide doesn't challenge her enough. The tougher the quest, the more she appears to enjoy it. I once told her she had a masochistic tendency and she threatened to beat me with a hose.

I think she was confusing masochism with sadism.

CHAPTER TEN

Southbound I-10, Tucson—September 5, 10:42 A.M.

The state tree of Arizona must be either the palm tree or the light pole—and I'm leaning toward the light pole. Aside from the occasional water tower, the poles seem to be the tallest structures we pass as we make our way south on Interstate 10 back to the motel.

A surprising number of low-water plants thrive in this climate and add their greens and yellows to the gray contrast of the highway. There are a wide variety of small trees, including acacia, rosewood, ebony, and mesquite. The palm trees are the most fascinating. Some are close, but most are seen at a distance, lording over parcels of Arizona brown.

It's a climate and terrain far removed from the Pacific Northwest, which is not just my home by accident of birth, but by inheritance and choice. Because of this, I've never been much for the drier climates of the southwest. Still, they never fail to surprise me, and whenever

I'm down here I find incredible beauty hidden in plain sight.

Jimmy's driving, but his mind is far away, absorbed in theories of murder past, present, and future. Engaging him in conversation would be pointless, and since the road noise is tediously familiar, I turn the radio on and hit the scan button. It rotates through several channels before landing on a song that instantly sits Jimmy up in his seat. He punches the scan button quickly to lock in the channel and then cranks the volume, shooting me a wicked grin.

It's Queen.

"Bohemian Rhapsody," to be precise.

Like trained seals, both Jimmy and I instantly break into song. To say that our contribution to the classic Queen ballad is music would be an affront to music, but traditions must be maintained and so we bellow out the words at the top of our lungs.

When we get to the *Wayne's World* part of the song, we start bobbing our heads just like in the movie. It's a tradition that goes back to our first assignment together.

I remember our first meeting.

Jimmy was handpicked for his position by FBI Director Robert Carlson. He had some skill as a tracker, even back then, and a master's degree in psychology. Uncle Robert said he was a natural profiler, which is true, but I guess I always suspected he was chosen so he could monitor me—make sure I don't walk off into that dark abyss that tends to follow us from case to case. We met at Hangar 7 on a cold January afternoon. The two-story office complex at the back of the hangar hadn't been built yet, nor had Betsy been delivered. Basically it was a giant, empty, poorly lit hangar, and we sat around a folding card table on four folding chairs: Director Carlson, Jimmy, me, and Dad.

This was still months before Diane joined the unit.

As we sat at the flimsy card table and Director Carlson tried to explain shine, Jimmy started glancing around at the empty hangar. Maybe he thought he was being punked; maybe he thought Director Carlson was an imposter and this was some type of trap; I don't know, but you could almost feel his apprehension—and you couldn't really blame him.

I was asked to leave the hangar three times, and three times I came back in and showed Jimmy everywhere he walked, everything he touched, even the dance step he did in the northeast corner.

It only convinced him that we had cameras hidden *everywhere* in the hangar and that I was watching his every move from a monitor outside.

The fourth test convinced him.

He insisted that I sit in the corner of the hangar with my coat zipped up and wrapped around my head. When I exited the corner and pointed out every single step and half step he took, he just sat down at the card table and stared at his hands.

It's a lot to take in, particularly for someone with Jimmy's extremely rational mind-set. He eventually accepted it, but only because he could find no alternative explanation and had no choice. It created an uncomfortable dynamic between the two of us. I was an illogical construct in his rational world.

The singing was Jimmy's idea.

He figured that since we were strangers in a strange situation, the best way to team-build was to tear down some of our natural inhibitions. His proposal was simple: when certain songs came on the radio, we would sing along.

And no humming or lip-synching.

It had to be loud and forceful, from the gut.

As to the selection process, our first day in the car together solved that. We agreed that every third song that came on the radio would go on the list. Since the station we were listening to played hits from the seventies, eighties, and nineties, we ended up with a cornucopia of thirty-seven tunes that kept us singing almost anytime the radio was on.

That lasted about three months before we pared it down to just "Bohemian Rhapsody," "Der Kommissar," "Livin' la Vida Loca," "Sweet Emotion," "Stairway to Heaven," "Pass the Dutchie," and "Girls Just Wanna Have Fun."

I'm not particularly fond of the last one.

As stupid as the whole thing sounds, it worked.

Our mutual humiliation at having to sing "Karma Chameleon" while stopped at a light at a busy intersection helped forge us into more than a team; it made us brothers.

Plus, we got some laughs along the way.

And some stares.

So when "Bohemian Rhapsody" comes on the radio, there's no dread or embarrassment or hesitation. Jimmy and I jump right in, singing at the top of our lungs. It brings with it a heartwarming sense of nostalgia and kinship, like walking through the front door of your childhood home after a long absence and smelling warm apple pie fresh from the oven.

We sing and we don't care who looks or stares. And when the song ends we both have a long laugh.

It feels good.

It feels right.

Best Western, Room 310—September 5, 12:14 P.M.

I've never been in the military and don't pretend to know what it's like, but I think I can relate to the hurry-up-and-wait syndrome. If Jimmy and I kept track of how much time we devote to the different aspects of each case, I'm betting at least a quarter of it is spent in motel rooms, police station lobbies, conference rooms, and dozens of other locations, just waiting for something to happen.

We could be waiting for a report, an escort, a local detective, a doctor, a coroner, a priest, a ride. It all comes down to just killing time. A good book helps. Jimmy sometimes plays games on his phone, but I just can't get into that; seems like a waste of time—but I guess that's the point.

Right now we're waiting for a call from Diane . . . and waiting.

I'm deep into *The Frozen Dead,* an intriguing novel by Bernard Minier, when there's a knock at the door. Jimmy doesn't budge from his game, so I replace my bookmark, set the paperback aside, walk to the door, and check the peephole. It's Les. He's cradling a sealed letter in his hands. The stationery is lavender and brown.

"You don't have a stamp, by any chance?" he asks as I swing the door wide.

I've always liked Les. He and Marty are yin and yang, and not just because they're pilot and copilot. Les is quiet and reserved; steady and reliable. With his perfect head of salt-and-pepper hair he looks the part of a seasoned pilot. He and Beth have been married twenty-six years and have three sons and seven grandkids.

Marty, on the other hand, is ex-Army: a former chopper pilot with combat experience in both Iraq and Afghanistan. He was married—briefly—but later swore off matrimony for all eternity . . . until his second marriage. That lasted about as long as the first. He's gregarious even on his worst days, and always upbeat.

The only problem with Marty is that his mouth only has two gears: fast and faster. There's no neutral—the guy just can't stop talking. I don't know how Les puts up with him on long flights. Maybe it's because Les does very little talking himself and doesn't seem to get frazzled by much; maybe he can just sit and listen. Or, more likely, he just tunes Marty out and the talkative copilot is so busy yapping that he never notices.

Like I said, yin and yang.

I hold the door open and wave Les in, then retrieve my leather bag from the closet and fish through the buckled pockets until I find two books of stamps. I pick one and hand it to Les. It's a heart stamp that the postal service calls *Sealed with Love.*

It was either that or one from the Harry Potter collection.

"Hey, Jimmy, look at this," I say in my best golly-gee voice. "Les is writing a letter to his wife. How romantic, huh? And what a great idea; wherever did you come up with that idea?" Les just chuckles and gives a wave good-bye, slipping into the hall before Jimmy can put up a defense.

Closing the door, I walk slowly back toward my seat. "Considerate guy, that Les," I say, thumbing toward the door. Picking up some of my stationery off the table on the way, I wave it in the air and add, "Look at this, some paper and envelopes. Isn't that odd?"

Jimmy finally looks up from his game and is about to say something when the phone goes off in his hand. He's startled and nearly drops it on the floor, but manages to catch and answer it in one swift movement.

Jimmy contacted Diane an hour ago and gave her the dump on our jail visit. From the half-conversation spilling out in three- and four-word sentences, I can tell she's whittled the list of ten down to just two—again.

She's good.

Some might be skeptical of such an audacious claim; some might question her analysis. On the other hand, some know better. If she says she eliminated eight of the ten candidates without ever leaving her office, then she eliminated eight of the ten candidates.

Period.

After an entire minute of supreme patience, I motion for Jimmy to put the phone on speaker, but he keeps brushing me off. I can be annoying when I want to be—or so I'm told—and persist until he holds a hand up in surrender.

"Hold on, Diane. I'm going to put you on speaker." He pauses a moment as Diane adds something to their semi-private conversation. "Pestering doesn't even come close to covering it," Jimmy replies a moment later, giving me a withering look. He presses the speaker function and sets the phone on the bed. "Go ahead, Diane. You're on speaker."

"Do you want me to repeat everything?" she asks.

"No, just skip to the possible victims," Jimmy says.

"Right," she says, and I hear a shuffling of papers. "The first is fifty-one-year-old Cecil B. Thompson, a transient with dozens of arrests for trespass, urinating in public, sitting or lying on the sidewalk, public drunkenness, that sort of thing. His last arrest was three weeks before the feet turned up on McAllister's living room floor."

"What did they book him for?"

"Defecating on the hood of a parked police cruiser."

"Good grief," I mutter in disgust.

"Yeah, he admitted to 'dropping the kids off at the pool,' as he put it, but claimed he was using a public toilet. Honestly, I don't think the guy has been sober in thirty years."

"I'm guessing he's not high on your probability ladder?" Jimmy says.

"Bottom rung, for sure," Diane says, "and he has no motive to hate McAllister; the guy defends him pro bono every time he gets arrested."

"Yeah, Jimmy has a theory, and this guy doesn't really fit," I chime in.

"Now, does he?" Diane says in a bored, show-me-what-you-got tone. "Well, out with it; what's the theory?"

"All in good time," Jimmy replies. "I don't want to ruin the surprise."

"Well, then I'll just have to remain breathless with anticipation," Diane says, sounding neither breathless nor anticipatory. "Suspect number two," she continues. "Travis William Duncan, age twenty-seven. Real winner, this one; he's a hard-core heroin addict, career burglar, and car thief. Almost two years ago he was in some dive trailer on a binge with a half dozen of his doper pals. Seems he and his partner in crime were celebrating after scoring a wad of cash from a small safe that had been bolted in place; they used a pry bar to get it out, destroying the floor and wall in the process. With cash in hand, first thing they did was re-up with an eight-ball of Mexican brown and set up a shooting gallery in the aforementioned dive trailer—a shooting gallery is a place where a bunch of junkies get together to shoot up," she adds.

"I know that," Jimmy says blandly.

"Ditto," I add.

I have no idea what she's talking about.

"A few hours later an ambulance responds to the trailer after dispatch receives a barely intelligible 911 call."

"Overdose?" Jimmy asks.

"No, I wish it were so. The medics found a five-month-old baby boy convulsing and suffering from trauma to the head, including a fractured skull. They found the mother passed out nearby with a needle still in her arm. Travis apparently made the call, and was the only one somewhat alert when the ambulance arrived.

"He claimed the mother must have dropped the baby when she passed out, but his story kept changing. Eventually he cracked and admitted to punching the baby in the head a couple times because it wouldn't shut up."

"Define *a couple times,*" Jimmy says.

"He said twice; the medics had a slightly different view. They said the baby had to have been punched eight to ten times, and not lightly."

"Did the baby make it?" I ask.

"No. He died the next day in the hospital."

"So Travis picks up, what, a murder second charge?" Jimmy says.

"Correct. His bail was set at a million, which he obviously couldn't afford, so he spent over a year in the Pima County Jail awaiting trial. The prosecutor offered plea deals on several occasions, but Duncan rejected them, against the advice of McAllister. Anyway, the trial didn't go well for the prosecution. I couldn't get a straight answer from anyone as to what went wrong, and the lead detective was either too embarrassed or too upset to even talk to me. Duncan was acquitted on March fifth."

"So McAllister represented him well," Jimmy says.

"Better than well," Diane says. "Now . . . this is the part where you tell me your great theory." She pauses for effect. "You know, the one about a vigilante hacking off the feet of people who have escaped justice."

Jimmy and I stare at each other, speechless.

I mouth, *How did she know?* But Jimmy just shakes his head; he's completely deflated, like a hot-air balloon lying on its side after all the air spills out. It's sad.

"I figured it out yesterday morning," Diane adds, interpreting our silence correctly. She exhales a contented sigh. "Sorry, hon. Gotta be faster than that if you want to beat this old girl to the punch bowl."

I give a little chuckle.

Jimmy doesn't think it's funny.

"Bottom line," Diane continues, "I'm betting your Mr. Gray is going to be Travis Duncan. Which reminds me: Why do you call him Mr. Gray?"

"Uhhh," Jimmy and I say together, followed by an awkward silence. When Jimmy makes no move to explain away the name, I jump in. "It's just one of those stupid names we come up with for our victims," I say. "So when Chuckles—that's the pathologist who wasn't helping us—when he set the feet on the autopsy table, they looked all dead and gray—"

"I'm guessing because they were dead and gray," Diane interrupts.

"Bingo! See, you get it; hence, Mr. Gray. That's how we do it in the field." I want to end with a hearty *Booyah,* but it seems a little over-the-top, so I restrain myself.

"Impressive," Diane replies flatly.

We sometimes forget that she knows nothing about shine. Little bits slip loose here and there, bits that should be more carefully guarded. Diane's wickedly brilliant with information, even when that information points to something as unlikely as shine. It's one of the reasons I've been thinking about bringing her into the inner circle, her and Heather.

If Diane suspects anything, she's not talking.

"Travis's DNA wasn't in CODIS," she continues, "so I tracked down his aunt, Penny Dellal."

"Is she local?"

"She is. Travis stayed with her on and off. She was the one who reported him missing in mid-July. Claimed she last saw him in early April, about a month after his acquittal, but wasn't worried about him initially since he has a tendency to disappear for days or even weeks at a time. After the months started to stack up without a word from him, she got worried and filed the report."

"Have you talked to her yet?" Jimmy asks.

"I was just getting ready to call. I doubt there's much she can add to what we already know. Why? Did you want to take a run at her?"

"You read my mind. What's the address?"

There's a pause, filled with the hurried shuffling of paper, then Diane reads off an address on South Presidio Avenue. "I looked it up on Google Earth and checked the county assessor's site," she says. "It's a single-wide trailer in a rough-looking trailer park at the southeast corner of the city. You might want to think about taking backup."

"I've got Steps," Jimmy says, glancing over at me.

"Your funeral," Diane replies. "Make sure you get a toothbrush or a razor so we have something to pull DNA from."

"Is—what did you say the aunt's name is?"

"Penny Dellal."

"Is she from the dad's side or the mom's side of the family?"

"I'm not sure; I didn't look that deep. You're thinking mitochondrial DNA, aren't you?"

"I just want to have a backup plan," Jimmy says. "His aunt may have tossed his toothbrush by now."

"You can't make identification with mitochondrial."

"I know that, but I might be able to eliminate him as our victim."

Mitochondrial DNA is located within the cell's mitochondria, outside the cell's nucleus. While a single human cell contains just two copies of DNA in the nucleus, known as nuclear DNA, the mitochondria can contain hundreds of copies of mitochondrial DNA, allowing for a much better opportunity to recover workable DNA, even from heavily compromised samples, such as old bone.

The odd thing about mitochondrial DNA is that it's inherited exclusively from the mother. Barring a mutation, a woman's mother, siblings, and children will all have identical mitochondrial DNA. This, however, limits its application in criminal investigations, because it doesn't provide a positive form of identification. In fact, one string of mitochondrial DNA—the most common one—is shared by 7 percent of American Caucasians. That's a lot of suspects. It also costs more and takes longer to analyze.

Still, it's another tool in the toolbox.

Jimmy and I don't need DNA to figure out if Travis is our man. I'll know that as soon as we get to the trailer and I see his shine. But a shine match isn't something that can go into a medical examiner's report. We'll need something legally and scientifically acceptable, and the best thing for that is DNA. That means a toothbrush, or a comb, or an old bandage; anything that might contain saliva, blood, hair, or skin cells.

On one case we even collected an old stool sample.

Correction: *I* collected an old stool sample.
Good times.

A Single-wide Trailer with Curtains—September 5, 12:53 P.M.

"What a hole," Jimmy says as he pulls the rental to the side of the rutted gravel road in front of the trailer on South Presidio Avenue and shifts into park. Glancing around at the sketchy neighborhood, he adds, "Maybe we *should* have brought backup."

"Too late now," I say. "Besides, we've seen worse."

Jimmy looks wary. "I'm not so sure," he mutters.

Popping the door open, I step from the gentle air-conditioning of the Ford Fusion into the ninety-eight-degree furnace that Tucson residents so quaintly refer to as "afternoon." As the air from my first breath half bakes my lungs, I pray aloud, "Dear Lord, let this humble single-wide have air-conditioning."

"Amen," Jimmy finishes.

Scrutinizing the other residences along the road, I'm reminded of the slums and shantytowns you see in Third World countries; neighborhoods patched together with plywood and corrugated metal roofing. It's not that bad, I'm sure, but standing among the filth and decay it's hard to separate the one from the other. "Make sure you lock the doors," I say, looking over the roof at Jimmy. "We don't want a repeat of Detroit."

I give him a grin.

"Really?" He hits the lock button on the key fob and

the car gives a short chirp. "I thought we weren't going to mention Detroit."

"*You* said we weren't going to mention Detroit," I remind him. "I made no such promise. Besides, you're making a big deal out of nothing; they found the car, didn't they? Well . . . most of it."

Taking my glasses off and placing them in their case, I glance around the property and give Jimmy a nod. There's a well-established path of gray mottled with carmine from the road to the trailer, and around the property.

No doubt about it, Travis Duncan is victim number two.

A pit bull chained to the trailer next door goes ballistic as Jimmy and I make our way across a parched piece of dirt outlined with rocks, presumably the front yard, and continue along the side of the trailer to a dented piece of faded aluminum that serves as Penny Dellal's front door. Jimmy gives it a couple raps and we wait and listen. There's no answer or stir of movement from inside, so Jimmy gives it his best law enforcement knock—loud and strong—and calls out, "FBI."

While Jimmy mans the porch, I scoot around to the front and try to peer in through one of the larger windows. Heavy curtains completely cover the inside, so I work my way around the trailer, checking window after window, and running into curtain after curtain. As I loop around the rear of the trailer and start back toward Jimmy, Cujo goes rabid again; he's even foaming at the mouth.

"*FBI, open up,*" Jimmy shouts, pounding on the door.

From my position at the corner I hear a distinct *clink* and what sounds like a footfall from inside. "We've got movement," I tell Jimmy. He knocks again. "Ms. Dellal, we're here about your missing nephew."

The footfalls are more pronounced now, and I hear the unmistakable sound of glass hitting glass as someone moves forward in the trailer. A moment later the aluminum door opens a few inches, and a voice croaks, "Whatchawant?"

"FBI, Ms. Dellal," Jimmy says, holding his badge up.

Her hand flops around in front of her face and she says, "Call me Penny."

Jimmy nods. "We're following up on your nephew's disappearance, Penny, and I was hoping we could take a few minutes of your time."

"Travis?" she mutters. "He's gone."

"Yes, ma'am. That's why we're here. You filed a missing-person report with the Tucson Police Department in July."

"No, that was in . . . July."

Jimmy looks at me out of the corner of his eye and I make a drinking motion with my right hand. I passed a pile of empty vodka bottles outside the rear window—probably tossed out as they were emptied—and the glass-on-glass clinking from inside likely means there are more scattered about the bedroom floor.

"Can we come in for a moment, Penny?" Jimmy presses.

The door is wide open now and I arrive at the porch in time to see Penny picking at something in her left armpit with a disoriented look on her face and wind-tunnel hair.

"I s'pose you can come in for a minute," she says. "If you're really the FBI." She gives each of us an inquisitorial stare before seeming satisfied.

Flopping down in a recliner covered by a lightly stained blanket, Penny invites us to sit. The only other piece of furniture in the room is a road couch: a piece of furniture so nasty that you leave it by the side of the road with a FREE sign hoping someone will take it. Jimmy politely takes a seat and the couch makes a squishy sound as he sinks into it.

I decide to stand.

"You find Travis?" Penny asks.

Hmm, yes and no, I think.

"No," Jimmy replies, always tactful in these situations, "but we're making progress." He opens his notepad and takes pen to hand. "Do you remember if Travis got any threats before he disappeared? Phone calls, notes left at the door, anything like that?"

"Sure, he got some nasty comments after he killed that little baby," Penny blurts, "but most people didn't know he was staying here, so it was mostly stuff on blogs and such, people who didn't know him. Travis had a heart of gold," she adds. "It's just the heroin done it to him. He couldn't keep clean, couldn't keep a job, stole from everyone he knew, including me. It's the drugs; it poisons the mind."

She picks up a half-full vodka bottle from the end table and takes a long pull, then offers Jimmy a drink. He shakes his head and says a polite, "No, thank you," so she screws the cap back on and lays the bottle in her lap.

"Did Travis have a car?"

Penny thinks real hard and then shakes her head. "He had lots of bikes. Every week it was a different one, it seemed, but no car, not for a couple years. He lost his license, you know. Same with me, but mine was a discarriage of justice. I know when I'm drunk and I wasn't drunk when they said I was."

"I believe you," Jimmy replies. "Tell me, are you related to Travis through his mother or father?"

"Through his mother, of course," Penny says impatiently. "I'm his aunt, not his uncle. His mother was my older sister, Paula."

"Was . . . ?"

Penny's face sours. "She died when Travis was nine. The heroin got her. And Travis didn't have no father; well, I guess he did at one point, but only for a night, if you get my meaning."

"I do," Jimmy says. "A lot of that going around." He makes some scratches in the notebook. "Did Travis leave any possessions behind?"

Penny stares at the bottle in her lap a moment, then sets it on the end table and gets up without a word. She disappears into the small bedroom off the hall, and the only thing that comes out for two long minutes is some banging and cussing. When she returns to the living room, her hair looks like the wind tunnel had another go at it, and she's holding a two-foot-by-two-foot box in her hands.

"That's it," she says, setting the cardboard cube on the coffee table. "That's all of it; everything he had, except the three bikes out back."

Something is wrong when a man's worldly possessions fit inside a small cardboard box, I think as I

cautiously peel back the four flaps at the top. Most
Americans use their garage to store all their extra junk,
and sometimes they rent a storage unit on top of it. The
fact that Travis's sum accumulation fits in this box is
sad. Where are the middle-school baseball trophies, the
favorite T-shirts, the books, the movie posters, the
music? Where are his high school yearbooks, or his
diploma?

McAllister's right: heroin didn't do this to him, he did
it to himself. Heroin was just the vehicle he drove on the
way to self-destruction.

There's an unappealing odor playing at the end of my
nose, but I'm not sure if it's coming from the box or from
the living room, which has a smorgasbord of its own
aromas, and none of them pleasant.

"Don't touch that," Jimmy warns me in a soft voice,
tilting his head toward the box. "I'm going to run out to
the car and get the kit." He's gone less than a minute,
serenaded by Cujo there and back. When he returns to
the living room he's carrying a small leather bag by its
short straps. He sets it next to the cardboard box and
unzips the top. Reaching inside, he retrieves a pair of
black tactical gloves.

Designed specifically for high-risk frisks and searches,
the gloves provide extra protection against cuts and jabs.
The biggest concern when dealing with an addict is
getting stuck by one of his used needles. It's a good way
to end up with hepatitis or HIV.

Pulling the gloves on, Jimmy begins removing items
from the box one at a time, placing each on the coffee
table. There's little of note and nothing of value. Halfway down he says, "Uh, I got something," and extracts

a used needle attached to an empty syringe. There's a touch of dried blood on the needle and the residue of heroin in the syringe. Jimmy opens the mouth of the kit and pulls out a small travel-sized plastic container designed for safe needle disposal in the field. He pushes the syringe through the hole, and then sets the trap aside.

Two more needles and a pair of dirty underwear later, Jimmy is getting close to the bottom of the box when he says, "Here we go; yeah, that's perfect," and extracts a blue toothbrush with the bristles wrapped in clear plastic.

"I wrapped it up 'cause I didn't want it to get dirty," Penny says, pointing at the plastic wrapped around the end.

"Good thinking," Jimmy replies generously.

Next he pulls out a hairbrush, a pair of nail cutters, and a used bar of soap wrapped in a stained washcloth.

"That's all the stuff he left in the bathroom," Penny says. "Except the toothpaste; I used that."

Jimmy holds up the hairbrush in his left hand and the toothbrush in his right. "Can we take these, Penny? We can send them to the FBI lab and they'll give us a DNA profile for Travis. It's very useful in cases like this, and could help identify him—find him," he quickly corrects.

Penny just waves the stuff away. "I don't care. It's just sitting in a box. Take what you need."

We finish inside and say our good-byes to Penny, who continues to sit in the recliner taking regular sips from the vodka bottle. We're halfway out the door when her words reach us, listless and flat: "He's dead, isn't he?" They're simple words from a beat-down woman, words from the bottom of an empty vodka bottle. "Otherwise he'd be back by now," she says. "He'd be back."

She tips the bottle to her lips and then realizes it's empty. Screwing the cap back on, she sets it on the end table and stares at it. "He wasn't much, but he's the only family I got left . . . far as I know."

There's a dump truck of unpleasant things associated with the job that Jimmy and I do: dead bodies, blood, fecal matter, vomit, serial killers, dismemberment, and the media, to name only a few. Dealing with grieving relatives is the worst. It's something you never get used to, and no words ever seem right.

"I'm sorry." The statement rumbles in my throat before falling onto the living room carpet, broken and inadequate.

Penny just stares at her bottle as the door closes behind us.

Some things can't be fixed.

Ten minutes later we're merging into traffic on Interstate 10 when Jimmy's phone rings. It's Detective Alvarado.

"Hey, Tony, what's up?" Jimmy listens and then his eyebrows lift and he gives me an encouraging look. "With both feet? You don't say." Moving the end of the phone away from his mouth, he says in a quiet voice, "They arrested Hector Ortiz last night, alive and kicking—literally," then turns his attention back to Tony. "So if Hector's still a ninety-eight-point-sixer, that just leaves what's-his-face. . . . Yeah, Larry Wilson. I'm guessing he's assumed room temperature somewhere—

either that or he's still in the same freezer that the feet were in."

Jimmy's listening; he nods, and then nods again. "No, that's great. How'd you track that down? Diane! What, she called you instead of us?" He listens and then chuckles. "No, she calls us stuff like that all the time."

There's a long pause this time. With the road noise, I can't even hear the static of Tony's voice. "Yeah, of course," Jimmy says. "We *were* planning on heading home in a couple hours, but another day won't hurt." He glances at me, but then looks away quickly. "Yeah, we'll be in the air within the hour. . . . No, it's not a problem. I'll call when we arrive."

"El Paso," I say, slowly nodding my head. He can tell I'm not happy.

"Diane came up with some info on Larry Wilson. Tony wants to start looking for him tomorrow." He gives me a sideways glance. "It's just one day."

"It's always just one day."

CHAPTER ELEVEN

River Belmont Hotel, El Paso—September 5, 5:37 P.M.

The flight from Tucson is uneventful and familiar, and as Les taxis Betsy to her parking spot, the dusty hills of the Franklin Mountains swing into view out the port window looking west. They look like the low foothills out of every Western I've seen: brown, dry, and saw-toothed.

Marty already has his heart set on the River Belmont Hotel, and though there's no hard-and-fast rule that Jimmy and I have to stay at the same hotel as our pilot and copilot, Marty is intent on getting a promise out of Jimmy that we'll stay there as well.

Jimmy finally relents. "But I'm not getting in the hot tub," he adds.

Marty just chuckles and waves him away.

We leave them to button Betsy down, and make our way to the lower level of the terminal, where we survey choices of rental car companies. Since this is Texas, we opt for Alamo and soon we're pulling out of the parking lot in a silver Dodge Charger.

It's a step up from the usual.

We barely have time to check in and dump our bags in our rooms before Tony calls and says he's waiting in the parking lot. He and Jimmy think we need a working dinner to go over what we have on Larry Wilson before we try tracking him down tomorrow. Plus, Tony says he wants us to experience a real Texas-sized steak, and he seems to know just the place.

We find him a few minutes later leaning against a black unmarked Ford Police Interceptor: a police utility vehicle based on the Ford Explorer. The rig is so new it practically glows in the late afternoon sun.

He grins as we approach, and motions toward the PUV. "Just picked it up this afternoon; what do you think? Dark and mysterious—just like me, right?"

"Nice," I say, giving an approving nod.

"Nice?" Tony replies indignantly. "Steps, this is a *Police Interceptor*. It's a thing of beauty. I've got three hundred sixty-five horses under that hood—that's one horse for every day of the year." He chuckles at himself. "It's got all-wheel drive and suspension *specifically* tuned for pursuit driving." He steps back and spreads his arms wide. "It's friggin' awesome! Even the wheels and tires are built for pursuit." Dropping his arms, he says, "We need to go chase someone."

Now it's Jimmy's turn to chuckle. "I'm game. Let's go chase down some dinner."

"Not exactly what I had in mind," Tony mutters.

Jimmy rides shotgun and I slide into the rear passenger seat, where I find a manila envelope with *Steps* penned across the front in large letters. The envelope is at least a half inch thick, and when I spill its contents into my lap I find a small trove of printed police data. The top eleven pages contain a summary of Larry Wilson's life for the last six years.

The verbiage and layout of the summary leaves no doubt that Diane was the author.

"Diane emailed that an hour ago," Tony says, glancing over his shoulder. "I haven't had time to read through it yet; figured we could do that over steak."

"Murder and steak," I mutter as I leaf through the package. "What wine goes with that, I wonder?"

Rather than go through the whole stack randomly, I decide to start with the summary and see where it takes me. I don't make it past the first paragraph before words start slipping out of my mouth. Words like, "You've got to be kidding me," and "Son of a bitch."

It seems there's more to Larry Wilson than a dead neighbor woman.

In fact, there's a lot more.

Jimmy and Tony are yapping back and forth in the front, completely oblivious to my mutterings, so I put them out of mind for the moment and devour the summary. When I finish, I rest the eleven crisp white pages on my lap and stare out the window as the street signs and cars zip past . . . then I read it again . . . and once more.

I'm still reading it for the third time as we make our way into the steakhouse. When following someone, it's not hard tracking them using your peripheral vision, that way you can read, or text, or dial a number and still make forward progress. The problem comes when paths cross. If you're paying attention you'll pick up on it and won't lose your way. If you're completely absorbed in what you're doing, however, you may end up following the wrong person . . . which is how I end up sliding into a booth next to three perfect strangers.

They're only slightly amused.

Making a hasty apology, I scan the restaurant and spot Jimmy and Tony at a booth next to the front window thirty feet away. They haven't even noticed I'm missing; I don't know whether to be insulted or relieved.

Taking a seat next to Jimmy, I browse the menu and settle on a ten-ounce filet mignon and a baked potato that Tony assures me will be "bigger than a buffalo turd," which must be a Texan phrase because he uses it twice.

Jimmy orders a New York strip steak and Tony opts for the top sirloin. The two of them banter back and forth for a few minutes, but the report is resting on the table in front of me, creating a presence of its own. It's a presence of unspoken whispers, of murder and mayhem; it drags their eyes repeatedly across the tablecloth and past the silverware, demanding attention.

A silent guest with a sinister tale to tell.

When the conversation finally lulls, the table grows small and uncomfortable. Jimmy gives me the nod. "What did Diane dig up?" he asks.

Where do I start?

Clearing my throat, I decide to start with the basics: the address where Chelsey Lane was killed, and Larry Wilson's place just three doors down. Next, I identify Larry's current residence: a dumpy apartment he shares with an ex-con named Fiz.

There are no surprises in any of this. It's all routine—expected.

But I'm just getting started.

When I drop the bombshell, it pulls Jimmy and Tony upright in their seats, like two old Marines in an epic stare-down, only now they're staring at me. "Say that again," Jimmy gasps.

"There's a second dead woman linked to Wilson," I say. "Or at least she's presumed dead, since her body was never found."

"Where?"

"Iowa—six years ago. Little town called Larchwood, just southeast of Sioux Falls. The woman's name was Corinne Winship. She was thirty-one. According to the report, Wilson had taken an interest in her after they met at a block party about a year after he moved to town. She went on one date with him and apparently found out everything she needed to know, because a month later she filed for an anti-harassment order."

"He was stalking her?" Jimmy says.

"Yeah, in a big way," I reply, "showing up at her work, at her home, even at her church on at least one occasion. At first she tried to be polite, asking him to stop, telling him she wasn't interested, that sort of thing, but he wouldn't let it go.

"A week after the harassment order was served things started getting bad. First it was a flat tire on her car, then the word *bitch* was spray-painted on her garage door—and in both cases Corinne remembered seeing Larry Wilson standing on his porch a half block away with a cup of coffee in his hand, smiling at her reaction."

"I hate him already," Tony growls.

I nod my agreement. "Larchwood is too small for its own police department," I continue, "so they contract with the Lyon County Sheriff's Office for their police services—even then, Lyon County is only eleven or twelve thousand people, so the sheriff's office isn't that large. When a deputy showed up to investigate the vandalism and the possible harassment order violation, Wilson just denied everything and there was never any evidence to prove him a liar, though they did start patrolling the area a little more frequently. She even had some of the neighbors checking on her and keeping an eye out."

"But somehow no one saw anything when she went missing," Jimmy says, finishing my thought word for word.

"Yeah, not one of them," I say. "Corrine just didn't show up for work one morning. Her car was still in the driveway and there was no sign of a struggle in the house; she was just gone . . . and Larry was on his front porch with a cup of coffee in his hand."

"And they hauled him in, right?" Tony says, completely indignant. "The girl lived thirty-one years on this planet without a problem and after one date with this joker she's gone? Please tell me they at least hauled him in."

"Oh, they hauled him in," I say, "but he told a convincing tale and even passed a polygraph—though there were questions later raised about how it was administered."

"And he got away with it."

"And he got away with it," I confirm. "Six months later he moved to Texas. Small town like Larchwood, I imagine the rumors spread pretty quickly and he probably didn't have much of a choice in the move. He managed to stay out of trouble almost five years, and then Chelsey Lane came along. Three months after they met she was found at the bottom of her stairs with a fractured skull and some contusions that weren't necessarily consistent with a fall."

"And he beat that one too," Tony fumes. He shakes his head and looks long at Jimmy, then at me. "This foot-chopper guy—what do you call him? IBK? He did us a favor; you know that, don't you?"

"We don't know yet that Larry Wilson is the victim," I remind him.

"Diane's usually pretty intuitive when it comes to connecting the dots," Jimmy insists, and though I tend to agree with his assessment, we'll know when we get to his house tomorrow.

Tapping his index finger next to the report, Jimmy asks, "How did Wilson meet Chelsey? She was a neighbor too, right?"

"She was, but there was no block party this time. He just went over and introduced himself."

"So if he's introducing himself, I'm guessing one of them was new to the neighborhood," Jimmy observes. "Which one?"

"She was," Tony chimes in. "She moved to El Paso from Albuquerque a few months earlier."

Albuquerque?

Why is that familiar?

"We had a storm of media vans descend on the city after her body was found and during the trial that followed," Tony continues. "Her aunt was a councilwoman on the Albuquerque City Council. It didn't go over well when Wilson was acquitted."

"I can imagine," Jimmy says. "Did Judge Ehrlich have anything to do with that?"

"No more than usual."

We spend the next two hours picking at our steaks and digesting the minutiae of the case. When we finally pay the bill and leave a hefty tip, we have a better understanding of the monster that is Larry Wilson.

Albuquerque.

There's something significant about the city, the name, the word—it's been eating at me all through dinner. It's just a little after nine when we return to the River Belmont, and instead of wandering off to my own room, I follow Jimmy to his.

Borrowing his laptop, I begin to sift through the IBK folder while he excuses himself to the balcony and makes a call home. I start with the Ehrlich report and skim the first dozen pages before realizing I can do a word search, which reveals . . . nothing.

Next is the McAllister report, which is short and concise, so I skim through it in a couple minutes, double-checking all the involved parties for any link to Albuquerque, but, again, there's nothing. Maybe it wasn't something I read; maybe it was something someone said.

The sense of relevance is too strong to let go.

I keep searching.

The Travis Duncan homicide report—all 743 pages

of it—is contained in a single, massive Word file. Opening the file with a swift double-click, I go to the word search function and type in *Albuquerque*.

The return is immediate and definitive.

I slump back in my chair and stare at the screen. Before me lies that single tidbit of information that's been playing on the cusp of my memory.

It's the link between El Paso and Tucson.

It's everything and nothing.

It's nothing.

And though both my instinct and my recollection have proven correct, there's no sense of elation as I stare at the collection of words on the screen. They are words borne by murder.

His name was Noah Gray.

His mother, Melissa Gray, was born and raised in Albuquerque, New Mexico. She was a cheerleader in high school, came from a good family, and found the wrong boyfriend. Three years ago she dropped out of high school halfway through her senior year and moved to Tucson to get away from the abusive, drug-addled boyfriend who got her hooked on meth and heroin . . . and ended up with another boyfriend just as bad.

Noah was born premature seven months later.

Despite the drug issues, Melissa somehow managed to get custody . . . and so ended the life of Noah Gray. Travis Duncan was the instrument of that death, but he wasn't the only guilty party. Born with the promise inherent in every new life, Noah found only death among the squalor and needles of a Tucson drug house.

Most seasoned detectives will tell you they don't believe in coincidence. For the most part, I agree, though

I have had occasion to stumble upon more than one unusual coincidence that could have led an investigation astray. Still, when it comes to murder, the maxim is usually correct: there are no coincidences.

Melissa Gray was from Albuquerque.

Chelsey Lane was from Albuquerque.

Both were victims: one directly, one indirectly. Both had friends and family in Albuquerque. Both tragedies would have been covered by the Albuquerque media.

These are not coincidences.

IBK is somehow linked to Albuquerque.

It's that simple.

CHAPTER TWELVE

El Paso—September 6, 9:12 A.M.

Today we hunt for shine: mocha brown with wisps of lime green and the texture of pumice stone spewed from a volcano. Whether the shine belongs to Larry Wilson or some yet-to-be-identified victim will be discerned by the end of the day.

Before we leave the hotel I make two calls. The first is to Tom McAllister to bring him up to speed on Travis Duncan. He's startled by the revelation, I can hear it in his voice, but he takes it well.

He takes it well.

What does that really mean?

He takes it as well as anyone would upon hearing that the severed feet found on his living room floor belonged to a former client. He takes it as well as anyone would upon hearing that a killer has a particular interest in his living room.

I suspect his wife may not take it quite as well. Tom

thanks me, his voice genuine and sincere. He again extends an open invitation to me and Jimmy.

I'd like to see the night sky the way he describes it.

I'd like to see stars so thick it's as if some astral giant poured out honey upon the blanket of night.

I'd like to see the McAllisters again.

We'll just have to wait and see; Fate is a fickle travel agent.

Next I call Diane and the office phone goes to the answering machine after three rings. I could call her on her cell, but it's Saturday morning, and Diane's the type who would drop everything and rush to the office. It's bad enough that Jimmy and I spend our days in a haze of temporal confusion; there's no need to drag Diane down with us.

After the answering machine beeps, I lay out my first request: get hold of the Lyon County Sheriff's Office and find out if Larry Wilson's DNA was collected for the Corinne Winship case.

My second request isn't work-related . . . not really. It's just something that's been bugging me, and if anyone can get answers, it's Diane.

On the way out of the lobby, I ask Jimmy to wait a moment and then veer off and make for the front counter. I hand a sealed and stamped letter to the brunette wearing the REBECCA name tag. "Can you put this with the outgoing mail?" I ask, getting a courteous nod and a big smile in return. When I turn around, I see Jimmy strolling my way.

"Wow, that took a while," he says.

"It took me, like, three seconds, what do you mean?"

"I was talking about the letter," he clarifies. "Isn't that the same one you were writing four days ago?"

"No, I mailed that the day before yesterday. This is a new one."

"Really?" It's less of a question and more of a verbal musing. "You don't think that's a little bit overkill?" he adds. "After all, we're heading home this afternoon."

"Doesn't matter," I say. "Whether I'm home or I've been gone a week, she's going to love getting it. Everyone likes getting mail, especially when time and thought have gone into it. That's what's missing from email and texts and tweets and all the other electronic noise out there."

"So it doesn't matter if she gets it and you're already home?"

"Not at all," I reply. I pat him on the shoulder and make my way past him toward the lobby door. "You know," I say, "if you and Jane were to— Jimmy? Jimmy?" I turn around just in time to see Special Agent Donovan, Super G-Man, blush as he hands a letter to Rebecca and softly asks her to place it in the outgoing mail.

I bite my lower lip trying not to grin.

Jimmy is full of surprises, the greatest of which seem to spring from his ability to admit when he's wrong. There are plenty of things I'd give Jimmy a hard time over, but writing letters home to his family isn't one of them.

When he catches back up at the lobby door, I place my hand on his shoulder and give him an encouraging smile.

"Shut up!" he says, cutting me off before my lips open. And just like that the moment is over and I'm hustling to catch up to him in the parking lot. Breathing the throaty Dodge Charger to life, Jimmy gooses it a bit as he pulls onto the main road. "What's the first address?" he says as he readjusts the rearview mirror.

I check my notes and read off the address on Rancho Tierra Avenue. "You want to get onto Highway 62 eastbound for eight or ten miles. When you see a massive Armed Forces archive and vehicle maintenance facility on the north side of the road, you'll want to turn south."

"Which house is that?"

"The one he was living in when Chelsey Lane had her little accident," I reply. "Is Tony meeting us there?"

"Something came up this morning. He said he'd call when he's free."

We ride in silence and soon find ourselves merging onto Highway 62. "What came up?" I ask.

"With Tony?"

"Yeah."

He shrugs. "Some chatter on the terrorist grapevine. They just got an alert out of EPIC," he continues, referring to the El Paso Intelligence Center that operates out of Fort Bliss. "September eleventh is just days away and this time it looks like Fort Bliss itself might be targeted." He shakes his head. "We picked a helluva time to come to El Paso."

"It's just another alert," I mutter. "Nothing will come of it, just like the one before, and the one before that."

"Maybe. Or maybe that's what they're counting on," Jimmy says. "What if they want us to get so numb from seeing one report after another—one alert after another—that we just start ignoring them altogether? Our guard would be down and we'd be easy pickings."

"That almost sounds paranoid," I say.

"You might be right; just don't forget the old saying."

"Yeah, what saying is that?"

"It's not paranoia if they're really out to get you." He grins at me and punches the accelerator, pushing me back in my seat. I'm starting to think this car is having a deleterious effect on him.

Larry Wilson's former home is a modest ranch, about fourteen hundred square feet, with nice landscaping and surrounded by a decent-looking neighborhood. There's a FOR SALE sign in the front yard when we roll to a stop at the curb. A separate placard underneath the sign reads FORECLOSURE. Larry Wilson made a good living as a truck driver, but he spent too much time in the county jail after waiving his right to a speedy trial. As the months ticked by and his mortgage went unpaid, it was only a matter of time before the bank moved in.

They also repossessed his car.

Almost makes you feel sorry for him . . . almost.

My eyes wander three houses to the east, to a teal two-story with the white shutters: Chelsey Lane's home. Or at least it was before she found herself at the bottom of the stairs with a broken neck.

Slipping off my special glasses, I fold the arms neatly into place and then slide them into their case. When I raise my eyes once more it's all around me, omnipresent and irrefutable: mocha shine as thick as hail from a summer storm. It fills my vision and sets the question to rest: Larry Wilson *is* the El Paso victim. Where the rest of him is we have no way of knowing, but his feet landed in a Styrofoam ice box on the floor of a prospective federal judge.

"Want me to call him?" Jimmy asks, pointing with his phone to the FOR SALE sign at the edge of the yard. Putting my glasses back on, I glance over at the sign and take in its overdone imagery. A mid-forties male real estate agent grins back at me from the two-dimensional surface with the words *Just Call Booth* scrawled across his chest.

"Booth," I muse aloud. "I thought that name went out of favor after Ford's Theater."

Jimmy studies the sign and the name. "I kind of like it," he says. "Why let one guy ruin a perfectly good name for the rest of us?"

"Would you name your kid Adolf?" I counter.

Jimmy starts to answer, but then thinks better of it. Holding the phone up, he says, "Is that a yes or a no?"

I take another look at Booth with his five-dollar salesman grin and Photoshop-perfect complexion, and then shake my head. "No. We got what we wanted here. Let's go see what Fiz the felon has to say."

As we rumble back onto Highway 62, I point Jimmy toward the center of El Paso, to Yancey Street and the apartment of Fiz Moshiri, Wilson's former cellmate. After circling the block twice looking for the address with no luck, I slip my special glasses off and quickly find Larry's shine on the sidewalk, which then leads to a two-story fourplex in the middle of the block. There's no street number on the building, but the mocha shine leaves the sidewalk and makes its way up the stairs to the apartment on the left.

There's more.

"He's been here," I tell Jimmy as the hair rises on the back of my neck. "IBK's been here." My eyes follow the ice-blue shine. "It looks like he walked right up the stairs to the apartment."

"That's bold."

I nod.

There are nine cars filling the tiny parking lot, of which only three look roadworthy, so Jimmy avoids it altogether and parks at the curb. I give him a look as we exit the Charger and he dutifully taps the lock button on the key fob.

We cross the stained parking lot, which is so full of oil drippings that Jimmy suggests setting up a fracking operation. Reaching the stairs, we ascend to the second story and turn left.

The doorbell button is hanging from two wires, so Jimmy knocks loudly and we listen for any sign of movement from inside: there's nothing. Jimmy knocks again, louder this time, but still there's no answer.

It's not really that unusual.

At the first sign of company, seasoned ex-cons like Fiz sneak a look through the blinds, or out a peephole, or at a security monitor. If it's someone they don't recognize, especially if that someone looks like a cop, they just hunker down and wait till they leave.

Jimmy hits the door again.

"FBI, Mr. Moshiri. We're not here for you; we just have some questions about your roommate?" He follows this with three more hard raps.

The door to the adjacent apartment opens a crack and a sliver of face peers out: just an eye, half a nose, and part of a mouth. You can't tell if it's a man or woman and the muffled voice that follows only adds to the confusion. "He's not there," the sliver says.

Jimmy steps toward the door, not too close and not too swiftly. People who open their door just a crack tend to spook easily. "FBI, sir," Jimmy says. "We need to ask your neighbor about his roommate. Do you know where he is?"

"He ran out," the omnigendered voice replies. "It's the bugs. He ran out because of the bugs."

"The bugs?" Jimmy says.

"They're in the walls; they're in the ceiling; they're everywhere. Can't get rid of them, I've tried."

I lean in close to Jimmy and whisper, "Fifty-one-fifty," and he immediately nods his agreement.

Every law enforcement agency has a code to describe subjects with mental disorders. It could just be some harmless and completely sober person who can't find his pants because he's wearing them as a hat, or it could be more serious, like someone hearing voices that tell him to kill.

Sliver appears to be more of the pants-on-the-head variety. Bugs in the walls and under the floorboards is not an unusual claim from those suffering from mental illness—and those could be the creepy-crawly type of bugs, or the electronic-listening type. Both are likely to produce a certain level of paranoia.

In California, the code for a mental is 5150, or fifty-one-fifty. Like everything else from California, the code has spread far and wide and has been generally adopted as slang for anyone who's a bit crazy or reckless. Tattoos containing 5150 are now common in jails and prisons, and some gangs have even added the code to their name: apparently it's scarier when the other gangs think you're a little cray-cray.

Oh, and Van Halen released an album titled *5150* in 1986.

It went platinum.

"What's your name?" Jimmy asks Sliver.

"None of your business; Bob, my name is Bob. Just don't tell anyone, it's classified."

"I promise," Jimmy replies. "Do you know where Fiz went, Bob, or when he'll be back?"

Bob's cyclopean eye darts to the left and then to the right before he answers. "He went to get the canisters. The canisters kill the bugs; kills them dead. He's bringing one for me too. He told me so. He always brings one for me."

"Do you know when he'll be back?" I ask, moving up next to Jimmy.

"Who are you? What do you want?" Bob fires back, as if seeing me for the first time.

Pointing at Jimmy, I say, "I'm with him," and start to back away, but Bob slams the door before I finish my first step.

"Great," Jimmy mutters, staring at the ugly door.

Stepping closer, he knocks several times, but Bob won't answer. Little noises tell us that he's still at the door, probably watching us through the peephole. I contemplate picking imaginary bugs off my arms and shoulders, but decide it's probably not wise to mess with someone's mental health. Jimmy eventually gives up knocking and we start down the stairs.

Bob has a parting gift for us.

"He has to pay tribute to the king," he shouts through

the door. "No one gets the canisters without paying tribute. Fiz has a special arrangement."

"Thank you, Bob," Jimmy shouts back.

Halfway down the stairs I turn to Jimmy and say, "'Thank you'? For what?"

He just shrugs.

Walking around to the passenger side of the Charger, I start to open the door and then pause. Getting Jimmy's attention, I tilt my head up the street. He studies the old man who's shuffling our way. "Isn't Fiz supposed to be in his mid-forties?"

"Forty-seven," I confirm.

"This guy looks closer to seventy. I don't think it's him."

He slides behind the wheel and sticks the key in the ignition . . . but doesn't start the car. Getting into the passenger seat beside him, I close my door and together we watch the scrawny, scruffy old man hobble up the sidewalk. He's stooped over clutching something tightly to his stomach, which only adds to the image of a hunched old man.

Sure enough, he turns into the grimy parking lot and starts up the stairs. Jimmy and I exit the Charger and hurry to catch up, just as Bob's door pops open a full foot and the old man passes a dark cylindrical tube through the opening.

Then, just like that, the door slams shut.

No words are spoken.

The old man—Fiz—turns and makes his way to the apartment on the left.

"Mr. Moshiri," Jimmy calls, taking the stairs a time in his rush to intercept the ex-con before inside his apartment. I follow close behind, taking the stairs one at a time; I'm pacing myself.

The old man turns and gives Jimmy a squinting stare. As I reach the second story it becomes clear that he's not as old as he first appeared, but on the other hand, I don't think I've seen forty-seven so poorly represented. The guy looks like he got curb-stomped by the Grim Reaper.

"Who are you?" Fiz barks.

"FBI," Jimmy replies, flashing his badge. "I'm Special Agent Donovan, and this is Operations Specialist Craig. We're looking for Larry Wilson. You wouldn't know where he is, would you?"

"Haven't seen him for nearly a month," Fiz says, still clutching the package close to his stomach. On closer inspection it appears to be a plastic grocery bag, and he's guarding it carefully. "Larry stayed here a couple days, then just up and disappeared. He was talking about a trucking job in Colorado, so I figured he was back on the road." Glancing at the door, he adds, "All his stuff is still inside if you want to take a look. I didn't touch none of it."

"Thank you," Jimmy says graciously. "We'd appreciate that."

Unlocking the door, Fiz leads the way into the one-bedroom apartment, followed closely by Jimmy. I linger at the door a moment and pull my glasses down the bridge of my nose just far enough so I can see over the top. Glancing about quickly, I see that the ice-blue shine doesn't enter the apartment, but it's obvious from the foot impressions and hand marks that IBK spent a few minutes at the door.

To what end I don't know.

It's puzzling.

Fiz steps into the kitchen and places his package on the counter. Looking at the bag, then at us, then at the bag again, Fiz reaches in and pulls loose one of the dark cylinders he handed to Bob.

"Want one?" he says reluctantly, holding the twenty-ounce beer up for our inspection.

"No, thank you," Jimmy replies. "We're on duty. Besides, I don't normally get my beer on until noon."

"A man of restraint," Fiz says. "I admire that." He raises the can in salute, clearly relieved that he won't have to part with any of his stock. Popping the top, he chugs down half the beer in one long undulating gulp before coming up for air. He wipes his mouth with the back of his hand and belches the words, "It's good," before remembering himself and quickly apologizing.

"Beer?" I say. "That's the bug killer you gave to Bob?"

Fiz looks confused. "Who's Bob?"

"The guy next door," I say, motioning with my thumb.

"That's Stu," he chuckles. He stares at me for a long moment and then shakes his head. "Bob," he mutters. The name comes out like the punch line to a bad joke.

Jimmy clears his throat. "About Larry; you said you still have his stuff . . . ?"

"Yeah, it's over here." He walks to the couch and pulls a dirty white pillowcase out from behind it. Before handing it to Jimmy, he wipes a whole warren of dust bunnies from the side and bottom, then shakes the filth from his hand and watches it fall to the carpet. "He didn't have much; least not here."

Jimmy takes the bag and upends it on the coffee table.

"Sure, go ahead," Fiz grumbles. "Dump it out."

Rather than retrieving his gloves from the kit in the car, Jimmy pokes at the pile with an unsharpened pencil he plucks from the mug on the counter next to the phone. About half the pile is clothing, which still doesn't amount to much: a couple pairs of folded socks, one pair of mostly clean underwear, two T-shirts, and a pair of shorts. There's also a toothbrush, a travel-sized tube of toothpaste, some wart cream, a new addition of *Hustler* magazine, three pennies, a nickel, and a ticket stub from the local movie theater dated August 10.

"I'm taking this," Jimmy says, plucking the toothbrush from the pile while being careful to stay clear of the bristles. "The rest of it is of no use."

"What you need a toothbrush for?" Fiz says.

The ex-con appears to have just three or four of his own teeth, one of which stands like a solitary gray stone at the front of his mouth, so the question is almost funny. I'm tempted to say, *Oral hygiene*, but Jimmy has a way of knowing when my internal filter and my mouth are struggling with one another, and he quickly says, "We need to check for his DNA." He points at the brush head. "If Larry really is missing, we may need his DNA profile to . . ." He hesitates, not sure how Fiz will take the next words. "Well . . . to make sure it's really him."

"DNA . . . yeah," Fiz says. "I heard some stuff about that. It's like science fiction come to life; *Jurassic Park* and all that."

"Just like that," Jimmy says, not even trying to set him straight. "So you and Larry were cellmates, right?"

Fiz nods. "Six months."

"Did he ever say anything about getting threats, either while in jail or after he got out? Nasty phone calls, letters, that sort of thing?"

Fiz shrugs. "That girl's family lit into him pretty good in court; least, that's what he said. He tried to act all depressed and upset about it, but I don't think he really was. You get to know a guy after six months in a cage together."

"I can imagine."

"What makes you think he wasn't upset?" I ask.

Fiz is preoccupied scraping some of the plaque off his front tooth with his thumbnail, and finishes before answering. I get the impression he doesn't think much of me. "Just other stuff he said about the girl," he eventually replies. "He talked about peeping at her through the window at night; even said he had a pair of her panties. Stuff like that."

"Do you remember what day it was that you last saw him?" Jimmy says, and then stresses, "The *exact* date?"

Fiz looks up at the ceiling and scratches under his chin. He turns his head half-cocked to the left, and a few seconds later he switches to the right. "That's a tough question," he finally says. Raising the beer to his lips, he finishes it off and then tries crumpling the can in his fist, but fails. "Pretty sure it was the twelfth or thirteenth." He nods. "Yeah, one of those two."

"That's almost a month ago," I say. "At some point didn't you think it was kind of odd that he disappeared just days after getting out, leaving all his worldly possessions behind, even his toothbrush, which he just might need?"

"Like I said, he was talking about a trucking job. It's none of my business what he does or where he goes. Besides, he paid his rent two months in advance."

"You charged him rent to sleep on the couch?"

"Better than on the street," Fiz says defensively. "A hundred and fifty bucks a month is cheap, even if it is just a couch."

"Yeah," I snort, "but this is HUD housing, isn't it? I met a woman not long ago who was paying two dollars a month for her HUD apartment—and it was a lot nicer than this. How much are you paying, Fiz? Ten bucks? Twenty?"

"Thirty-seven dollars," Fiz grumbles.

"So, you charge Larry a hundred and fifty—which I'm pretty sure is against HUD regulations—and after paying your subsidized rent you clear a hundred and thirteen dollars. That's not a bad racket. I'd think you'd want to keep a closer eye on your meal ticket."

"Screw you, Fed!"

"All right," Jimmy intercedes, trying to calm things down. "We're not here to cause problems for you, Fiz, we're just trying to get some answers."

"I told you everything I know," Fiz blurts.

"So you don't remember any threats, no nasty phone calls or letters. How about any visitors? During the few days that Larry was here, did anyone stop by to see him or ask about him?"

Fiz immediately shakes his head vigorously from left to right, but then he stops abruptly, an odd expression on his face. "There was this guy that stopped by," he says, scrunching up his eyes. "Said he needed to talk to

Larry about a debt. He was dressed in a suit, so I figured it was legit."

"When was that?"

"The day after Larry moved in. I remember because when it happened I thought it was just bad luck that Larry would get out of prison after more than a year, and here's this guy claiming he owes money."

"Did Larry talk to him?" Jimmy presses.

"No, no. He wasn't home. Dude kept asking me when he'd be back and I finally told him to get lost. He didn't say another word, just gave me this weird smile and started whistling this song—kept whistling it even as he walked back to his car."

"Whistling? What was he whistling?"

"I recognized it, I just don't . . ." Fiz screws up his face, obviously thinking hard. "It was the song from one of them James Bond movies, the Paul McCartney song. I remember 'cause I always liked the Beatles."

"'Live and Let Die'?" I say hesitantly.

He brightens. "That's it. That's what he was whistling."

Jimmy gives me an ominous look. "Can you describe this guy?"

Fiz shrugs. "He was about my height."

"Five-foot-seven?" Jimmy guesses.

"Five-foot-eight," Fiz corrects. "I'm not good at guessing weight, but he was about average, maybe a little on the leaner side, and he had short sandy hair."

"How about an age?"

"Maybe thirty."

"Good, good," Jimmy says, scribbling on his note-pad. "Caucasian, Hispanic, African-American?"

"He was a white guy."

"Is there any chance he gave you his name?"

"No, and I wasn't asking."

"How about his car? Do you remember what he was driving?"

"I never saw his car," Fiz says, shaking his head. "I assume he drove one, though. This isn't exactly the kind of neighborhood where guys in suits wait for the bus. He walked out to the street and turned right, that's all I know. I didn't watch where he went."

Jimmy pumps him for additional details, but there's nothing more to give. Fiz looks spent, exhausted. God help him if he ever has to stand up to a real interrogation. He watches me suspiciously as I retrieve a twenty-ounce can from the Quik King bag and pop the top. I hand him the beer and he gives me a big grin. "Guess you're not so bad after all," he says, then downs the bug killer.

We leave Fiz at the door, cradling his beer in both hands, and start down the stairs to the shabby parking lot below. A thought occurs to me and I turn around and wave at the door to the adjacent apartment. "See ya, Bob," I say, giving a big smile. There's a small thump, like someone banging their knee on the door, or maybe jumping back from the peephole in surprise.

I don't know why I do some of the things I do.

Northbound Betsy—September 6, 3:13 P.M.

There's something enchanting about the hum of a jet engine.

Even after so many hours and miles in the sky, it's

impossible not to relish the sound. For within it lies power, and not just the brute force necessary to thrust a seven-ton aluminum tube through the sky. No, there's power to enchant the mind with promise of adventure; there's power to deliver one to new places and new experiences. There's power to change everything one believes, feels, and knows.

It's an impossible allure.

I've tried to hate Betsy, and for good reason: she delivers me to the dead, again and again and again. Like Charon the ferryman, she carries me across the rivers Styx and Acheron to that far dreary coast wherein lies the underworld realm of Hades. Corpses, empty of souls, await me at the end of too many flights. They may as well have coins upon their eyes: a tribute to Charon and payment for passage.

Still another thought torments me.

Perhaps Betsy is just the boat . . . and I am Charon.

To say that I've gotten used to tending the dead would be a lie; to say that I've learned to tolerate it is closer to the truth.

It's been an hour since we lifted into the sky above El Paso, filled with that familiar feeling of going home. Jimmy has been reclined in his chair with his eyes closed almost as long, his breathing comfortable and relaxed. Meanwhile, I'm absorbed in the pages of a wickedly clever book.

"I've got one for you."

The words startle me; even more so because they come from the sleeping man. Glancing over, I note that he hasn't moved; both eyes are closed. I chalk it up to sleep-talking and go back to my book.

"I've got one for you."

My head snaps up, and this time I see one eye open and gazing in my direction. It's a bit creepy at first; something out of a Poe story: *The Tell-Tale Eye*.

"I thought you were asleep," I say.

"In and out," Jimmy replies with both eyes now closed. A second later he raises the seat to its full upright position and he's suddenly wide awake and fully alert. I don't know how he does it. Must be something they teach you at the academy.

"I've got one for you," he says for the third time.

"One what? What have you got?"

"Plane Talk," he says. "I still owe you a subject. You did the torture tree—"

"Manchineel tree," I correct.

"And I didn't have a subject. Now I do."

I push forward in my seat and lean on the armrest.

"Have you ever heard of something called Swahili Time?" he says, overemphasizing the last two words like I've never heard them before. I shake my head no.

"Well, it seems that in a number of East African countries, time is calculated differently than in the rest of the world. For them, the day starts and ends at dawn rather than midnight, so if it's August third, for example, it doesn't become the fourth at midnight like it does here, but at six A.M. And where our one o'clock is an hour after noon or midnight—depending on which side of the day you're on—one o'clock in Swahili Time is seven o'clock our time. Likewise, if you tell someone from, say, Kenya, that you'll meet them at eight, that means two in the afternoon."

"How confusing," I say. "What happens as the year

goes by and dawn arrives at five A.M. instead of six, or at seven-thirty, for that matter? Does their whole time-and-date system shift with it?"

"You're thinking like a nonequatorial person," Jimmy says.

"I *am* a nonequatorial person."

"What I mean is that dawn is pretty much six A.M. *every* morning. We're talking about countries that are on or near the equator, like Kenya, the Congo, Tanzania, parts of Somalia, and even Uganda. We're used to days growing shorter or longer, but that's not the case along the equator."

"It's still confusing," I say.

"Just wait, it gets worse. It seems that this system of time only applies if you're speaking Swahili. If the conversation is in English, even if you're in an East African nation talking to a local, then standard date and time are used. The time reference is dependent upon the language spoken."

Jimmy leans back, puts both hands behind his head, and just smiles. He knows this kind of thing drives me up the wall. It's the illogical nature of it; midnight is such a commonsense breaking point between the days that it's hard to imagine why it wouldn't be embraced by all.

I mull it over until my head starts to hurt, and then mutter, "I'll never complain about daylight savings again," and go back to my book.

Across from me, Jimmy continues to grin.

CHAPTER THIRTEEN

Lynden, Washington—September 7, 1:22 P.M.

It's DD1: Down Day One.

Usually we'd be relaxing and catching up on sleep the first day back from a mission, even a mission not yet complete, but there's a new remodeling sheriff in town, and her name is Jane Donovan.

At five-foot-seven and 125 pounds, Jane is a Zumba-infused, auburn-topped whirlwind of energy. Her movements are those of a dancer, balanced and smooth, and she has a simple, natural beauty that doesn't come from a bottle.

Jimmy met Jane while stationed at Fort Carson, Colorado. His roommate was dating Jane's best friend, so they were constantly crossing paths. At first they pretended that they couldn't stand each other, but there was an instant and powerful attraction between them. The magnetism was so unexpected and irrational that they wasted months feigning disdain for one another before the walls between them finally came crashing down in a spectacular manner.

That was the beginning.

Jane's most endearing trait is an abundance of kindness. It's a rare quality in our hurry-up world. Like most who are abundantly kind, she seems to have an extra gas tank full of patience tucked away someplace for emergencies.

Therein lies our problem: Jimmy and I sucked the first tank of patience dry several months ago, and have been working on number two ever since.

We've put the kitchen remodel off as long as we can—longer than a calm, intelligent woman like Jane would normally allow. We've worn out excuses, retreaded them, and worn them out again. Jimmy bought us an extra three weeks when he insisted on the acquisition and prepositioning of all the necessary materials.

"I don't want to be on a roll and then have to stop and run all the way into Bellingham because we need a piece of molding or some nails or a faucet," he said.

It was brilliant!

But that was three weeks ago.

His garage is now packed full of crated kitchen cabinets, custom-cut granite countertops, high-end appliances, tile, grout, paint, even a gorgeous—and expensive—farmhouse kitchen sink of fourteen-gauge hammered copper.

Yep, we're out of excuses.

And Jane made sure we know it.

Betsy was still taxiing to Hangar 7 last night when Jimmy's phone rang. It was Jane, of course. I knew it was Jane because her ringtone is the theme to *Jaws*—personally, I'd be offended, but she thinks it's funny. I didn't hear the conversation, but Jimmy's head was nodding up and down and every once in a while he'd throw in an "Okay" or a "Sure thing, hon."

When he hung up the phone he wouldn't even look at me. "Boss says we start at eight A.M.," he said. And that was it. Our stall tactics had ultimately failed. We were doing this remodel whether we liked it or not.

I showed up at 8:07 A.M. on purpose and Jane gave me a disapproving look, glancing at the clock on the wall, then back to me, then back to the clock. My more audacious plan was to show up at eight-thirty, but I'm just not that brave.

Five hours into the project we're actually making good progress. All the old appliances have been removed and shuffled out to the garage. They're a little dated and dented, but still work fine, so a local charity is picking them up on Monday.

We also have all the upper cabinets off the walls and are just finishing removal of the countertops when Jimmy's phone rings. It's Diane. The theme from *The Pink Panther* echoes through the dismantled kitchen. Jimmy has separate ringtones for everyone.

Jimmy has separate ringtones for everyone!

It suddenly hits me: I've never heard *my* ringtone—I'm never there when I call.

I listen to the lopsided conversation, trying to discern meaning from Jimmy's one- and two-word replies. "Sure," he finishes. "We need to run to the hardware store anyway." He looks at me and shrugs. "We'll swing by the office and you can fill us in. Okay. See you then."

He hangs up the phone and slides it into his back pocket.

"She knows it's Sunday, right?" As the words leave my mouth I wonder why I even bother. "She should be out paragliding, or knitting mittens for squirrels, or something—anything—just not at work."

"I reminded her."

"So what's so important?"

"Tony called; sounds like they just got another hit on the RFI. Someone dumped a body in Baton Rouge, minus its feet."

"Baton Rouge? That's a long way from El Paso."

"It's got to be a thousand miles," Jimmy agrees. "That's a little far for someone to drive to dispose of a body. Who knows, maybe it's just coincidence. Still, we don't know what we're dealing with yet. Tony's emailing the report to Diane as we speak."

I glance around at the destruction zone that used to be Jimmy's kitchen. "So, either we stay here and try to put this all back together, or we go to the office. How's that going to play with Jane?"

"We . . . have to go to the hardware store?" Jimmy offers.

"Right." I nod. "The hardware store. What do we need at the hardware store?"

"Uhh . . ." Jimmy glances around the kitchen quickly. "Tape," he says. "We need masking tape."

"That's what you're going to tell Jane?"

"Masking tape," Jimmy repeats, "and we had to stop by the office for an important break in the case." His face suddenly brightens. "It could take all day. Besides, Jane is running errands with Pete. She could be gone for hours. I'll just leave her a note."

Jimmy scribbles something barely legible on a white napkin and tapes it to the side of one of the lower cabinets.

"It's going to be hard explaining our need for masking tape when you used some to hang up the note," I point out.

Jimmy pauses, but then just waves away my concern.

As we're heading out the front door I dial Jimmy's number. Seconds later, Judy Garland begins to belt out "Somewhere Over the Rainbow" from the confines of Jimmy's back pocket. Startled, he fumbles for the phone and rips it from his pocket, quickly stabbing buttons in a desperate attempt to silence the naïve Toto-toting farm girl. It's too late.

"Really?" I say, incredulous.

"Oops," Jimmy replies with a shrug.

"No—really?" I insist.

"Ah, come on, Steps. I picked that ringtone five years ago when I was first assigned to the STU. I didn't even know you. I picked it because of the . . . you know"—he leans in close and whispers—"shine," even though there's no one around.

"You just got a new phone last year," I challenge.

"So? I kept the ringtone. I'm a creature of habit."

I'm shaking my head and my finger at the same time. "No way," I say. "We—*no, I*—I'm going to find a new ringtone. And you're going to like it . . . whether you like it or not."

"Fine." Jimmy laughs.

I make my way around the curvy walkway connecting the porch to the driveway and I'm halfway to the street before I realize Jimmy's not with me. He's at his car door holding both hands up in the air and looking at me like *I'm* the idiot.

"Uh-uh, we're taking mine," I say, pointing at the dark green 2003 Mini Cooper snuggling the curb. Jimmy looks at my Mini, then back at his banged-up silver 2004 Kia Spectra, then back at the Mini. Without a word, he closes the driver's door—a little too hard, because the whole car shakes and rattles—and scoots across the parking lot.

With a chirpy *boop boop* I unlock the doors with the key fob and slide behind the wheel. Jimmy is still settling into the passenger seat when Gus—that's my Mini—clears his throat and begins to growl. I wait for my partner to buckle up, then slide the little British beast into first and start up the street.

Jimmy's playing with all the buttons on the dash, as usual, and keeps looking in the backseat for some reason. "Whenever I open the door on this thing," he finally says, "why do I get this odd feeling that ten clowns are going to suddenly jump out?"

"It's not a Volkswagen."

"Yeah, well, it's about the same size."

"Hardly," I shoot back. "Besides, it's better than that death trap you call transportation, all dented up and falling apart."

"In fairness, I'm not responsible for any of those dents. They were there when I bought the car; and I bought it cheap, probably because of the dents, but that hasn't affected its functionality. It's great on gas and has been mostly reliable. You see someone driving a car like that and it says something."

"Yeah, it does." Cupping both hands around my mouth, I yell, "Get out of the way!"

Jimmy laughs. "No. It says you're smart with your money. You don't strap yourself with a payment on something that goes down in value every year you own it. You avoid debt. You're thrifty."

"You mean cheap."

"No, there's a difference between cheap and thrifty. The cheap person bases his decision on cost alone and tends to be stingy; the thrifty person manages his money carefully. He doesn't just look at cost; he looks at value, he looks at return on investment."

"I paid cash for Gus," I remind him. "And I got him for less than Blue Book."

"See, that's thrifty."

"So how come my thrifty purchase is ten times better than your thrifty purchase?"

"You'll want to take a right at the corner," Jimmy says, pointing at the stop sign where I've turned right a thousand times before. He goes back to fiddling with the buttons and knobs on the dash.

Jimmy's a master at changing the subject.

As we make our way past the cipher lock and into the heart of Hangar 7, we immediately notice a wall of seven-foot-high screens clustered around Betsy's nose, completely obscuring the front of the plane. Marty is settled in a chair at the far end of the screens reading a book, but looks up and waves when he sees us enter.

Jimmy stops dead in his tracks at the sight. "Marty, what are you up to now?"

I hear Les chuckle from behind the barrier, and Marty says, "*This* is a restricted area, need-to-know and all that stuff. You will be summoned at the appropriate time, which will likely be—" He tilts his head to the backside of the screens and says, "How much longer you think?"

I can hear Les consulting with a third person before saying, "Maybe an hour."

"An hour," Marty says, tilting his head back toward us . . . like we couldn't hear Les. "Maybe," he adds.

Jimmy just shakes his head and makes for the office. Marty shoots me a half-pie grin and I can't help returning it.

Diane lingers on the second-story balcony outside her office as we approach. She has a cup of coffee in one hand and a fistful of chocolate-covered macadamia nuts in the other, no doubt from the less-than-secret stash she keeps in her bottom drawer.

"What are they up to?" Jimmy demands, thumbing toward Betsy.

"Not a clue," Diane replies. "They've been at it for hours."

As Jimmy's right foot lands on the bottom step and he starts to take the stairs two at a time, Diane points with a commanding index finger, saying "Conference room," in a curt voice. She points at the room of glass with her macadamia-nut hand.

"What?" I say indignantly, touching my hand to my heart, "no *Good afternoon* for your favorite crime fighters?"

Her smirk twists into a half smile, which lasts but a second before crumbling away. "Conference room," she repeats in a dry monotone.

The report from Baton Rouge PD is waiting for us. It's thorough, and occupies more than a hundred pages, not including the dozens of photos now laid out on the long mahogany table.

The click of Diane's heels is right behind us and she bustles into the conference room a moment later, saying, "You want to read it yourself, or do you want the abridged version?"

"Abridged," Jimmy and I say in unison.

"I figured as much."

She'd never admit it, but Diane loves narrating cases for us. It helps her connect to the action. Her martyr complex, however, demands that she groan, huff, or roll her eyes at least seven times a day—and she never misses a quota.

"So, let's start down here," she says as she moves to the far end of the table and taps the first photo with the tip of her finger. "The body was discovered in Bluebonnet Swamp on September third—"

"That's the day after the feet showed up at Ehrlich's," I interrupt.

"Coroner had no estimate for time of death because the guy was refrigerated. If this *is* the rest of Larry Wilson, your suspect drove a thousand miles across Texas and dumped him in Louisiana for a reason."

"Maybe he was hoping the gators would dispose of the evidence," I offer.

"I don't think so."

"Why?"

"Because of this." She picks up an eight-by-ten from the center of the table and lays it in front of us. The photo reveals the body after it was removed from the swamp and laid out on a black body bag at the edge of the water. Most of the enlarged image is focused on a letter-sized piece of paper pinned to the victim's shirt. One word occupies the blank page, scrawled out in four large letters.

"*Soon*," Jimmy reads aloud.

"What's that supposed to mean?"

Jimmy glances at me. "It means this was just the warm-up act. He's got something else in mind." Turning to Diane, he asks, "How far outside of Baton Rouge is the swamp?"

"It's inside the city."

"They have a swamp in the city?"

"It's the South, brother," I say with a drawl. "They have swamps all over the place."

"The fact that the swamp is surrounded by city is the very reason the body was found so quickly," Diane continues. "Even with that lucky break, we still come away almost empty-handed . . . but this is where it gets interesting." She points to the next nine pictures one at a time. "Someone went to a great deal of trouble to hide the victim's identity, cutting off the fingertips, pulling all the teeth, and peeling the skin from his face. Nice, huh?" She takes a big gulp of coffee. "That leaves DNA as our only option for identification."

Jimmy picks up the pictures one at a time for a closer look. "I'm assuming they already collected a sample and sent it for analysis. Any idea where we stand with that?"

"Limbo," Diane replies.

"Let me guess," I say. "The crime lab in Louisiana is as backed up as everyone else in the country, and we'll have to wait until the statute of limitations for murder runs out before we see any results."

"Close," Diane replies. "The state police crime lab is in Baton Rouge, and they're actually really good—from what I've heard. The problem is they never received any DNA samples."

Jimmy starts to say something and Diane holds up her hand. "Let me finish the story. I already called Baton Rouge PD and they're on top of it. The two detectives working the case each thought the other had sent in the samples; simple mistake. They assured me the lab will have them by Monday—tomorrow. After that it could be weeks or even months before we see any results. The lab tech I talked to was sympathetic to our situation, but they're just swamped. . . ." A spontaneous smile erupts on her face and she adds, "No pun intended."

"Good one," I say with a nod and a half-cocked smile.

Apparently, Jimmy doesn't think it's funny.

"What else?" he says without looking up.

"The coroner's report indicates that the clean, precise cuts on the fingertips and face suggest they were removed with a very sharp object, possibly even a scalpel. Our guy was dead when they were removed, fortunately for him. As to the cause of death, it was exsanguination after his feet were lopped off. I'm guessing he bled out pretty quickly."

She scans the collection of photos and then grabs an eight-by-ten from the end of the table and hands it to Jimmy. I crowd over his shoulder to get a look.

"Notice the bones," Diane says, pointing.

Jimmy squints and looks closer. "Clean cuts," he says, "just like the feet in Tucson and El Paso."

"Exactly," Diane replies. "No saw marks; no hack marks like you'd get from a cleaver. Coroner says the cut was likely made by some type of industrial-grade machinery, something with a lot of force that moves swiftly."

Jimmy studies the photo, and then works his way through the others on the table. Soon he's leaning on one hand and rubbing his chin with the other, the way he does when he's tossing something around in his head. "We need to go to Baton Rouge," he finally says, glancing up at the clock on the wall. "If we leave first thing in the morn—"

"No way," I say firmly, crossing my arms in front of me.

Jimmy looks at me. "It's just Baton Rouge," he says. "We'll fly down in the morning and be back by evening."

"Until something else comes up," I say, "and that will lead to something else, and on and on. I'm all for chasing the leads, Jimmy, but we *just . . . got . . . back*." I shrug and throw my hands up. "We can't keep doing this. It seems like we spend more time in the air than we do on the ground."

"It's just this case—" Jimmy begins, but I cut him off.

"It's always just this case or that case. I have plans with Heather tomorrow. We're finally taking that day trip up to Mount St. Helens—you know, the one we planned to take in July? I've already canceled on her twice and it's not going to happen again."

Diane watches me silently as I speak, her eyes shifting to Jimmy, then back to me.

"I need some kind of life outside the STU," I insist. "*You* need a life outside the STU. If Jane gets tired of you and throws you out you'll end up sleeping on my couch, and that's just one too many bachelors under the same roof." I turn my gaze on Diane. "That goes for you too."

"I have no intention of sleeping on your couch," she replies quickly.

"You know exactly what I'm talking about," I say, ignoring her coy little smile. "As it is, you spend way too much time here in the office—and we don't get overtime."

Diane and Jimmy stand like two Ionic columns, glancing back and forth at each other like guilty coconspirators. At last, Jimmy clears his throat. "How about Tuesday—the day after tomorrow?"

I don't answer.

"That's two days of down time—well, not counting this meeting," he says. "That's almost like a regular weekend for normal people."

"After all, it's not like the dead guy is going anywhere," Diane says, trying to sound reassuring. She's looking at Jimmy, but her eyes keep darting my way. "One more day won't hurt."

"Good point," Jimmy says, a little too enthusiastically. He watches me a moment and then adds, "How about it, Steps? Fly out Tuesday, back the same night?"

I let him hang a minute, then nod and say, "Fine. Tuesday."

The room is silent for a long moment. "Well," Diane

finally says, "speaking of the body . . ." And just like that we're neck-deep in swamps and ice boxes and severed limbs once more. We forget about the clock on the wall and immerse ourselves in the case. Ruminations stack upon theories, and speculations become the silent wallflowers of this analytical dance.

Jimmy has his ideas, Diane has hers, and I'm playing with a few of my own, but we're united in our belief that these are vigilante killings. There's a purpose behind IBK's actions and how he picks his victims. If we figure that out, we'll be one step closer to finding him.

We're completely absorbed in this debate—three heads pushing and pulling at one another like a three-way tug-of-war—when a swift *tap-tap-tap* on the window next to the open conference room door pulls us back to the present.

"Hmm-hm-hm," Marty says, clearing his throat. "The captain requests your presence outside the cockpit." He gives a slight bow.

"This ought to be good," Jimmy says, tossing an eight-by-ten back onto the table.

We follow Marty back to the wall of screens, where he joins Les and some guy with a shaved head and two full sleeves of tattoos on his arms. After some banter back and forth, Les holds up his hands for silence.

"So," he begins, "Marty and I . . . but mostly Marty . . . decided it was time to take our relationship with Betsy to the next level."

"Oh, dear," Diane says.

"There is a time-honored tradition among aviators, a rich and colorful history perhaps best illustrated during World War II. To that end, we conscripted Darrin here"—he gestures toward Mr. Tattoo—"to create a piece of nose art for Betsy worthy of her mission." He nods at Marty and Darrin, and the three of them move the cloth partitions aside, revealing a stunning two-foot-by-two-foot airbrushed image on the nose of the plane, just forward of the cockpit windows.

Marty stands posed, like a magician gesturing toward his assistant after a particularly brilliant piece of magic. He's greeted by silence.

"Is that . . . Betsy Ross?" Jimmy asks after an uncomfortable pause.

"Of course it is," Marty says impatiently. "See, she's sewing the flag."

I don't know what textbooks Marty and Les had when they were going to school, but my mental image of Betsy Ross is that of a gray-haired grandma huddled over her needle and thread—not a young vixen busting out of her colonial blouse.

But who am I to complain?

"That's impressive work," I say to Darrin, and I really mean it. The picture is rich with detail, and the name *Betsy* arching over the top finishes the piece in handsome fashion.

"Very nice," Jimmy admits, giving a little clap. "Technically speaking, you just defaced government property, but I'm good with that."

There's nothing but silence from Diane.

She's still studying the nose art, her eyes walking over it in random patterns as she takes in every detail. She huffs, crosses her arms with her coffee cup perched on her finger, and then huffs again. Finally she speaks: "Could you make her breasts any bigger?" She takes another sip of coffee, shakes her head, and then turns and starts back to the conference room.

She's halfway across the hangar when Marty blurts, "Uh-huh! Yes, we could!" throwing as much indignation into the words as he can muster.

Diane keeps walking.

An hour later, Jimmy and I are driving back to Lynden when we remember the masking tape. Swinging Gus through a U-turn, I steer the Mini Cooper toward the nearest hardware store.

We ride in silence for a few minutes, each absorbed in our own thoughts. There's something I want to run by Jimmy—partly for his opinion, but mostly because I don't want to blindside him. He's my partner. I've been searching for the right time and the right words, but they haven't come, so I just blurt it out.

"About my trip with Heather tomorrow—"

"I really am sorry about that," Jimmy says, cutting me off. "You're right about this ridiculous schedule we keep. Sometimes it's just hard—"

I stop him midsentence. "We're good. I'm not mad."

"Then . . . what about your trip?"

I look at him in the passenger seat and realize that I'm biting my lower lip. Taking a deep breath, I exhale all at once, blowing out seven words with the wind: "I'm going to tell Heather about shine."

There it is; fast and simple.

His reaction isn't what I expected.

"That's your call, Steps. You know how much I like Heather, so I wouldn't even think of trying to talk you out of it." He suddenly grins. "What that girl sees in you I'll never know, but you have a good thing going. She's a rare person. Someone you can talk to when it gets rough." He looks out the passenger window as the buildings flicker by. "It's a big secret to carry around." His voice is subdued, introspective. "It gets old sometimes . . . don't you think?"

"Yeah." It's a simple affirmation, but Jimmy knows my heart and soul are in that single word. Then I drop the next bombshell: "I'm going to marry Heather."

"You asked her?" Jimmy practically howls, reaching over the stick shift and punching my arm repeatedly. His eyes are giant crystal marbles, and if he smiles any wider his cheekbones are going to have to contort.

"No," I say with a chuckle, rubbing my arm, "it's too soon. But she's the one—sometimes I think she knows me better than I know myself."

Jimmy's hand is on my shoulder and he's still grinning. "Well, if you need my blessing, you have it."

"Gee, thanks, Dad."

He slaps the back of my head. Then his eyes suddenly go big again. "Wait till Jane hears! And Diane! Holy crap, she's going to come unglued."

"Don't you dare tell either of them, not yet."

"My lips are sealed," Jimmy says solemnly. He runs an imaginary zipper across his mouth, which he then locks, placing the invisible key in his pocket. With some friends, such a promise would be broken within the hour. But Jimmy and I live in a world of secrets. This one's easy by comparison.

CHAPTER FOURTEEN

Belen, New Mexico—September 8, 1:30 A.M.

Concealing darkness lies upon the street.

The homes thereon are cast into shadow, with only the angles showing real depth. All else falls away into the grays and blacks of night, the intangible veil that separates the seen from the unseen, muting color, and erasing detail and contrast. Quiet reigns, for it is well beyond the witching hour.

Yet not all is still.

Some shadows move.

The opening between the door and the frame gapes wide, providing ample room for the thin blade as it scrapes across the brass strike plate. Finding the latch, the tip of the knife digs in, wiggling and prying until the bolt loosens its grip and slides free. The door groans as it swings open an inch and abruptly stops. Quiet follows . . . waiting . . . listening. At length, the soft hiss of

compressed gases issues from the top hinge, and is repeated at the middle and bottom hinges.

The air suddenly tastes of oil.

As the door begins to move again, the hinges are
silent. The opening widens into blackness, pressed there
by a dark hand. When it comes to a stop, the house lies
still. For a full minute this unmoving silence continues,
as if the very night is listening for disturbances within.

And then the shadow steps forward.

For a moment, the doorway is filled with his silhou-
ette, and then he fades into the interior, shadow into
shadow. Without a sound, he crosses the hardwood floor,
as if gliding rather than walking . . . as if he has no feet
at all.

When Carlos sits up in bed at 1:33 A.M., he's not exactly
sure why he's awake. He listens for a car or a barking
dog, but there is nothing . . . and something at the back
of his mind is coiled, defensive. Fear rushes through him
and he doesn't know why. A dream, he reassures himself. It's only a bad dream.

Yet still he sits, hardly daring to breathe for the noise
it makes.

Several stints in prison had allowed Carlos to hone
his lizard brain, that collection of primal instincts cen-
tered in the brain stem that signal danger, even when
none is immediately apparent. Right now his lizard
brain is on fire, and it shows in the sweat beading on
the back of his neck and in his palms.

"Is someone there?"

He feels foolish as soon as the words are out of his

mouth. If anyone had actually answered, he would have run screaming from the house, but he really didn't expect anyone to answer. It was a reflex comment, something to break the quiet and reclaim night. Hearing his own voice should have calmed him, reassured him, but it doesn't.

The same overwhelming sense of apprehension continues to claw at him, and he forces himself to breathe slowly, deeply. It's just the night, he tells himself, just the utter quiet of the house, nothing more. But there's a patch of darkness in the open doorway to the walk-in closet that he didn't notice before; a darkness deeper than normal—deeper than it should be.

His eyes are now fixed on the spot, almost to the point of tunnel vision, and then he sees it: the barest reflection of light on metal . . . and the metal is moving.

Terror-stricken, Carlos recoils against his headboard in an instant, pulling his legs tight to his body and kicking over a lamp in the process. He opens his mouth to scream, but the shadow is upon him. Electricity snaps and sparks, strobing the room with miniature lightning bolts. Convulsing, the scream dies in Carlos's throat before ever reaching his lips.

In the darkness that follows, the shadow goes about his business.

CHAPTER FIFTEEN

Big Perch—September 8, 8:38 A.M.

It was a rough night.

Jimmy and I worked on the kitchen until just after ten, and only stopped when our muscles went on an involuntary sabbatical. When you can no longer grip a screwdriver, you know you've pushed your body past its tolerance level.

When I arrived home just before eleven, Jens was playing Xbox with Darius and Spider, his friends and frequent companions from Western Washington University. Fall classes don't start for two weeks, so they're making the most of what vacation they have left. They needed a fourth for their game and tried shaming me into it, but I was too far gone. My fingers wouldn't have worked, even if I wanted to.

Before going to bed, I took three ibuprofens and washed them down with orange juice. They helped . . . and then they didn't.

By three A.M. even my eyebrows were aching.

* * *

Jens, Darius, and Spider are still playing when I stumble out of my bedroom a little after eight-thirty, walking like a ninety-five-year-old man on a hunger strike.

"Morning," Jens says without looking up.

I mutter, "Morning," in response, though it sounds more like some otherworldly moan. Jens doesn't seem to notice. The coffee table is covered with empty soda cans; they stand like a small forest around five open, half-eaten bags of chips. I grab a single chip from one of the bags as I stumble by, and Spider decides to give me grief about my hair, which is standing up like a rooster's comb.

Like he has room to talk.

He's got the whole nerdy-punk thing going on, with his thick-framed glasses and odd clothes, not to mention his constantly changing hair color and the plugs in his ears. I try not to judge too harshly. He's as odd as they come, but has a heart the size of Texas. Plus, he's a brilliant programmer.

Ignoring the dig about my hair, I pour a glass of milk from the jug in the fridge, and then glance at the calendar. Opening the slider, I walk out onto the large west-facing deck and I lean on the rail, taking small sips from the glass. My eyes walk across the great expanses of Puget Sound and the many islands peeking up from her depths. It's a beautiful view and one of the things I like most about Big Perch, my home.

I bought the 2,400-square-foot two-story home in a foreclosure auction three years ago and never changed the name, probably because it's such a fitting title. Nestled in the cliffs above Chuckanut Bay, Big Perch sometimes seems like an eagle's aerie, a great perch in the sky with the whole world laid out below.

The auction included a second, smaller house called Little Perch. At just over thirteen hundred square feet, it was built by the former owner, Ellis Stockwell, as an in-law apartment for his mother-in-law . . . well, his ex-mother-in-law. The home is in the same style as its big brother, just one level instead of two.

It's now Ellis's home.

I like the old guy; it didn't seem right kicking him out of the two homes he took so much care designing and building. In exchange for maintenance around the property, I let Ellis stay in Little Perch rent-free.

He's become family.

Still, he's an odd fellow. He frequently speaks in a British accent, and lately has been learning to speak like a Texan, with particular emphasis on the drawl. He also has a peculiar penchant for nude sunbathing and for hats—all types of hats. He has an impressive collection of historic headgear on display inside Little Perch, but he also has scores of hats that he wears on a daily basis, sometimes wearing three or four different hats throughout the day, depending on his mood.

Jens and I have made a game of this obsession. We try guessing which hat or hats he'll wear on any given day. Those guesses get marked down in two-letter codes on the calendar hanging from the side of the refrigerator.

Today I selected the fedora, code FD, and Jens selected the beret, code BR.

Ellis is an early riser, so I was hoping to catch a

glimpse of him before getting a shower and driving to Heather's apartment in Seattle, but it doesn't look like that's going to happen. Waiting another minute, I gulp down the last of the milk and head inside.

"No sign of Ellis," I say as I close the slider behind me.

"I'll send you a photo when I see him," Jens says.

"Just make sure it's a photo from today."

"Right, like I'm going to cheat," little brother says. "Now, if there was some money riding on it . . ." He looks up from the game just long enough to shoot me a grin.

Johnston Ridge Observatory—September 8, 2:12 P.M.

On a pristine Sunday morning on May 18, 1980, at 8:32 A.M., Mount St. Helens, which had been rumbling for months, erupted in a spectacular way that stunned the nation. It began when an earthquake triggered a massive avalanche of rock and debris that swept down the north face and slammed into Spirit Lake. In moments, the lake was buried under hundreds of feet of debris, and the flow swept on, up and over a 1,300-foot ridge, before rushing down the Toutle River, destroying everything in its path.

The slide was just the beginning.

It triggered the release of pressurized gases within the volcano, and the resulting explosion destroyed 150 square miles of forest. Most of the trees were blasted to the ground by the force of the explosion; a few remained standing, scorched and dead—silent tombstones in the bleak landscape that came after.

Night descended at noon as the volcano spewed gray ash thousands of feet into the air, blocking out the sun. Superheated pumice issued from the crater, scorching the landscape further as the mountain continued its grand geological performance for the next nine hours.

The tally of destruction was immense: fifty-seven dead, 250 homes destroyed, forty-seven bridges gone, 185 miles of highway erased, and fifteen miles of railway buried.

David A. Johnston, a thirty-year-old volcanologist, was stationed at Coldwater Ridge to observe the mountain. He was too close. When the volcano erupted, and just moments before the swift-moving pyroclastic flow swept over his position, he radioed his famous last words: "Vancouver! Vancouver! This is it!" Pieces of his trailer were discovered by a road crew thirteen years later, but his body was never recovered.

Johnston Ridge Observatory was opened in 1997. It sits on a ridge just five miles from the hollowed-out crater that is the north face of Mount St. Helens. Named for Johnston, it was built near the observation post the young volcanologist was manning when he died.

"It's magnificent," Heather says. She's standing at the railing just outside the observatory complex, and looking across the valley to the fractured mountain beyond. It rises before us, large and imposing.

There are a number of interesting places to stop on the drive up to the Johnston Ridge Observatory, but Heather and I have both been here before, so we skipped the sideshows and headed straight for the main event. The unopened picnic basket beckoning to us from the backseat may have had something to do with that decision. If time permits, we'll stop at the visitor center on the way down. There's also a Forest Learning Center that has some nice displays.

With our bellies full, the sun nestled in the sky, and the raw power of the mountain on display before us, I wrap my arms around Heather and rest my chin on her shoulder a moment. Now would be the perfect time to tell her about the odd ability I have that may or may not freak her out.

Not knowing what to expect is the worst part.

I know Heather well, but everyone reacts differently to shocking news. It can range from calm and accepting, all the way to Lizzie Borden on ax-sharpening day. I tried telling her on the long drive south from Seattle, and again as we made the fifty-two-mile drive from Interstate 5 to the mountain.

The first time, the soft melancholy of Aerosmith's "Dream On" began to bleed from the radio just as I opened my mouth to speak. It's one of her favorite songs—along with about two hundred others—and she immediately closed her eyes and soaked up the music. Then she began to sing in soft, barely audible tones.

It was remarkable, sexy, and powerfully moving.

On my second attempt, she had her head laid back with her eyes open behind her sunglasses, and a small smile on her face. The wind teased the top of her hair through the open sunroof, and the sun caressed her face.

She caught me looking over and slipped her hand into mine. In that instant, any thought of shine or the Special Tracking Unit slipped quietly into oblivion. If I could have frozen time I would still be there, lost in the moment.

Two attempts, two failures.

If this was baseball, I'd be feeling the pressure.

Moving to the rail beside Heather, I turn away from the mountain and lean my back against the concrete and steel barrier, partly so I can look at her, but mostly so I can see if anyone wanders our way. About two dozen people are milling about, though none are within earshot.

Resolving to be bold, I brace up, take a deep breath, and open my mouth.

"There's something—"

"Didn't you say—" Heather begins in the same instant.

Our words fall over each other and we laugh.

"You first," she says.

"No, please, after you."

Her mouth curls up on the right side, and her dimples jump. The look is alluring, but it's her eyes that always captivate me—the wells to her soul; like staring into the bottomless depths of the ocean and wondering at its mysteries.

"I was just going to ask about your dad," she says. "Didn't you say he was near the mountain when it erupted?"

"Well . . . *near* is a relative term, I suppose. He was at Holden Village, a Lutheran retreat in the mountains above Lake Chelan. Everyone heard the boom as it raced over the camp that morning, but to him it sounded like two separate explosions."

"Two?"

"I think it had something to do with the way the

mountain exploded, the lateral blast, and then all the atmospherics. Witnesses much closer to the mountain remember how utterly quiet everything was, like they were watching a silent film. Scientists called it the quiet zone. That was the case even in Portland, which is fifty miles to the south."

"It's so hard to imagine," Heather says, shaking her head.

"We sometimes forget what nature is capable of." I take Heather's hand. "That Sunday was Dad's last day at Holden after a weeklong stay, and the only way in or out was on a lake ferry that operated out of Chelan. It was a two-hour boat ride back to civilization, and about halfway there the captain came over the PA system and said there was a wall of ash headed their way."

"And they went into it?"

"They didn't have a choice, not if they wanted to get home. Even if they went back to Holden Village, there was no escaping the ash, so they pushed on. By early afternoon, the sun looked like a shrouded moon and there was an inch of ash on the ground. Some areas were hit much harder. In Eastern Washington, they were pushing ash off the road with snowplows. It was crazy."

We start strolling slowly along the railing, hand in hand, heading west toward the outdoor amphitheater. Our conversation wanders from Mount St. Helens to Pompeii, and Heather admits that she's always been a bit haunted by the body-shaped castings they've pulled out of the ash at Pompeii.

My mind begins to drift back to shine, and what I need to tell Heather. I feel my stomach begin to ball up again as I summon the will to do what must be done . . . and then my phone rings.

"It's Diane," I say, glancing at the screen. "Do you mind?"

"No, go ahead. I'm going to take a look through the giant binoculars." She gives me a peck on the cheek, and heads for the observation binoculars permanently mounted on an upright support at the railing.

"Hey, Diane," I say.

"Sorry to interrupt," she replies, sounding sincere. "Thought you might want a quick update on those two things you asked for when you were in Tucson."

"You find something?" I say, as I begin frantically searching my shirt and pants for a pen and some paper. I come up empty on both counts.

"I found something," Diane echoes.

"On which one?"

"Both."

"Okay, let's start with the DNA."

"I tracked down a detective at the Lyon County Sheriff's Office: Miller or Mulder or Middler or something like that. He was the lead detective on the Corinne Winship disappearance. The short answer to your question is no, they don't have Larry Wilson's DNA. They couldn't get a warrant because they didn't have enough for probable cause. On a couple occasions they followed him around for the better part of a day, hoping he'd discard a cigarette butt or soda can, but never had any luck. Then Wilson moved and the case died."

"That's . . . disappointing."

"Yep," Diane agrees. "But if it's any consolation, I had better luck with your second request."

"How so?"

"I found Penny's cousin." She lets the words sink in before finishing. "He wants to help."

Penny Dellal has been haunting me since we visited her dingy trailer in the run-down trailer park. Travis Duncan may not have been much of a nephew, but he was the only family she had. With him gone, I don't give Penny a year before Tucson PD is responding to a bad smell at her trailer.

If the alcohol and drugs don't kill her, she'll find another way.

"Tell me everything."

"His name is Mike Keiding from Provo, Utah. He remembers Penny and her sister, Paula, from when they were kids, but says none of the family has heard from them in decades—they didn't even know Travis existed."

"Wow, how do you just lose family?" I say.

"Good question," Diane replies. "I didn't press, but Mike said that their mother died when Penny was thirteen and Paula was eighteen. After that, their stepdad moved them to Arizona looking for work and the family slowly lost touch."

"Does he know that Paula died of an overdose years ago and that Penny's not doing much better?"

"I told him. He seems like a good man; has a large family of his own. I gave him Penny's address and he said he'd be on the road within a few hours. He's going to bring her to Utah and get her into a program."

"Nice work, Diane," I say, feeling for the moment as if I had just sloughed a battleship anchor off my shoulders.

"I just tickled the databases," she replies. "This was all you."

On the drive back to Seattle, I make six unscheduled detours.

I've been slowly checking off addresses on a list that Dex gave me in late June after I discovered Leonardo's shine on the ground at Bellis Fair Mall in Bellingham. The crime analyst was able to identify the make, model, and even year range of Leonardo's car from surveillance video, and printed out a list of all the black 2000 through 2002 Saturn L-series sedans registered in Washington State.

It didn't take long to go through all the addresses in and around Bellingham, and I've been picking off those throughout the rest of the state as I'm able. Day trips like this are perfect opportunities to reduce the list even further. Each address takes but a moment. If Leonardo lives there, his shine will be overwhelmingly evident upon the ground, on the front porch, and along a wide swath to and from the mailbox; whether the car is there or not is irrelevant.

Heather is everlastingly gracious.

I tell her that I'm hunting for a black Saturn with a large white decal running across the top of the windshield—something easy to spot during a quick drive-by. There is no decal, of course; Leonardo's Saturn is as plain as any other. The lie may be harmless, but the aftertaste is foul nonetheless.

I should have told her when I had the chance.

I should tell her now—at this moment. If it means I'm

a monster in her eyes, so be it. Better to know than to wonder. I tell myself these things, and I pluck at the edge of my courage, and the sun warms my face, and I try . . . I try.

But it's been such a lovely day. . . .

Night is upon the city when I steer Gus into the underground garage below Heather's lofty apartment complex. Arm in arm, we amble our way to the elevator, the picnic basket dangling from the crook of my right elbow.

Tucking ourselves into her cozy apartment, we empty the contents of the basket onto the table and make a snack of what remains—with a few additions from the pantry. Heather's apartment is on the ninth floor of Empire Tower, with sweeping views to the north and the west, so when we step out onto the balcony all of Seattle is laid out below us, and beyond it the mysterious depths of Puget Sound. We stand together, wrapped in a single blanket, my arms around her.

It's a perfect night.

Minutes fall away one by one, meaningless in this moment and place. Our eyes find each other from time to time, as do our lips, but it's the distant noise of the city, the milling about of people, and the afterglow of our day together that occupies my mind.

"There's something you need to know," I say.

The words surprise me, but now they're out and there's nothing to do but press on. "That's . . . not exactly what I mean. What I should have said is there's something I *want* you to know. It's about what I do; about—how I do it."

She's looking up at me, studying my face as the shimmer of the city highlights her cheeks, casting them in a golden hue. With slow deliberation, she presses her index finger to my lips and says, "You're not ready. It's okay, wait till you're ready. I'm not going anywhere."

Heather has a special ability of her own: she reads body language better than any seasoned detective or FBI interrogator I've ever met. I should have guessed she'd see how conflicted I am.

Pushing up on her tiptoes, she kisses me softly on the mouth and then lays her head against my chest. "Stay the night."

The back of my right index finger brushes lightly under her chin and then up her cheek, etching her features into my memory.

"Stay," she says again.

"I can't." The words are filled with disappointment, regret. "We're flying out at seven A.M." It's an excuse and she knows it, so I give her the real reason, the one she's already guessed. "I'd never hear the end of it from Jens."

She smiles and nods. "Your brother is a moral man," she says after a moment. "That's a good thing, and rare these days. I don't know how he does it," she adds with a shake of her head. "Especially with the way women are drawn to him."

"Yeah, I have the same problem," I whisper in her ear.

The night deepens, the din from the streets below quiets, and two hours pass by with no regard for hearts or young lovers. I finally pull myself from Heather—away from the warmth and comfort and peace that come with forgetting the dead.

We really are flying out at seven A.M.; I wasn't kidding about that. By noon we'll be in Baton Rouge, and neck-deep in murder once more; another morgue, another pathologist, another body . . . and a swamp. The only thing I can be certain of is that it's going to be a long day, made longer by Heather's absence.

The drive home is lonely; the only sounds are the undertones of road noise, the soft growl from under Gus's hood, and the melancholy tunes of a Seattle soft-rock radio station issuing from the speakers.

It must be the night for sappy love songs.

Yeah—not helping.

CHAPTER SIXTEEN

Baton Rouge—September 9, 1:01 P.M.

"Who's Aaron Kosminski?" Jimmy asks.

"He was supposedly a hairdresser or barber who lived in Whitechapel when the murders took place," I say. "He ended up in an insane asylum in 1891."

"And he's Jack the Ripper?"

"That's what the article says." Jimmy's driving, so I hold up the day-old paper and tap the column on the right side, which includes a black-and-white image of Kosminski. "They claim they solved the case using hundred-and-twenty-five-year-old mitochondrial DNA."

"Please!" Jimmy exclaims. "First off, that's a bit hard to believe. Second, where's the chain of custody for the evidence? Where'd they get the DNA sample?"

"It came off a shawl that belonged—well, that supposedly belonged to one of the murdered prostitutes." I scan through the article looking for the name. "Catherine Eddowes. The legend behind the shawl was that it was found with her body and taken by a police officer named Amos Simpson."

"He just took it?"

"I guess he wanted a souvenir." Jimmy looks at me and I shrug. "They did things different back then; I don't know. Anyway, the shawl was passed down through the Simpson family and eventually auctioned off in 2007."

Jimmy shakes his head, and I read him several paragraphs from the article. He's still not buying it, but after a few minutes of reflection, he asks, "Do you think you could use shine to track down Jack the Ripper?"

"Maybe," I reply, "depending on what kind of access we had to evidence and how much of the old streets and buildings are still intact. Even if I could, how would we explain it?"

Jimmy grins. "We'd figure something out. We're pretty good at coming up with a believable story." He palm-punches the top of the steering wheel twice in his enthusiasm and says, "I think we need a vacation to England."

"Okay, Sherlock, but if we're going to the UK, I want to take a side trip to Scotland. My dad still has family there."

"I'm serious," Jimmy insists.

"I know you are," I say with a chuckle, and then point at the road sign ahead. "You're going to miss your turn."

"Crap."

Somehow he manages to steer the beige Ford Escape across two lanes of heavy traffic and down the Route 408 off-ramp, where the road spills into a cluster of buildings housing the mayor's office, Homeland Security, and other elements of local and federal government.

The East Baton Rouge Parish Coroner's Office is at the back, and, ironically, right next to the airport runways.

"Looks like we took the long way around," I say as a corporate jet reaches speed and lifts off with a roar. Jimmy swings the SUV into an empty spot near the front door and we make our way to the lobby window.

It's the usual routine: hold up credentials, apologize for not having an appointment, then wait for the medical examiner or coroner, who may or may not be in the middle of an autopsy. In this case, it doesn't take long.

"I'm Dr. Kenny," a young pathologist says. "I understand you have an interest in our mystery man?"

"We do," Jimmy replies. "We're investigating a pair of severed feet that were left on a judge's living room floor. Your colleague, Dr. Cosentino, advised El Paso PD that you might have a possible match—a body found in a swamp last week without any feet?"

Dr. Kenny nods. "That would be Trey Cosentino. He's not a doctor, just an overeager intern. I hope he didn't jump the gun on this and have you fellas fly all the way out here for nothing."

"You don't think this is our guy?"

"Well, the body we recovered was clearly mutilated to obscure identification. It's possible the feet had tattoos or some other features that might be recognizable, so the suspect just cut them off. They probably got dumped in a separate swamp a few miles away."

"Possible," Jimmy agrees. "But we put out an RFI for bodies missing feet and yours is only the second call we've taken. The first call was from Tucson with another pair of feet, so now there are *two* bodies out there with missing feet. I like our odds."

Dr. Kenny smiles and shows a row of perfect white teeth. "It's a thousand miles from here to El Paso," he says, feathering his words with skepticism. "I've never heard of someone going to such lengths to dispose of a body."

Jimmy shrugs. "Steps and I have seen some strange things, haven't we, Steps?"

"Strange," I say with an affirming nod.

"So if we could just take a look at the body, we'll be out of here in no time."

"Your call," the doctor says indifferently. He hands Jimmy a clipboard. "Just need you to sign in." He grabs two visitor badges from behind the counter and hands them to us, noting the number on each badge and writing it on the sign-in sheet next to our names. "This way," he says, holding open the blue door with the RESTRICTED sign.

The morgue is like every other I've visited in the last five years. It's sterile, yet has an undertone of putrefaction that not even bleach can eliminate. A twelve-body cooler dominates the back wall, three rows high and four wide. Dr. Kenny opens the middle door, second from the right, and pulls out the loaded stainless steel tray.

"I warn you," the doctor says, snapping on a pair of gloves, "it's not pretty."

"It never is," I mutter.

Unzipping the body bag, he pulls it wide, revealing the skeletal features of a face with no teeth. You can see the clean incisions where the suspect trimmed along the hairline, down the back of each cheek, and then under the chin to remove the flesh from the skull, leaving the corpse faceless and grotesque.

But there's something else: mocha shine.

The mutilated corpse is Larry Wilson, beyond a doubt. I catch Jimmy looking my way and give him a furtive nod. Officially, we'll wait for DNA results to make the announcement, but we have the answer we were looking for.

The doctor unzips the bag further and lifts each arm free, displaying the raw fingertips where the skin has been removed. Then we're on to the ankles and the missing feet, where we find clean, precision cuts, just as the report indicated. The position of the two cuts is the same, suggesting the feet were taken at the same time with the same instrument, not separately, as one would suppose. The cut is just above the ankle, and includes about an inch each of the tibia and fibula, the two lower leg bones.

Dr. Kenny restates what we already know from the police report, and Jimmy pays close attention as the forensic pathologist walks him through the postmortem mutilations, before returning to the cause of death: exsanguination after the feet were chopped off.

"So he bled out?" Jimmy says.

"Fairly quickly, I'd say."

"And the body was found in a swamp?"

"Correct," Dr. Kenny replies. "Bluebonnet Swamp; it's five or six miles from here. Pleasant as far as swamps go."

"I thought *pleasant swamp* was an oxymoron."

The doctor chuckles. "This is Louisiana. We have different grades of swamp here. And when it comes to fishing a body from one of them, you could do a lot worse than Bluebonnet."

Jimmy unfolds his map of Baton Rouge and lays it out on the table adjacent to the husked remains of Larry Wilson. "Can you show me where, precisely, the body was found?"

I'm only partially listening as they examine the map, and when they start discussing the body again I tune out completely, imagining myself back at Mount St. Helens with Heather.

Oddly, my daydream includes Jimmy this time. His voice floats at the surface of my imagination, drowning Heather out. It seems he's examining the missing tip of the mountain and commenting on the way the blast cut the rock, peeling parts away and leaving jagged edges that make it unrecognizable as its former self.

Mountains become bodies, and bodies become mountains.

Imagination helps pass the time.

"One last thing," Jimmy says as their discussion winds down. "Can I get a DNA sample for our lab?"

"We just sent a sample to the state lab," Dr. Kenny replies. "I can send you a copy of the report when we get it, if you'd like?"

"I'm guessing that could be a while?"

The doctor wobbles his head from side to side, a pensive, noncommittal look on his face. "The lab's not as backed up as it used to be, but, yeah, it's probably going to be a few weeks."

"We have a dedicated DNA tech at the FBI lab in West Virginia who can have an answer for us in a day, not counting shipping time. And she already has a sample to compare it to . . . so what do you say?"

Dr. Kenny doesn't hesitate. "As long as I can get a

copy of the report," he replies. "The sooner I can free up the cooler, the better."

Jimmy writes down the address and point-of-contact info and hands it to the doctor. When he grabs it, Jimmy doesn't let go right away, but points to the second line of the address. "Make sure you include 'Attention: Janet Burlingame.' If you forget, the sample will end up with the general caseload samples and we'll be waiting weeks or months."

"Janet Burlingame," the doctor says. "No problem. I'll prepare a blood card and get it in the mail this afternoon. Anything else?"

"No," Jimmy replies. "That's more than enough. We really appreciate the help."

Dr. Kenny walks us back to the lobby, making small talk on the way. We hand over our badges, sign out on the clipboard, and say our good-byes.

As I'm shaking the doctor's hand, he says, "You two have fun at the swamp." I don't know if it's the *hardy-har-har* way he says it, or the huge Louisiana grin on his face, but I get the feeling he knows something we don't.

Jimmy tells me I'm distrustful of strangers.

He may be right.

As we're leaving the ME's office, I hold the door open for Jimmy and he says, "Thank you," instinctively, as is his habit. I continue to hold the door for the two people behind him, who are close enough that the courteous thing to do is to wait for them. The first, an older female, brushes past me without a word and barely a glance, though she does toss me a snarl—which I presume was meant to be a smile of some sort.

The second person in line is even worse.

He's in his late teens or early twenties and is dressed like a slob, despite having a county ID card clipped to his shirt—which you would think might imply some level of dress code. He's wearing earbuds that dangle down to the cell phone in his hand, and he strolls out the door without a glance or a word—like I'm his personal doorman. I watch him as he shuffles down the sidewalk, the crotch of his pants hanging halfway to his knees because he can't seem to get his pants up all the way.

Either that or there's a sudden shortage of belts.

"You're welcome," I call after them, but neither of them hear me, nor care. They're far too important to pause and say thank you.

My parents raised Jens and me to always say please and thank you, to hold doors open for women, even though that's now frowned upon, and to show common courtesy in everything we do. I'm starting to think that we're archaic anomalies in this new and watered-down world.

Jimmy has a knowing smile on his face as we make our way to the car. We've had this conversation before, so he has an idea of what's coming. "Maybe she thought you were being a chauvinist," he says with a shrug.

"It was common courtesy," I reply dryly. "And what about Pig Pen? Was I being a chauvinist to him as well?"

"It would seem so."

"I must be an equal-opportunity discriminator."

"That would be my guess."

I often wonder what happened to the polite society that was once America. So much has changed, and so quickly, even from my parents' time.

Part of the problem, I suppose, is that America became a transient society, and not just because we move around a lot and have lost our sense of home and community. Everything we do seems temporary. Even our pictures, once collected in albums and passed around at family gatherings, are now just bits and bytes in our cell phones or laptops. And when a cell phone gets lost or stolen, or a laptop dies, we suddenly realize that we don't have copies of those photos.

They're gone forever.

There's nothing to pass on to the next generation.

Our jobs are transient; our truths are transient; our friendships and marriages—transient. Everything is disposable.

I wonder if that's why the Travis Duncans of the world find themselves dabbling in drugs, alcohol, or other self-destructive behavior. I see the same rot and despair everywhere; I see it reflected in our growing prison population. Society seems to have lost its rudder, and we keep looking to find it in all the wrong places.

Sliding into the driver's seat and starting the car, Jimmy cranks up the air-conditioning and patiently listens as I rant on for another minute. He doesn't interrupt; he's had his fair share of time on the soapbox, and he's pretty good about taking turns.

When my words start to falter and eventually cease, he gives me a broad smile and says, "Better?"

"Ehh," I say with a shrug.

* * *

We make our way south on I-110, which soon branches and turns into I-10 eastbound. Whether in Arizona, New Mexico, Texas, or Louisiana, we can't seem to get away from this road.

"Exit 162A," I say, pointing at the approaching overhead sign.

"Bluebonnet Boulevard," Jimmy says, reading the words slowly and methodically. "I guess they name their roads after swamps around these parts."

Angling to the right after exiting, we make our way past the Mall of Louisiana, and then continue another two miles to the Bluebonnet Branch Regional Library on our right. The parking lot is only partially full, which is probably normal for an early Tuesday afternoon.

As Jimmy starts to pull into the first available space near the sidewalk, I sit bolt upright in my seat, my spine suddenly as straight as a construction level. My eyes dance along the sidewalk, the parking lot, the grass between the sidewalk and the building.

It's everywhere.

Throwing my seat belt off, I bail from the SUV before it's entirely stopped.

By the time Jimmy catches up to me, I've already walked the sidewalk and found my way to the grassy strip bordering the swamp at the back of the library. I'm down on one knee next to an ancient tree with the girth of a Russian babushka.

My eyes and concentration are on the ground, but I hear Jimmy approaching; I sense him when he stops ten feet behind me. He leaves me alone, lets me finish, allows me to digest the scene and make sense of it.

Eventually I rise and brush the debris from my pants.

"He was here . . . and not just when he dumped the body. He's been here a lot, but it's all old—years old. The only recent track is the one leading out into the swamp."

"How old are the others?"

"Hard to say for certain: maybe eight to ten years." I run my hand down the hard bark of the old tree, the rough texture playing at my fingertips. "I don't think he was alone," I say.

Jimmy's head snaps around hard, so I step back and point to the ground at my feet. "This was their spot. Sometimes they'd be facing each other; sometimes they'd be leaning up against the tree, or sitting at its base. It was someone close to him—someone he was intimate with."

"Have you seen the other shine before?"

I shake my head.

"You're sure?"

"Pretty sure; I think I'd remember this one. It's an amazingly bold bronze with what looks like—I don't know—maybe acid green swirled through it."

Jimmy walks a slow circle around the tree, perhaps imagining he sees what I see. "So, what brought them here again and again—the library?"

"Or the swamp," I offer. "From this position, it seems like they're looking out into it. The library is well off to the left, almost behind them."

"Was she with him on the most recent trip, when he dumped the body?"

"She?"

Jimmy shrugs. "Most serial killers are male; you know that. And most males are heterosexual, so I'm just making the most logical assumption."

"The odds are in your favor," I say, "but I wouldn't rule anything out."

"You haven't answered my question."

"No. *She*—or *he*—wasn't here when IBK dumped the body."

"Begs a few questions, doesn't it?"

"Yeah, like why would you dump a corpse at a spot that held fond memories—unless the relationship didn't end well? And what about the note pinned to the guy's chest? That message was directed at someone, and we better figure out who and why in a hurry. You don't write *soon* on a piece of paper and leave it on a mutilated corpse unless you mean it. This is some type of warning."

Jimmy has a different idea; I can see it in his face.

Turning to face the swamp, he takes it in. I leave him be; it's his turn to puzzle things out. When he finally turns back, his eyes are on the tree. The words are soft, but come with all the force and awe of thunder on the mountains.

"It's a tribute."

My spontaneous leap from the SUV when we pulled into the library parking lot broke our normal protocol, which tends to be more about analysis and less about arms waving in the air and running about wildly. In such circumstances, Jimmy can usually be counted on to get me back on course.

I'm better now.

"Right here," I say, pointing. "It looks like he backed the car in."

"How do you know that?"

"He got out on the left side, not the right. If he pulled straight in the driver's door would be to the right. Plus, it looks like he had the body in the trunk, or in the back of a van or truck, because he walks . . . here." I stop on the sidewalk directly in front of the parking spot. "This is where Larry's shine first shows up. He laid him on the ground a moment, then he must have picked him up and carried him, because all I see is ice-blue shine heading that direction." I point into the swamp.

"What do you think Larry weighed?"

I shrug. "A buck ninety-five, maybe two hundred—minus the feet."

"So we're talking someone with a decent amount of physical strength; probably someone younger and fairly active."

"But old enough to think this through," I offer. "The crime scenes aren't sloppy; he's organized, and disciplined enough to be conscientious about evidence."

"Agreed," Jimmy says, nodding. "Do you have a good trail?"

"Yep," I reply. "It leads straight into the snake-infested swamp." I slap my neck, then my arm. "Pterodactyls," I warn.

"Pterodac—*what?*"

"Pterodactyls," I repeat, slapping at the other side of my neck.

"You mean mosquitoes?"

"That's what they *want* you to believe," I say slowly.

"Take a look at the size of these things next time one comes near."

Jimmy just shakes his head. "You want to lead the way?"

"Not really."

Jimmy's patience tends to come in small measures when we're in the field, so he gives me a brief moment, and when I make no movement toward the swamp, he issues a less-than-subtle *Ah-hmm*. And since it's pointless to argue with him, I exhale deeply and begin putting one foot in front of the other.

From the parking lot, we follow the ice-blue trail 180 feet to the west, through what appears to be a greenbelt, which isn't so bad. Then we reach the swamp proper. I linger for a moment, eyes casting about for any small movements that might indicate the presence of snakes or alligators or rodents of unusual size attempting to devour wayward princesses, but the swamp doesn't give up her secrets.

IBK likely dumped the body at night.

Perhaps that's why he only ventures some forty feet into it before stuffing Larry Wilson's mutilated corpse under the low-hanging boughs of swamp vegetation.

His steps lead to the dump site, then there are three or four additional steps stacked one over another as he sloughs the body off his shoulder and lets it fall where it may. Repositioning the body against the branches and vegetation, IBK leaves Larry upright but slouched over.

In the darkness that comes to swamps in the night, he may have considered the body well concealed, but Larry Wilson's bright red shirt was clearly visible by day, a beacon among the greens and browns.

If concealment was his intent, IBK had failed.

Perhaps during the long drive from El Paso he forgot Larry was wearing the shirt. In the shadows of a Louisiana night, all color would have reverted to a thousand shades of black and gray, and the shirt wouldn't be a factor. That changed with the coming of the bright southern sun. By midmorning the red smear in the swamp was a beacon that easily caught the eye of a library worker on a smoke break.

Bad luck for IBK.

Our trip to Louisiana generates more questions than answers.

We suspected the body from Bluebonnet Swamp was that of Larry Wilson when we left Bellingham this morning, so finding his shine, and that of IBK, isn't a big surprise, and there's no real gain from an investigative standpoint.

On the other hand, the discovery of the bronze shine opened up a new box of puzzle pieces and dumped it right on top of the old puzzle. As we drive away from the library, a host of questions jump out at me, but three in particular are picking at the scab in the corner of my brain.

First: Why drive a thousand miles to dump a body?

Second: Why choose a swamp behind a library?

And third: Why Baton Rouge?

The bronze shine is the key to all of this, I'm certain. But I'm starting to feel the pressure of time, and with bodies and feet starting to stack up, I wonder if the answer will come too late. The note on Larry Wilson's chest is ever-present in my mind: *soon,* it read—but what's soon? The next body, the next victim, the final retribution? The single word provides no answer, only more questions, and the promise: soon.

We check into the Baton Rouge Reserve, a four-star hotel just off I-10 and near the geographical heart of the city. After dumping my bag in the nondescript room, I wander two rooms down and give three loud raps on the door. Jimmy's phone is to his ear when he opens the door and waves me in: he's talking to the lab. More specifically, he's talking to Janet Burlingame, our dedicated DNA tech at the FBI lab, and one of the most competent in her profession.

"No, that's perfect." Jimmy listens for a long moment. "You're awesome. I'll talk to you in a day or two. If for some reason you can't reach me, just call Diane." There's another pause. "No, we're flying back in the morning. Not much else we can do at the moment; besides, I have a kitchen to finish."

Some lighthearted banter ensues and then Jimmy disconnects the call and sets his phone on the small table in the corner, where he takes a seat. "Janet got a match on the feet from Tucson," he says casually as I park myself on the edge of his bed. "Travis Duncan is now—officially—our second victim." He looks up suddenly. "Not that we didn't know that," he adds almost apologetically. "It's just *now* we have the DNA to prove it."

I just nod. "Without evidence there's no evidence."

Jimmy shoots me a grin. It's a joke we came up with years ago. Some would call it a coping mechanism to deal with the fact that, because of shine, we often know who our suspect is, but have no evidence to prove it. Anyone in law enforcement will tell you that knowing something and being able to prove it in court are like lovers trapped on opposite sides of the Grand Canyon.

It can be maddening.

"She also got a good male profile off the toothbrush from Fiz's apartment, so once Dr. Kenny gets that sample to her we can list Larry Wilson as victim number one."

"She should get the blood card tomorrow," I say. "Provided it went out right away and was shipped overnight delivery."

"Right, but between the vagaries of overnight delivery and the complexities of in-house mail service at Quantico, Janet may get the package first thing in the morning, or right as she's turning off the lights tomorrow night. Which means we might not get an answer till— what's today?"

"Monday—no, Tuesday."

"So we should have confirmation by Thursday at the latest," Jimmy says. "That'll take care of the victims, but we're still no closer to identifying IBK. In fact, we've got nothing. He's smart, I'll give him that."

"They all screw up eventually," I say. "He will too. Maybe he already has."

"I don't know," Jimmy replies skeptically. "I hope you're right."

Me too, I think. And then my own words slap me in

the face: *Maybe he already has!* In that instant, a parade of wretched thoughts marches through my brain, led by the all-eclipsing question: How many bodies are still out there?

CHAPTER SEVENTEEN

Baton Rouge Metropolitan Airport—September 10,
7:32 A.M.

After taking our seats on Betsy, and while Marty completes the preflight check, I lean toward Jimmy and hold out my closed hand.

"What?" He looks at me suspiciously—like I've ever given him cause to be suspicious. Well . . . maybe some cause, but it was all in good fun.

"Open your hand," I say.

"Why?"

"Just do it."

He hesitates, but eventually opens his hand, palm up. Uncurling my fingers, I place a small, folded white piece of paper in his outstretched palm and then lean back in my seat.

Jimmy stares at it. "What's this?"

"Read it."

"If it's your resignation, I think they prefer it on letterhead."

"Just read it."

Jimmy peels apart the three folds of the note and reads the message aloud. "*George Thorogood. 'Bad to the Bone.'*" He looks at me. "What's this?"

"My new ringtone."

"George Thorogood?" he says with a raised eyebrow. "'Bad to the Bone'?"

I just nod.

"Bad to the Bone." Uh-huh.

I feel empowered just saying it.

Jimmy doesn't argue, he just finds the ringtone and downloads it to his phone. Then he plays it—loudly. I can see him getting into the music. After an encore, he bobbles his head and says, "That's actually a pretty good ringtone."

We sit and listen a moment as he plays the ringtone a third time, and then a fourth. Finally, he puts the phone back in his pocket, leans back in the seat with his hands behind his head, and says, "I'm gonna miss Judy Garland, though."

An hour later we've exhausted all attempts at Plane Talk, and we still have a long stretch of sky before Bellingham. Jimmy's going over some updates on a case we worked last month in North Dakota, so I pull out my folder and do some reading and writing of my own. Thirty seconds into it, without looking up, Jimmy says, "Another letter?"

The question is casual, almost rhetorical, as if he'd be just as satisfied without an answer as with. His voice carries the soft edge of a distracted mind. Even as I look up to answer he doesn't break eye contact with the words before him.

My retrieval of the folder, the shuffling of papers, perhaps even my breathing as I read and correct and take notes, are all things he perceives at the periphery of his senses. He doesn't have to look to know that I have pen in hand and paper before me.

Jimmy's senses are well honed . . . all six of them.

"It's my will."

The words take a moment to pierce the wall of concentration, but then I see his eyelashes flutter, his mouth twist, and then he looks up. "Your will?"

"First Pat McCourt, then Sad Face," I say with a shrug. "Seeing a shotgun rise up on you not just once, but twice, is enough to get you thinking about putting your affairs in order . . . just in case."

"That was just bad luck on both counts."

"Yeah, bad luck." I nod emphatically. "If I remember correctly, that's the type of luck that gets you killed."

"Not exactly what I meant," Jimmy replies. I can tell he's got his psychology hat on, because he's suddenly studying my face and body language, looking for tells, and trying to read my feelings. He does it in a casual way that most wouldn't catch, but he and I have been through too much together.

We know each other's moves.

"I know what you meant," I reply, letting a little gratitude coat the words. "It's good. Don't worry about me. This isn't some fatalistic meltdown; I'm just trying to be practical. We don't exactly have desk jobs, after all."

"No, we don't," he replies. Then he grins and says,

"So what are you leaving me? Anything that might encourage me to push you out of the plane?"

I clear my throat and in a very stoic, lawyerly voice say, "I'm leaving you one of my most prized possessions; I'm leaving you Gus. That way you won't have to ride around in that shameful, beat-up heap you call a car."

"Nice," Jimmy says, grinning.

"Keep in mind that I don't plan on dying anytime soon, so it may be an antique by the time you get it."

"All the better," Jimmy says. "I'm assuming you're leaving the house to Jens . . . or maybe Heather?"

"I'm kind of stuck on that one. If—*when*—I marry Heather, the house would obviously go to her, but I want Jens to always have a home as well, so that's where I'm hung up."

"Why not leave Little Perch to Jens and Big Perch to Heather?"

"No, that doesn't work. I'm leaving Little Perch to Ellis."

"Really?"

"He's like family," I reply with a shrug.

"Yeah, but Jens *is* family."

"I know." I strum my fingers on the folder. "Who would have thought it would be so complicated to die? Maybe I should leave Little Perch to Jens with the stipulation that Ellis gets to stay there as long as he likes. They get along like brothers anyway, so I doubt there'd be any problems."

"So Jens would inherit Little Perch *and* Ellis."

I chuckle. "Yeah, I guess so."

"What about your books?"

"Heather loves them, always has. I think she should have them."

"How many do you have now?"

"Five hundred and eighty-seven; all first editions, and most are first printings."

"Good grief. I'm surprised you have shelving for them all."

"I don't. At some point I need—"

Jimmy's phone rattles, interrupting my words.

I follow the one-sided conversation, deducing what I can from the distilled words. It's Tony, of that I'm certain. The other words tell me that something has happened, something significant. Jimmy's questions contain the basic ingredients of a criminal investigation; words like "where," "when," and "how."

When he hangs up, he simply says, "Death and dismemberment," and then makes his way to the cockpit. "Slight change of plans, guys," he says as he pokes his head between Les and Marty. "We need to divert to El Paso."

"El Paso. Roger that," Les says, always the professional. He immediately starts recalculating their flight path and adjusting the flight plan.

"Sweeet," Marty says from the copilot's seat. "River Belmont, here we come." He does an exaggerated arm pump, and then raises both hands to an imaginary cheering crowd. I'm starting to think we need to drug-test him more frequently.

"We're not staying," Jimmy advises. "We're picking up Detective Alvarado, renting a smaller plane, and flying to Fort Stockton. One of you will have to fly. You can flip a coin or something."

"I'll do it," Les says dryly and without hesitation. "Marty has some kind of love affair going on with that hotel. I wouldn't want to come between them."

Marty just grins like an idiot.

Back in his seat, Jimmy breaks out a map of Texas and quickly finds Fort Stockton, which is some 230 miles east of El Paso as the crow flies. "Pecos County Sheriff's Office called Tony about ten minutes ago," he explains. "It seems they found a freshly dumped body that's missing its feet. Some trucker spotted it lying in a ditch just a couple miles west of town."

"How fresh?"

"They think it was dumped last night or early this morning. Not a lot of details, but it sounds like the same MO. Pecos County has the scene secured and is leaving the body in place until we get there. Tony called ahead to the airport to see about renting a Cessna or some other prop job, so we should be able to take off again as soon as we reach El Paso."

"What if there's no plane available?"

Jimmy shrugs. "I guess we'll have a four-hour drive ahead of us. Fort Stockton's airport is too small for Betsy. The good news," he continues, "is that the body is likely Travis Duncan."

"How do you figure?"

"His are the only feet we haven't matched up."

"What if it's a new victim?"

Jimmy's skeptical. "In both cases, IBK left the feet first; why break pattern?"

"Because this one's smarter than others we've hunted."

Jimmy persists in his belief that the body will be that

of Travis Duncan, and I play devil's advocate and we discuss the ramifications of the new body dump. We're not the only ones on the plane in disagreement. Marty's voice pours from the cockpit as he extolls the virtues of the River Belmont to Les, who isn't having any of it.

"I wish I could get so excited about a hotel," I mutter.

"It's Marty," Jimmy says with a grin. "Remember when we gave him that box of old maps and travel guides for Christmas last year? It was supposed to be a joke, but he was ecstatic and spent a week studying them. Said he was looking for any aquariums he hadn't heard of."

"Yeah, for his aquarium quest," I say.

Jimmy and I shake our heads and say, "The aquarium quest," in unison.

CHAPTER EIGHTEEN

The gloom suits him.

It's the middle ground between light and dark; the haze between worlds, where shadows are plentiful and deep. He embraces this middle ground, perhaps because he knows that darkness exists where there is no light, just as evil exists where there is no good. Light a candle, darkness withdraws. It's the same with good and evil.

"I'm a shadow," he whispers to the gloom, knowing that he is no longer what he was, and not yet what he'll become.

The words bring an ironic smile to his lips, but he has no time to dwell on it. Setting the wooden high-backed chair on the concrete floor, he lowers himself onto the seat and leans into the back. The wood is cool against his skin, seeping through his thin T-shirt. It's a pleasing sensation.

He doesn't feel much these days. Pleasure, pain,

empathy, pity—they're all just words, so the fact that the coolness of an old chair could give him pause is surprising, even to him.

Lifting his eyes, he stares straight ahead, making sure the angle is correct, the view complete. It isn't, so he rises and moves the chair two feet to the right, and then turns it ten degrees to the left. Reclaiming the seat, he once again raises his eyes and stares directly in front of him.

It's better.

"You'll sit here," he says to the empty room.

He's never had an audience before, so the placement of the chair is of the utmost importance. He could move it a few more feet to the right, where its occupant would be privy to every mechanical movement, horrified facial expression, and convulsion, but the chair would then be too far from the focal point, and that's just not acceptable.

Presentation is everything.

Turning his eyes from the mechanism to the bench, he scans the length of it, noting that every strap is visible: feet, hands, and head. Moreover, the entire device is meticulously clean, all trace of past performances washed away. The leather appears new, the metal buckles shine, the steel frame is pristine—though much is hidden by the gloom.

The only indication that the machine has ever been used lies at the end closest to the chair. There, upon the ground, is a three-foot pool of congealed blood, intentionally left as an offering, a tribute, or a harbinger. The smell of it circulates the room, but the sight of it captures the eyes as one draws near, and that's exactly what the shadow wants: a focal point.

He looks at his watch and counts the days forward. Satisfied that all is in place, he leans back in the chair and takes in his creation, admiring its fearsome beauty and terrible power.

He smiles . . . but there's no joy in him.

He smiles because death is coming.

"I'm ready," he whispers.

CHAPTER NINETEEN

West of Fort Stockton, Texas—September 10, 12:32 P.M.

The roads of America are haunted.

Wilted flowers and small white crosses mark the places of the dead, tributes to those tragically taken too soon and for no reason. Most died without malice, the unintended victims of motor vehicle accidents that took them suddenly and without warning. At worst, they were victims of the drunk or the stoned, drivers too absorbed in themselves to worry about the lives of others until it was too late.

Stupidity isn't malice.

When it comes to roads, we tend to forget that the automobile was not the first reaper, just the most efficient. Death and roads have walked hand in hand long before even the Appian Way or the Silk Road came to be. As long as humans have put one foot in front of the other, death has walked beside them. Starvation, dehydration, banditry, warring tribes, riding mishaps, and chariot accidents all added to the deadly tally long before the inventions of gas and internal combustion fueled the reaping to higher levels.

The first fatal motor vehicle accident in America was on September 13, 1899. Since then, more than three and a half million others have followed.

America's roads, freeways, underpasses, and turnouts are also favorite dumping spots for killers, and not just the more experienced, the serial killers. Novices and onetime amateurs are welcome in this club. Some of the victims are killed at the scene, but most are murdered elsewhere and dumped a distance from the original crime, complicating the investigation.

If ghosts exist, or ever have, surely they haunt the roads of America.

At almost five thousand square miles, Pecos County, Texas, is roughly four times the size of the entire state of Rhode Island, and more than twice as big as Delaware. Scattered throughout this thinly populated territory are less than sixteen thousand county residents. That's about one person for every two hundred acres.

Half the county residents live in Fort Stockton itself.

With such a small population, and therefore a small tax base, the county can neither afford nor justify a full-time medical examiner. In those rare instances when a homicide occurs, the Lubbock County medical examiner takes jurisdiction of the body and conducts the autopsy on behalf of Pecos County.

That's Dr. Juan Mendoza-Cruz.

He's slim and short, but greets us with a handshake twice his size as we step from the unmarked Pecos County SUV.

With a wave of his hand, Juan leads us off the road and north into the low brush and grass bordering the east-west throughway. "Normally, I don't get out in the field a lot," Juan says over his shoulder. "Too much work stacked up at the office. Besides, I like to think we have some of the best certified medicolegal death investigators in Texas, and I trust their work. They're like my eyes and ears out here. Still, I had to see this one for myself."

As we draw near a loose cluster of deputies, Texas Rangers, and forensic techs, I get my first view of the Ice Box Killer's telltale shine. I give Jimmy a subtle nod, which he returns.

"You gotta be kidding me," Tony breathes through clenched teeth as his eyes fall upon the discarded corpse. He instinctively steps back a pace. "*Que Dios lo perdone,*" he says, crossing himself.

It's worse than Larry Wilson . . . and it's not Travis Duncan.

When Jimmy glances my way, I hold up three fingers and he understands: we now have three victims. IBK just became a serial killer, and the case just became more complicated.

Jimmy pauses a moment, letting Tony collect himself, and then, without a spoken word between them, they move in for a closer look. It takes a lot to shock a seasoned homicide investigator.

"What the hell . . . ?" Tony says, shaking his head.

"That's one way of putting it," Dr. Mendoza-Cruz replies.

The body lies on its side, slightly contorted, as if someone had tossed it there like so much garbage. It's naked except for a pair of boxer shorts and the cut and frayed upper portion of a single sock that clings to the stump of the right leg like a sweatband.

The rest of the sock is with the foot—wherever that is.

"Large patches of skin have been cut from the arms, legs, chest, neck, and back," Dr. Mendoza-Cruz says, "leaving these troughs in the flesh that are anywhere from an eighth-inch to a quarter-inch deep." He waves away the flies gathered around one such wound, revealing a raw piece of flesh filled with a congealed brown slurry. "Gives new meaning to the words *tattoo removal*, doesn't it?" the doctor adds.

Crouching next to Tony, he points out the hands. "The fingertips are also missing, plus the face was peeled like an orange and every tooth was yanked from the guy's head, so we can't use AFIS, and dental records are a no-go."

"We saw the same thing with our victim in Baton Rouge," Jimmy says, "though it wasn't this extreme. This is . . . well . . . brutal. Thank God he was already dead."

"I'm not too sure about that," Juan says. "I'll know more once I get back to the lab, but I think the tattoos were removed first, and then the feet, and I think he may have been alive for both of them. There's something else. . . ." He rises and walks to a bin resting several feet away on the other side of the body. Retrieving a plastic evidence bag from inside, he hands it to Tony. "Does that mean anything to you?"

Detective Alvarado peers through the clear plastic,

and turns the bag over to check the back. "Where'd you get this?" he asks as he hands it to Jimmy.

"It was pinned to his chest."

"Was he wearing a shirt when you found him?"

"No, it was pinned to the skin," Juan replies. "Does it mean anything?"

Jimmy sighs and says, "Yeah, it means we're running out of time."

"For what?"

"That's the problem: we don't know." Jimmy hands the evidence bag to me and I see the single sheet of paper inside. It has IBK's shine all over and reads in large letters: *JUSTICE MUST BE SERVED*, followed by the words *TIC TOC* scrawled across the bottom.

"He left a note in Baton Rouge too," Jimmy continues. "All it said was *soon,* whatever that means. He's clearly building up to something more significant . . . or counting down."

"If it's more significant than this, I'm not sure I want to see it," Tony says. Crouching once more beside the body, he closes his eyes and shakes his head. His lips move silently, but I can't tell if he's cursing or saying a prayer. When he opens his eyes again, he just stares at the remains . . . and then his posture suddenly shifts. He cocks his head to the side and leans in close, squinting at the corpse, but not in horror. He's curious.

Jimmy notices it too. "What's wrong, Tony?"

The detective looks up at us with a crooked grin on his face. "I think your Ice Box Killer screwed up."

Jimmy lowers himself to a crouch and moves closer, until he's little more than a foot from the debased corpse. My curiosity is less compelling, and I have no intention of following his lead. I've seen plenty of bodies over the last five years, both fresh and foul, and in different states of decomposition—but this one freaks me out.

I don't know why.

It looks like a discarded prop from some B-rated horror movie, but more than that, it strikes me as the physical manifestation of humanity's ability to inflict pain and suffering on others, a relic within our DNA dating to our deepest ancestors.

Throughout the history of civilized society, there has always been a line you do not cross. This body lies on the other side of that line.

"What do you see?" Jimmy asks.

Tony offers only a clue. "Take a look at the back of his head."

When Jimmy finds nothing, Tony scooches in and draws something in the air next to the scalp. Procedure dictates that the body belongs to the medical examiner; we can't touch the corpse in any way, even if it's just to push some hairs aside to get a better look.

I'm okay with that.

"See it now?" Tony says.

Jimmy's neck is stretched all the way out, his eyes are squinting hard, and he's biting his lower lip. Then, in an instant, every muscle in his face and neck slackens and his features soften. "Really?"

Tony just grins.

Turning to Dr. Mendoza-Cruz, Jimmy says, "What are the chances you can give this guy a haircut, at least on the back of his head?"

Juan shrugs. "How much do you need taken off?"

"Down to stubble . . . if you don't mind?"

"There should be some clippers in the van," the doctor replies. "Give me a couple minutes; I'll see what I can find."

As he picks his way to the road, my eyes walk over the back of the victim's head inch by inch, but still I have no idea what Tony and Jimmy are looking at.

A minute later, Juan trudges back toward us. Seeing all eyes turn his way, the good-natured pathologist hoists a pair of standard hair clippers triumphantly in the air and gives us a grin.

I like him.

He's like Doogie Howser—only older and Hispanic.

Careful not to contaminate the scene, Dr. Mendoza-Cruz kneels next to the body and slowly begins trimming the hair from the back of the victim's skull, catching the clippings as they fall and depositing them in a paper evidence bag. As he works, bold lines start to reveal themselves, a half inch thick in most places. Soon a five-inch-tall *X* tattoo is exposed, with a matching *3* right next to it.

"*X3*," I say. "He's a banger."

"Yeah, Sureño," Jimmy confirms.

Juan has a puzzled look on his face. "How can you tell from one tattoo?"

"Thirteen," Tony says, pointing at the tattoo. When the doctor stares at him blankly, it's almost too much for the detective. "Seriously? Your name is Juan, you live in Texas, and you're not familiar with Hispanic gangs?"

"Sue me," the doctor shoots back. His face is slightly contorted and his words are itchy with indignation. "We don't get a lot of gang activity around these parts. Besides, my grandparents emigrated from Mexico fifty years ago—what would I know of Hispanic gang culture? I grew up in Virginia and didn't learn Spanish until college. My taste in music leans toward Toby Keith, Tim McGraw, and Lady Antebellum." He shrugs. "I watch *Duck Dynasty.*"

Holding up a shielding hand as if to ward off a blow, Tony chuckles and says, "Fair enough, *ese.*" Standing, he brushes his clothes straight. "Guess we grew up in different varrios, homie. Here, let me walk you through this." He waves his open palm over the tattoo. "A Sureño—which means *Southerner*—uses the number thirteen as an identifier, a way of recognizing fellow Sureños. Mostly you see it as tattoos or graffiti."

"Why thirteen?"

"Simple," Tony says. "Gangs are big on swapping letters for numbers. The Sureños are affiliated with the Mexican Mafia—or El Eme, which means *M*—and so they use the number thirteen as a kind of tribute to the Mexican Mafia, a sign of respect, because *M* is the thirteenth letter of the alphabet."

"It's the same with their rivals," Jimmy adds. "The Norteños, or Northerners, are associated with Nuestra Familia, so they use the number fourteen—"

"Because *N* is the fourteenth letter of the alphabet," the doctor interjects.

"Exactly right: it's a tip of the hat to Nuestra Familia. Just remember that if you see a tattoo that has a number or a Roman numeral, odds are that it's gang-related. Not in all cases, but in most. Same goes for graffiti."

"Not just Hispanic gangs either," Tony says. "They're the worst offenders, but when it comes to substituting letters for numbers, most gangs do it: Bloods, Crips, Gangster Disciples, Vice Lords, P Stones—even white supremacists like the Aryan Brotherhood."

"So when I write this up I can say this guy was likely a member of the Sureño gang?" Dr. Mendoza-Cruz says, searching for clarification.

"Not exactly," Tony says. "What you've got to understand is that there's not *one* Sureño gang, it's more of a collective term for all the gangs affiliated with the Mexican Mafia. In fact, in Los Angeles County there are over five hundred Sureño gangs, or clickas. These include the big ones like 18 Street, Florencia 13, and MS-13, plus a whole bunch of smaller ones."

"So how do we know which *specific* gang this guy belongs to?"

Tony shrugs. "That might be a little difficult, since his tattoos are missing in action. In any case, he's probably not an active member—not for a long time."

"Why do you say that?"

"He wouldn't have grown out his hair and covered up that tat. You only do that if you've left that life behind—or you're trying to hide your gang affiliation, which is a possibility, I suppose." He stares at the body a moment, and then his forehead creases and he eyes the doctor. "I don't suppose you can shave the rest of that hair off?"

"Why not?" Juan says. He kneels next to the body and works the trimmers in slow, controlled movements, careful not to contaminate the crime scene. As soon as he starts on the left side of the head, the black shadow of hidden letters begins to emerge. He trims closer and the word takes shape.

"Smiley," Juan reads aloud. "What's that, his nickname?"

"Close," Tony replies. "It's his gang moniker."

"We might be able to do something with that," Jimmy says, his phone already in his hand. "I'll have Diane get started on it."

"Tell her to start with those that have a link to Albuquerque," I say as he dials. Nodding, he steps away to a quiet spot beyond the murmur of voices that surrounds the crime scene.

He's gone barely three minutes, and when he returns he has company. A lanky fellow in a black cowboy hat, weathered jeans, and a tan Western shirt walks beside him. His leathery skin speaks to the years he's spent in the Texas sun, and his thick Sam Elliott mustache goes perfectly with the badge on the left side of his belt and the gun on the right, which is a six-shooter. Considering that most law enforcement agencies switched over to semiautomatics years ago, the gun is an anomaly. The holster is even tied down.

All things considered, he looks like he just stepped out of Texas circa 1880.

"Steps, Tony, this is Sheriff Roland Grimm," Jimmy says when the stone-faced lawman stops in front of us. After shaking hands and the usual pleasantries, Sheriff Grimm gets straight to the point.

"So you're telling me this is the third body you've linked to this killer?"

"It is," Jimmy replies.

"That makes him a serial killer, right?"

"There's a lot of debate as to what qualifies as a serial killer," Jimmy starts to explain, but then he stops himself, looks the sheriff in the eye, and simply says, "Yeah, he's a serial killer."

"It's a cryin' shame," the sheriff mutters. "Last thing the county needs right now."

"If it's any consolation," I say, "Pecos County was likely just the dump site. We're pretty sure he was killed far from here."

"That doesn't make me feel much better, son," the sheriff replies sternly. "I still got a dead man dumped on one of my roads and a population that's still on edge from a homicide two years ago. Folks 'round here don't forget things like that." He tips the brim of his hat at the body. "I'm serious, now, when you boys figure out who did this, you let me know ASAP. You'll have whatever cooperation you need from my people."

"I appreciate that, Sheriff," Jimmy says. He spends several minutes discussing the tattoos with the sheriff, both those that were cut out and those on the victim's head, and then explains the similarities between this case and the homicides of Travis Duncan and Larry Wilson.

"And you figure this is another ex-con who got away with something?" the sheriff says when Jimmy finishes. "Thwarted the system, so to speak, and this Ice Box fella decided to settle the score?"

"I do."

"Well, hell," the sheriff says with a deep laugh. "He's not a serial killer, son, he's a public servant."

There's a smattering of laughter from those nearby.

"Anything else tying these cases together?" the sheriff continues.

"Interstate 10," I say, pointing loosely at the road.

"How so?" the lawman says, turning his gaze on me.

"I don't know yet," I reply, "but we've found bodies and body parts from Baton Rouge, Louisiana, to Tucson, Arizona, and places in between, and they're all connected by Interstate 10." I shrug. "Might just be a coincidence."

"I don't take much to the idea of coincidence," the sheriff interjects. "And to be accurate, *that's* Interstate 10." He indicates the highway a hundred feet to the south. "This is just the I-10 service road."

"Close enough," I mutter. He's right, of course, but the road runs parallel to I-10 and, frankly, that's all I care about.

It's about location.

If I had a pin on a wall map for each body and pair of feet we've found so far, Interstate 10 would be the brightly colored yarn stretched between them, connecting them. It's what we in law enforcement call a clue. Albuquerque is another clue. Then there's ice-blue shine, Styrofoam ice boxes, severed feet, cryptic notes, vigilantism, bodies disfigured to conceal their identity, public defenders, and the fact that IBK wants to send a message.

But what's he saying?

It's a convoluted nightmare of misdirection and obfuscation.

Excusing myself, I move away from the crime scene, letting Jimmy and Tony contend with the sheriff and ME, while I track IBK's shine to its origin.

It's an odd journey, and not what I expected.

The trail doesn't go to the road, but runs parallel to it, moving east some thirty feet to a scuffed-up patch of earth where he first laid the body on the ground. My first impression is that he was tired and only set the body down to take a quick break. But then I see Tattoo Man's orange shine in a wide swath where he was rolled under some low brush.

For some reason IBK wasn't satisfied with that.

Orange drag marks show where he grabbed Tattoo Man by the arm and pulled him back out. I see where IBK knelt next to the body, perhaps to get a good grip before hoisting him up again and walking him farther west to his current location, where he's exposed to the world.

There was no effort to hide the body, and it was easy for a passing trucker to spot it that morning at first light. The placement was deliberate: IBK wanted the body found quickly—just like Baton Rouge.

Tic toc.

Continuing the track, I follow the ice-blue shine as it takes a ninety-degree turn and heads south to the road some twenty feet away. There it stops. As odds would have it, the folks from the Odessa Mobile Crime Lab parked their RV directly over the spot where IBK pulled over and got out of his vehicle. The shine just disappears under the massive rig.

Dumb luck!

I could ask one of the lab techs to move the vehicle, but I suspect that would generate some uncomfortable questions, particularly if they take an interest in my tracking and want to see the supposed heel marks and toe impressions.

It's time to get dirty.

Everyone is busy at their various tasks or engaged in

conversation. No one's looking my way, and it's doubtful they would care one way or the other even if they were.

Dropping to my belly next to the mobile lab, I look under the RV to the east, then to the west. The clearance is high enough, so I scoot under a few feet.

It's the same as Baton Rouge.

The vehicle was facing west and the body was in the trunk. I'm pretty certain now that it's a car. I've seen enough shine at the backs of cars, trucks, and SUVs to know that people move differently for each, especially when off-loading heavy items—like bodies.

There's no sign of the victim's orange shine on the ground, so IBK must have lifted him straight out of the trunk and slung him over a shoulder. That takes strength. If you've ever had the unfortunate circumstance of having to lug a body around, you know they can be unwieldy. Fighting to get a good grip is a constant problem, which only makes the body seem that much heavier.

"Where are you?" I whisper to IBK, though I know the real question is, *Who are you?* The asphalt of Interstate 10 feels cool against my back as I lie under the RV staring at the undercarriage. It's actually quite comfortable under here. The crime lab has been parked since early morning, so any heat the road had absorbed is long gone, leaving only the refreshing, clarifying ambient temperature of earth.

And, lying on my back under the RV on the side of Interstate 10, something suddenly occurs to me—as if I'd known it all along. It's the answer to the mystery; the solution to the puzzle; the missing part we've been looking for.

I know how to identify IBK.

As the realization sweeps through me and adrenaline sets my muscles to tingling, I forget my surroundings. In my rush to get to Jimmy, I try to sit straight up and nearly knock myself out on the undercarriage. Half dazed, I scramble and claw and pull myself out from under the RV. My clothes are covered in filth, front and back, and blood oozes in a steady flow from the gash on my forehead.

It doesn't matter.

Staggering to my feet, I prop myself up against the mobile crime lab for a moment, arms outstretched against the side until I feel steady enough to walk. Pushing off from the RV, I vector toward Jimmy, Tony, and the cluster of people still gathered around the body. It seems like they've all become one globular mass; I can't make out any faces.

"Jimmy," I yell, waving an arm. "Jimmy!" The world begins to spin and a comfortable blur lightens my head. I can't think straight, but—wait!

I know this feeling.

Yep. Here comes the ground.

CHAPTER TWENTY

The Long Grind—September 11, 11:17 A.M.

"Stop picking at it."

"It itches."

"Of course it itches," Jimmy says dryly. "Bandages are supposed to itch. They're designed that way to torment people who knock themselves out."

"I didn't knock myself out."

"Oh, okay," he says with a sarcastic smirk. "What, then? Let me guess: you were sniffing the ground for clues. No, wait! You were studying the microscopic qualities of IBK's shine close up."

I don't reply. No sense in encouraging him.

"STOP PICKING!" Jimmy roars.

My left hand is back up at my forehead, fussing with the bandage. I didn't even realize it. I drop the hand back into my lap and hold it there with my right hand. It's not so much the bandage that's driving me crazy, but the five stitches underneath. I've had stitches before and don't remember the bandage being so gigantic, but Jimmy picked it out personally and insisted.

Now I have a three-inch-by-four-inch bandage covering the troublesome stitches. Worse still, it's one of those industrial-strength hospital bandages, the type that takes a layer of skin with it when you rip it off.

Roofing tar is easier to remove.

Since our adventures yesterday west of Fort Stockton, we returned to El Paso for the night, and then flew to Baton Rouge early this morning. We landed an hour ago. Jimmy's in the driver's seat of a midnight-blue 2014 Dodge Charger that we rented at the airport. I'm guessing he really liked the silver Charger he rented in El Paso, because this morning he wouldn't even consider other options at the rental counter.

We're rolling down Interstate 10, westbound, with some thirty miles already between us and the city. After crossing the Atchafalaya River, Jimmy pulls off at a rest area just beyond the bridge.

This is where our search begins.

There are a thousand miles of metal signs pointing out rest areas, motels, and hotels between Baton Rouge and El Paso. We intend to stop at every one, if that's what it takes. This rest area is stop number one, though technically we don't actually stop; we just roll slowly past the parking area and the restrooms looking for ice-blue shine.

We find none.

I have no doubt this is just the first of many disappointments. The theory is simple: IBK dumped Larry Wilson in the Bluebonnet Swamp after driving the entire length of Texas, likely with few breaks—maybe just some coffee here and there, and a few bathroom breaks. That's kind of what you do when there's a body in the trunk and the hot southern sun is baking the outer skin of the car.

The point is that he drove at least fifteen or sixteen hours, probably more. That's a lot of road miles. After dumping Larry, he would have been exhausted, but our guy is smart enough to put some distance between himself and the body.

He wouldn't have stayed in Baton Rouge.

On the other hand, there's no way he makes it all the way to El Paso without stopping somewhere to rest. Could be that he tried to catch some winks at one of the many rest areas along Interstate 10, but a lot of jurisdictions don't allow that. And, frankly, by that point he would have been sick of being in the car. The thought of sleeping in the same seat he'd been sitting in for so long would have been unbearable. Still, we have to check.

Our real hope lies in the probability that he checked into a motel or hotel, and he wouldn't have strayed too far from I-10 to do so. Motels and hotels mean a room registration, maybe a license plate number, and, almost certainly, a credit card.

I intend on checking every motel and hotel between Baton Rouge and El Paso until we find his telltale shine. It may mean a thousand miles, hundreds of stops, and days with little rest, but that's the path to IBK.

Jimmy calls it *the long grind.*

It's a perfect metaphor.

The prospect is daunting, but we have three bodies stacked up and we're no closer to our killer now than when we started. The next twenty-four to seventy-two hours could make all the difference.

For now, we grind our way west.

Hour Three

Afternoon finds us a few miles beyond Lafayette, having put just twenty miles between us and the visitors' center at the Atchafalaya River. We find a scattered half dozen motels and hotels off the highway between the river and the city, but it isn't until we get into Lafayette proper that the real work begins.

Exit 103A proves to be the mother lode.

There are about a dozen franchise motels less than a half mile from I-10, and dispersed on both sides of a divided throughway. We work one side, then the other, methodically driving past the entrance to each lobby in search of shine, but find nothing.

There's a bit of momentary excitement as we cruise past the lobby of an inn on Northeast Frontage Road. I swear it's IBK; it's the same tint of ice-blue shine.

My heart races.

I don't know if it's shock or excitement or just stupidity brought on by my weakened condition (on account of my head injury, which I intend to milk for all its worth), but I manage to jump out of the Charger before Jimmy gets it fully stopped.

It's hard to look cool and not draw attention when you're windmilling your arms and trying not to do a face-plant.

Again.

On closer examination, the shine's color is similar, but there are no black flecks, and the texture is similar to that of a traditional Berber carpet, very different from IBK's plastic-like sheen. These are details that can't be distinguished until one is close.

Hour Four

Diane calls.

She's drilling Jimmy pretty hard, wondering why we're driving our way across Louisiana and Texas when we should be at home or in El Paso trying to sort this mess out. It's at times like this that I regret not telling her about shine; her, Heather, and Dex. It would make everything so much easier, and, frankly, I'm tired of keeping it from them.

Jimmy goes back and forth with her for a full two minutes and never breaks from the script. The cover story is simple: we're checking with the medical examiner in each county between Baton Rouge and El Paso looking for similar cases.

It's the type of boots-on-the-ground detective work that solves cases; the grease that works the clues free. It even sounds somewhat logical. If Diane's IQ were just thirty or forty points lower, we might actually be able to sell it, but as things stand right now, that lie won't fly.

She thinks the world of us, but right now she's so mad she can barely conceal it.

It's not the first time we've lied to Diane, nor will it be the last. Every mission involves some type of deception, though most tend to be the benign white lies explaining, for example, how we found a single drop of blood that was somehow missed by seasoned CSIs.

The more difficult and complex the case is, the deeper the lie.

Three years ago it didn't bother Diane as much: we pretended to tell her the truth and she pretended to believe us. It was like a dysfunctional marriage. Two years ago we would cloud the truth and she would pretend not to care.

A year ago, the dysfunctional marriage started hanging out at divorce court.

Time is no longer on our side. I'd say we have six months, a year at the most. Diane knows there's something else at play, and if we don't come clean soon it's going to get ugly with a capital Ugh.

"Did you just call to harass us," Jimmy says, "or was there an actual purpose you dialed?" He's a pretty good match for Diane. They can both dish it out harsh and eat it cold.

Clearing her throat, Diane says, "I think I've identified your victim from Fort Stockton. His name is Carlos Juan Hernandez, age thirty-seven. He's from Belen, New Mexico, which is where he was reported missing a few days ago."

"Where's Belen?" I ask.

"About thirty miles south of Albuquerque," Diane replies.

Jimmy shakes his head in disbelief. "Albuquerque—again."

"What's his story, Diane?" I ask.

"Guy's a real peach; registered sex offender with extensive criminal history going back decades. Property crimes seem to be his forte, the most serious of which was an armed robbery conviction when he was nineteen. Then, a year ago, he was arrested for rape and assault after he grabbed a twenty-nine-year-old female out of the back parking lot of a bar and drove her out into the desert, where he beat and raped her over several hours.

"There wasn't any DNA to link him to the crime," Diane continues, "and the victim was fairly intoxicated, so the case was shaky to begin with. Then, two months ago, the whole thing got blown apart. Defense learned that the victim was arrested ten years earlier for prostitution. She's had no arrests since, but it was enough. The victim got wind of it and was afraid it would come out in trial, something she didn't want, particularly with her husband sitting in attendance."

"So the whole thing got tossed," I say.

"Charges dismissed," Diane confirms. "Carlos walked."

"Well, someone was paying attention."

Jimmy and I are silent a moment. It's not an uncomfortable silence, as one might expect, but the quiet wrestling match of teammates mentally tag-teaming a problem.

Jimmy's the first to speak. "Do we have any idea how he went missing?"

"The report suggests he was grabbed out of his home in the night." The crackle of shifting paper seeps through the speakers from ten different directions and then Diane finds what she's looking for. "There was evidence of a struggle in his bedroom, and then he didn't show up for work the next day. I talked to his boss twenty minutes ago. He said that Carlos may have been a real piece of work, but he always showed up for work on time. That didn't happen Monday morning."

"That's two days between the abduction and the disposal of the body," Jimmy muses. He's tapping the steering wheel with his left index finger while he puzzles it out. I usually pace when I think, but that's a little hard to do while rolling down Interstate 10 at seventy miles an hour. Instead, I mimic Jimmy's tapping—only I do my tapping on the armrest built into the door and use my right index finger.

I try to keep time with Jimmy.

Tap—tap-tap—tap.

Diane has little more to add, so she makes some final comments about wasting time in Louisiana and then ends the call. Jimmy's still in his own little world.

The exits for Lake Charles are coming up, and with them close to fifty hotels and motels. I point the sign out and Jimmy looks at it indifferently before putting his blinker on and moving to the far right lane.

It takes another minute before he notices my tapping. By this time I'm playing the armrest like a drum, and the exit is fast approaching.

"Come on, Steps! That's irritating."

I don't say a word. With a raised eyebrow, I tilt my head sideways at him, look purposefully at the strumming finger on the steering wheel, and then back at him.

"Oh." That's all he says; no less, no more. Sometimes the simplest statements are the most powerful.

Regardless, the finger stops.

A moment later the right blinker starts again; the grind resumes.

Hour Nine

By the time we grind our way through Beaumont, Texas, and its offering of hotels and motels, the sun has made its gracious exit from the sky, and vestiges of its radiance have all faded from the long horizon.

Interstate 10 carries us away from the city in a southwest direction and we pause just long enough to grab some burgers from a fast-food joint off the highway. One of our must-sing songs comes on the radio, but we're too exhausted to pay proper tribute, and by silent mutual agreement we let the song bleed out without the benefit of our voices.

Jimmy wants to drive until at least midnight.

I'm too tired to argue.

We grind on.

Hour Ten

Fourteen miles west of Winnie, at exit 815, the blue sign for a safety rest area leads us back off I-10 near Hankamer, Texas. The spot is hidden behind the trees, but as we draw near, the rest area emerges from the darkness ahead and stands as a beacon in the night. My first impression is that it's one of the nicest rest areas I've been to—and I've been to a lot. The main building is well lit, as are the scattered pavilions and outbuildings. There's even a state-of-the-art playground for kids.

"Nice," Jimmy says, parking the Charger and shutting it down. He points: "They have free coffee."

Then I see it.

Not the coffee stand—the ice-blue shine leading to the coffee stand.

I throw the door open so hard it rebounds and catches me hard in the shin. Despite the pain, I jump out and chase the shine. I imagine I look a bit ridiculous, like a bloodhound on a fresh scent, turning this way, then that.

Jimmy's right behind me, not asking questions, just following. Like me, the find seems to have put energy back in his steps. After several minutes that take me all over the complex, I stop at a picnic table.

Jimmy lets me breathe a moment, lets me digest what I see. He doesn't have to wait long before it comes bubbling out.

"He parked over there," I say, pointing to a spot near the main building, about ten spaces farther down from the Charger. "He probably went to the men's room first, then got some coffee. After that he walked around and looked at pretty much everything; he even stopped at the fence around the play area and watched the kids— though I image it was still early morning, probably even dark when he was here, so he may have been staring at an empty play area."

"Maybe that's relevant," Jimmy offers. "Maybe that's what drives him."

"You think he turned vigilante because he lost a son or daughter?"

"Think about it," Jimmy presses. "If something was going to send me off the deep end, what would it be?"

"You want a list?"

He gives me a smirk that says *Touché,* and presses

on. "For me it would have to be something involving Jane or Pete—for you it would be Heather and Jens, your mom, your dad . . . maybe even Ellis."

"I like Ellis," I say, "but not enough to go full schizoid for him."

"Okay, but you get my meaning. The worst for me would be if something happened to Pete. I love Jane with everything that's in me, and would kill or die for her, but with Pete there's something else. I suppose it's that primal parental instinct to protect, and the fact that he's so vulnerable."

"Maybe it wasn't a child he lost," I offer, "but the hope of a child. Maybe something happened to his girlfriend or wife. Or maybe he's just angry at the world because he can't get a girlfriend or a wife. Could be he's socially awkward, or there's something else about him that drives women away . . . assuming he's a guy."

Jimmy's shaking his head. "Female serial killers are rare enough; one that could cut off feet, yank teeth, and carve out tattoos is hard to imagine. No, most serial killers are white males, and I'm guessing this one is between, say, twenty-five and forty years of age." Jimmy's voice is suddenly low, quiet. "Something happened to him."

I don't argue the point. Jimmy is uncannily accurate when it comes to profiling suspects, and I've learned to trust his instincts.

"At some point he ended up right here," I say, pointing at the seat in front of me. "He sat at the picnic table and drank his coffee. I can see where his right hand kept lifting up and coming to rest in the same general spot on the table. The shine from his hand is in a reverse-C shape, or maybe a close parenthesis, indicating he had it cupped around the coffee. He was here a while."

"This is good," Jimmy says, gently hitting the table three times with the ball of his closed fist. "This proves he was on I-10 . . . just as you predicted." He gives me a grin. "Not that I doubted the logic behind your idea, but I was starting to wonder if maybe he took a different route."

"I never had a doubt," I reply in a haughty tone.

Jimmy knows it's a lie and we both smile broadly, then he says, "No, this is really good. He was obviously tired—he had to be. And it's still a long way to El Paso. He's going to stop somewhere, and probably soon."

Hour Eleven

The coffee from the Hankamer rest area proves inadequate and by the time we reach Mont Belvieu twenty minutes later, Jimmy and I are both ready to call it quits for the night.

A certain peace came with the discovery of IBK's shine.

We now know we're on the right track and that, from here on out, it's simply a process of time and elimination. We don't have to find where he stayed tonight, or even tomorrow night. We're at ease because we know we'll find it.

After checking the sixteen hotels and motels in and around Mont Belvieu, we cross the San Jacinto River. All of Houston lies before us—our biggest challenge yet. Even though our search will be limited to those lodgings within a mile of I-10, the sheer number is staggering. This will require fresh minds and fresh eyes.

Houston is a battle best fought in the light of a new day.

CHAPTER TWENTY-ONE

Houston, Texas—September 12, 9:05 A.M.

"Where's the battle station?" Jimmy says to the teenage barista with the stained HANK'S COFFEE apron tied sloppily around her waist. She stares at him blankly a moment, and then her head shakes back and forth rapidly in a one-inch range that makes it looks like she's having a meltdown.

"Where do you keep your cream and sugar?" Jimmy clarifies.

"Oh," she says. "It's right over there." She points to a shelf hidden against the adjacent wall. "Battle station," she snorts. "That's cute."

Jimmy stirs two packs of sugar into his coffee and takes a sip from the obsidian broth. His face grimaces horribly and he sets the cup back on the counter. "Back home they'd run you out of town for serving swill like this," he mutters. Dumping two more packs of sugar into the cup, he chases it with a long pour of creamer.

Jimmy's a coffee snob.

He's had coffee all over the country, at roadside dives and fancy restaurants, and half the time he places it in one of three categories: awful, terrible, or just disgusting. I always agree with him, of course, but then—*I hate coffee.* Still, I'm forced into coffee shops everywhere we go, north, south, east, and west, so over time I've perfected a drink that camouflages most of the bitter coffee taste, plus it tastes pretty good. I'd even say it tastes pleasant.

Jimmy calls it the *why-bother*; I call it a twenty-ounce mocha with a single shot of decaf, one-percent milk, and no whip.

It's a glorified hot chocolate.

Good or bad, this coffee stop is our last oasis this side of sanity. Having reviewed and studied our varied collection of maps and travel books this morning, I suspect that Houston is going to chew us up and spit us out in little chunks that resemble wet cat food.

But that's just me; I'm an optimist.

Sunset arrives at 7:26 P.M. and as dusk settles, the evening lights of Katy, Texas, arrive outside my window, flashing by and then slowing as we exit to do our checks. It's a relief to arrive in the town, because it means that we're finally beyond the sprawl of Houston and its suburbs.

After getting back on I-10, we travel another seven miles and see a sign that reads BROOKSHIRE CITY LIMITS, POP. 4702. There are three motels, all within a thousand feet of the freeway. We check the Executive Inn, the Super 8, and, farther west, the La Quinta Inn, and find nothing.

We're almost back to the I-10 on-ramp when Jimmy suddenly pulls a U-turn and heads back to the La Quinta.

"I don't know about you," he says, "but if I have to look at another hotel or motel I'm going to scream. What do you say we check in, have a beer, and sit in the hot tub for a while?" He looks at me and tries to grin. "It should be safe; Marty's not with us."

"Works for me."

Having looked at perhaps two hundred hotels and motels in the last thirty-three hours, and being sick and tired of even the look of them, and disheartened by the mere thought of them . . . we check into a motel.

Brookshire, Texas—September 13, 9:05 A.M.

After the therapeutic effects of the hot tub, a couple beers, and nine hours of sleep, Jimmy and I are both alert and invigorated, though neither of us is excited about another day of hotel hunting. Jimmy insists on a sit-down breakfast, and, since this is Texas, I decide to have steak with my eggs and hash browns.

What arrives is bigger than the steaks I normally have for supper, and as I work my way through it I decide that I could get used to this.

"Diane called this morning," Jimmy says between mouthfuls of omelet.

"Let me guess, she wants to know what we're doing wasting our time driving through Texas?"

Jimmy chuckles. "Yeah, that was part of it."

"And the other part?"

Jimmy shifts uncomfortably in his seat. "She's got missions stacking up. Two cases in Ohio that might be related, one fresh, the other a year old—they want our opinion. She also mentioned a missing pair of hikers in the Olympics."

"How long have they been missing?"

"Two days."

I sigh and push the half-eaten steak to the center of the table; I was full anyway. "One more day," I say. "If we don't find something by this evening we can have Les and Marty pick us up and fly us straight to Port Angeles. We can be in the Olympics early tomorrow morning." I give Jimmy a hard look. "We've come this far."

He nods and pushes the balance of his omelet away. His fingers strum the tabletop three times, and then he says, "That's exactly what I told her." Picking up the blue cloth napkin from his lap, he wipes his mouth, then his hands, and tosses it on his plate. "We've got twelve hours to prove your theory. What do you say we hit the road?"

Fifteen miles west of Brookshire is the town of Sealy, Texas.

Ask a hundred people if they've ever heard of the town, and ninety-nine will likely say no. The irony is that almost all of them know the town; they just don't *know* that they know the town.

That's because in 1881, cotton gin builder Daniel Haynes, a resident of Sealy, began making mattresses filled with cotton for friends and family. By 1889 he had patented an invention for compressing cotton for mattresses and his product eventually became so popular that the term "Mattress from Sealy" was coined. The Sealy-brand mattress is with us still, and the Sealy Corporation, now based in North Carolina, employs close to five thousand people—the rough equivalent of the entire population of present-day Sealy, Texas.

As we pull off I-10, Jimmy asks, "How many?"

I glance at the list. "Looks like eight, all within a mile of each other. We should be able to get through them quickly enough."

We start on the north side and work south. As expected, we run by the first six in less than fifteen minutes . . . and then we reach number seven.

The Southern Cross Inn on Main Street doesn't have the appearance of a franchise motel, the type with cookie-cutter architecture and neutral colors. Instead, the inn blends well with the surrounding buildings, asserting its place as a long-standing member of the community, not some recent interloper.

Formerly a two-story commercial building dating to the early days of Sealy, the inn has been nicely refurbished and stands as one of the grander structures on the street, but it's not the glass work, the old lamplights, or the oiled wood that draws my gaze.

No.

It's the trail of ice-blue shine that walks up the sidewalk and right through the hundred-year-old double doors leading into the lobby.

A surge of adrenaline dumps into my system, pumping through my veins with the force of a garden hose so that I hear my own heartbeat in my ears. Unbidden, my left hand clamps onto Jimmy's arm even before it's off the steering wheel, startling him.

"We found him," I say. Then, exhaling deeply, I slump in my seat for a moment, closing my eyes, feeling the relief.

"You're sure?" Jimmy's as excited as I am, but won't show it.

"I'm positive."

I can feel him staring at me, and when I open my eyes he's grinning broadly. Without a word, he springs from the Charger and rushes toward the front doors as I scramble to follow, nearly knocking over an old woman who's dragging a rat terrier around on a short leash. There's no one in the reception area, so I follow the shine up the stairs and down the hall, where the trail disappears under the door of room 113.

But that's not all.

"He stayed here before," I whisper to Jimmy. "There's new shine—very recent, plus a faded track, probably from the same time frame as the older shine we found at the swamp. Eight to ten years, give or take. Both times he stayed in *this* room"—I point at the door with both index fingers—"and she was with him the first time."

"She? You mean the *she* from the swamp? Bronze?"

"Bronze with acid-green swirls," I whisper with a single firm nod.

Jimmy's mind is churning; my mind is churning. His fingers are strumming his pants while I pace five steps up the hall and then five steps back. A moment later we speak simultaneously: "We need to get into this room."

The front desk has one of those old-fashioned bells where you tap the knob on top to summon assistance. I tap it—a few times. The woman whose head pokes out of the office isn't amused. Nonetheless, she puts on a welcoming Texas smile and comes around to greet us. Her name tag reads ANGELA.

"What can I do for you gentlemen this morning?"

Jimmy badges her, holding his credentials up long enough for her to get a good look, then says, "We're going to need some help from you today, Angela."

"Wh-whatever I can do." She's biting her lower lip now, which means she's either nervous we're going to arrest her for something, or she finds me attractive—or she finds Jimmy attractive . . . I suppose.

"We're in the middle of a very important investigation," my partner explains in an official tone. "Can you tell me if there's anyone currently registered in room one-thirteen?"

"Normally I could tell you that off the top of my head," Angela says, "but my shift just started an hour ago and I've only checked two out and one in during that time." She sidles over to the computer at her left and brings the monitor to life with a wiggle of the mouse. Her fingers twitch at the keyboard as she begins to type. "Shoot," she says a moment later, hitting the backspace button several times.

She tries it again with similar results and finally makes a go of it on the third attempt. "Just don't know what's wrong with me today." Her eyes quickly scan the results. "No, that room is currently vacant. It was last occupied yesterday."

The words spill from Jimmy's mouth: "We need a list

of everyone who stayed in room one-thirteen from September—" He's snapping his fingers.

"They found the body on the third," I say.

Angela's eyes suddenly look like white porcelain saucers. "B-body?"

"Make it the third through the sixth," Jimmy says.

Angela's fingers click the keyboard for several seconds. "I have two names for that time frame. Mrs. Shepard was in the room on the fifth and sixth—she was here from Tallahassee visiting her grandkids. Sweet lady. The second guest was Lawrence Wilson from El Paso."

"Lawrence Wilson?" I say, dumbfounded. "*Larry* Wilson?"

"That's correct. He checked in late on the third, and stayed just one night."

"That's quite a trick, Angela," Jimmy says, "since Larry Wilson was dead on the third. In fact, he'd probably been dead several weeks by then."

"Oh, my!" Her right hand moves up to cover her heart, as if wounded, and her eyes stare accusingly at the words on the screen. "But the computer . . ." She lets the words fall into a silent grave.

"What's your check-in procedure?" I ask.

Angela retrieves a form from under the counter, which is printed on a half sheet of regular printer paper, and hands it to me. "We have them fill out the form themselves, and we enter it into the computer later, after they're registered. It speeds up the process. That way we can get them taken care of quickly and have them on their way." She smiles.

"So they fill out the form themselves. Do they have to show identification?"

"Only if they're paying with a credit card or check—though we don't see very many checks these days."

"And how would I find out if he paid cash or used a card?"

"We would have marked it on his registration form," Angela says, nodding at the paper in my hand. "But then it would have been entered into the computer." As she's speaking her hand moves to the mouse, which she repositions and clicks several times. She types in Larry's name and almost immediately says, "Uh-oh." Grimacing, I'm sure for our benefit, she says, "It looks like he paid cash."

She glances at me, then at Jimmy, then back at me. "I . . . I don't have any other information. If this isn't the real Larry Wilson, I don't know who he is—I mean *was*!"

Jimmy taps a box in the lower right corner of the registration form. "You have an area here for the guest's license plate number. Did Larry Wilson fill that out?"

"I'm sure he did," Angela says. "It's required." Her fingers go to work on the keyboard and then she smiles. "It's a Texas license plate, number 2FT2L8."

Jimmy scribbles it down and immediately walks away from the counter to make a call. "That's exactly what we needed." I beam, giving Angela's hand a little pat, which sets her cheeks on fire.

Jimmy paces the lobby a moment and then heads out the door, probably for better reception. He's gone a full two minutes. When he returns I can see it on his face before he utters a word. "Tony says it's a bad plate." He tosses the piece of paper with the scribbled license number onto the front counter. "There goes our best shot."

"There's still the room," I offer.

Jimmy says something in return, and though I hear the individual words I don't piece them together into a coherent sentence because I'm suddenly distracted by the very paper he tossed on the counter.

"Jimmy, take a look at this," I say, cutting him off in midsentence. The tone of my voice gets his attention and he moves closer and looks down. Turning the piece of paper with the scribbled license number toward him, I ask him, "What do you see?"

"Two-F-T-two-L-eight," he replies. "What am I supposed to see?"

"What is FT an abbreviation for?"

His eyes widen. "Feet," he says. "Two feet—but that could just be a coincidence. What's the Two-L-Eight part?" I give him a moment and he doesn't disappoint. "Two feet too late," he says, sounding breathless. "Is it a message, or is he just toying with us?"

"It's a message," I say. "Everything keeps coming back to feet. But is he talking about Larry Wilson's feet, or someone else's?"

Jimmy ponders this a moment, and then he turns to Angela. "Any chance we can take a look at that room?" Thirty seconds later we're taking the stairs two at a time with a room key dangling from Jimmy's closed fingers.

At first glance there's nothing remarkable about the room—at least nothing remarkable that pertains to the case. The room itself is spectacular. From the bedding to the wallpaper, and from the carpet to the furnishings, the living space is Texas to the core. It pulls you in, and for a moment, except for the modern conveniences, you imagine that you're in old Texas. A passing car sounds for a moment like a stagecoach rattling by, and I swear I hear a piano playing.

Wait.

I *do* hear a piano playing.

Stepping over to one of the large windows, which is cracked open a few inches, I look down and across the street and, sure enough, there's a guy in a tan cowboy hat playing an old upright piano just inside the door of a restaurant. "Texas," I say, shaking my head. If I didn't like the Pacific Northwest so much, I'd consider moving to the Lone Star State.

"So . . . what are we looking for?" I ask, glancing around the room.

"Latent prints. Check anything he may have touched," Jimmy replies. "This is our last shot. . . ." He lets the words dangle, like the Sword of Damocles.

As I'm turning left to the bathroom, with its double sinks and small closet, my focus is on light switches, the built-in hair dryer, various door handles, faucets, and countertops, so much so that I almost miss it, even though it's bold and big and right in front of me.

"Jimmy?"

He finds me staring at the large mirror over the double sinks. When I don't immediately say anything, he looks at me, then at my reflection, then at me again, saying, "Yes, I'm afraid that's your real hair."

I punch him in the arm and then point at the mirror. "She wrote on it," I say.

"She wrote . . . Oh?" He looks at the mirror and sees nothing. "What'd she write?"

As I speak, I trace the words and the shapes in the air

without touching the mirror. "*TW* and then a large heart"—my finger sweeps widely over the face of the glass—"and on the other side an *IW*."

"*W* on both sides—like a last name? So they're married!"

"Seems so, and since she's writing it, I'm assuming the *T* belongs to her: Tina, Tasha, Tammy, something like that."

"How do you figure?"

"It just makes sense. If *you* were writing it, you'd write Jimmy loves Jane, right; your name first because you're the one declaring it? You wouldn't write Jane loves Jimmy—that's like putting words in her mouth."

"You're right," Jimmy agrees. "So, that makes Mr. IW our suspect."

"It does. Oh, and one more tidbit for you." I wave my hand around the bathroom suite. "He wiped down everything: countertop, doorknobs, faucets, even the toilet seat and lid. He was pretty thorough too. Either that or the cleaning crew is really good."

Jimmy's not so easily dissuaded. "Check the rest of the room."

I spend the next few minutes examining the room, every aspect of the room, but all of the recent shine has been carefully and completely wiped for prints—even the snooze button on the clock radio. Prospects for the old shine are even worse. Over the past eight to ten years every surface, button, knob, and drawer pull has been handled thousands of times and cleaned by the maids almost as often.

There's a single exception.

Waving my partner over, I frame an area on the wall with both hands. "How do you feel about trying to recover a print that could be a decade old, from a porous, textured wall?"

"Like I'd have better luck winning the lottery." I give him a long stare and he sighs. "Go on. Tell me what you have."

"It's both of them, IBK and our mystery lady; right here." I emphasize a section of the wall for him. "She's got her back flush up against the wall—just her back, nothing else touching. The only part of him I see is a full left palm print with fingers and thumb splayed. It's right over where her shoulder would have been."

"So she's got her back against the wall and he's close enough to . . . Oh."

"Yeah." I nod. "I don't think he was helping her put her shoes on."

"Show me exactly where the handprint is."

Circling the spot with my left index finger, I step to the side and let Jimmy take a closer look. The invisible print is about five and a half feet from the floor. I can't use shine to determine if any dermal ridges are present; it just doesn't work like that.

"Iodine fuming is obviously out. We can't use normal dusting powder either; the print is just too old. Silver nitrate is going to be our best option—I think—though it's going to leave a stain." He weighs the options one more time in his head, then nods and says, "Can you run out to the car and get my kit?" I'm almost out the door when he adds, "Make sure the UV light is in the bag."

I wave at Angela on my way out, and then again on

my way back in. She returns my wave both times, curiosity eating her up. I'm at the top of the stairs when something occurs to me, and I make my way back down and over to the counter.

"Do you have any touch-up paint for the walls?"

"Touch-up paint? What for?"

"It's nothing to be concerned about, we just found a spot on the wall that might have a latent print."

"A latent print?"

"A fingerprint—from our suspect. The only problem is that no matter how we try to recover it, we could end up with a small mess on the wall. We can't use dusting powder—the stuff you see on TV—because the print is too old; there's nothing left for it to stick to. Special Agent Donovan is going to try silver nitrate, which reacts with the chloride in salt molecules left behind in print residue, even if those prints are really old and dried out. The chemical reaction creates silver chloride, which, when exposed to ultraviolet light, turns black or brown."

Angela has a confused look on her face.

"The bottom line," I say hurriedly, "is that you're going to have a small stain on the wall, possibly one that won't come off easily, if at all."

She still looks confused. Her mouth is half open, like she wants to say something, but has no idea what it is.

"I really don't want to waste time getting a warrant," I add in a congenial tone, planting the seed that we're going to get this print one way or another. "Since you're our new best friend, I just thought, you know . . ." I shrug, giving her a big grin, which she can't help returning.

"How big of a stain are we talking about?"

I hold up my index fingers and leave a three-inch-gap between them.

Angela sighs and waves away any concern. "I'll just hang a picture over it."

"Thanks, Angela," I say, flashing my best smile. "You're a peach."

You're a peach?

I don't know why I said that, except it sounds like something southern folks would say. Angela doesn't seem offended and she's still smiling at me as I make my way up the stairs, so maybe I got it right. Either that or she's wondering what kind of citified Yankee idget is messing up her motel.

I set Jimmy's bag on the carpet and dig out the UV light, along with an eight-ounce clear plastic spray bottle with 3% written in black marker on the side: it contains silver nitrate diluted down to a 3 percent solution using distilled water.

Since the shine shows me exactly where any possible prints might be, I get the honor of spraying the handprint. Once that's completed, we unfold a metal stand and attach the UV light so that it's about a foot away from the wall.

Now we wait for the silver nitrate to do its job. It could be ten or twenty minutes; it could be as much as an hour. Jimmy flips on the TV and clicks through a couple dozen channels before turning it off again.

"Three hundred channels and nothing worth watching," I say.

"Mmm."

I mention Angela's hesitant cooperation to Jimmy so

he can heap on some praise when we leave. And from there we end up talking about investigative procedures, forensics, and detective work in general.

Fifteen minutes into our science experiment the chemicals finish processing, and the faint outline of a hand appears on the wall. Jimmy moves in with a jeweler's lens and studies the fingertips one by one.

After a minute, his arm drops to his side. "Nothing," he says, defeated. "The walls must have been wiped down or washed at some point. There's barely anything left of the print."

It's a hard blow.

We tear down the UV light stand and pack everything back up. Just like that, the long grind falls on its face and breaks into a thousand pieces. I feel sick to my stomach, like someone just gut-punched me.

Back in the lobby, we return the key to Angela and share our disappointing results. "Thanks," Jimmy says in a deflated voice. He hands her his card. "You've been great." The words are flat, hollow, lifeless. "If you think of anything, can you please give me a call?"

She nods, her lips pressed tightly together as if she can feel our pain . . . which would be impossible, since her backside wasn't planted in a car seat for the last two days scouring hotels, motels, and rest stops from morning till night.

Jimmy's go-bag is dangling limply from his right hand as we exit the inn and meander toward the car.

"Hey, we got something," I say, searching for the bright side.

"Yeah, what's that?"

"Initials. *TW* and *IW*—it's more than we had before.

Maybe Diane can cross-reference some databases, align some satellites; you know, do her thing. Plus we have the cryptic 'two feet too late' message."

"Another needle in a haystack of needles," Jimmy replies.

He's right, of course. The ugly reality is that we failed; the long grind failed. We may have found where IBK stayed after dumping the body in Baton Rouge, but with no prints and no name we've gained little to nothing.

We're going home empty-handed . . . and Diane's going to give us an earful that'll make waterboarding look like a pleasant distraction.

Jimmy throws his bag into the back none too gently, and then slides into the driver's seat and fires up the beast. He's just backing out when the front door of the Southern Cross flies open and Angela races after us, waving a piece of paper in the air.

"I found it," she pants when Jimmy rolls down the window. She thrusts a piece of paper through the opening, and then points at the bottom right-hand corner. "I was thinking about your Mr. Wilson, and I suddenly remembered that when he checked in, he wrote down his license number wrong. We check the plates in our parking lot every couple hours," she explains. "There's limited parking downtown, and we get customers from other businesses parking here all the time; it's a constant battle. I did a lot check shortly after he arrived, so I remembered what his car looked like—only, his plate wasn't on my list. I figured he might have written down a plate from one of his other cars by mistake, so I just added it to my list and wrote it on his registration form when I came back in." She holds up the form, IBK's form, and points to the scratched-out 2FT2L8 in the bottom corner. Next to it is a standard seven-digit Texas plate number.

"So this is his real plate number?"

Angela's half smile is hopeful. "Does that help?"

"Oh, Angela," Jimmy purrs, "I could just kiss you." Her cheeks light up red and she tries to contain her blossoming smile, but fails.

Tony picks up the phone on the first ring, and when asked to run the plate, he doesn't question the why or how of it. He just reads the number back, and when Jimmy confirms it, he says, "Let me call dispatch. I'll have a name and address for you in a couple minutes."

But a few minutes pass, and then a few more. When Jimmy's phone finally chimes, it's not a call, but a text. He slides his finger across the screen and the message materializes: *Slight delay. Complicated.*

"What's that supposed to mean?" I ask.

Jimmy shrugs resignedly. "Just another roadblock."

The next fifteen minutes are agonizing. By the time the phone rings, Jimmy and I are so on edge that we flinch involuntarily.

"Tony? What's up?" Jimmy puts the phone on speaker.

"Ran into a little hiccup, but before you get your shorts all wadded up, I got it sorted out—you're welcome, and you can buy me a beer. The plate comes back to a rental, a white Ford Fusion. Normally we'd have to find a judge, get a warrant, blah, blah, blah, but fortunately for you I just so happen to have a contact at the rental agency. I made a call, then my contact made a call, and we got an answer. You ready for this? The guy's name is Isaiah Webster, thirty-four years old according to his New Mexico license, and he lives in Albuquerque."

Bam! That's how it happens.

If someone were to ask me how Jimmy and I solve homicides, I'd have to paraphrase Hemingway and say, *Two ways: gradually, and then all of a sudden.*

"Albuquerque," I hiss at Jimmy, nudging his shoulder.

He waves at me like I'm some kind of mosquito.

"Do you have an address?"

Tony rattles off an address on Carlisle Boulevard Southeast and then pauses so Jimmy has time to scribble it down. "I already ran this guy, Jimmy. He's about as clean as they come. I couldn't even find a parking ticket. You sure he's the one?"

"Pretty sure," Jimmy says, giving me a look.

"What's your next move?"

Jimmy gives a one-word reply: "Albuquerque."

CHAPTER TWENTY-TWO

Brookshire, Texas—September 13, 12:17 P.M.

Brookshire.

We're right back where we started this morning.

It's actually a bit of luck. We thought we'd have to drive all the way to Houston to meet up with Les and Marty, but, as it turns out, Brookshire plays host to the Houston Executive Airport, which has a runway just long enough to accommodate a Gulfstream G100.

It's only a twenty-five-minute drive from the motel in Sealy to the airport, so we arrive well ahead of Betsy and crew, which gives us time to place calls and prepare for whatever awaits us in Albuquerque. Jimmy's on the phone with a contact at Albuquerque PD. Words like "SWAT" and "surveillance" are being tossed around like dough in a New York pizza parlor.

It's safe to assume that APD will have surveillance on the house within the hour; probably a couple scruffy-looking detectives in doper cars, courtesy of some flavor of local drug task force. In my experience with agencies all across the country, drug and vice detectives are almost always the best surveillance option. They have cultivated looks that range from Mr. Goodtime, to neo-homeless, to hard-core tweaker; whatever fits the particular bill.

I've been trying to get through to Diane for the last twenty minutes with no luck. She's not answering the office phone or her cell, which is unusual for her. I'm calling every minute now; first the office, then her cell, then the office again.

This time I hear a click.

"Diane?" I say as soon as the phone picks up. "Diane?"

"'Es," a voice says, sounding similar to Diane, but only if you stuffed a sock in her mouth.

"Diane?"

"'*Es!*" The voice is impatient this time, making it sound even more like Diane.

"What are you doing?"

"Eadding."

"Eating?"

"'Es."

"Do you want me to wait until you finish chewing?"

"'Es."

Diane chews while I wait. She chews and chews and chews, until I start to imagine that she's the reincarnation of Horace Fletcher, the Great Masticator, who used to chew each mouthful a hundred times and attributed his health and long life to the practice.

"Better?" I say when she finally swallows.

"Mm-hmm," she replies. Only Diane can make *Mm-hmm* sound sarcastic.

"Was that the entire elephant, or just one of the legs?"

"It was a blueberry-and-cream-cheese bear claw."

"It took you that long to chew a pastry?"

"Do you want an update or not?"

"Please."

I hear papers shuffle and the tapping of a keyboard. "Isaiah Webster," she begins, "is *not* a likely serial killer. You two better be sure of this before you proceed. The guy has a top-secret security clearance with a special background investigation and higher access than I have."

"Top-secret clearance? Who's he work for?"

"He *was* a cybersecurity expert at the Cyber Engineering Research Laboratory. I've never heard of it, but it's part of Sandia National Laboratories."

"You said he *was*?"

"Yeah, he worked there for a couple years, plus another nine years for Sandia National Lab before that. He was friends with everyone he worked with, and even went on vacations with some of them from time to time. Then, in February, he just up and quits. He hands in his resignation, empties his desk, and no one has seen him since. Bottom line: they don't know where he is."

"Is he still in Albuquerque, at least?"

"I don't know yet. I'm working on it. That address you got from Tony is iffy, though, so before you go storming in there with SWAT, I suggest a knock-and-talk."

"Iffy in what way?"

"It may have been his boyhood home. I found records

linking him to that address all the way back to his college years. It's now owned by a Lisa Webster, but Isaiah used to have an ownership stake. He granted a quit-claim deed about seven years ago and gave it all to Lisa."

"Ex-wife, maybe?"

"I don't think so. It looks like they inherited the house jointly from Martha Webster in 2006. I think she must have been their mother, which makes Lisa Isaiah's sister. Also, the county assessor shows that Isaiah owned a home not far from his work, only it went up for sale in mid-February and sold in April, which puts us back where we started."

"What's his boss's name at the cyber lab—whatever you called it?"

"Ross Feldman, and it's the Cyber Engineering Research Laboratory. He's expecting you at four."

"They're open on a Saturday?"

"He said they operate twenty-four/seven. Try not to upset them. From what I hear, these guys can hack your bank account, quadruple your mortgage, and wipe out your retirement account just for fun."

"I'll try not to insult them."

"Mm-hmm."

Sandia Science & Technology Park—September 13, 3:47 P.M.

The front of the building stretches the length of the sidewalk, with the main entrance off-center and with a slightly higher roofline that jumps up in two steps. The left and right wings are of earthen red, with the entrance a darker blue, flanked by tan. Trees line the street on both sides, and an abundance of indigenous bushes and plants populate the immaculate landscaping. To the northeast, a low desert mountain rises from the horizon.

All around the facility, on the sidewalks, in the parking lot, and in the street, is the presence of ice-blue shine, IBK's shine, folded and woven through other shine and stacked in impossibly thin layers.

It is the accumulated sum from years of passage.

Things aren't looking good for Isaiah.

We park on the side of the building and make our way along the sidewalk to the entrance, which has CERL in large letters overhead, and CYBER ENGINEERING RESEARCH LABORATORY in bold, raised letters underneath.

Jimmy badges the kid at the front window. A call is made, and a minute later we're being escorted down a maze of halls, right, then left, then right again, until our guide stops at an office door and leans his head inside. "Yo, Ross, your visitors are here."

I learned a long time ago not to stereotype jobs to specific types of people. I say I *learned* this; I didn't, however, say that I properly embraced this knowledge. Ross Feldman is a good example of why stereotyping doesn't work.

Generally speaking, those who work in the computer sciences readily refer to themselves as geeks; they're actually proud of the label. It wasn't long ago that the term implied pocket protectors, thick glasses, mismatched clothing, and repressed social skills.

Things have changed.

These days, computer repair companies even use "geek" in their name to stress their level of competence. Diane's a computer geek, my brother Jens is a computer geek, Dex is a computer geek.

Ross Feldman doesn't look like a computer geek.

He's a fisherman, or a grounded, alcoholic crop duster.

Maybe he's just a well-groomed vagabond.

He's at least six-two, and two hundred and fifty pounds. His brown hair reminds me a bit of that famous Einstein poster, the one that looks like the mega-genius just crawled out of bed after a rough night with some tasty equations.

"Hi, I'm Ross," the big guy says, coming around the desk and thrusting a hand at us. His voice is higher-pitched than I would have imagined. It doesn't seem to fit his body.

"Special Agent James Donovan," my partner says. "This is Operations Specialist Magnus Craig." I take his hand and give it the obligatory two pumps. "We need to find Isaiah Webster," Jimmy continues, not wasting any time. "I know he doesn't work here anymore, but we were hoping you could tell us where he might be."

"I wish I knew," Ross replies earnestly. "Truth is, he left in such a hurry it caught us all by surprise."

The tech manager's office is elevated above the others, and the back and side walls are all glass, giving him a clear view of the workstations and employees he supervises. He waves his arm past the field of glass. "Most of us here are more than just coworkers—we're like family; that includes Isaiah. Frankly, we've been worried about him."

"When was the last time you heard from him?"

"July. Every year we all get together for the Fourth, kind of a blowout celebration, you know? I pestered Lisa—that's his sister—until Isaiah finally returned my call."

"Did he say where he was or what he was doing?"

"No. It was an odd conversation, lots of awkward silence, like we hadn't been the closest of friends for the last eleven years." He shakes his head. "I talked to Lisa afterwards and she just started crying. She *did* tell me that he's living somewhere near Deming, New Mexico, and doing work as an independent contractor—mostly SQL programming and website development, which is like taking a skilled heavy equipment operator out of his excavator and handing him a shovel."

"So he's good at what he does?"

"One of the best," Ross replies. "But he's that way about everything. You know the type: they get interested in something and so they read up on the subject and practice until they've perfected every aspect. That's Isaiah. After Tracy's accident, he got heavily into prosthetics, mostly experimenting with new designs using CAD."

"Accident?" Jimmy says.

"Who's Tracy?" I ask.

Ross looks from Jimmy to me and then back to Jimmy. "Tracy's accident . . . that's his wife—*was* his wife," he quickly corrects. "Sorry, I thought you knew. It was in his last clearance review."

"We haven't seen any of his clearance paperwork," I say.

Ross looks confused. "I thought you were here to

read him out of his special projects and close out his clearance."

"No," Jimmy says. "We're here on a different matter."

"Which is?"

Jimmy shakes his head. "Sorry. Need-to-know." He gives Ross a moment, and then continues. "Can you tell us about the accident?"

The supervisor studies us, unsure of what to make of our presence, but after a moment his face softens. "Yeah, sure," he says, "why not?" He motions us to a pair of chairs on the other side of his desk.

Returning to his own seat, he swivels to face us. "Most of those working here knew each other before the Cyber Engineering Research Lab was established. Isaiah and I worked together for Sandia National Labs for about eleven years. Same with Scott and Hoover." He points to a large shared cubicle off to the right.

"Others, like Oscar and Pip, joined us later." He pauses, as if a deep pain were slowly working its way up from his stomach, only to settle in his chest, pressing and gripping. "It was about nine years ago. Isaiah was working late—we all were. I don't even remember why. Seems there was always something. Anyway, Tracy made up some sandwiches and brownies and dropped them off for us around nine.

"About twenty-five minutes later Isaiah got a call. He was panicked when he got off the phone; his face was white, his hands were trembling. He told us that some drunk driver in a pickup truck crossed the centerline and hit Tracy's car head-on. It's not even the cops or paramedics that called, but Isaiah's sister. Lisa's an emergency room nurse at the hospital, and one of the responding paramedics recognized Tracy's name and gave her a call.

"Well, Isaiah was in no state to drive, so Scott and Pip and I loaded him into my car and started for the hospital, only it turns out she wasn't at the hospital yet. We came upon the crash a few miles away. We could hear her screaming as soon as we got out of the car. Her legs"—he motions toward his own legs—"were pinned under the dash. The force of the collision was so strong that the engine was pushed partway into the passenger compartment, crushing her feet, and, and . . ."

Ross falls quiet for a long moment; when he looks up, his eyes are wet glass. "They had to amputate both her feet—right there in front of us."

The words land like a slap to the face.

They had to amputate both her feet.

Jimmy and I exchange a piercing look.

"They were mangled and crushed beyond saving," Ross continues, "and it was the only way to get her out of the car. If they were going to save her, they needed to get her to the hospital." He dabs at the corner of his eye, wiping away the memory. "Tracy was in and out of surgery for a month. In addition to losing both feet and facing a future with prosthetics, she had seven broken bones, and her face was disfigured and heavily scarred when the airbag deployed incorrectly—some factory glitch."

Tears are openly streaming down Ross's face, but he continues. "Even after the wounds healed, she was in constant pain; doctors couldn't figure out why. In the end, it was all too much for her. Eight months after the accident, she killed herself."

He pulls a tissue from the box in his second drawer and wipes his face.

"I'm sorry," Jimmy says in a quiet voice.

Ross nods and stares at his desk, composing himself.

"Do you believe in soul mates?" he eventually asks. "My wife does. She's pretty adamant that we each have a single soul mate and that fate or God or just circumstance will always allow the paths of soul mates to cross; giving them the opportunity to meet."

He wipes at his eyes again, and then chuckles. "She gets so mad at me when I suggest that if I hadn't moved to Albuquerque twenty years ago—when our paths crossed—that I would have met a different soul mate back home in Sacramento." He forces a smile. "I have a little fun with her now and then; see if I can get her spun up."

He looks at me, then at Jimmy, and then brushes the words from the room with a wave of his hand. "My point is that with Isaiah and Tracy you could believe the idea of soul mates." His demeanor shifts and I notice he's staring at a small crystal cat resting at the corner of his desk.

"After . . . he was never the same without Tracy. We tried getting him out and involved—all of us." He waves a hand to encompass the entire office and the dozen or so employees at their various workstations. "We managed to get him out on a few unofficial double dates, stuff like that, but nothing made a difference. It was the same Isaiah, but the spark was gone."

Ross shifts forward in his seat and lowers his voice. "It's like he went cold inside. It didn't happen all at once, but over years. Like his emotions—love, hate, fear, sympathy, all of them—were a fire slowly dying, if that makes sense."

It does make sense; perfect sense, I think.

How else could he have done the things he's done, carve up humans like a butcher takes to a cow? He had to kill off his soul first; empty his emotions and turn himself into a sociopath.

"What happened in February?" Jimmy asks. "What set him off?"

"Bill Blevins, that's what happened," Ross practically spits.

"Bill Blevins?"

"The drunkard who hit Tracy." The words force themselves through a cage of teeth. "One day Isaiah storms in absolutely furious; I mean, it was scary. I've never seen him like that. We only got bits and pieces out of him before he up and leaves for the day, but we found out that afternoon that Blevins was in another drunken accident. This time he killed an eight-year-old boy who was crossing the road at a marked intersection with his mother. The mom barely survived—and then she probably wished she hadn't.

"Next day, Isaiah came back to work like nothing happened. We tried talking to him about it, but he refused to discuss it. He was completely different from the day before, like a switch had been flipped. There was no emotion in his words, and his eyes—you know how they say that a shark has dead eyes? Well, that's what I thought of when I made eye contact with Isaiah that morning."

"How soon after did he quit?" I ask.

"About two weeks later. Blevins had a bail-reduction

hearing a week after the accident, and got his bail dropped from a million to a hundred thousand, which he was somehow able to raise. When Isaiah heard about it he didn't even react, he just nodded, like he expected it."

Ross shrugs. "Maybe he knew. Suppose it doesn't matter now, either way. The bail hearing was on a Friday, and it was the very next Friday that Isaiah came into my office and handed me his prox badge. I tried talking him out of it, but he seemed set on whatever course he was on."

As he says these final words, Ross's face twinges, suddenly fearful. He looks at Jimmy and then at me with a certain foreboding in his eyes. "I don't suppose you can tell me why the FBI is interested in Isaiah?"

Jimmy hesitates.

"He sounds like a good man," I say.

"He is. One of the best."

I nod and give him a reassuring smile. Then something occurs to me. "Did he ever live in Baton Rouge?"

Ross seems startled. "Yeah, right after he and Tracy got married—before I even met them. He wrote code for a small software company right out of college; it was only for a year or so, then he and Tracy moved back to Albuquerque."

"Any particular reason they moved back?"

"I don't remember them ever saying, but I suspect they probably missed the place. Isaiah didn't have any trouble getting hired on by the labs. In fact, I was on his oral board, and I liked him right away. He was smart beyond measure, and that's saying something in this line of work. As for Tracy, she ended up working for the Bernalillo County Library System. She worked part-time at a library in Baton Rouge, and just loved being around books."

"The library in Baton Rouge," I ask, "was it by a swamp?"

"Oh, I don't recall," Ross says.

Jimmy has a few more questions, and when we're sure there's nothing else Ross can add, he escorts us to the entrance and we shake hands all the way around.

"Talk to Lisa," he says adamantly. "She and Isaiah have always been close. If anyone knows where he is, it'll be her."

When we reach the door, Ross calls after us: "Agents!" His tone is sharp, but you can hear the pinpricks of pain ebbing back into his voice. When we turn, he says just three words: "He needs help." Without waiting for a response, Ross Feldman enters the door behind him and disappears into the heart of the high-security facility.

We don't reach the sidewalk before Jimmy has Diane on the phone. "Yeah, Blevins," he repeats. "B-L-E-V-I-N-S; first of William. He would have been arrested for vehicular homicide earlier this year, but the incident I'm interested in is a vehicular assault about nine years ago." He listens a moment. "Yes, Albuquerque. Both of them. At the very least I need a current address for Blevins. Do your magic."

As he's about to hang up, another thought comes to him. "Diane, find out who his attorney was in the vehicular assault. . . . Right. . . . No, that'll be perfect."

"Smart," I say as he slides the phone into his pocket.

"What's smart?"

"Asking about the attorney," I reply. "Isaiah blames them almost as much as the suspects. Maybe he'll get tired of just sending gift boxes."

Jimmy's staring at me with an odd expression.

"What?" I say defensively—he can be unnerving sometimes.

"You called him Isaiah, not IBK."

"It doesn't feel right anymore." My words are quiet, reserved. "Main Vein, Proctor, Sad Face, the others; they were monsters; they didn't deserve the dignity of their real names. Isaiah's not like them."

"Have you forgotten what he did to his victims?"

"No, I remember, but people break. What would you or I do if something happened to Heather, Jane, or Pete?" This seems to knock him back a step, and he doesn't say anything until we're both inside the car and buckled up.

"I wouldn't end up like Isaiah," he finally says.

I look him straight in the eye. "Are you sure?"

CHAPTER TWENTY-THREE

Nob Hill, Albuquerque—September 13, 5:32 P.M.

Isaiah Webster wasn't always a serial killer.

Once, not long ago, he was a husband, a son, a brother. He was a successful and skilled cybersecurity expert with a security clearance reserved for only the most trusted, or perhaps just the least corruptible.

Isaiah went to college, took his studies seriously, stayed away from the pitfalls of drugs and excessive alcohol, and married his true love. Isaiah was the architect of all the great things in his life, and none of the bad.

A drunk driver took it all away in a moment.

Isaiah Webster wasn't always a serial killer.

The Nob Hill area of Albuquerque is near the city's center and serves itself up as an eclectic area of shopping and nightlife with nothing less than historic Route 66, the Mother Road, running through the heart of it.

The aging Craftsman-style home on Carlisle Boulevard Southeast, just blocks south of Route 66, still sports the faded earth tones from a paint job with too many years behind it. Despite the deplorable paint, the home itself is in immaculate condition, as is the cubistic landscaping.

Ross Feldman said that Lisa Webster is an RN at Lovelace Westside Hospital; more importantly, she's an emergency room nurse. That generally means that she's going to be logical and pragmatic . . . and she's going to want answers.

Answers we can't give, or don't have.

Jimmy parks on the street and I slip my lead-crystal glasses off as I exit the passenger side. The home is awash in ice blue, breathtakingly so. Not just decade-old shine like I saw at the library in Baton Rouge and the Southern Cross in Sealy. No. This shine is much older, stretching back to Isaiah's youth. I see it on the roof, around the vegetation, brushing against the side of the house, and ensconced in the very soil.

Here he played.

Here he grew up.

I'm still entranced by the blue neon glow as Jimmy makes his way to the front porch and presses the doorbell. A white screen door with five vertical bars on the lower portion is all that stands between us and the interior of the house, and the pleasant door chime that drifts out to us.

"Just a minute," a voice calls from within.

Moments later, a woman comes around the corner,

still teasing her hair with a brush as she prepares either for work or a night on the town—it's hard to tell which, since she's wearing the pants from her hospital scrubs, topped off by a white chiffon blouse.

She slows when she sees us, and it's clear she was expecting someone else.

"Ms. Webster," Jimmy says, pulling out his badge, "I'm Special Agent James Donovan; this is my partner, Operations Specialist Magnus Craig. You *are* Lisa Webster, aren't you?"

"Yes," she says hesitantly, and then her tone becomes inquisitive. "Can I help you with something?"

"We have some questions about Isaiah, if you can spare ten or fifteen minutes. It's important."

She nods skeptically. "It usually is." She takes a good look at Jimmy's badge, then at Jimmy, then at me. Pushing the screen door open, she waves us in and guides us to the small and sparsely furnished living room. There's no couch, just the recliner that Lisa sinks into, and an old floral-pattern love seat which Jimmy and I end up sharing.

We're so close the smartphone in his pocket is jabbing me in the leg.

"If this is about his clearance update, you should know that he doesn't work at CERL anymore," Lisa begins.

Isaiah's shine is so thick in the house that it's almost overwhelming, like someone painted it on the floor in broad strokes. What I notice in the living room, however, isn't on the floor or the walls. It's on the ceiling: two handprints with the thumb tips touching and the fingers splayed out like wings—a bird in flight.

They're not adult hands; Isaiah would have been maybe nine or ten when he made them. How he reached the ceiling . . . well, that'll have to remain a mystery.

"We're not here about his clearance," Jimmy replies. "We just need to talk to Isaiah about some work he's been involved with." *It's not exactly a lie, but it's not exactly the truth either.* "Do you happen to know where Isaiah is living these days? I understand he sold his house a few months ago, but we weren't able to locate an updated address on him."

Lisa shakes her head. "I have his P.O. box in Deming, that's about all. He moved down there in March, before his house even sold. I offered to help him move, but he refused. And when I asked for the house address, he gave me the post office box number and some excuse about the house being too difficult to find."

"So you haven't been to his new place at all?"

"No," she replies. "Sorry. I figured he just needed a little space, so I gave it to him, but I don't know how much longer I can keep at it." She pulls her long brunette hair over her right shoulder and begins to run her fingers slowly through the silky strands as her eyes drift slowly away from Jimmy and find me watching her. The way she plays with her hair is silently seductive, though probably not a conscious move on her part. Still, it pulls the eyes in and teases the mind.

At Jimmy's prompting, Lisa retrieves a pen and writes the P.O. box number on a scrap of paper. When she finishes, she hands it to him and he slides it into his shirt pocket.

"Where, exactly, is Deming?" I ask.

"It's a three-and-a-half-hour drive south of here," she

replies. "Just hop on I-25 and follow it south to Hatch. Then you want to get on State Route 26 westbound. Deming's hard to miss. There's not much out that way."

"Do you have *any* idea why he moved there?"

"I've been asking myself that for months," Lisa replies. "Isaiah's had a rough time of it since Bill Blevins killed that little boy in February. I'm just trying to be there for him as much as possible, but he keeps pushing me away. I only hear from him once or twice a week, and only when he calls me. All my calls to him go straight to voice mail. He's got me worried."

"How so?" Jimmy says.

She shrugs, and in doing so the mask of confidence she's been wearing since we arrived begins to slip, revealing a sliver of fear underneath. "It's nothing," she says quickly.

"He hasn't been himself, has he?"

Her face melts and she almost goes to tears. "No," she replies, and then the words come fast. "I've never seen him like this; not after Tracy died; not after Mom died. He tries to pretend that everything's all right, but I know it isn't—is it?"

Jimmy and I exchange a glance, and as if by some unspoken agreement, I'm the one who delivers the bad news. "He may be going after Bill Blevins." I don't mention the other three victims; she'll hear about them soon enough.

"To hurt him?"

"To kill him."

She shakes her head firmly. "No, you don't know him. Isaiah couldn't do that; it's not in him."

"You'd be surprised what perfectly normal people are

capable of, Ms. Webster," Jimmy says. "We all have our breaking point. Some tune out and disconnect from society, like Isaiah. Some turn to drugs or alcohol. Others turn mean or even violent; still others snap completely and stare at a wall all day. I've seen every manner of mental break in my time with the Bureau, and nothing surprises me anymore."

Lisa props her right elbow on the side of the recliner and rests her forehead in her hand. The soft sounds of tears—the sniffling, the bubbling—issue from her bowed head and we let her digest the information uninterrupted. As hard as it is delivering such news, it's even harder receiving it.

A box of tissues sits on the end table next to me, so I rise, pull two of the tissues from the box, and hand them to Lisa. She stares at them for a moment, as if she doesn't recognize them, and then takes them into her hand and dabs at her eyes.

When she finally speaks again, her head is still bowed and her words are monotone. "I was the one who found her, you know," she says.

Jimmy and I remain silent.

"We were supposed to go out for breakfast. She didn't want to, of course, but I was the pushy sister-in-law. I was always forcing her to go to the mall, the grocery store, even the pub down the street, anything to get her out in public so she could get over the fear of wearing her new feet around others."

Lisa pauses and dabs at her eyes. "Maybe I pushed too hard. She hated those prosthetics, like somehow they made her less of a person."

She looks up now, her eyes red. "I told her how brave

she was, every day—I told her, and I meant it. To endure what she had and to come out the other side; to have to learn to walk all over again using different feet—it's superhuman. It's remarkable and honorable and noble . . . but it wasn't enough."

Lisa falls quiet.

The house, too, lies silent, save for the faint murmur of street noise outside. I can hear the steady ticking of a clock from the kitchen.

"When I got to the house that morning," she continues, "I let myself in, as always. I called out to her and she didn't answer, so I just figured she was in the bathroom or still getting ready in the bedroom.

"I rinsed off the dishes in the sink and put them in the dishwasher while I waited, and then emptied the trash. There was still no sign of her, so I called out again and went to see if she needed any help. I cut through the dining room to get to the back hall and that's when I saw her."

She gasps involuntarily, and then forces herself to inhale deeply.

"I'd been in the kitchen cleaning dishes . . . like an idiot . . . when the whole time she was dead on the other side of the wall . . . fifteen feet away." Lisa visibly shivers, almost convulsively. Tears begin to stream down her face as she continues.

"She was just sitting there with her head on the table, her eyes closed, like she was sleeping. And at first, that's what I told myself—but I knew.

"Then I saw the blood." She blinks hard and covers her mouth. "She had slit her wrists all the way up the forearm and her hands were resting inside a cooler between her legs. I suppose she did that so blood wouldn't get all over the carpet—and not a single drop did. She wouldn't have wanted to make a mess."

Jimmy's posture changes at the same moment as mine, both reactions cued by a single word: cooler.

He clears his throat and in the most gentle of voices asks, "What kind of cooler?"

Lisa looks up, puzzled, or perhaps just caught off guard by the odd question. "It was one of those disposable white Styrofoam coolers you get at the convenience store for a couple bucks." She expels a series of involuntary sobs, but then grows angry with herself over the outburst. She balls her fingers into tight fists and holds them against her stomach. When she speaks again, her voice is flat and eerily low, each word controlled absolutely. "Do you know what she did with those prosthetic feet she hated so much? She put them inside the cooler; she bled all over them."

The Styrofoam ice box!

The feet!

He's doing it for Tracy. He's doing all of it for her.

As Lisa finishes, her face falls into both hands and she weeps loudly and uncontrollably for a long while. Jimmy moves over to the chair and stands next to her, his arm across her shoulder, silent, but present.

How do you console what is inconsolable?

It's well after six when we leave Lisa to the spoiled squalor of a ruined evening, with worries for a brother whose soul has drifted far from shore. She still doesn't know anything, but she suspects much, and fears the worst. We promised we'd do everything in our power to help Isaiah, but I don't know if that's a promise he'll let us keep.

Right now we're still not sure where he is. We think Deming, but, honestly, he could be anywhere. He could be parked down the street or a thousand miles away in Baton Rouge.

Jimmy calls Diane and puts her on speaker as we pull away from Lisa's quaint home and park at a convenience store two blocks away.

"Apartment 202," Diane clarifies after rattling off an address on Chestnut Street. She sounds as tired as I feel, and the sarcasm we know and love is lacking from her weary words. "It's Blevins's last known address."

"Thanks, Diane," Jimmy says. "We'll head there—"

"You won't find him," she interrupts. "He's been gone a while. He posted bail on February eleventh, and then picked up a felony warrant after he failed to appear on the vehicular homicide charges. Albuquerque PD has checked the apartment a dozen times looking to arrest him, but it's like he dropped off the face of the earth."

"Or someone *else* dropped him off the face of the earth," I say under my breath.

"I talked to Detective Susan Rigo," Diane continues. "She's lead detective on the vehicular homicide and says that no one has seen him at the complex since February."

"They could be covering for him."

"That's what she thought, so she stuck a paper clip between the door and the frame to see if anyone was coming and going, and it stayed in place for a month, until she removed it. It was enough to convince her. She thinks he's on the run, maybe Mexico."

"When did she start looking for him?" Jimmy asks.

"It wasn't until after he missed his court date on April ninth, but she said there were rumblings before that. His attorney tried reporting him missing in March after not hearing from him since his release."

Jimmy perks up at the mention. "Speaking of attorneys . . ."

"The attorney from the Webster accident is Paul Anderson," Diane says. "He's a condescending, uptight . . ." She pauses. "He's difficult. I also found out that he got Blevins off on a technicality after the accident with Tracy Webster. The Breathalyzer hadn't been calibrated recently, there was a problem with the blood sample, the usual. Anyway, he said he hasn't dealt with or talked to Blevins in years, and wouldn't tell me anything if he had. I tried to convince him to take on a security detail, but he wouldn't agree to any precautionary measures, not even an extra patrol in the neighborhood. 'It's not my first rodeo,' he told me," Diane says, putting on her best Southwest accent.

"What part of *severed feet* and *serial killer* didn't he get?" Jimmy utters in disbelief. "Did you explain to him that this is a very real threat; that his life might be in danger?"

"Till I was blue in the face," Diane replies.

"Maybe I should have a talk with him," Jimmy offers.

"I appreciate the offer," she says, "but the day I can't handle an uptight defense attorney is the day I turn in my resignation. Besides, I asked Rigo if she would have APD provide some extra patrol on the sly, and she's on top of it. They'll drive through the neighborhood every twenty or thirty minutes. That should provide a bit of deterrent."

"Good enough, I suppose," Jimmy replies. "Steps and I will go check out Bill Blevins's apartment, see if there's anything worth seeing."

"I told you, it's empty. He's not there."

"Yeah, I know you did," Jimmy replies, and then terminates the call.

We sit in the idling car for a full minute, both of us staring out the front windshield in silence. Jimmy has both hands on the wheel and he's slowly twisting them up and then down as he thinks about Isaiah, Blevins, and Tracy.

"Blevins's apartment?" I say after another minute passes and the fading sun begins to threaten the long horizon.

Jimmy nods—just nods, and then slips the car into gear.

The sky is hazy gray, and quickly surrendering to the dark shades of dusk, by the time we reach the dumpy apartment complex on Chestnut Street. At first glance, it looks like an old two-story motel with the rooms opening onto outdoor walkways and stairs all the way around. There's even a swimming pool, but it stands empty and neglected. If ever it was a motel, those days are gone. The rooms now rent by the week and the month.

As we start up the stairs to room 202, a prostitute in her late teens brushes by us on the way down. We're not in uniform, we're not even dressed professionally, but somehow she makes us for law enforcement and says, "I didn't do nothing," as she averts her eyes and starts taking the steps two at a time, which is hard in heels.

There's a light on in 202, and the sounds from a TV issue through the door and wall, so Jimmy knocks; Jimmy knocks loudly. There's a scuffling inside, and then a face appears at the window, peeking through the curtain.

"What do you want?" the face demands.

Jimmy holds up his badge and does the usual introduction. "We're looking for William Blevins. We understand this is his apartment."

"Not no more," the face says. "This is *my* apartment. I moved in last month. Never heard of no William Blevins."

"Would you mind if we come inside and check for ourselves? It'll only take a moment, and then we'll be out of here."

"Get a warrant, bitch. This is my place." At that, the face disappears behind the curtain, and the TV gets cranked up to full volume.

Jimmy stares at the empty window.

I stare at the floor.

"Orange and silver," I say, holding my glasses in my hand.

"Huh?"

"Orange and silver." I repeat. Then, in almost a whisper, I say, "Your new best friend there, he's got orange and silver shine. He's not lying when he says he's only been here a month or so." I tilt my head down at the walkway. "I'm betting Blevins is more of a burgundy.

It's all over the ground, it's on the handrail; he probably lived here for a couple of years."

Jimmy sighs. "Still doesn't tell us where he is now."

"Wherever he is, he's dead," I say in an even quieter tone. "The shine is flat—no vibration. There's something . . . else."

"What?"

"Isaiah."

"He's been here?"

I nod and point at the transition at the base of the door. "His prints go right into the apartment and it's not just one visit. He was here again and again. The time frame matches up with his mental break."

"Dammit!" Jimmy presses his palms into his temples.

"Tssstt."

The sound comes from two doors down on the right, one of the apartments we passed on the way in. The door is ajar and a mid-forties Hispanic male with a beach-ball gut under his T-shirt is standing there waving us over. His eyes keep shifting around, making sure no one is watching. I imagine this is one of those neighborhoods where everyone hates cops until they need one.

"You guys looking for Bill?" he says under his breath as we draw near.

"Yeah, we are," Jimmy says. "Who are you?"

"Mexican Tom," the man says, extending a friendly hand.

"Mexican Tom?"

"Tommy Peralta," he clarifies. "But everyone here calls me Mexican Tom to avoid confusion on account of we have two other Toms. There's Fat Tom on the first floor near the front office"—I glance at Mexican Tom's stomach and wonder how he dodged that bullet—"and there's Rodeo Tom across the way over there." He points to the other side of the complex. "We call him Rodeo Tom 'cause of his hat."

"So . . . about Bill?"

"Yeah, APD was out here a couple times a week looking for him, but they stopped coming in June or July. I never said nothing to them 'cause I figured Bill was hiding somewhere, but it's been too long now. After they moved his stuff into storage it got me to thinking that maybe he was in trouble."

"Who moved his stuff?" I ask.

"I heard from Cheryl in two-oh-seven that they evicted him for nonpayment. They must've called his emergency contact to come get his crap. That's the best I can figure." He snaps his finger. "You should talk to Aaron; he's the manager. He would've been the one to make the call."

"How do we get hold of Aaron?" Jimmy asks.

Stepping around us, Mexican Tom leans out over the railing and points past the empty swimming pool to a room right next to the shuttered and locked front office. "That's his apartment there: room 101. It's the nicest one in the complex—least that's what everyone says. I've never been inside it myself."

We thank Tom and make our way down the stairs.

Aaron doesn't invite us in when he answers the door. In fact, he seems eager to get us away from his apartment, so eager that he's wearing nothing more than a pair of boxer shorts, a T-shirt, and some flip-flops as he leads us to the front office, jumbles through a weighty ring of keys, unlocks the door, and flips on the light.

"Bill Blevins," he mutters to himself. "Bill Blevins."

The computer is only in sleep mode, so in less than a minute we have the name of Bill's brother, Donnie Blevins, and his address. No warrant, no schmoozing, just *boom*: here you go. After writing the name and address on a slip of paper and shoving it into Jimmy's hand, Aaron practically shoos us away and then watches us from the office door, silhouetted by the light behind him.

We're almost to the car when a head pops through the door opening to room 101. "Aaron!" the girl calls. "Aaron?"

It's the prostitute we passed on the stairs. When she sees us, she quickly ducks back inside.

"Rent must be due," Jimmy says.

CHAPTER TWENTY-FOUR

Albuquerque, New Mexico—September 14, 8:17 A.M.

"It still doesn't make any sense," I say as Jimmy turns off Montgomery onto San Mateo Boulevard, and then starts scanning addresses for Donnie Blevins's residence. "They don't give out top-secret security clearances to defective people. How could Isaiah have gone so wrong?"

"Well, first off, *you* have a top-secret security clearance."

"What are you saying? That I'm defective?"

"You're afraid of trees."

"I'm afraid of forests, not trees. There's a difference."

"And Styrofoam."

"Go ahead, make fun. But just so you know, it's estimated that a quarter million people in the United States are afraid of Styrofoam."

"You looked it up?"

"Of course I did. And, for me, it's not really a phobia;

it's more of an intense dislike. Regardless, it doesn't answer my question. How does a guy like Isaiah—normal, hardworking, responsible, stable—suddenly turn into a psychopath? How's that even possible? And if it can happen to him, couldn't it happen to anyone?"

"Probably," Jimmy answers, which isn't reassuring.

"Probably? That's all you have to say?"

Jimmy shrugs. "All roads run straight . . . until they don't."

I push back in my seat and ponder the words. It's either the most brilliant answer ever given, or the stupidest thing I'll hear all day.

I'm undecided.

The dilapidated house on San Mateo Boulevard sits on a full basement that protrudes out of the ground to such an extent that you have to walk up a four-foot flight of wooden stairs to get to the front door. There's a raised deck along most of the front of the house, and it wraps around the right side, presumably to a much larger deck in back.

At some point in the distant past it was stained.

Now it's just weathered.

As we climb the stairs, someone peeks through the dirty white blinds covering the big window to our right and then quickly disappears. Before Jimmy has a chance to knock, there's a clamor inside, followed by the sound of a sliding glass door slamming open at the rear of the house.

"Runner," Jimmy calls out, and sprints across the deck and around to the back. An instant later there's a loud yelp—the sound an animal might make as a steel trap closes on its foot.

"To your left," I yell at Jimmy, pointing through the sparse trees behind the house.

Donnie Blevins has had better days.

He's limping badly as he tries to flee through the back of the property, but he's clearly in no shape to walk, let alone run. Jimmy catches up to him with his gun at the low-ready, while I circle around to the other side.

"Donnie?" Jimmy calls out.

"Yeah," the big guy answers in a defeated voice. He leans into a tree and tries to hold his left foot off the ground with limited success.

"Why'd you run?"

"You're here to arrest me, right?"

Jimmy doesn't answer, but tips his head toward Donnie's ankle. "How'd you hurt yourself?"

"Jumped from the back deck."

Jimmy nods. "I took the stairs."

"Yep. That would've been the smart thing to do."

"Can you lift up your shirt for me, Donnie? Show me you're not armed?"

He complies, wincing as he loses balance and has to catch himself on the wounded left ankle.

"Now the back," Jimmy says, circling around. "Okay. That's good. You're not going to give us any trouble, are you, Donnie?"

"No," the big guy groans. He's sweating profusely now, either from the pain, from the drugs in his system, or from the lack of drugs in his system.

After frisking him, Jimmy says, "I'm going to holster my gun, and then you and I are going to have a little talk." He slides the Glock semiautomatic back into its holster, and then studies Donnie a moment. "How bad is it?"

"Hurts a lot—feels like stuff is grinding together; I think I broke it."

"Okay, we better get it looked at." Jimmy dials 911 and requests an aid unit, then we help Donnie to the ground and prop his foot up. Response time is good, and within a few minutes three emergency medical technicians are huddled around Donnie examining the ankle. One of them comes over to give us the bad news.

"We need to transport," she says. "It doesn't look broken, but we need to get it X-rayed just to be sure."

Jimmy nods. "I guess we'll meet you at the hospital."

Donnie hears this and cries out, "Ah, hell, no! If you're not here to arrest me, what do you want?"

"We're looking for your brother," Jimmy shoots back.

"Haven't seen him."

"We thought as much. I understand you moved his belongings from his apartment into a storage unit?"

"Yeah, like three months ago— Ow! Easy, there," he snaps at one of the EMTs.

"Did you find anything unusual or odd? Anything missing?"

"I wouldn't know. I just took it all as is and threw it in a locker. Figured if he showed up again he could sort it out himself."

"You don't seem too concerned about his disappearance."

Donnie just shrugs, and the gesture says it all.

"We'd like to take a look at his stuff," Jimmy says, "see if we notice anything out of the ordinary. We're good at that type of thing. Any chance we could do that?"

Donnie digs in his right front pocket and pulls out a ring of keys. Peeling a small padlock key from the ring, he tosses it at Jimmy. "Merch Storage, just up the road," he says, bobbing his head toward San Mateo Boulevard. "Unit G27."

Jimmy gives him an appreciative smile. "We'll mail the key back to you."

"You can keep it, for all I care."

We're up the stairs and making our way around the deck to the front of the house when Donnie suddenly remembers himself and calls after us. I hear "thanks" and "broken ankle," but the rest of the words are lost in the distance between.

It's probably for the best.

His tone was anything but thankful.

Merch Storage—September 14, 9:46 A.M.

As the overhead door rattles up, the interior of the twenty-by-fifteen storage unit sees daylight for the first time in months. Stagnant air spills out as a gentle morning breeze pushes its way into the locker, rustling magazines, old mail, and miscellaneous paperwork left loose on an upright kitchen table.

"Is that . . ."

"Decomp," Jimmy finishes for me.

"It's not very strong; not strong enough for a body, right?"

Jimmy shakes his head, but he's hesitant. "Could just

be a rat or squirrel, something that crawled in through a vent in the roof."

"I don't see any rolled-up carpets," I say. It's meant as a joke, but I'm half serious.

"It's stronger farther in," Jimmy says after squeezing past some furniture. "Help me move some of this stuff out."

The back of the unit is packed tight, but it appears that the closer the movers got to the front of the unit, the less concerned they were about stacking and fitting. Perhaps they realized they would have enough room for the whole load and placing the boxes together like a well-cut puzzle was no longer necessary.

Perhaps they just got tired.

Jimmy and I are able to dig our way well into the unit simply by pulling out a few of the larger furniture pieces, beginning with the small kitchen table, and following up with a bedroom dresser, a recliner, a love seat, miscellaneous boxes of bedding and towels, and three kitchen chairs.

Everything we touch is covered in the dead shine from Blevins's apartment. The news doesn't faze Jimmy. "Any sign of IB—" He stops himself, and then says, "Any sign of Isaiah?"

But the ice-blue shine is conspicuously absent.

We shuffle boxes and furniture another fifteen minutes, and find ourselves past the halfway point with an increasingly high and tightly packed wall of boxes, crates, and bins before us.

Pausing for breath, Jimmy takes a seat on a plastic storage bin and wipes the sweat from this brow while I lean back against an upright dresser.

"Keep going or call it quits?" I say.

Jimmy doesn't answer right away, but sits silently, taking several deep breaths. At first I think he's winded from moving too many boxes, but then I realize he's sampling the air. I take a deep breath myself.

The smell of decomp *is* stronger.

"*Can't* be a body," I say. "We'd be gagging, even after three months. It's got to be a mouse or a rat."

"Could be a pair of feet," Jimmy offers.

Feet.

I hadn't thought of that.

"So . . . keep going," I surmise.

Jimmy nods, and pushes himself up.

"Help me with this," I say, slapping the top of the upright dresser. I grab the top edge and tip it down and to the side so Jimmy can grab it from the bottom. With cautious half steps we shuffle the heavy piece out of the unit and set it on the asphalt in front.

That's when I see the trunk.

It was behind the dresser, hidden from view the whole time. It's an eighty- or ninety-year-old steamer trunk with a small amount of ice-blue shine on the lid and clasp. Instantly a shiver runs down my spine and into my legs. I feel its tingle in my neck, my cheeks, my scalp.

"Jimmy," I hiss.

My tone tells him what.

My pointing finger tells him where.

Together we pull and yank the old trunk out from under the stacked remnants of Bill Blevins's unfortunate and destructive life. The job is made more difficult by the extreme weight of the trunk; it's certainly heavier than a pair of feet, or even a body.

Books, I tell myself. *It's just books.* But my inner voice lacks conviction.

"You want to open it?" I ask Jimmy.

"Not really. You?"

"Uh-uh," I say emphatically. "You're the special agent; I'm just your minion."

"You're the tracker. I thought I was *your* minion."

In the end we do it together.

Jimmy frees the locking clasp. We both take a deep breath. He lifts the lid from the right corner, while I lift from the left.

An instant later the lid falls closed with a heavy thud as Jimmy screams and we both scramble away from the trunk and out into the morning light. In hindsight, I suppose I was the one doing the screaming.

"Are you kidding me?" my partner yells into the cavernous mouth of the storage unit. "Are you kidding me?"

"Is that what I thought it was?" I say.

"Yeah, it's what you thought." Jimmy's already on the phone to Albuquerque dispatch. He relays the address and requests CSI, someone from the ME's office, a couple uniforms, and a detective or two.

Three minutes pass before we hear the first of the distant sirens. In the meantime, we keep our distance from the trunk.

The Office of the Medical Investigator, or OMI, is New Mexico's statewide medical examiner system, with specially trained investigators in every community ready to respond to sudden or unexplained deaths. If the investigation requires an autopsy, the body is transported to the University of New Mexico School of Medicine in Albuquerque, regardless of where the body was found.

Jessica Loomis and Matt Segershaw are the field deputy medical investigators, or FDMIs, dispatched by OMI to investigate the steamer trunk at Merch Storage. They arrive in a white OMI van at 11:32 A.M., by which time APD has the storage facility locked down tight.

Both of the detectives and several of the officers have gloved up and taken turns peeking into the trunk to confirm our findings. You can't blame their curiosity; it wouldn't be the first time something was called in that turned out to be a Halloween decoration.

After clearing a space on the asphalt outside and laying down a thick blue tarp, officers and detectives alternate pulling, lifting, and carrying—but mostly pulling—the heavy trunk out of the storage locker and onto the tarp.

Jessica Loomis lifts the lid and folds it all the way open, grimacing at the trunk's contents as she examines it from several angles. Looking up, her eyes glance around at the various crime scene faces before stopping on me and Jimmy. She waves us over.

"You the FBI?"

"How'd you know?" I reply.

She smiles. "You're the only faces I don't recognize." We make introductions and then she continues. "Can I ask what led you to this storage locker?"

I let Jimmy explain; he tends to be more concise.

"A serial killer?" Jessica says after he finishes. "Seriously?"

Jimmy gives a single, exaggerated nod.

"Well, that's something," she says, seemingly amused at the prospect.

"How are you going to handle this?" Jimmy asks.

"We'll do the extraction here—that's what the blue tarp is for. The trunk is just too heavy and awkward to load up and take to the lab in its current state."

"I was hoping you were going to say that. Would you mind if Steps and I observe the extraction?"

"Not at all—just don't touch anything."

With the lid of the steamer trunk open and exposed to the full light of the noon sun, the desiccated face is revealed, particularly where the lips have pulled back to reveal the gums and teeth. The mouth is agape, the eye sockets sunken.

The trunk is filled almost to the top with what initially appears to be white sand, but is quickly discovered to be a combination of salt and lime. All that is visible of Bill Blevins's corpse is the upturned face with its open mouth and the four fingers of his left hand.

The image is horrific: right off the poster of some low-budget horror flick.

As Jessica and Matt begin to remove the salt and lime mix in teaspoon-sized scoops, Matt looks at us and says, "This could take a while. You may want to run and get lunch or something."

Lunch. Right.

"We're fine," Jimmy says.

A half hour later, the chest still looks full and my patience is nearing empty. I ask to borrow the car keys from Jimmy, and tell him I'm going to check out Paul Anderson's residence on the other side of the river.

My reasoning is simple: with Blevins dead, his defense attorney could be next on the list.

Jimmy argues with me, pointing out that Isaiah has only killed ex-cons. He's right about that, but he's forgetting that Paul Anderson is the reason Blevins escaped justice for Tracy's maiming and ultimate death, at least in Isaiah's mind.

That, and Isaiah is working up to some grand finale. Until we figure out what it is, we need to cover all bases.

Tic toc.

Jimmy hands over the car keys when I point this out.

Either he sees the logic in my words or he realizes I won't shut up until he concedes. The result is the same, and I leave the macabre mess at Merch Storage behind— even if it's only for an hour or two.

Paul Anderson's single-story adobe home on Dali Avenue, which he shares with his wife, Elizabeth, is spitting distance from the west bank of the Rio Grande River, which dissects Albuquerque north to south, leaving a majority of the metropolis on the east side of the river.

The neighborhood is exactly what one would expect of a successful defense attorney. The homes are exquisite, a number are gated, and all enjoy some of the best views to be had. Dali Avenue is a dead-end offshoot of Vista Grande Drive. It's barely the length of a football field and ends in a cul-de-sac at Anderson's driveway.

As I swing into the turnaround and pull to the curb near the attorney's house, I pull my glasses off and hold them in my right hand as I study the road, the sidewalk, the brown earth of the yards to the left and right. I start counting in my head: one . . . two . . . five . . . seven.

It's not good; it's not good at all.

Of the seven separate ice-blue tracks around the residence, four were left within the last few months. Isaiah's been busy. Whether he has bigger plans for the attorney or he's just scouting his next delivery, it's hard to tell.

The front and sides of the home are almost completely obscured by high vegetation, leaving only sections of the adobe structure visible in earth-tone patches peeking out here and there.

The trees and bushes are nice.

They look great, they lend shade to the residence during the hot New Mexico summer, and they thrive this close to the Rio Grande. They're also a criminal's best friend, providing cover to jimmy the lock on your kitchen window, or boot open the side door to your garage.

Isaiah likes the vegetation.

His most recent tracks are visible on all sides of the house, but most prevalent among the trees on the south side—the right side if you're at the curb. The driveway is empty and the other four houses on the truncated street show no sign of life, so I decide to risk it. Hopping out of the driver's seat, I hurry up the sidewalk and follow Isaiah's shine into the southern clump of trees.

The only opening behind the green foliage is a high frosted bathroom window. It's bigger than most bathroom windows, which means Isaiah would have little difficulty getting through, and bathroom windows are sometimes overlooked when security systems are installed.

"How are you getting up there?" I mutter to myself. It's a good seven feet from the ground to the window, and the trees are too far away from the house to be of use. He'd need something to step on, a folding stepstool or something similar.

Regardless, the hurdle is easily remedied.

Back in the car, I waste no time exiting the cul-de-sac. I turn right on Vista Grande Drive and wonder how things are going at the storage unit . . . and then it happens. One moment the street is empty, the next I've got an APD unit behind me with his lights flashing and the *blurp blurp* of his siren warning me to pull over. At the same time, another unit approaches from the front and pulls his vehicle across both lanes at an angle, blocking my way.

Moments later, a third vehicle appears behind me, seemingly out of nowhere, and pulls in behind the first. It's only then that I remember the request for extra patrol.

I'm close enough to Isaiah's age and physicals, and we both have the same sandy blond hair. It would be easy to confuse us at a distance. I make sure my hands stay on the steering wheel, and I refrain from any sudden or furtive movements.

Right now they're running the plate and learning the car is a rental, which is only going to heighten their suspicions. The officer in front of me has his shotgun in hand. He's doing a good job of concealing it, but the barrel peeks under the open door of his patrol car every now and then.

Here they come.

One moves up the driver's side, one the passenger's side, guns at the low ready. Just behind the rear doors they pause, scrutinizing everything in the back of the vehicle while I stare straight forward with my hands on the wheel.

I could identify myself as FBI, but anyone can make that claim—why should they believe me? Besides, someone obviously saw me snooping around the house. I've been through this dance before and find that during a high-risk stop, the fewer distractions the officers have, the better. There'll be time enough for badges and identification later.

My only job right now is to sit tight and try to avoid lead poisoning.

Officer One and Officer Two are just behind the doorposts now, scanning the front of the vehicle for weapons. Satisfied I have nothing within my immediate reach, they have me exit the car, hands first, which I then place palm down on the roof until they finish frisking me.

We sort it out.

They take turns looking at a picture and comparing it to my face until they decide that I don't look anything like the picture of Isaiah that was distributed department-wide, and when I show them my FBI credentials and explain why I was checking the outside of Paul Anderson's house, they suddenly relax.

Then it's all smiles and questions.

Everyone wants to know more about the serial killer.

I'm still having a hard time lumping Isaiah in with all the other serial killers we've dealt with, but then I remember the desiccated face peering out from a pool of salt and lime back at the storage unit.

Before leaving, I commend the officers for the extra patrol, and, without going into detail, advise them that Isaiah has been to Paul Anderson's residence recently. I make it clear that the concern for his safety has increased, not decreased.

I have a couple Special Tracking Unit patches in my bag that I keep for such circumstances, and as I hand one to each of the officers you'd think I was handing out hundred-dollar bills.

The steamer trunk is still full of lime and salt . . . and Bill Blevins.

Clearly, I wasn't gone long enough.

Between driving to Paul Anderson's house, prowling the outside of the residence, getting made by the Albuquerque PD and almost taken down at gunpoint, and driving back, you'd think a guy could kill more than an hour.

Activity at the storage unit continues.

Jessica and Matt are steadily working their teaspoon-sized scoops; two detectives watch as the medical investigators work; a half dozen uniforms stand perimeter, and CSI is slowly extracting every item in the locker piece by piece, documenting each, and looking for prints, blood, or evidence of any kind.

Another hour passes, then two.

At length, Jessica and Matt stand simultaneously and brush the debris from their clothes. They exchange words I can't make out, and then Matt goes to the van for a body bag and a gurney.

As he makes his way back, Jessica scans the area quickly and spots Jimmy and me sitting in the rental car a hundred feet away. Both front doors are wide open, and every window is down. I'm sure it's just another refreshing Albuquerque afternoon for her, but eighty-eight degrees is fainting weather in the Pacific Northwest.

She waves us over.

"You might want to see this," she says when we're closer. "Looks like the salt and lime did a good job of mummification. There's still decomp in some of the tissue, but it's minimal. I bet the whole body doesn't weigh much more than eighty or ninety pounds."

As I stare down at the desiccated corpse, the words of an old poem come to mind and I find myself speaking them aloud:

"And all the while the burning lime
Eats flesh and bone away,
It eats the brittle bone by night,
And the soft flesh by day,
It eats the flesh and bone by turns,
But it eats the heart away."

"Oscar Wilde," Jessica says with a grin, "'The Ballad of Reading Gaol.' A long poem, but not unknown to pathologists. Only Wilde had it wrong—along with a whole bunch of screenwriters and novelists and even a good many murderers."

"Lime doesn't dissolve flesh and bone," I say, beating her to it.

Her grin broadens. "No, no, it doesn't. It's actually a very good preservative. If you want to get rid of a corpse you need lye; that'll do the trick."

"Do you think that's what was intended here?" Jimmy asks. "Dissolve the body; destroy the evidence?"

"Not a chance," Jessica says without hesitation. "Your guy knew exactly what he was doing. If he was trying to destroy the body, why add salt? No, he wanted him found, just not right away."

Placing the body bag on the tarp next to the trunk, Jessica and Matt lift the dried-out husk of Bill Blevins from its makeshift coffin and lower it to the pavement. The knees are pushed up to the chest and the arms are contorted to fit in the steamer, so the FDMIs slowly extend the limbs until the body lies flat.

The feet are missing.

I should have expected that.

Jimmy is already crouched down looking at the stump of each leg, first the left, then the right, then the left again. "Take a look at this, Steps," he says.

"I can see it fine from here," I reply. "Let me guess: clean cuts, probably from some kind of industrial equipment."

"No," Jimmy says with a shake of his head. "Not this time. But we've seen this before, on other cases. It looks like he used a hacksaw."

"That was our thought too," Matt says quickly.

"Hacksaw?" Before I can stop myself, I'm on my knees next to Jimmy.

"Hesitation marks, false starts," he says as he points them out.

He's right, but this is a break from methodology. I lift my glasses an inch and cast my eyes upon the calves, just above the cuts. It's there, and it makes me shiver: Isaiah's shine pressed into the flesh. I can see the handprints where he held the legs down as he hacked through flesh and bone. "This was the first victim," I say with conviction, though I can't yet tell Jimmy about the shine because the curious medical investigators are standing over us.

"This is sloppy, time-consuming, even disappointing," I continue, waving a finger at the cuts. "This was his first; he learned from it. He figured out a better way. That's why all the other cuts are precise and clean."

"I think you might be right," Jimmy concedes.

I stand and look one last time on the shriveled corpse of Bill Blevins.

I know I'm right.

CHAPTER TWENTY-FIVE

Albuquerque, New Mexico—September 15, 5:37 A.M.

The sound waves come like the low concussions of bombs dropped on distant cities. Their *woomp, woomp, woomp* is felt as much as heard, coming in rapid succession, then followed by another wave.

It's a familiar sound—a hated sound.

It's the harbinger of bad; the prelude to things unpleasant.

It's Jimmy pounding on my hotel room door.

At first I imagine it's a dream—hope it's a dream—but the carpet-bombing continues, so I force an eye open and glance over at the clock just as the red LED face flips over to 5:38 A.M. Even Jimmy isn't this fanatical; he wouldn't be at my door at this hour unless something had happened, and the increasing urgency of his pounding fist tells me it's not something I'm going to like.

"Steps," he hisses through the door, trying not to wake the other guests.

"Yeah, yeah," I mutter as I roll out of bed. "I'm coming," I say in a louder voice, anything to make the noise stop.

When I open the door he pushes past and starts going on about Paul and Elizabeth Anderson. I comprehend about every third word, and then he turns the light on, which temporarily blinds me.

"Are you listening?" Jimmy presses. "You need to get dressed—fast."

I'm rubbing my eyes. "Say it again, and slow down this time. I heard 'Anderson,' and something about another box."

"They're *gone*," Jimmy snaps, "taken from their home at gunpoint an hour ago."

"Both of them?"

"Both," Jimmy replies curtly as he starts picking clothes from my bag and throwing them in my direction faster than I can put them on: underwear, socks, pants, and shirt, topped off by a black FBI windbreaker. Then he rinses my toothbrush and squeezes out some toothpaste as he continues his narration.

"I didn't have time for details, but his neighbor called it in after the house alarm went off, even got a license plate number."

"Isaiah's not that sloppy."

"No, he's not. Albuquerque PD had units in the area in two minutes, and on-scene in three, but there was no sign of the suspect vehicle." Jimmy shakes his head. "After stuffing Anderson and his wife into the trunk, he paused and waved at the neighbor. Can you believe this guy?"

"He's been building up to this," I tell Jimmy. "The

messages—*soon, tic toc*—he was telling us something was coming. This is it. The Andersons were his target all along."

"Let's not get ahead of ourselves," Jimmy says.

"Why else?" I argue. "Every other victim was solo; now we have two. Every other victim was snatched without a trace, they just disappeared. But with the Andersons, he makes a show of it, intentionally parading them in front of the neighbors."

"What's his plan, then? Kill them both?"

"I don't know," I say with a shake of my head. "I don't know."

Brushing quickly, I run a wet comb through my hair. It's not my best look, but it'll have to do, considering the circumstances. As I'm doing this, Jimmy rummages around at the bottom of my leather travel bag and finds my Walther P22 in its holster. Slapping in a loaded magazine, he chambers a round and puts the safety on before sliding it back into the holster.

He hands the gun to me as we make for the door, and I clip it to my belt with a sense of foreboding. Generally I don't pack, but when I do, it's always when things are the most dangerous and least predictable, which is almost always during the last minutes and hours of a case.

I've thought about getting a different gun, a lighter gun; it could even be the exact same make and model . . . just different. The Walther P22 weighs a mere fifteen ounces, but it's not the physical weight that concerns me. It's the weight on my conscience every time I carry.

I killed a man with this gun.

And no matter how much I tell myself that he deserved killing ten times over, I have an image stuck in my mind. It's the image of serial killer Pat McCourt lying in red snow, a steaming shotgun by his side, an ironic smile on his face. Another permanent impression in the catalog of horrors I call my memory.

Pat McCourt's gone.

Lives were saved.

My guilt remains.

The early hour means that traffic is light and our progress is swift, even without the benefit of lights and siren.

I was just at the Anderson residence yesterday and know the way, so Jimmy lets me drive while he starts making calls and waking people up. The first call is to Les.

Both Jimmy and I agree that Isaiah will most likely take his captive to Deming. He didn't move to the small town without reason, and despite this morning's surprising lack of caution, he remains a secretive creature, a man of routine and ritual. With a good vehicle description and plate number, our best hope is to throw up a wall of state troopers, deputies, and police between him and his destination.

If that fails, we'll need Betsy.

Time is wasting—*tic toc*.

We had intended on flying to Deming yesterday afternoon, but finding a partially mummified and dismembered corpse in a steamer trunk tends to wreak havoc on travel plans, and we thought another night in Albuquerque wouldn't hurt.

We were wrong.

*   *   *

The circular cul-de-sac on Dali Avenue is awash in red and blue lights as we walk in from the closest available parking space on Vista Grande Drive. All of Dali Avenue is a crime scene, and the who's who of the Albuquerque criminal justice system have gathered to wait for news—any news. These quiet observers include a fair number of judges and attorneys who, despite their standing in the community, must watch from the other side of the yellow police tape like everyone else.

Their presence here doesn't necessarily imply appreciation or admiration for Paul and Elizabeth Anderson; it's more a point of professional courtesy: mess with one attorney, mess with them all.

Jimmy and I show our credentials to the officer standing perimeter, and he lifts the police tape for us to pass. Beyond the yellow line is a huddle of brass, to include the chief of police, the assistant chief of police, and both deputy chiefs. As we pass, they're being briefed by a lieutenant and two sergeants.

They'll have to step in front of reporters soon, so they listen to every detail, and question everything.

Despite our black FBI jackets, we show our credentials a second time to get into the house. The ice-blue shine on the pristine entry tile tells me that Isaiah exited out the front door, but that's not how he came in.

A white Styrofoam cooler sits in the middle of the living room floor; the feet inside belong to Bill Blevins. I half expect them to be mummified, but that's not the case. The foul water at the base of the cooler tells me they were frozen, just like the others.

I follow Isaiah's ice-blue trail to the door of the master bedroom and observe CSIs collecting evidence within. An overturned nightstand and a few drops of blood on Paul Anderson's pillow are the only evidence of a struggle.

"Where'd the blood come from?" Jimmy asks one of the CSIs.

"He was probably pistol-whipped."

We watch in silence as they work, and then I tug at Jimmy's elbow and point up the hall with a toss of my head. As I follow the blue path deeper into the house, it leads directly to a bathroom with a high window.

The bathroom.

The one Isaiah had scoped out in one of his surveillance runs, and the very one I stood under just yesterday.

Stepping up onto the toilet seat, I push the window up and find pry marks on the lower edge. Though the house has an alarm system, there's no sensor visible on the window, either on the frame or on the frosted glass.

"This was point of entry," I tell Jimmy as I step down from the toilet, "which begs a question."

"What's that?"

I point up at the window. "No alarm. That means he made it inside the house without alerting the Andersons. He was armed; we know that from the neighbor's statement, so he wouldn't have had any trouble controlling them in the bedroom. I'm guessing he held Paul at gunpoint and had Elizabeth bind his hands, and then bound Elizabeth himself."

"One is easier to control than two," Jimmy says.

"Exactly."

"So, what's the question?"

I curl my index finger at him a couple of times in a come-hither motion and lead him back to the entry. "Why'd the alarm go off?" I say, pointing at the security system control panel.

That stumps him. "They had a panic button?"

"If they had a panic button they would have pushed it as soon as Isaiah entered the bedroom, before he had them under control."

"How do you know they didn't?"

"You said it yourself. The neighbor heard the alarm go off and immediately got up and came out to his front porch, arriving just in time to see Isaiah marching Paul and Elizabeth out to the car. He said it was maybe fifteen seconds."

Jimmy suddenly understands. "If the Andersons had a panic button, they would have tripped the alarm as soon as Isaiah appeared in their bedroom, but that doesn't play into the neighbor's timeline. It probably took two or three minutes for Isaiah to bind and gag them, especially if he was forcing one of them to bind the other at gunpoint. Then there's the time it took to get them to their feet, herd them through the house, and out the front door." He nods. "That's a lot more than fifteen seconds. Isaiah set off the alarm on purpose."

"He wanted the neighbors to hear it," I say. "He wanted them to come to their windows and their porches. He wanted them to see."

"Exposing himself like that—it doesn't make sense."

"It does if this is his endgame."

"Meaning what? Kill Paul Anderson while his wife looks on?"

I shake my head. "Worse, I think."

* * *

Jimmy and I plant ourselves just outside the front door of the residence, waiting for word that the Albuquerque police located the red Mercury Milan and rescued the Andersons from the trunk.

Fifteen minutes pass, and that scenario becomes unlikely.

Next, we wait for word that the New Mexico state police have stopped the car along I-25 south of Albuquerque, freeing the victims and taking Isaiah into custody.

Thirty minutes pass, and still we wait.

We wait for word—word of any kind, good or bad, but forty-five minutes pass and silence is our only company. With increasing frequency, I glance at the black dial on my Movado watch as Jimmy strums his fingers anxiously on the front railing.

At three minutes past seven, a murmur runs through the gathered law enforcement both inside and outside the residence. It's sparked by a single radio transmission, and words that change everything in an instant.

The red Mercury Milan, the suspect vehicle everyone has been looking for, was just located a half mile from the Anderson residence parked in the driveway of a random house—as if it belonged there.

The realization hits hard: he switched cars.

It was all a diversion.

Isaiah must have figured out there was extra patrol in the neighborhood, so he ladled out his own brand of disinformation in the form of a witness, a license plate number, and a suspect vehicle.

Responding units would have been so focused on

finding a red car—*any red car*—that after dumping the Milan he could have driven right by them without a second glance.

Any illusion of intercepting Isaiah before he reaches Deming just popped like soap bubbles on a breeze, and that's assuming Deming is even his destination. Right now we have nothing else to go on, so Jimmy and I jog to the car and speed to the airport.

"Driving time is about three and a half hours," I tell Jimmy. "That'll put him there about eight."

"What's our flight time?"

"If we take off immediately and push Betsy hard, we can be there in thirty or forty minutes. Les and Marty are standing by with the engines running." Buildings and bushes flick by my window at eighty miles an hour as a marked unit clears the way for us with lights and siren.

"We don't know how long he keeps them alive," Jimmy says absently, searching for hope. "Maybe he toys with them for a while first; letting them imagine what's coming. If so, that buys us time."

"Webster's not a sadist," I remind him. "I don't imagine him toying with any of them; he just dishes out his own version of justice. Anderson will be dead within a few hours. If we're lucky, he'll spare the wife."

I let the words settle a moment, and then voice another concern. "Without an address in Deming, how are we supposed to find him?"

Jimmy fishes in his pocket for his phone. "It's time to wake Diane."

CHAPTER TWENTY-SIX

Over New Mexico—September 15, 7:44 A.M.

The only drawback to flying around the country in a Gulfstream G100 is that not all airports have a runway long enough to accommodate her. Landing isn't the issue, it's taking off again. Betsy requires just 2,500 feet for a clean landing, but 8,395 feet to take off at sea level.

The longest runway at Deming Municipal Airport is 8,018 feet, plus the elevation is 4,314 feet, so that bumps our takeoff distance out to almost 8,700 feet. The next closest suitable airport would be El Paso, but that's just not acceptable.

Paul and Elizabeth don't have that kind of time.

We're already on descent to Deming Municipal when Les runs through the numbers one last time and decides to risk it. Marty looks around and gives us an okay sign and assures us that the published takeoff distances "are just suggestions anyway."

Now I'm genuinely concerned.

*   *   *

Les wastes no time putting the plane on the ground, and immediately parks next to a white unmarked Crown Victoria sitting at the end of the runway with its lights flashing. Detective Sergeant Pete Villanueva introduces himself, and we pile into the Crown Vic.

During the short flight, Diane managed to find us a local liaison, get us a ride, and have a search run through local records. Not bad for a grandma in her bathrobe and pink pig slippers.

Jimmy rides shotgun, and I'm in the narrow back-seat of the Crown Vic with a thick Plexiglas partition between me and the front seat. One of the sliding panels on the barrier is open, so I lean forward to listen.

"Nothing in locals," Pete says. "Honestly, I've never heard of the guy, or anyone like him. Are you sure he's in Deming?"

"That's the word from his sister," Jimmy says. "Only problem is she's never been to his house; he's never even given her the address."

"So how are we supposed to find this guy? Do you know what he drives, at least?"

"No. Not a clue. It's probably not registered in his name anyway."

I can tell the detective is growing frustrated. His hands keep clenching and unclenching on the steering wheel as we roll down the road at seventy miles an hour—a whole lot of hurry to nowhere.

"Swing by the post office," I say.

"What?" Jimmy's tone is overly abrupt.

"To rent a post office box in the United States," I explain, "you need to provide proof of your residence, like a rental agreement or utility bill. So if we want to find Isaiah's physical address, all we need is his box number."

Jimmy hesitates. "We have that."

"We have that," I parrot.

We reach the Deming Post Office a few minutes before eight, but a half hour before the government facility is due to open. A single car graces the parking lot, which must belong to an employee—or so we tell ourselves. Jimmy and I take turns pounding on the door and calling out "FBI," but there's no response from within.

It takes a full three minutes of door-bruising before a figure appears in the distant hall and makes her way toward us, growing larger with each step until she fills the window.

"We don't open for another"—she squints at her wristwatch—"twenty-eight minutes," she says, then turns and starts to walk away.

Jimmy and Detective Villanueva pounce on the door, shouting and pressing badges to the glass. That gets the woman's attention and she returns, gives a disapproving stare, and then reluctantly fishes out a key from the lanyard around her neck. She unlocks the door, but only opens it wide enough for her face to peer out.

"Like I said, we're not open yet." She's at least six feet tall and half as wide, and her lips are pinched in the disapproving manner of a shushing librarian as she stares through her bifocals and down her nose at us.

Jimmy glances at the name on her access badge. "This is an emergency, Ms. Henshaw. I'm Special Agent James Donovan with the FBI, and this is Detective

Sergeant Pete Villanueva with Deming PD. We need the physical address associated with one of your post office boxes, and it's urgent."

"Of course it is. It's always urgent," Ms. Henshaw says. "You have a warrant?"

"We don't, but—"

"Well, I'm the postmaster here, and I'd have to look it up, but I'm pretty sure we need a warrant to give out that type of information."

"Ma'am, I assure you there's no time for that. Exigent circumstances exist when someone is in imminent danger, and that negates the need for a warrant. This is well established in criminal procedure law, so, for example, if I hear screaming coming from this building and believe someone is being harmed, I could make entry without a warrant, even if I had to kick the door in, understand?"

The words fly at the postmaster so fast she takes two steps backward. She looks at Sergeant Villanueva, confused.

"That's exactly correct, ma'am," Pete says with a nod.

"This *is* an exigent circumstance," Jimmy continues, "and lives *are* in imminent danger, so I must insist: I need that address information, and I need it now." The postmaster stares at him, mouth hanging open. "Please," Jimmy adds, forcing a smile.

That seems to break through to Ms. Henshaw, and she swings the door wide, saying, "This way." She shuffles deep into the building and down a hall, her steps urgent, either because she truly gets it or because Jimmy scared her. I'm not sure which.

"Box number?"

"Six-six-seven-seven," Jimmy replies, reading from the scrap of paper that Lisa gave him during our visit to Nob Hill two days ago.

It only takes Ms. Henshaw a moment.

"Paul Webster," she says, and then provides an address on Relay Road.

Paul Webster.

"He used his middle name," Jimmy and I say together.

"Relay Road; that's about ten miles outside of town off the 418," Pete says.

We leave the postmaster without so much as a thank-you or good-bye. Rushing down the hall, we burst through the front door of the post office and practically bolt for the patrol car.

"Do you have a SWAT team?" Jimmy asks as he reaches the passenger door.

"We have seven members of our Special Response Team standing by," the sergeant replies, "plus two negotiators. Relay Road is outside the city limits, which means we don't have jurisdiction, so I need to run this by the Luna County Sheriff's Office. All our guys are cross-commissioned by the county, but we don't operate outside the city without notifying them."

Reaching into his pocket, Pete tosses a ring of keys to Jimmy. "You better drive," he says. "I've got some calls to make." Before pulling out of the parking lot, Jimmy punches the address into the dash-mounted GPS.

The yellow track on the map heads west.

Pete's first call is to the sergeant in charge of the Special Response Team, updating him on the situation and location. Typically, a threat assessment is conducted before an SRT or SWAT team is activated. If the incident scores high enough, the activation proceeds. A serial killer is enough to spike the assessment numbers, but the imminent risk to Paul Anderson and his wife eliminates the scoring altogether.

As Jimmy steers the patrol car out of the city and westbound on I-10, we pass a sign warning of possible dust storms, and then the speed limit kicks up to seventy-five and we find ourselves racing out into a world described in two words: *flat* and *dry*.

There are breaks in the otherwise level horizon—small hills bumped up against the distant sky—but they're as infrequent as teeth in an old vagrant's mouth.

Pete's next call is to the Luna County Sheriff's Office. He ends up on hold a minute, and then the call is forwarded directly to the sheriff. After explaining the situation and discussing options, he disconnects the call.

"The sheriff is going to send a couple SWAT-trained deputies to augment. I told him we'll be staging a mile east of the residence." The sergeant glances at the time on his phone. "It's going to take them about twenty minutes." He hesitates before asking, "How much time do we have?"

Jimmy's voice is low, hard. "He's already there. We're out of time."

The staging area is concealed behind an abandoned barn a quarter mile off I-10. Standing at the southeast corner of the barn looking west, I see Isaiah's place in the distance. The residence is a single-wide trailer, but it's nestled in the center of forty acres with numerous outbuildings, including an old Quonset hut that's in considerably better condition than any of the other buildings, most of which appear on the verge of falling over.

Approaching is going to be a problem.

A gully in the terrain, possibly from an ancient river or the washout from a flash flood, will get us partway there, but after that we'll have to leapfrog forward using the limited vegetation as cover.

Jimmy's just finishing a call to Tony in El Paso when I pull him off to the side. "I need to get in closer and take a look," I insist. He opens his mouth, most likely to say no, but I cut him off. "For all we know, this could be a bogus address, and we don't have the time to wait for verification. Just get me close enough to see Isaiah's shine, and then we can hunker down until the cavalry rides in."

"You remember what happened the last time you needed to take a closer look?" Jimmy says impatiently. The ghost echo of a shotgun blast rings in my head as the image of Arthur Zell—the Sad Face Killer—wavers in my mind.

"This is different."

"Why? Because you think Isaiah won't shoot you?"

I shake my head. "No, I know better than that, but this is also about Paul and Elizabeth. If I can get close enough I can tell if they're here, and maybe which building they're being held in."

Jimmy studies me as he works it through. "This is a bad idea," he says after a moment. "If we do this, you stay behind me and follow my lead."

"Behind you." I nod. "Follow your lead. Got it."

Sergeant Villanueva is less than pleased with the

idea. "Backup is fifteen minutes out," he says. "If something goes sideways . . ."

"It won't," Jimmy says with false bravado. "This is what we do."

As we make for the dip in the terrain, Pete suddenly calls after us. "Hold up a sec." He pops the trunk to his patrol car and digs through several bags. Like most cops, his trunk is filled to capacity with every manner of support gear and equipment. He even has a built-in gun vault for his AR-15, but it's not the assault weapon he's looking for.

When he emerges from the depths of the trunk, he has a small black bag in his left hand and a pair of tactical binoculars in his right. He hands the binoculars to Jimmy, saying, "For far away," and then hands him the black bag and says, "For up close."

Jimmy peeks into the bag and gives Pete a grin. "I don't think we'll get that close."

"Just in case," the sergeant replies.

The gully no longer resembles a dried-up riverbed, if ever it was one. It's now just a scar on the earth, a low impression carved out in the distant past by water and gravity, or perhaps just wind and time.

It was made for this moment . . . and we use it to our advantage.

The first half mile is easy, and we do most of it at a half run, but then the gully abruptly ends. Emerging slowly into the open, we huddle behind a small desert tree, dangerously exposed.

With the binoculars pressed to his eyes, Jimmy scans

the trailer and outbuildings for almost a full minute before handing them to me. "No sign of Isaiah," he says. "I see five cars, but only one that looks drivable. The porchlight at the trailer is on, same with the light above the door to the Quonset hut."

Scanning the compound, my view is different from Jimmy's. I still see the trailer, the cars, the scattered outbuildings, the Quonset hut, and several disconnected stretches of fence lying about in various stages of disrepair. But because the lenses on the binoculars are regular glass, not lead crystal, I also see shine everywhere I look.

Some of it is ice blue.

"This is it," I say. Turning the binoculars on the blue Dodge Intrepid parked outside the trailer, I add, "The Andersons are here. Their shine is on the trunk."

"Is it pulsing?"

"Yeah, they're alive, at least for the moment."

"Can you tell where he took them?"

"I can't see the ground that well from here. I need to get closer."

Jimmy looks back toward the staging area behind the barn, then at Isaiah's compound and its many outbuildings. Retrieving his cell phone, he sends a text to Pete: *Suspect and victim likely on scene. Moving closer.* After hitting Send, he says, "Okay. Follow me and keep close."

We advance from cover to cover, and soon find ourselves on the east side of Isaiah's trailer. Jimmy peeks through the window above our heads, but the room is empty. We come around the front of the trailer to keep it between us and the nearest outbuildings, then Jimmy has me wait at the corner while he checks each window.

Nothing.

Satisfied that the trailer is empty, he waves me forward. As I draw near, I'm immediately struck by the layers of blue shine filling the gap between the trailer and the Quonset hut. Then I see Paul Anderson's shine, and beside him the distinct dirty tan belonging to his wife; the same dirty tan that was so prominent in their bedroom, their bathroom, their house. It all goes just one direction: into the Quonset hut.

"Remember that industrial cutter we've been trying to identify?" I whisper to Jimmy. "Well, whatever it is, it's in that Quonset hut."

"How do you know?"

"Footprints go in and don't come out. I see Larry Wilson, Travis Duncan, and Carlos Hernandez."

This time it's Jimmy's turn to say it: "We need to get closer."

There are no windows on the Quonset hut, so we take risks we normally wouldn't. With guns drawn, we step lightly across the baked earth until we reach the door to the hut, and then crouch down.

A single voice emanates from within.

Most of the words elude me, a jumble of consonants and vowels distorted by the arched ceiling and muffled by the door.

Jimmy fishes inside Pete's black bag and withdraws a device that looks similar to a GPS attached to a handgrip. Protruding from the unit is a thin black cable that stretches several feet, at the end of which is a tiny camera.

Moving slowly, Jimmy slips the snake camera through the horizontal slit at the base of the door. Making some adjustments, he points the head in the direction of the voice.

"I see Isaiah," he whispers a moment later. "He's near the back, next to a tall . . . I don't know . . . shelf, maybe?" His voice is suddenly more urgent. "I see Paul. He's tied to a chair."

"What about Elizabeth?"

Jimmy shakes his head. "I don't see— No, wait! Oh, dear God!" He holds the cable steady and hands the viewer to me, saying, "Tell me that's not what I think it is."

It takes me a minute to sort the images and recognize what I'm looking at, but then I see it. We should have guessed as much—*I* should have guessed as much. It's funny how things make perfect sense once revealed, as if no other option was logical or possible. One more piece of the puzzle just became crystal clear.

"There's your surgical cut," I whisper, handing back the viewer.

"We need to move back and see if the Special Response Team—"

The voice is loud and clear this time, though no longer addressing Paul and Elizabeth. "I said come on in," Isaiah repeats. "The door's open."

Jimmy and I remain frozen in position. Maybe it's a bluff. Maybe he heard something, or thought he heard something, and is flushing out the culprits.

"I saw you three minutes ago," Isaiah says loudly. "There's a camera in the fence post next to the driveway, and another by the rock to your left. There are others, but no sense wasting time on that when Mr. and Mrs. Anderson have been so patient."

Jimmy's text is brief: *Contact. Move now!*

"Who's the text for?" Isaiah's voice calls. "Is that your backup? By all means, have them join us."

"What do we do?" I'm surprised at the calm tone of my voice, especially considering that my insides are hopping around like grease on a skillet. Adrenaline serves a useful purpose, but there are times I wish I could just shut it off.

"We need to stall," Jimmy whispers. "Stay behind me and pay attention to muzzle discipline. If you have to shoot, do so over my right shoulder, but if it comes to that I'd prefer you just hit the ground and stay down until help arrives."

"He's just broken," I remind Jimmy.

He nods heavily, as if a great weight were suddenly pressed upon his shoulders. "I know, but we save the ones we can. Right now that's Paul and Elizabeth." Turning the door handle, he yells, "We're coming in."

The Quonset hut is dimly lit and mostly empty when we enter. In the corner to our right is a stack of four old tires, and halfway up the right wall is a chest freezer. There's an upright tool chest to the left, along with a workbench, a welder, and some miscellaneous cardboard boxes.

Then there's the guillotine.

It's in the center of the floor toward the rear of the building, and I immediately notice that the polished steel blade is raised and locked in place. It's like every other guillotine I've seen in pictures or movies, but where those were built to chop off heads, this one works from the other direction. Even now, two delicate feet are clamped into the bracket, their pale soles facing us.

They're Elizabeth Anderson's feet.

Though we can only catch glimpses of her beyond the guillotine's drop mechanism, she's strapped to the terrible bench, still in her nightgown. Isaiah stands next to her, a Colt model 1911 .45-caliber semiautomatic in his right hand, which hangs limp at his side. In his left hand he holds the pull cord to the guillotine.

"Don't do it, Isaiah," Jimmy says gently. "There's a better way." The muzzle of his Glock is locked on Isaiah's chest. There's no waver or shake in the barrel. It's steady.

Isaiah just laughs.

It's a genuine laugh, with no fear, no hesitation, no regret. It's the laugh of someone who's accepted his fate. "Do you honestly think this is going to end well?" he says with a dead smile.

"Yes," Jimmy replies immediately. "All you have to do is drop the gun and let go of the cord. No one else has to die."

"Let go of the cord," Isaiah muses, looking up at his left hand. "Yeah, that might be a problem."

In the dim light of the Quonset hut, I missed it when we first entered, but now it stands clear and prominent. A sense of dread sweeps up my body. "His hand is duct-taped to the cord," I warn Jimmy. It's a crude version of a dead-man switch, but it'll get the job done. Isaiah's determined to pull the cord, even if it takes the weight of his dead body to do so.

"I see it," Jimmy replies, the words steeped in conflict.

Isaiah looks up and gives the cord a gentle shake. "Eight ounces," he says. "That's how much pressure it takes to send the blade on its way; just the smallest of tugs." When he looks once more at Jimmy, the dead smile is back on his face, frozen, leering.

"Why eight ounces, Isaiah?"

The question takes the killer by surprise. "What makes you think there's a reason?"

"It seems important to you—why else would you mention it?"

Isaiah is quiet a moment, and then he smiles. "Very good," he says, nodding approvingly, "very good, indeed. I'd say you've earned the answer to that one, wouldn't you?" He pauses, first looking at his duct-taped left hand, then at the gun in his right hand. "I was going to pat my heart, but it seems both my hands are occupied—and you might mistake my intentions if I raise my gun hand." He chuckles, and then his voice grows sinister. "That would be a shame, because then Mrs. Anderson would die and you wouldn't get your answer."

He pauses a long moment . . . and the smile returns.

"Eight ounces?" Jimmy presses.

Isaiah's response is almost lyrical: "Such is the weight of the human heart, with all the tragedies of the world poured therein."

"The heart?"

"The average adult human heart," Isaiah confirms, "my heart—just eight ounces. Eight ounces that can sometimes feel like the moon, the stars, and all the heavens are resting upon it, yet the scale still reads eight ounces. How is that possible, I wonder?"

"Life isn't easy or fair," Jimmy says, and I hear the echo of my mother in the words. "I'm sorry about your loss, Isaiah. I'm sorry about what happened to Tracy. It's not right, it's just life. There are people you can talk to—"

"People I can talk to!" Isaiah rages. "What do they know? Most of them can't even sort out their own lives, let alone tell me how to deal with mine."

"Then think about Lisa," Jimmy insists. "She's worried about you. She's lost enough already—your mom, Tracy. You don't want to do this to her."

"This isn't about Lisa," Isaiah replies coldly. The smile is gone, leaving just a blank canvas where his face used to be. It's like he flipped a switch and turned everything off: Lisa, Tracy, love, fear, even hate.

For the briefest moment I picture him as the embodiment of the computer code he so loves to write. It has no passion, no emotion, no will of its own; it's just a collection of values, variables, and functions culminating in the source code of a singular human app with but one function: make Paul Anderson suffer.

The input is complete.

The output is imminent.

"What's your name, FBI?"

Jimmy tells him, and in a gesture no doubt meant to win some goodwill from Isaiah, he drops the Glock to a low ready position. Every move he makes, every comment, is about deescalating the situation. Calling Isaiah by name, invoking his sister, his mother, and his wife—all meant to personalize their contact and break through the determined shell in which Isaiah has encased himself.

It's not working.

Isaiah has dug his own grave and intends to use it. His next words are hollow and lifeless: "Let's make this easy, Jimmy."

In the blurred instant that follows, I see Isaiah's right arm rise up. Fire belches from the barrel of the .45-caliber handgun. Jimmy instinctively fires back, pulling the trigger three times. The shots echo through the Quonset hut, thunder stumbling upon thunder.

I hear the *twang* of a bullet piercing the metal siding above our heads.

From his position next to the guillotine, Isaiah spins hard to his left, staggered by the bullet that rips through his chest. Wavering on his feet, he turns his face our way one last time. Already, blood taints his lips and leaks from his mouth . . . and then he smiles.

In the split second that follows, Jimmy fires again, this time at the execution cord where it connects to the pulley at the top of the bench. One bullet strikes the pulley; another nicks the cord . . . but it's not enough.

As Isaiah falls silently to the floor, eight ounces are all the leverage needed to move the world.

The guillotine stirs.

The blade falls.

And from his chair, Paul Anderson screams through the gag stuffed in his mouth. He screams as he watches the blade fall to its utter end . . . and then he's joined by his wife. Together they scream . . . and scream . . . and scream.

As Jimmy races to Isaiah's side, I rush over to the guillotine, unstrap Elizabeth, and pull her back from the wet blade. She claws at me—begging for help—and I have to wrench her hands away to free myself. Running to the toolbox, I find a roll of duct tape. Ripping fabric from her nightgown, I wrap the wounds and then bind each stump tightly in four turns using the duct tape. The blood loss slows as I wrap, and then stops altogether.

I have another problem.

Elizabeth's severed feet lie on the floor.

I need to get them on ice immediately to have any hope of reattaching them. Remembering the chest freezer, I rush over and throw open the lid, praying that it actually works. There's no ice, but bag upon bag of frozen vegetables litter the inside, along with some meat cuts, and four bags of frozen blueberries. The vegetables will work in place of ice, so I begin to scoop them into my arms . . . and then I notice the two clear plastic bags in the right corner.

The shape and shine are familiar: they're Carlos Hernandez's feet.

I recoil at the sight, staggering back, and as I do, my eyes fall to the stack of three Styrofoam ice boxes resting on the floor next to the freezer. They still have price stickers attached. Composing myself, I pull one loose, throw some frozen peas and carrots inside, and rush back to the guillotine.

By this time the Special Response Team has made entry and I hear the wail of an ambulance siren. It's an unexpectedly fast response time considering how far we are from town, but it turns out that while Jimmy and I were working our way up to the property, Sergeant Villanueva decided it might be a good idea to have an aid car standing by.

He was right.

I kneel on the floor, and the activity in the Quonset hut takes on a surreal tone as I pick up Elizabeth Anderson's severed left foot and place it in the ice box. I don't have gloves, so I'm careful not to touch any blood, which is challenging. As I lift the warm foot I want to scream; I want to drop it and run, but I don't. I'll have nightmares about it later, in the long hours of the night, where the horrors of my job collect into a dark pool of unwanted images, but for now I do what must be done.

Packing a half dozen bags of frozen vegetables around the still-warm foot, I repeat the process with the right foot, and then top off the ice chest with more vegetables and the Styrofoam lid.

The EMTs arrive and two of them rush over to Elizabeth, their steps faltering momentarily at the sight of the guillotine and the blood on the floor. I brief them quickly on the feet in the ice chest and the improvised tourniquets, and then turn my attention to Paul Anderson.

His wailing has degenerated into shock, and he slumps to the floor as I free his restraints. I help him to his feet and guide him to Elizabeth's side, where an EMT checks him out and calls for another gurney.

When I join Jimmy, he's kneeling next to Isaiah. The .40-caliber round from his Glock punched through Isaiah's chest an inch left of his heart and he's fading fast. EMTs work feverishly to stop the bleeding and stabilize him, but the damage from the round is too great.

Jimmy's eyes are glossy.

He sits at Isaiah's side, holding his hand, as the unlikely killer's life drains out on the floor. When his heart begins to give out, the EMTs try to bring him back with the defibrillator, but it's no use.

Isaiah dies as he intended.

Jimmy's quiet when he walks by me and out the front door. I leave him be. He'll disappear behind the Quonset hut or wander out and around the other outbuildings, clearing his head, coming to grips with the fact that he just took a life. Contrary to what we see on TV, it's no easy thing to kill someone. Nor should it be.

Suddenly the hut seems stuffy, claustrophobic. I need air and light and the warming heat of a New Mexico morning on my face.

As I approach the door, I glance up, looking for the bullet hole from Isaiah's high shot. It's easy to find. There's a perfectly round hole two feet above the door with a stream of pure light flowing through it.

It's not just a wild shot.

The hole punches through a large piece of recently hung paper. Isaiah's shine is on the paper at all four corners where he taped it to the wall, and the bullet hole is almost dead center. It's a paper target, and the hole in the center is the result of an expert marksman, someone who doesn't miss his target except on purpose.

It's a final message from Isaiah: he had no intention of harming us.

I point out the poster to Pete so he can photograph it and document it for his report. I hurry him along by removing the poster and helping him bag it for evidence; I ask him not to mention it to Jimmy.

He doesn't need to know.

What purpose would it serve?

* * *

Every case, no matter how it starts and ends, must be closed out. That means paperwork, statements, interviews, observations, and the army of minutiae that gather throughout the investigation, waiting for explanation and clarification.

Over time, the details collect like dust and dander on the floor, and by days and hours we sweep them together into piles and gather them up. Some are relevant, others are not. In most cases, the comprehensive report that is the end product of such a case must be flawless and ready for its day in court.

This is not such a case.

There is no one left to convict.

The shooting death of Isaiah Webster will be investigated; that's standard procedure. It will rip open wounds best left undisturbed, but it can't be helped. Aside from that, there are no loose ends.

The inches-thick case report on the Ice Box Killer will close out active cases in El Paso, Tucson, Albuquerque, Deming, Baton Rouge, and Fort Stockton. A hard copy will be sent to each jurisdiction, where it will be placed on a shelf. Eventually, it will find its way into an archives building, unneeded and forgotten.

Elizabeth Anderson was airlifted to Albuquerque and by three P.M. we receive word that the operation to reattach her feet is going well. She won't have full use of them, but she'll never have to wear prosthetics like Tracy Webster.

Despite their cocky demeanor and Marty's assurances that runway takeoff lengths are only suggestions, Les and Marty don't want me and Jimmy on the Gulfstream when they try taking off from the runway at Deming Municipal.

"It's just a precaution," Marty says with a stupid grin.

As it is, they use up every bit of the runway getting Betsy back into the air, and somehow avoid calamity. With our ride airborne and northbound, Pete offers to drive us to Albuquerque, even though it's a seven-hour round trip for him.

He's a good man; a good cop.

We meet his kind on every case, in every big city and small town across the country. The media may relish news of bad cops, of which there are a rare few, but it's the Pete Villanuevas and the Tony Alvarados that they should find hope in.

I do.

CHAPTER TWENTY-SEVEN

Bellingham—September 15, 9:57 P.M.

Four figures wait for us at Hangar 7.

As Les noses Betsy through the wide door, the wing lights illuminate their faces momentarily and set them apart as they stand motionless to the side. The jet slowly maneuvers to its place and then stops, engines winding down.

Jimmy was quiet the whole way back. I talked about everything imaginable, slowly burning up the time between Albuquerque and Bellingham, and doing my best to keep him from dwelling on Isaiah and the fatal shot.

I talked about the future of DNA, including the idea that one day we'll be able to reconstruct a suspect's face from nothing more than his DNA profile, right down to his hair and eye color. Composite sketches will be a thing of the past.

I talked about Jimmy's desire to get Petey a pet of some type, most likely a dog. I argued that cats are a better option. People have miniature goats and miniature horses, I told him, but cats are like miniature lions. Who wants a dog when you can have a miniature lion?

I talked about natural law, and Benjamin Franklin's assertion that only a virtuous people are capable of sustaining freedom.

I talked too much.

I'm hoarse when we land.

When Marty lowers the front ladder, I let Jimmy descend first. Jane and Petey are right there, their arms around him, loving him. Heather's face smiles up at me from the bottom of the ladder and I melt into her, holding her for the longest time. Part of me wants to cry, part wants to live in this moment forever, but the biggest part is just grateful to be home.

Diane remains on the sidelines, a soft smile on her face.

Her boys are home.

When moments have folded into minutes, I peel myself from Heather and take her by the hand, leading her over to the steady and reliable matriarch, our work mother. I embrace Diane, and then kiss her on the cheek. "Welcome home," she says gently. Her eyes drift to Jimmy. "How is he?"

I shake my head. "He needs time."

Eventually, Jimmy, Jane, and Petey break from their huddle. Jimmy needs to get out of here; I can see it in his face. He walks over and smiles at Heather and Diane, and then puts a hand on my shoulder.

He wants to say something, but the words don't come.

I give him a single nod—a thousand words wrapped up in the gesture: respect for the man, appreciation for my partner, love for my brother.

No words are necessary.

He turns to go, and as he slips his arm around Jane and they start for the door, Petey breaks away and comes over to give his Uncle Steps a hug. "Take care of them," I tell Petey. He grins at me, and pulls the lobe of my ear before running to catch up.

"They'll be all right," I say. "We've seen worse."

Before leaving, I stop and thank Les and Marty. The seasoned pilot just nods his appreciation; the less-seasoned copilot starts telling me a joke about a rhino, a parrot, and a bicycle built for two.

Don't ask me how it ends.

I didn't stick around.

EPILOGUE

Lake Jocassee, South Carolina—September 30,
12:27 P.M.

It's hot in South Carolina—over ninety degrees.

Detective Danny Pritchett of the Pickens County Sheriff's Office was one of the first on scene when the body of Tasha Miller was found under the power lines, just east of Lake Jocassee.

That was a year ago.

"Most of the lake area is Oconee County," Pritchett explains. "It's only the eastern third that falls within Pickens County. The Jocassee Dam is to the south, and from it you have power lines running to the northeast and southeast." He leans toward the windshield and points out the lines overhead.

The SUV slows and then stops at the edge of the pavement. Beyond is rough terrain, with only a semblance of road leading away from the parking lot.

"We walking?" Jimmy asks.

"Nah," Danny says, "just switching into four-wheel drive."

A moment later, we're moving again.

"They found Tasha Miller under the power lines about two miles northeast of the dam," Danny continues. "She couldn't have been there more than a day or two. Some linemen were doing a routine inspection, and spotted her while they were up in the air working on one of the towers. That was August seventeenth last year."

"Good memory," Jimmy says.

"Well, honestly, we don't get many homicides. It's not something you forget. Besides, when I saw your request for information I had another look at the case report." He glances back and gives me a wink. "My memory isn't what it used to be."

The drive to the crime scene is rough and slow, but not without entertainment. "You boys ever see *Deliverance*?" Danny asks, and immediately continues without waiting for a response. "Part of that was filmed right here. You remember the cemetery scene? Where they dig up the bodies and relocate them because a dam is going to flood the whole area? Well, that was shot right here at the Mount Carmel Baptist Church. Course, that's all underwater now," he adds with a wave of his hand.

"A year or so after the film crew left," he continues, "the Jocassee Dam was finished, and when it came online it flooded a huge area, including the church. You'd have to swim down a hundred and thirty feet or so if you wanted to see it now."

"So the scene in the movie where they're moving the bodies was real?" Jimmy asks.

"As a heart attack," Danny replies. "Irony is that *Deliverance* takes place on a fictional river in Georgia that's also going to be flooded by a new dam. The scene was shot to show the steps they were taking to relocate the bodies, but at Mount Carmel they left some of the dead where they lay. Lucky the whole place isn't haunted, if you ask me, like in *Poltergeist*, or some of them other shows."

Danny, who appears to be the talkative type, chatters on about the dam and the lake it formed. He mentions he's retiring in a year and starts telling war stories about his time on the force. This is cut short when the rutty road abruptly ends. "We're on foot from here," he says.

The hike is little more than three hundred yards.

I know we're getting close when I see Leonardo's distinctly hideous ebony shine oozing upon the ground—and then we're on top of the crime scene. I see where Tasha Miller was laid out on the ground, her shine so beautiful, her legs pointing south, her arms east and west with a wide circle of ooze around her.

The elements are all here; the calling cards of Leonardo.

I sigh and hold up three fingers for Jimmy.

He knows my meaning: first Jessica Parker in Bellingham eleven years ago, then Ally McCully in Fairmont, West Virginia, just last month, and now Tasha Miller in South Carolina. Her connection to Leonardo almost went unnoticed—and would have, if not for the RFI.

Three victims, and, God help us, there may be more.

"That makes it official," Jimmy says. "Leonardo's a serial killer."

Over the years, the elusive killer's hideous shine has

become difficult for me to look upon. Its color and texture so perfectly match the evil it leaves on display that, for me, a vision of hell is not flames and smoke, but stygian black and the texture of oozing blood.

I slip my glasses back on, clearing it from sight.

A year has come and gone, and you'd never know a body had been here. Time marches on, the bushes and trees continue to grow, the wind blows, the sun shines, life continues—but not for some; not for Tasha Miller.

"Leonardo," I whisper.

And the wind whispers back . . . only the wind, nothing more.

ED LEISURE·CULTURE